Dislocation

Kat Dale

Kat Dale is a writer and sculptor who interprets nature and the human condition in her own individual way.

In Dislocation she draws on the conflicting emotional experiences of being raised on a farm and spending her adult life in an urban environment. Her writing reflects her interest in human interaction and the strategies women develop to survive and flourish.

Kat lives in York, where she has her ceramics studio. Wander along her sculpture trail through legend, dream and allegory at www.katdale.co.uk

Published by Myopia

A CIP catalogue record for this book is available from the British Library.

ISBN 978-0-9927041-0-0 (Paperback)
Ebook formats available through Amazon.

To my children, Edward and Susanna,
who have taught me so much about life and beyond.

Dislocation

Kat Dale

Footsteps were closing in. She felt the weight of his body against her. Felt his warmth seep away through denim into snow. In the distance she could hear the wail of a siren. She stroked his head and he lay still. If this was the end of it all –

then there must, sometime, have been a beginning...

She could not remember when she'd first noticed the geese. They hadn't been there when she'd started coming along this road, when the verge was thick with poppies as well as plastic bottles. She liked watching them, in that wasteland between the carriageways. Watches them now, as they waddle to the fence, peering at the drivers in their metal cages.

Soon she'll be at the front of the queue, pushing through to the next set of lights. But for these few goose-filled moments she's free to stretch and preen and – foot down, fast forward. Amber turns red. To the right, forty tons of revving metal, enough to send V-reg Festina to that great scrap yard in the sky, or, God forbid, the council tip behind their double-bedded flat. Will he, won't he? Flash a smile and catch the driver's eye. He blasts his horn, ups two fingers: she presses on – but not without a sideways glance.

Chapter One

The starter had its head on. Jane shook open the starched waterlily – or maybe it was a bishop's mitre with one fold too many – and spread it across her lap. She took another swig before setting about some necessary flesh removal.

The skin lay on the side of her plate, tail tucked under, like a mermaid who'd swapped her soprano scales for a few hours' salsa. Silent but not legless. Jane fingered her glass. Oli would be thinking she'd half emptied it already, when it was really half full.

'I understand,' Mrs Brailsford was saying – was saying to her, she must concentrate – 'you moved up here with Oliver. Have you found work?'

'Yes. Up Your Street. It mainly handles town properties so I –'

'And is that what you've always done?'

'Yes, I was with one of the national chains when I –'

'Glad to hear it. Young people are too eager to chop and change nowadays. Simon's been with us for nearly three years.' Mrs Brailsford looked across the table. Her smile faded as she heard Simon launch into details of a deal the firm was trying to clinch. All the anti-wrinkle cream north of the Watford Gap wasn't able to smooth the Brailsford frown.

Oliver topped up Simon's glass with a few words. The men laughed.

Jane didn't catch the remark but she couldn't avoid Oliver's say-something-for-God's-sake look.

'I see,' said Jane, 'that you're an admirer of Elliott Kiddle, Mrs Brailsford.' She nodded at the painting above the fireplace. 'That must' – fingers crossed – 'be one of his Underground series.' Because the picture behind the Edgware hot desk in Maloney's office had been crammed with similar strap-hangers on the Northern line.

'The Kiddle? An investment, of course. I only wish it went with the wallpaper. But that's Art for you.'

'But why,' asked Mrs Carson, 'haven't the people got any faces?'

Mrs Brailsford's frown redoubled its efforts.

'I think,' said Jane, slowly, to make it look as though she really was, 'it's an expression of life in the big city, isn't it?' That's what Jack Maloney had told her anyway. 'The loneliness of the individual within the crowd.' Best not repeat any more. He was an estate agent, after all.

'Exactly,' said Mrs Brailsford. She smiled at – what was the girl called? Jane Something-or-other. The girlfriend of that new chap, the good-looking one. She liked to see a well-matched pair, even if he was a bit older. Mrs Brailsford glanced at Mark, partnerless as always. It wasn't particularly that he made the numbers awkward for dinner; in fact she didn't go along with alternating men when it came to whose rear went where. But there was something about a man alone. Oliver, however, seemed a straightforward decent sort, like Simon. But Simon's girlfriend – too much flesh on show by half. Mrs Brailsford looked at her husband, getting to grips with the topside. Traditionally reared; she'd checked the label before loading her trolley. She caught Harry's glance as Sophie bent to

2

retrieve her screwed up bishop's mitre and shook her head.

'I resisted the temptation,' said Mrs Carson, 'to stick my easel outside this morning. Nothing beats a cold back-end.'

'Another week of these frosts, then it'll be a mild winter,' said Mrs Brailsford. She took the lid off a dish of sprouts boiled twenty minutes after al dente. 'You know that old Yorkshire rhyme, *When the ice in November*, which it very nearly is, *will bear a duck, then the rest of the winter is* –' She passed the dish to Jane. 'I forget how it ends.'

'*All slush and muck.*' Which came out a dollop of brassicas louder than Jane intended. But Oliver had told her the weather was a safe topic, so there was no need for that look. As piercing blue as a pair close to the fence that morning. 'I pass a field of geese on my way to work. They don't seem to feel the cold, even with bare feet.'

'Geese?' Frank Carson homed in. 'They don't feel a damned thing. It's the poor blighters taking a pot-shot that suffer. Knocking off a few ducks after a day's shoot's one thing, but that time you dragged me up to Stranraer, Harry. Stood by a blasted loch at 5 am. Damned near froze to death.'

'But you've got to admit those geese were a sight to see. I was spot on about where they'd rise. Must have been a thousand, flying up in great vees.'

'And we didn't bag one!'

'Early morning light conditions can be difficult,' Oliver said.

Almost, smiled Jane, as if he knew.

'Should have had rifles, Harry!' Frank shook his head. 'Never again.'

'I'm off up there at the weekend as it happens. Knew you'd not be interested, Frank, but one of you lads might enjoy it.' Harry nodded round the table. 'Up before it's light, tramping across the fields, testing your aim. Nothing like it to give you an appetite for breakfast.'

'It's altogether a damned unpleasant activity. And a bloody unsociable one. Give me a pheasant shoot any day.'

'Nonsense. You're getting old, Frank.'

'Course he isn't, are you, Frank?' said Sophie. 'It'll be more fun killing them in spring. It's always worth waiting till things start to warm up.' She lifted her glass and winked at him.

Mrs Brailsford's bosom strained in three directions against its double D upholstery.

'How about it, Oliver?' said Harry. 'Are you up for a bit of sport?'

'Sounds great, Harry, but we're off to Jane's parents this weekend. Another time –'

WHY did footwear always shrink two sizes come midnight? Jane nudged her left shoe back onto its stiletto heel and squashed in her foot. So, Cinderella managed to have one fall off after dancing all evening. A likely story. Probably just a line for the fairy godmother. Ten to one – or earlier, if you went along with the tale – she was doing something quite different with the prince, and knew when to leave him gagging for more. She heard Oliver clearing his throat. Everyone else, except Mrs Brailsford, was on their feet. Even Sophie was having a second stab at it. Where was her other shoe? Jane swept her foot across the carpet. Oliver's eye-flashing in her direction wasn't helping a bit. She wriggled further down her chair.

She touched the shoe and managed to hook it nearer. Her foot slid in. She rose beamingly, then made a grab for the edge of the table. Somehow her right heel had become five inches lower than her left. Was that why Oli's lips looked lopsided? Bad enough for her to lose a shoe under the boss's dinner table, but to filch one of his wife's –

Jane sat down, sliding forward till she was verging on the horizontal. She smiled serenely, while below the surface her foot wiper-swished the floor. Then she felt it, moving towards her, and saw that Mrs B had also taken up eye-twitching. Jane pushed the flattie as far forward as she could, without actually disappearing under the table. She crammed a double layer of toes into her own shoe and stood up.

'Thank you so much, Mrs Brailsford. It's been –'

'No, my dear.' Mrs B offered her cheek. 'Thank you.'

Jane would have given her a big smacker on the lips as well, if the old dear hadn't pulled away, because, between Mrs B's earlobe and shoulder, Oliver was glowing.

HE flicked the headlights to main beam. 'This should just about clinch the promotion, Jay. To be honest, I was wondering –' Oliver paused.

So was Jane. Maybe this wasn't a good moment to set about unscrunching the soles of her tights.

'– how you'd perform tonight. But you seemed to fit in, no problem.'

Into Mrs B's size eights? Jane leaned forward to serve her return smile while she pulled off the other stiletto. No problem. Though it was more tricky prising apart fifteen denier soldered to skin while keeping the smile in place.

'Takes a bit of skill,' he said. 'You know, this social interaction thing.'

Of course she knew. Beneath the tablecloth, her feet and Mrs B's had been getting along just fine.

'A bit like playing chess, sussing out what the other's thinking. It's these little things that make all the difference. Between chugging along –' he slid into overdrive '– and really getting somewhere.'

And Jane, squidging toes into the sponge strip on the ice scraper, remembered from those games with Daddy that a pawn can end up king. Depending, of course, on who was making the moves.

HE unbuttoned her dress and let it fall. Burrowing fingers into hair, he pressed down until she was kneeling. She dug nails into buttocks, pulling herself nearer. He was omnipotent. She traced the line where his golden tan dissolved to silver in the onyx lamplight. She was the sacrificial virgin, selected to submit to his divine will. Hands slid across bronzed thighs. He was a Greek statue, the Artemision Poseidon. The maiden's palms worked their way down the sea god's hamstrings, over the iron contours of his calves. All the way to the welt of his terracotta socks.

SIDE stepping mud and puddles, Jane hurries to the car. Engine splutters, wipers screen-scrape. Edge into the flow.

Muted headlights crawl towards her, tail lights brighten, traffic signal echoes red. Join the queue.

Eyes stray right. There's no sign of them. On such a morning they'll be huddled inside the goose ark near the stackyard fence. Then, through the haze, an undulation of white. She rubs the glass.

Lights change, cars jolt forward. Stop.

The billowing mass moves closer.

Wind down the window. Who cares about a bit of rain?

She watches them sway to and fro, necks dipping and rising, feathers smooth under sliding raindrops. Impervious, they patrol their world.

Rain pelts shoulder, collar, face. She holds out her arm through the window. Ice spears bounce off outspread palm. The geese are curious. They rock towards her, orange beaks leading, orange-rimmed eyes alert. Fence-close they waver, cackling. One approaches the rail. Girl and goose gaze as equals.

The traffic moves on.

'THIS,' Roy said, 'is more than the usual five-thirty glow. Don't tell me – you've shifted the Jubilee Terrace heap. The Chrysalid will be over the moon.'

'Sure. It was snapped up by another flying pig.' Jane shuffled some sheets together and shoved them in a drawer. She liked to leave the desk tidy. You never knew when a myopic bus driver might take a short-cut through the staff car park.

'Okay –' Roy pulled the free newspaper from the letterbox and shook out the inserts. 'If it's not our waste of space boss, it must be Oliver's. But of course –' he kept his eyes on the flyers '– you were sensational.'

'Absolutely.' Jane snapped shut her brief case.

Early-bird two for one at the Curry Pot. 'I don't suppose –' said Roy.

But she was putting on her coat.

He flicked over to the next sheet. *Book early for the Christmas panto.*

Already she was digging out her keys for the getaway coach.

'See you tomorrow, Roy.'

'What's on tonight's agenda?' *Special rates for mid-week performances.* 'Dancing at the palace? Mind you don't lose a shoe or you won't get far.'

'You'd be surprised.' She jangled her keys. 'Although I am doing the fairy godmother bit on Sunday.' She walked to the door. 'My sister's new baby, remember? And the best bit is –' hand on handle '– Oli's coming with me. That'll be his second visit to Mum and Dad's in a month.'

And her second in five years.

'That'll take away all the excitement.'

'Whatever do you mean?'

'The thrill of wondering whether you'll make it there and back. I take it you won't be going in your old Fiesta now?'

'Course not,' Jane said. Her, Oli and Festina? It would be like a threesome. And anyway – 'Oliver always likes to be the driver.'

JANE let herself into the flat and began pulling out pans. The cooking was his job – his inventiveness with Greek-style yoghurt on a Saturday night was amazing – but during the week she helped him out. She couldn't match his Béchamel sauce but she knew the fourteen ways with mince. Which more than covered a whole fortnight of getting in first.

Although – could she hear water running?

'Hi, I'm back,' she told the bathroom door.

'Gudah?' Or something similar.

'Showed someone else round Jubilee Terrace.' Jane began unzipping her anorak. 'Thought of five more words to describe the seventies DIY.' Including two she'd made up. 'Did I tell you the tiles have got psychedelic flowers?' Not to everyone's taste, unlike the Ships We Know and Love transfers some previous showerer had thought a good idea to stick up in a certain bathroom –

'You coming in?'

'You bet.' The zip snagged. 'Just give me –' she tried forcing it the other way '– two secs.'

Off with boots, tights, skirt, knickers. This is your final chance, zip.

She managed to get her arms out and began shoving up the coat from the inside. It had stuck just under her ears. There she was, framed in the long mirror, encased nose to navel in green padding, sleeves sculling air – like that mermaid-in-reverse on the cover of volume 5 of *Art for the Uninformed*, second shelf down. A creature of another mind's creation transposed on glass. No, not 5. Oli had cancelled the subscription after the fourth book had filled the gap. Magritte to Someone-Else who dealt strictly in two dimensions. Talk about weird –

'Oh, Oli, it was so funny. When Roy was on a viewing this morning, he opened the bathroom door and –' she upped the decibels a notch '– the curtain was drawn across the bath. Roy could sort of make out a figure through it, but the shower wasn't on or anything. I would've been spooked but he put his head round the curtain and – you'll never guess.'

Through the wall the water flowed on.

'There was a body, hanging up!'

Which at least drew a wheezing gasp.

'Don't freak out – it was just a mermaid, life-size, blown up.'

'Jane, this shower stuff's empty.'

She wrenched the coat over her head, along with her jumper, and half an earring. BOGOF. So there must be another bottle in the bathroom cupboard. Dolphin friendly with essence of kelp.

The spray got her full in the face as she handed it through. So she might as well...

Fibres swelled as she dragged the loofah across his back and two or three of those little flat things – funny how you always seemed to get them with a new one – dribbled out onto the dimples on the bottom of the bath. The water swished them this way and that, dashing them against the wave-ripples on the sea bed, far below a horizon measured out in six inch squares, where the curled-edge *Cutty Sark* sparkled on the drink – but now was not the time to think of tea. Not when sweat was filling her nostrils and, above the taps, the *Argo* had its sights on snaffling the gold-haired ram's fleece, or any other body part that came to hand. The loofah slid from her grasp. Two rows up and seven tiles along, the good ship *Endeavour* was set to round Cape Horn. Spray doused eyes, splashed over breasts, spattered down her gleaming scales. She no longer breathed air. Her tail slithered between his thighs. The mermaid had been netted. Salt water stung her tongue, scalding nostrils with the sense-consuming smell of... synthetic seaweed, as he squeezed out a dollop of two-in-one.

Oliver, thoroughly rinsed off, got out, leaving the loofah in a sog at the bath floor and groping Jane wondering what happened to the other towel.

'FANTASTIC.' Oliver dug in and wound round half a metre of selected durum wheat. 'Last night spelled success –' he raised his fork '– with a capital S.'

The Spaghetti paused, mid-dangle.

'It won't be long before I'm offered a partnership. The place needs a complete shake-up for Brailsfords to survive. Harry's been fretting for some time about the lack of little Bs to take over. Then I came along. Called me a breath of fresh air.' He steered the spag bol mouthwards. 'And now Ma Brailsford's taken a real shine to you. He takes a lot of notice of her. You know, behind every brilliant man –'

'There's a woman with a can of Pledge?'

Oliver lowered his fork. 'Harry sets a lot of store on family values. Marriage and all that.' His face came closer. 'You and me, Jay – we make a great team.'

His eyes were, Jane thought, almost azure in this light. Like in that poem... *He clasps the crag with crooked –*

Oliver took her hands across the table. 'Getting out of London was the best move I ever made.'

Close to the sun in lonely lands, Ringed by the azure world – or what was that other sky colour? Somewhere it was etched on her brain, proof that thirteen years with a

10

homemade name tape rubbing against the back of her neck hadn't been entirely wasted.

'Stick with me, Jay, and your future's made.'

Something like surrealian, but not quite. Blue skies forever. The stars had been shining on her the day those eyes had caught hers... Except, of course, stars only showed at night. But now his eyes were definitely darker, watching... waiting for her to say something.

'Brailsfords was lucky to get you.'

'You're very loyal, Jane. I like that.' He let go of one hand – 'The way you dropped everything to come with me, though we'd only known each other a few weeks –' and patted the other.

Silly darling. She'd have followed him anywhere. Jack Maloney couldn't understand it – just when he'd pinned *Lettings facilitator* on her chest, which meant, despite the big red L, she usually managed to bring home more than Oli at the end of the month. She was, Jack told her, throwing up a promising future. Even Maddy had been against it. There's only one word for you, Goggle, Mad had said. 'Nuts.' Jane mouthed it across the table.

Oliver dropped the remaining hand. 'Not quite the reply I was expecting.'

'What –' did she just say? More to the point – 'What did you just say?'

'Now feels the right time to make a permanent commitment.'

All belongings should be labelled with an indelible marker.

'I knew,' picking up her hand again, 'you'd be the one, soon as I clicked on you.'

'Oh, I did, too, Oli.' She sighed. It was a wonderful moment, so tender, so intimate... so enigmatic. 'Oliver, when you say permanent –'

He pressed her fingers to his lips. 'Don't spoil the magic.' Kissed each one in turn.

A permanent magnet retains its magnetic properties...

'Let me put you under my spell.' Moist lips traced a path across her hand.

...even in the absence of an inducing force...

'I'll whisk you away to the land of enchantment, far away from reality.'

...remaining stable against outside influences that could demagnetise it.

'It'll soon be Christmas. And when Christmas comes, my angel...' His tongue flicked over her third finger, eyes upturned.

They were to die for, those long dark eyes, peeping out from those pale blue lashes... Idiot. She meant, of course, his pale –

Oliver picked up his spoon. 'Is there any pudding?'

HE'D proposed! Jane stacked the dirty pots next to the sink. It was so romantic. Well, as good as. She held her finger under the tap, waiting for the water to run hot.

Christmas. End of the old, start of the new. Near enough. A perfect time to make it permanent... *made from material that stays magnetised for ever...*

Not that marriage would change anything, she told the little lump in her chest.

Water was spilling over the rim of the bowl. She turned off the tap, watched the cascade subside to a trickle. Thought of geese with rain running off their backs. The little lump followed them round the perimeter fence. A lifetime of confinement, never to fly up from a lake into the early morning sky. Never even to get as far as dabbling a toe in the pond.

'SO you're free after all?' she asked, as he scraped up the last bit of custard. 'I've had my fingers crossed the whole week.' But not her toes. They'd been too scrunched up with going-back angst. 'Because it was you who said I – we – should go.' And everything would be all right if Oli was there. 'I so want you to come.'

She nudged the dish along the carpet and nestled her head into the warmth of his thighs, but not too far. She didn't want him to get sidetracked away from a definite –

'Yes.' He squeezed the volume button on the remote. 'I know you do. And obviously I'd love to come.' The hero mouthed his words in glorious technicolour. 'But I haven't time, now Harry's about to commit. You understand, don't you, angel?'

The answering yes, mumbled into the seam of his trousers, sounded 30% genuine, 60% synthetic. Because there might still be a 10% chance of changing his mind. She should have gone in deeper at the start. After all, she knew exactly –

'What that man wants –' he pressed pause '– is something that really grabs him. That's why I need to work on my restructuring strategy. Precisely how it'll come together doesn't matter. Presentation's everything. How to wow in a non-scary way.'

She lifted her head. 'Nothing too in your face then.' She smoothed the creases in his trousers. 'I guessed it was just an excuse not to have to go shooting.' She sat up. 'I actually pass some geese on the way to work. They're lovely to see, magnificent really. I always look out for them when I'm waiting at the roundabout.'

'Are they Brent or Canada?'

'I don't know. They're white.'

'Just table birds then, waiting for Christmas. I must get in some practice with clay pigeons before then. I've been reading up about handling a shotgun with open sights. When you're new to it, you need to focus with both eyes for accurate depth perception. It all comes down to analysing the situation correctly. Those dummy sessions won't come cheap but I'll be prepared next time Harry asks me.'

'But you might kill one!'

'I'll need to put away more than that for the old sod to take notice. The secret of bagging the perfect goose, apparently, is to aim for the head. Just imagine, at shooting distance that's like hitting a pea on the end of a loose wire.'

With closed eyes, Jane imagines.

'The funny thing is, even with its brains blown out, it might soar up another ten metres. It's all down to catching a nerve. But I reckon, use a bigger diameter shot and aim for the body. A goose doing about forty-five to fifty will only get hit by two or three pellets. Or you might be lucky and get it in the wing. A drop from around seventy metres with a broken wing's going to finish it off sure enough.'

Grounded on the carpet, Jane's hand lies untwitching.

'And you heard what the man said. There are thousands of them. The few we take out won't make any difference.'

On screen, a ginger tabby pushes through the cat-flap.

'Anyway, everyone knows only blood sports prevent the whole countryside being covered in concrete.'

Cat sniffs at the bowl.

'The woods'd be ploughed up if they weren't used for pheasant rearing. Three quarters of the world's moorland's in Britain, what's left of it. Remember, there are a lot of furry animals out there that owe their lives to the twelve-bore.'

As the dish is licked clean, Jane makes a big effort to remember.

'Women are getting a taste for it, too. And doing their bit to preserve heather moors while they're at it.'

Cat rubs against leg.

'Think of all the spaniels that would be out of work on benefits if there were no grouse to pick up.'

He pulls her onto his knee. She snuggles close.

'You do love me, don't you?'

'You bet.'

Fade out to sound of purring.

'HOLD it, Jane.' Christian came through waving a post-it note. 'Another punter for sixty-six.'

'Jubilee Terrace?' It was Friday afternoon, for God's sake. Her coat was zipped past half way. Should she remind him she wouldn't be in tomorrow?

'That's the only place that's been on the books so long we're on first name terms. See if you can get a definite this time, sweetie.'

Probably best not to bother. 'I do try.'

'Oh, I'm not saying you don't stir up plenty of interest.' He pressed the post-it note across her zip pull. 'But I take it no-one's made you a firm offer?'

He took another swill of tea and managed to swallow most of it before saying, 'Trust me, sweetie, one schlimazel is all it needs. Gloss over the dross and push the best features. Shove them in his face, give him an eyeful.' He swiped the back of his hand across his mouth. 'Make sure he appreciates the full potential. Know what I mean?'

'I understand you perfectly, Christian.' She picked up her bag.

'Thought you would, bright little thing like you. Remember what they say: there's a sucker born every minute. Mind you, in my experience –' he drained his mug '– it's not every day you'll come face to whatzit with a swallo-'

But Jane had already shut the door.

'I SUPPOSE I'd better get going.' She fingered the blended polymer fur of her new coat. 'I've left stuff in the fridge.' Scarcely a week old. 'I'm going to miss you so much.' Almost a newborn.

'Me too, angel.'

'Wish you were coming with me.'

'Another time, eh?' He looked at his phone.

'I'll be thinking of you every minute.'

The phone squirmed.

'I need to take this.'

Three, or maybe fewer, fingers waved as he disappeared into the lounge.

Jane lugged her bag to the front door. The paper, plus half a kilo of supplements, was sticking out of the letterbox. She pulled it through and sandwiched in the torn bits. But should she take it through and disturb him when he'd said –

'Keep it quiet.'

He had his back turned when she peeped round the door.

'Lucky you spotted it, Simon. Proves what dead wood Mark is, like I said. But don't mention anything to Harry.'

Without speaking

'Best leave all that to me, mate…'

Jane balanced the paper on the arm of his chair

'So things don't tip the other way…'

where all four sections slithered out

'Because I'm sure I can turn this round…'

the paper itself only sliding to the floor as the front door banged

'And do you a bit of good on the quiet…'

as soundlessly as a front door could bang.

SHE'D only done it once before this way. It had been his idea: she needed – and of course he was right, she could see that – to re-establish contact. He'd come along too, to give her a bit of moral support. And get to meet her family. Which, as it happened, pleased just about everyone.

Obscure place names gave way to the familiar, the ones she'd left far behind. Because she wasn't, she told the driving mirror, going home. Absolutely not. Just visiting. With a get out of jail free card rubbing shoulders with the easycare label in her pocket. The game was over, the flat iron back in the box.

Anyway, the village was different now. It wasn't just that the Friesians – all Holsteins now – were no longer allowed to splotch down Main Street twice a day. Now there was a link road, 5-bed commuter cottages were the new milch cows. The butcher's had gone and, sandwiched between the Shoulder of Mutton and the Spotted Pig, was a Bengal Tiger, with the surgery opposite. No point in calling, not today.

Round the next corner and... clay clogged beds in the lawn, clipped-back ivy, windows set in stone, front door bolted on the inside... there it was.

'HELLO, Mum.'

Floury hands were held mid-air. 'I didn't hear you come.'

Jane kissed the nearest cheek, as though there hadn't been a five year gap between now and dumping her school bag on the –

'Don't put it there, Jane. You can see I'm baking.'

Because the Big Reconciliation didn't really count. Not with Oli there. There'd been a distinct whiff of Insincerity, special reserve. Now it was unmasked odour of Mother-and-not-the-right-daughter, seeing as – 'Diane not here yet?'

'It's not so easy for her.' Pastry trimmings gathered into a ball, 'There's always so much to do with children,' a light touch with the rolling pin, 'so there should be just time to finish these and get cleared up before they arrive,' followed by a press and twist with the scone cutter. 'What does the clock say now?'

Jane looked. It said she needed two spoons of caffeine to get through till lunchtime. 'Shall I put the kettle on?'

'I thought we'd wait till they come. Why don't you take your bag upstairs? You can have your old room, though Stephanie usually sleeps there. She'll have to make do with the fold-up bed in with Diane. Helen's in the box room.'

'Isn't Rob coming?'

'Yes, of course he is. It would be helpful if you would take up your things, Jane. Before Diane gets here.'

SHE steps inside and shuts the door. Her room. There's the bed, with the same covers, the same rug beside it. There's the window, hung with the same curtains. There's the bookcase, with the books arranged in the same order, and the alarm clock and the bedside lamp. All her old things. So why is there nothing to connect her to this room?

Then she sees him. On the windowsill, nose against the glass. She takes him in her arms, sinking fingers into fur. *My ship sailed from China...* Jane and Booboo, rocking back and forth... *with a cargo of tea...* safe from everything horrid... *all laden with presents...* She turns his face towards her. Two glinting beads stare back, not blinking, not seeing. Not Booboo.

She takes off her coat and puts it on the bed. It lies there, cuffs in the air, a polar bear beached a thousand miles from home. She opens the wardrobe. Where's all her stuff gone? She hangs up the Snow Baby, leaving twenty empty hangers swinging on the rail as the door closes. She leans back against it, counting the beats until the pendulum jangle only rattles in her head, louder and louder... a motor running. Stopping. Doors opening, slamming, kick-starting the morning.

THE smile is Frosted Garnet. Today's make-up snubs its nose at understatement. Diane flashes back a stiletto of Scarlet Ice.

'Have you a kiss for your Auntie Jane, Stephie?'

'Hello, Stephie. I've just been talking to someone upstairs, in your bedroom.' Jane crouched down, watched through slit fingers. 'Do you know who it was?'

The fingers widened.

'He's furry and has a ribbon round his neck. I can't remember what colour it is –'

'It's red!'

'He asked me if he could open the present he saw in my bag. But I said no.' Jane deepened her voice, maybe a couple of octaves too low, because 'Well, who is it for?' came out more tyrannosaurus than teddy. Nevertheless the Stephie-shriek was, Jane decided, as fake rabbit as her new fur coat.

'What an actress,' said Rob. 'She'll be on telly when she grows up.'

'No, Daddy, I'm going to be a doctor when I grow up, like Grandpa.' She turned to Judith. 'Where is Grandpa?'

'At the surgery, making poorly people better.'

Diane raised one eyebrow. 'Couldn't the locum' – or any other Jesus with an index-linked pension – 'have taken it this morning, Mum? It's not every day we're all gathered together...' in the sight of – She glanced at Jane. Baby Sister was definitely back, though whether or not God was looking on was debatable.

'You know your father,' said Judith. 'He doesn't like to put anyone out without good reason. Come along inside. You must be gasping for a coffee.'

'And I,' said Stephie, hopping from one foot to the other, 'want a piss!'

'Stephanie! Ask properly, if you need the toilet.'

'I did. Uncle George told me what it meant.'

'It's not a nice thing for little girls to say,' said Judith.

'Mummy says it. I heard her. She said to Daddy to piss off.'

Trust Jane not to laugh. Diane sighed. Another riotous weekend in store. So they might as well get on with it. She opened the car door.

Jane watched her unstrap Helen from the carry cot on the back seat. Rob was pulling out a Tardisful. Blankets, nappies, toilet seat and toilet step. Bags of rompsuits, sleepsuits, playsuits. Plastic duck, patchwork doll... and Uncle George, eyes disappearing into grinning folds of flesh.

'Janey! Long time no see, eh? Come and give your Uncle George a cuddle. By, you've grown into a big girl, and no mistake.'

Uncle bloody George.

'SHE would have had just as much fun opening it if you'd snipped the sellotape first, Diane.'

'No, she wouldn't, Mum.'

'I always used to cut your presents open,' said Judith. 'Then the paper wasn't wasted.'

Frosted Garnet, now decidedly smudged, and Scarlet Ice, almost licked away, exchanged smiles.

'All doctor's fings!' Stephie rummaged in the red case. 'Look, a fernometer! Open your mouth, Daddy... Oh, I know what this is – a balloon to blow up your arm.'

'You need this as well.' Jane unwound some plastic tubing. 'It's how doctors test blood pressure. Let me show you.'

Stephie snatched it – 'I know that. Grandpa showed me –' fixed in the ear pieces '– because he's a real doctor,' and shoved the diaphragm between Jane's breasts. 'What's this called, Grandma?'

'A stethoscope.'

'A Stephie-scope!' She pranced round the room, repeating the name in a high-pitched sing-song till they gave up trying to correct or stifle it.

Or her, thought Jane.

'I want to show Grandpa my Stephie-scope!' and she turned towards the window. Brocade curtains swept straight across the carpet, shutting off the bay and the dazzle of low sun. Stephie made a gap and poked her head through. 'Where is he?'

Night after night the little girl had stood there, in the wasteland between mildewed cotton linings and damp-hung panes, watching the same trees shaking the same darkness, waiting for the same man.

Sensing audience unrest, Stephie delved into the case again, and when she pulled out the next bit of plastic they all looked. All except one.

Unnoticed, the little girl crept back into her in-between world to watch and wait.

'I DIDN'T think he'd be coming.'

'George? Don't worry, he isn't staying to wet the baby's head tomorrow.' Diane turned both taps on full. Water spattered the Pop Art calendar hanging by the sink, adding another dimension to Hockney's *Bigger Splash*. 'You know what he's like when he's had a few drinks.'

Jane moved herself – moved her cashmere sweater – a step back. 'Ogling every female within groping distance, you mean.'

'Georgie's harmless. He's all talk.'

'Men like him make me cringe.'

'You must be permanently screwed up, then.' Diane flipped up the cap on the Fairy. 'They're all the same.' She squeezed in a week's worth – 'They tell you what they'd like to do in case you don't notice when they're actually doing it' – though 2.4 squirts was usually enough.

'Oliver isn't –'

'I was talking about men generally, as a sub-species, not your personal paragon. Lumping men together. Best thing to do with them.' Diane dunked the nearest pile of pots. 'Put them in a bag marked "God's booby prize" and tie the neck with a reef knot, or a double Granny if they didn't graduate from cubs.'

'I bet Christian was a boy scout.'

'Who's Christian?'

'My waste of space boss.'

'Bit of a woggle-fiddler, is he? There's at least one in every office.'

'Apart from the WOS Boss, they're a great set of guys.'

'So there's just you and more than your fair share of talent?' Diane's left eyebrow twitched. 'Not enough detail.'

'I was the only female, but Christian took on a new intern a few weeks ago. Well, she's more of a general factotum really.' And someone else to be on the receiving end, thank God.

'A general what?'

'A Jack-of-all-trades.' Lukewarm pots were piling up faster than the national debt. 'Or rather, a –'

'You mean the office dogsbody.' The crocks were winning hands down. 'What did you call it?'

'Factotum. You know, from the Latin.'

'No. I don't,' said Diane. 'Sounds like another word for treating someone like shit. I expect you all do, too.'

'I certainly don't. Nor does Roy –'

'Roy? He's got a GCSE in Latin as well, I suppose. Amazing what qualifications you need to flog houses nowadays.' And there was everyone thinking it would come in handy at medical school. Except Baby Jane copped out. What's the Latin for Loser, little sister?

Two dribbles of water slow-raced down the Hockney print. Jane watched them meander across the disturbed surface of the swimming pool.

'You should see the framed certificates in the front office,' she said.

At the edge of the diving board the dribbles merged into a single channel which trickled down Nov-Dec, leaving the image as it was, a moment impossible to capture in reality.

'Christian's main qualification's in Liberal-with-the-Truth Studies.'

'Lying and touching up?' Diane's brows met across her nose. 'The standard all-rounder.' She must remember to borrow some tweezers tonight. Or not scowl for the rest of the weekend. Which was asking a bit much.

'He's not hands-on, just smutty.' Jane rubbed at some lipstick on the rim of the glass. 'Doesn't bother me, of course.'

Course it doesn't, said the scarlet smudge.

'But he makes Xanthe blush, which only makes him worse.'

'Georgie's the same,' said Diane. 'Don't let him see you're bothered.' She scowled at the burnt-on rice pudding round the dish and pushed it under the water.

'The thing is –' Jane scratched at the glass because the Marilyn pout was proving stubborn '– he's almost family. He's even seen us in the bath.'

'Yes, you must have been all of three, Mum was there, and we were covered in bubbles. The water used to be quite deep with two in, remember? Could well have been an educational experience for Georgie. He was probably having a Eureka moment.'

'I bet he was.'

'Well, he won't be around tomorrow to spoil the Big Occasion.'

'You don't sound very keen on it.'

'Oh, I want Helen baptised.' Diane paused, mid-dunk. 'She could've been done at our local church, of course.'

'Didn't think you'd know where that was.'

'I go along most Wednesdays, actually,' said Diane. 'Mother and Toddler Communion. The best part's when we're squashed round the rails, with all the little paws trying to grab the freebies. You know, those wafers that clog the roof of your mouth, and wine that tastes like Jesus hadn't quite got the hang of it when he did his first miracle. The vicar's sash is fair game, as well, so it's a bit of a laugh –' as well as a smidgen of something other, but she wasn't letting Jane in on that piece of info '– and it doesn't last long.' Neither did the feeling of otherness. It all seemed to evaporate once the blessing had been said, as though the also-with-yous gave the touched-soul feelings back to the vicar, to be kept under wraps along with the chalice and plate. Like this God rep wanted to keep everything under his control. Just another man after all. 'The whole thing's over and done with by the time the kids are scaling the altar rails. There's coffee afterwards so we can have a natter.' Competing with playgroup duty for high spot of the week. Diane jabbed a knife at the rice pudding crust.

'So why aren't we all at yours tomorrow?'

'Mother Dear wouldn't miss an opportunity like this. Half the village coming back to the house and the other half wishing – oh, sod this.' Diane lifted the dish onto the worktop and left it to soak. 'I can't think why she doesn't get a dishwasher, like everyone else in the world.'

'I haven't got one.'

'Take it from me, it needs to go pretty near the top of your must-have list.'

'I've got the only thing I want.'

'Give it another six months. There comes a time in every relationship when there's a need for gadgets.'

'I'd rather have what I've got than a fitted kitchen.'

The washing-up bowl bobbed on a greasy sea, considering the alternatives, while the wash mop had a stab at shifting the lumps in the plug-hole. And decided that, all in all, it'd settle for built-in convenience.

'Mummy!' The door slammed against the table.

Taken off guard, the mop cocked a snoop at Hockney, putting the superlative on *Bigger Splash* as it plunged into the bowl. Greasy water sloshed over Diane's arms and soused the draining dishes.

'Oh, fuck to them.' Diane flipped over the bowl and left it drowning in the blocked sink.

'What did you say, Mummy?'

'Look at this! Sopping wet.'

'What did Mummy say, Auntie Jane?'

'Factotum.'

'What's a factotum?'

'It's someone who has to do five hundred things at once,' snapped Diane. Then, seeing Stephie's face, 'It's what Mummies do, sweetheart. Lots and lots of jobs.'

'And what do Daddies do?'

Water trickled up the inside of Diane's sleeve as she tried to squeeze it out. 'Factotum all.'

'NAUGHTY girl!'

'I was only looking, Mummy!' But the chameleon tongue wasn't long enough to lick off all the pink icing round her mouth.

'Grandma's going to be so cross with you!'

'Auntie Jane!' Stephie burrowed her face into the cashmere.

But though Jane stroked Stephie's head, the other little girl couldn't control the smile that played around her lips, or suppress a bubble of excitement at what was to happen next.

All three froze at Judith's step. But Stephie had heard something else.

'Grandpa's here!'

She ran across the kitchen, but Jane beat her to it. Flung open the door. And there he was.

'PASS Charles the mint sauce, Rob,' said Judith.

'I'll do it!' Stephanie snatched up the dish. 'There you are, Charles.'

'Grandpa,' hissed Diane.

'But he is called Charles, isn't he, Grandma?'

'Most people call him Dr Challis.'

'You're not into this familiarity with your patients, then?' said Rob.

'I should hope not,' said Judith. 'It would be hard to disclose intimate details if you're on first name terms.'

'Might make it easier. Warm your hands, Charlie, before you stick two fingers up my – nostrils.'

'Do some people call you Charlie, Grandpa?'

'Sometimes. But I can't say it's my favourite name.'

'Is Charles your favourite name?'

'I expect it's Grandpa, isn't it?' said Diane. 'That's a very special name.'

'It certainly is,' said Charles. 'In fact, there's only one person who calls me it.'

'Me! But Mummy has a special name for you, too. Well, it's a bit special, but not special like Grandpa, cos –' she reached across the table '– she has to share it with Auntie Jane' – to pat Diane's hand.

'Careful, Stephie! Mind you don't knock over the –'

In the moment between the warning and the chair scraping, plate shifting, cloth sousing, calf slapping

26

inevitable, Jane mouthed the word. Just for him. And he smiled. Just for her.

Because the squeaker was wrong. Diane had a stock standard Dad. Daddy was all hers. Whereas Grandpa – Jane looked at Stephie, whose face had clouded over with sudden realisation...

'When Helen learns to talk, I won't be the only one with a special name for him.'

No you won't, smiled Jane. But I will.

SHE left them playing happy families. Taking out her phone, Jane went straight into the message – *Did u no llamas r only animal that can lick own ears??* As if she needed reminding about last night. She clicked reply. *Hey sexy lama I can think of somewhere Id like 2 b lickin rite now xx* Pressed send. Read his message again, every bit. Realised it was from Roy.

Oh, sh- e couldn't go back through, not now. Anyway the kitchen had always been her favourite room. Evenings by the Rayburn, hunched over right-angled triangles... reshelving the copper jelly moulds, black-ringed fingernails smelling of Brasso... filling the fat-bellied barrel with still warm biscuits, lick-fingering crumbs from under the baking rack... choosing which apple from duck-billed Martha with the missing eye, now flying up into her arms. Jane stroked the woven willow wings, remembering...

'Nice pair of juicy melons you've got there.'

Uncle George pushed the door to behind him.

Beneath the clinging cashmere, Jane felt her flesh shrink. She tried to put the basket down, but her jumper had caught on the side. Stitch-snagged to wicker feathers, it stretched itself between Jane and Martha, while the talking head looked on.

Kept on talking – 'Need any help there, Janey?' – kept on looking, till every barb was freed.

Don't let him think you're bothered. Concentrate on the unblemished skins of irradiated fruit. Look but don't touch, because the garden pippins will be back in the basket once the guests have gone. Good enough for family.

George had switched his attention to a ring-pull.

A childhood of nibbling round the surface bruises: taking a bite with fingers crossed that the codling moth hadn't got there first. Well, tonight she was going to have a class one Pink Lady, guaranteed maggot free. Although... bananas had more than twice as much potassium. Not forgetting the selenium.

She remembered George as she took her first bite. George, standing by the door, bitter sliding down the outside of his glass as banana turned to slime ball in her mouth. George, waiting for her to –

The door whammed into his shoulders. Beer slopped down his trousers as Reliant Rob came whistling in. George shuffled out, dab-hankying the telltale patch of damp.

'All right, babe?' as she struggled to swallow the lump of mush.

'Don't' – she peeled back more skin – 'you ever' – waved the stump in Rob's face – 'call me babe.' Stuffed it in the grinning hole.

'AT last.' Diane squeezed onto the sofa. 'I've got her off.'

And Stephie – Jane shifted along to make room – had been dispatched long ago, thank God. If she'd had to sing *My Ship Sailed from China* one more time she'd have rammed the cargo of tea down Little Miss Bliss's throat, like this, like this, like this... And as for the doctor's set, in future she'd make sure presents were only given for Christmas and birthdays – if Stephie lived to see another, there was tomorrow to get through – and then strictly by post.

'Is that the time?' Judith looked up from the something she was doing with string. 'And George still to take home.' It seemed to involve knots. 'You'd better drive him, Diane, as you've not had a drink. You can take the Mondeo.'

Diane almost smiled. 'Better get off, then, or it'll be time for her next feed,' because life was just – 'Wake up, Uncle George, it's bedtime' – one pyjama party after another.

'Perhaps someone ought to go with you.'

Diane booted an outstretched foot. 'You coming then?'

'In a minute.' Rob had to shift right over to see round her. She could be an awkward cow, could Di. 'This free kick could clinch it.'

'I'll come,' said Jane.

'Just as you like.' Diane shrugged. 'Bring the paper. In case he's sick.' In the Mondeo with a bit of luck.

THEY propped George against the wall while Diane searched out his latchkey, or whatever he called it. Jane kept him pinned, right where the jutting brickwork met the small of his back. No doubt the Victorians had a name for that as well.

Diane pushed open the first door from the hall.

A switch flick and the front room was sprung into sepia, under the dust-shade dangle of a bulb so low-energy a wash-over in Lucozade wouldn't have made any difference. Most of the space was taken up by the bed. Was that where the pong was coming from, or was it the damp clothes spread over the sideboard? Concentrated essence of rotting Uncle George, now engaged in his favourite game of fly clutching. Thank God Di was steering him out.

'It's like a morgue in here.' Diane lit a match and bent to coax a flicker from the gas, kneeling on the circle of floorboard before the armchair, where, way back in the summer of love, the shag pile had given up the struggle.

Whereas the carpet in front of the box enjoyed a sheltered existence under the heap of DVDs. Jane picked one up. 'My God!' Began to turn them over – 'Di, have you seen these?' – case after see-through case.

'The old bugger!' Diane squatted down beside her. 'Let's see what else there is.'

'I wouldn't have believed it was possible –' for us to ever be as close as this, nudge, nudge.

'Ssh! I think he's coming.'

He shuffles chairwards, wrongly buttoned. Sinks down, saliva etching a channel from his jowl. Without a word, Diane leans forward and unties his laces. Eases last week's socks along aubergine feet. Unhooks caked wool from sickle nails, thick as horn. Overlapping devil toes, seeping pus onto transparent skin.

How can Di put her hand between those sheets? Yet out they come: cardie, bed socks, balaclava, pyjamas with a dangling cord.

Jane can't bear to watch the shedding, can't look the other way. Please let it stop, the long-stretch long-sleeved vest, on its forever journey. Alleluia it's off, the hidden layers made flesh. Great lolling rolls of it. Scrawny arms are pushed into sleeves and something sharp is puncturing her knee. Diane's inching off stink-stained underpants and all Jane can do about it is grind her kneecap into the edge of the DVD case. Hard.

For one moment it hangs there, that shrunken skin-shroud of his brain. Then it's parcelled up in candy stripes.

'Give me a lift, Jano.'

She can't move. Not when her knee's fractured in three places.

'Jane.'

Uncle George is frogmarched to the bed. He perches on the edge, waiting for Diane to lift his legs and swing them onto the mattress. She extracts teeth. Checks the pisspot for easy reach.

'Fire, Jane.'

'What?'

Diane opens the door. 'Don't forget the light.'

Jane turns off the fire and hurries across the room, eyes fixed on the doorway. As she presses the light switch, a volley of bullets lacerates her back. She stands, frozen, waiting to crumple to the floor. The door swings shut. A moment of total blackness, a creeping tinge of red. She turns. The gas fire's glow fades, the firebricks' contractions peter out. Nothing remains except the breathing bed.

'I DON'T suppose he's ever actually done it.'

'You think?'

'Well,' said Jane, 'he never married. And women didn't, then, unless.'

'You think not?' Ms Einstein getting hold of the wrong end again. 'Perhaps his one true love was a bra-burner way back. Forerunner of you.' Though, Diane had to admit, Jano had come on a lot since her stuffing socks in a Wonderbra days. 'Hundred and ten percent elastic, no strings attached.' Cross your heart and hope.

'It's not like that,' said Jane. 'Oli and I have an equal relationship. We put the same into it and get the same out.'

'Like a joint bank account? Except – sod you, how much bloody road do you want? – one of you'd still have to sign – up yours too. Don't talk to me about equality.'

Which left things a bit on the quiet side. Except for a familiar tapping against the steering column. Jane couldn't see the fob dangling from the ignition key. But it would still be there. She'd spotted it at the Forestry Centre, on a school trip. There'd been a box of them, short lengths of thick twig, sliced diagonally across at one end, two little beads and an upturned mouth on the slanting edge, a hat on top: baseball caps, Comanche feathers, Robin Hood titfers. One with a golden crown. It cost almost all her spending money but she had to have it. A rubber would do for her mother. Daddy must have his forest fairy princess to keep him safe over the miles with an always smile, reminding him his real little princess would love him, and she couldn't help saying it aloud, 'forever and ever.'

'You're forgetting one thing, said Diane. 'You're not a paid-up member of the till-death-us-do-part club. Oliver could be sizing up some fresh talent right now.'

'We're free to make contact with anyone else, but we happen to love each other.'

'Call that love? If Rob tried to "make contact", as you put it, I'd cut his bollocks off, no questions asked.'

'Oh, I thought when he said he didn't –' French Connect. Me and my big mouth. Not that she'd even wanted to know. Rob and his big –

'Been giving you the hard-on story, has he? Trouble is, men's brains being located where they are, they've got short memories.'

'You're not too sore, then?' Did she really want to know?

'That excuse lasts about a fortnight.'

'Do you need an excuse?'

'Course I don't.' Not really. Because it didn't take long; he had to be quick before she fell asleep. Sheep didn't come into it nowadays. Diane sighed. Had there really been a time when his touch had been nuclear? When every snatched moment alone together had been flesh fusion with a double F? Another time, another borrowed Mondeo. She'd given Rob the keys. Her mother would never know. Doing a ton – well, eighty-five, it was a Ford – spray churning, face burying, teeth tugging at the zip... engulfing, gorging... In the wheel-gripped sway of the moment, death would have been the never-ending climax. God, the thought of it was enough to make you want to do your pelvic floor exercises there and then.

Diane changed gear and took the corner at twenty-three. 'I take it the smug silence means your child-free existence consists of back-to-back multiples? More detail needed.'

Jane tapped her nose. Which was a bit wasted on Diane, with a pair of headlights coming straight at her on full beam.

'Must be a bit of a strain, having to be perfect every time. Forget to stock up on aspirin and you go your separate ways.'

Jane yawned. She'd had her five-a-day from sour-grapes Di. 'You can't ever stop resenting me for getting away, can you?'

Diane had to admit, to herself, that Jano's bunk-off had been a bit of a bombshell. Who would've thought the mouse would've had enough spark? Her mother had nearly had a fit. Winged-it Jane became centre stage. It'd needed something mega to cap that – like telling her mother she was getting hitched. And then telling Rob. Exit Jane. But satisfaction, she'd found, was short-lived. Lately she'd even begun to suspect that Mum almost liked him. Meanwhile Jane had got away. Landed herself a dishy bloke, as well. Although there was something about him, not just that he was older, but something else...

'Enjoy it while it lasts, Jano, because –' how could she put this tactfully? '– you must know, deep down, that Oliver's not as fantastic as you make out.' Tact wouldn't do it. 'Be honest, don't you think he's a bit of a –'

Jane jabbed Audio On. Radio Yawn still churning out Dylan and all the answers still blowing in the sodding wind.

WHY hadn't he replied to her text? It was a bit late to try phoning again. The baby was crying. Why hadn't he picked up? She heard Di going in, heard the comfort murmurings. Why hadn't he rung back? In the stillness Jane could make out the sound of suckling. Tiny nostrils would be squashed against Diane's breast, tiny lips vacuumed to Diane's nipple, tiny cheek stroked with the back of Diane's finger.

The earth goddess. Could that be her, a few years from now? Would Oliver want children? Course he would. A son first, naturally – with the aid of a thermometer accurate to three decimal places plus shellfish for dinner. Most likely breakfast as well. Was post-coital legs-on-the-bedpost in or out? It'd be their own bedpost by then, of course. In somewhere a tad more rural than behind the old gas works. Maybe a pony grazing in the paddock. A guinea pig on the back lawn, anyway. All part of the Plan. And it would start to fall into place at Christmas.

She tossed over onto her stomach, bunched and plumped the pillow, rested chin on hands. Maybe she should she try – no, the battery was low. She'd put it on charge first thing. Which couldn't be that far off, and the frigging baby was at it again. A pillow over the head wouldn't be enough.

Might as well see if she could help. Jane edged open her door though surely the whole house, plus the hamlet's forefathers, even the half decent ones, must be awake by now. And there was another sound... where had she heard that tune? She couldn't make out the words. She didn't need to. *There's a ship sails away, at the close of each day... her lips couldn't stop... Sails away to the land of dreams. Mummy's baby –*

Rob stumbled across the landing without seeing her.

'Give her to me.'

From the doorway Jane could make out tears on the circles above Di's cheekbones, the hair sticking out in clumps, the nightdress damp over harnessed breasts. Rob moved round her chair, shushing and cooing and patting the tiny back. 'Get back to bed, love. I'll get her settled. Little Helen, giving hell, aren't you, my precious? Go on, girl –' he kissed the topmost clump '– you're about all in.'

Jane crept to her room and put her head back under the pillow.

'LUCKY there was a wedding yesterday,' said Judith. 'Flowers are so expensive this time of year. You can take your car to the church, Jane. There're bound to be people needing a lift. Mrs Wainwright will, for a start.'

'No problem. I'll take her home, too.'

'That won't be necessary. Jonny's coming to pick her up.'

'Oh. What's he up to now?' Since the days he did a different sort of picking up.

'He got married a couple of years ago, to some town girl.'

'I took Stephie down to see them come out,' said Diane. 'She gave the bride a lucky horseshoe. She looked so sweet – she was just off to toddle. They split up soon after. Spoon your soup away from you, Stephie.'

'Should have got your money back, Di,' Rob said.

'Stephie, don't slurp.'

'Trade Descriptions Act,' said Rob between mouthfuls. 'Not fit for purpose.'

'Or you.'

'Young people today,' said Judith. 'No sense of commitment.'

That's it, Mother Dear, thought Jane, do a bit of stewed prude head shaking.

'Anyone could see it wouldn't last,' said Diane. The vicar had no doubt opened a book on it. 'They weren't at all suited.'

'If they'd lived together first,' said Jane, 'they'd have found out.'

'Don't see why,' said Diane. 'You haven't.' Well, no-one else was going to say it.

Or look at her. Not even the MD, ladling out second helpings. The dish was scraped into Diane's bowl.

'Oliver and I are getting engaged at Christmas.' Who'd said that? Too late now to switch on her brain, with a barrage of Os coming from all directions. Even from the end where Daddy was sitting.

'You must bring him here again soon,' said Judith. 'We'd like to get to know him better, wouldn't we, Diane?'

'Sure.' She grinned. 'Join the club.'

THE scene was set: baby on the rug, camera at the ready. But only the lace petticoats were saying four generation cheesecloth. Over the key-jangling, toy-rattling, tongue-clicking coochy-cooing, Helen was screaming like a banshee babe who'd just realised her outfit was so last century.

Diane unhitched her bra and plugged the squalling mouth.

'You've got the gown crumpled up.' Jane watched as a tiny hand rose to touch skin, then fell again. How could an empty breast be so satisfying? The baby's hold on the nipple had become so relaxed that the suckling only resumed when Diane tried to ease it away. Mother love or maternal instinct – at six weeks were these the same thing? When could you tell the difference? When did it begin to matter?

'There,' said Diane. 'With a bit of luck she'll sleep through the service.'

'But she'll miss what's going on.'

'She's not going to be doing a right lot. The godparents do all the talking. Renouncing the world and the flesh, et cetera.'

Jane looked at the tight-shut eyes. 'Perhaps she doesn't want to renounce them.'

'She can always change her mind later on.' Everybody did, when it came down to it.

ST Mary's was untouched by modern alternatives. The congregation – for never a Sunday went by without someone turning up – wouldn't have it any other way. When all was safely gathered in, what was left of the farming community sheeted up their combines and came along for the annual singsong about ploughing the field and scattering, with a nod to the unfathomableness of God and their feet on the stone floor. The commuters took the nostalgia they'd taken on with their three-figure mortgages a bit more seriously. When it came to the default box, *C of E* did away with any doubts about whether the *I* came first in *ATHEIST*. Because they hadn't dabbled in their pockets to support the Pillar Lime-wash Appeal to find the mason's mark nothing more mysterious than a Plain English Crystal symbol. And now they'd called a ban on the Manor Farm dairy herd pat-spattering down Main Street, it was satisfying to hear, once in a while, that cleanliness was next to godliness. Especially in the sure and certain hope that, the vicar's next service being eight miles away, it wouldn't overrun.

Dost thou, in the name of this child, renounce the devil and all his works, the vain pomp and glory of the world, with all covetous desires of the same, and the carnal desires of the flesh, so that thou wilt not follow, nor be led by them?

Jane looked down. Thank God it was still asleep, this incarnation of original sin. She couldn't detect any signs of depravity as yet, but neither could she see anything Rob-like, even though everyone said Helen had his ears. Why this insistence on the baby looking like its Dad? Surely the milkman was above suspicion nowadays, with Asda running semi-skimmed as a loss leader.

She glanced at the other godparents for a cue, but Colonel and Mrs Hirst plunged straight in, one after the other. *I re I re I them all nounce them all.* Should she try and time it somewhere between the two? Maybe just keep her mouth shut. That was usually best.

She wasn't sorry to hand the baby over. Her arms felt numb. The vicar poured water, cloth ready... *manfully to fight under his banner against sin, the world and the devil, and to continue Christ's faithful...* Gradually the feeling returned... *unto her life's end.*

Unto her life's end. Helen was six weeks old, for God's sake. Three score years and ten was short change nowadays. But however long, a complete life. Butterfly equals oak tree, and who's to say which one will find Nirvana – did enlightenment come after? What did come after? Jane looked down the church, at the bodies turned in their pews. 'Let us sit or kneel to pray.' As if anyone's not going for the soft option.

Our Father... words taken up in a muffle of bowed heads...*thy kingdom come...* Certainty or hope? She wouldn't think about it. Wouldn't have to, once she'd escaped from this place. *Behold, the Kingdom of God is within you.* Jane pulled at her collar. It was stifling. Where was reality when you needed it?

The organ made a false start on the final hymn and someone's mobile stepped in to fill the silence. Oh, God, please don't let it be – Oli. She switched off her phone, the organ ground into the last verse and Helen was handed back. The tiny face puckered.

'Shush,' said Jane, rocking in double time. 'Nothing to cry about. It's all over now.'

'THERE'S the sun,' said Judith. 'Just when we've finished taking the photos.'

'Light conditions don't make any difference nowadays, Mum, with all those pixels.' Diane pulled the shawl further round the baby's head. 'Let's get going. It's Arctic out here. Come on, Stephie, we're going back to Grandma's.'

Judith wound down the window. 'Don't forget you're taking –'

But Mrs Wainwright was already in Festina's front seat, knees splayed and at the ready. Jane got in and started up.

'Oh, drat it, I've gone and left me gloves in church. Would you mind getting them, honey? It'll not take two shakes of a duck's tail.'

'Of course.' Jane switched off the engine. 'Whereabouts did you leave them?'

'In me usual spot.'

The church pervaded gloom. Jane scanned the pews and there they were, third row from the pulpit. Pink stretch nylon, ruched wrists, a neat darn down one finger. As she turned to go her eye was caught by a gleam of light. Not the visitors-be-sure-to-note stained glass on the east window, directly in front. The guidebook didn't mention that, at this time of day, it ran the whole gamut from grey to black. Because the low sun was now coming through the side window, rippling the altar, drawing her towards it. The brass cross winked where the rays touched, throwing a long shadow behind.

Afterwards she couldn't say – not that she would ever tell a soul – why she'd knelt. Or even that she had. *God the Father Almighty.* Forgive my unbelief. *In Jesus Christ*

His only begotten Son. An invisible creator beamed down from the polished crucifix. *In the Holy Ghost.* All this I steadfastly believe. So she'd said. *And in the remission of sins: the devil, the world and the flesh.* I renounce them all, so she'd read; had concentrated hard on getting the words right. Never mind the message.

So then they that are in the flesh cannot please God. Believe it and you're condemned. *For to be carnally minded is death...* The cross dissolved, the lilies blurred... Funeral lilies, lying on oak veneered chipboard years before, and Grandma Bates inside, dolled up like a courtesan in pink nylon froth – *Eeh, I wouldn't be seen dead in that* – with a thin line of red lipstick like she never wore. *Kiss Grandma goodbye, Jane, before they fasten down the lid...*

She dabbed her eye with Mrs Wainwright's glove. Yesterday's lilies, nothing more. Cut to sanctify the kowtowing bride, now left to wilt at the altar, while the licence to lust was shoved under the knickers in the bottom drawer. Each one flawless, marble carved. Too perfect. Jane picked one, no different from the rest, and stroked its inner edge. Knuckles brushed against a stamen, knocking suspended pollen dust onto milky skin. *Make sure those bits have been cut off, Jane, to save any mess.* She looked at her stained hand and wiped two fingers on the palm of the glove.

A scraping from behind made her turn. She peered into the gloom. There was someone at the back of the church, nicking the collection.

'Hey, you!' She hurried down the aisle. 'Stop!'

The vicar stopped.

So did Jane. 'Just came back for these.' She waved the gloves.

'You'll be needing them.' He touched her arm. 'You seem rather upset.'

Behind him and his little bag of money was the great door, black against an arch of light round the edge.

'Something's troubling you.' He caught hold of her sleeve – 'Whatever's worrying you –' held on like a Jack Russell trying out a new set of teeth '– we can talk it through. Rent arrears, mortgage default, unpaid utility bills, unauthorised overdrafts, credit card debt, pay day loans...'

God, didn't this guy think of anything other than – of anything other? Jane shook herself free, made for the door. Before he got onto fines for trespass. She twisted the iron ring, tried it both ways.

'You can't get out that way.'

She could feel terrier breath damp on her neck.

'It's locked.'

She rattled the ring, pulled with both hands.

'And bolted.'

He reached his arm round her. From the huge door a little one swung open. Jane ducked her head and stepped over the bottom plank into the low sun.

'You've tekken your time,' as Jane tossed the gloves into the old woman's lap.

Mrs Wainwright gave them a cursory glance. 'Them's not mine.' The gloves were tossed back. 'Your mother always said you never could do owt right.'

'NOW what you fetched me?' Mrs Wainwright looked at the last cup on Jane's tray. 'I can't drink that. As weak as water and twice as wet.'

Oh, just take it, can't you, you old crotchet, then I can dump this and find Daddy.

'But then, your mother's as stingy wi' tea bags as owt else.' Mrs Wainwright winked.

'I'll go and make you a stronger cup.'

41

'And when you've med it, come and sit wi' us a while.'

Great. Still, it would kill some time while everyone got settled and she could get him on his own. Because she was damned if she was going round again with another tray. All that snide it's-ages-since-anyone's-seen-you-didn't-go-to-be-a-doctor-after-all-they-did-for-you-aren't-married-yet-I-see... I see. The knowing nods. They hadn't a clue. It was like being in a time warp. Not a frigging clue. She slopped the tea down the sink, dropped three bags in the cup and gave them a thorough mashing.

MRS Wainwright sipped noisily. 'A cat'd live here better a week than a fortnight.'

Jane frowned.

'Blueblob.' Mrs Wainwright nodded at the cup.

'Oh, the milk,' said Jane. 'It's skimmed. Better for your heart than full-cream.'

'Aye, I seen folk in t'supermarket, paying t'same for it as proper milk. When me and Jack first started up, we had to buy so much back from t'Milk Board as skimmed just so's they could get rid of it. We fed it to t'calves, poor beggars. I wouldn't have it in t'house. Mind you, I remember me Da saying when he worked at Farm Place t'lads got blueblob instead of tea.' She drained her cup.

The old bat would be after a refill now. Which meant running the risk of being collared by the other Brooke Bond junkies. 'So he thought he was badly done to, being given skimmed milk?' Was that Daddy, across the room?

'He'd be lucky if it weren't smoked, an' all. The lasses got up and lit the fire while t'men were feeding the 'osses, and put milk on to warm afore it were properly going.'

'Oh, yes. A pan on the fire.' It was Daddy, and the crones were closing in. The usual small talk: varicose veins and sluggish bowels.

'Nay, lass. They hung a pot from t'reckins.'

What the frig were reckins? And what was the old besom looking at, through the lights reflected on the pane? Two pinpricks of red glowed from the shadows.

'T'fire'd be smoking away...'

Rob and one of his pals who'd come over, out for a fag.

'A couple of thick slices of cold fat bacon on each plate...'

No, not Rob, because the tea and sandwiches brigade was approaching, with Rob at heel bearing milk jug and new season piccalilli.

'I can see Jane's been neglecting you,' said Judith. 'What will you have, Margery?'

Mrs. Wainwright helped herself to a pork pie and a good spoonful from the jar. Plastic teeth bit into raised pastry. A glob of gelatine slid down her chin, dropping between the paisley collar and the cultured pearls.

THE bought stuff had run out. Now they could start on the homemade. Pear, elderflower, parsnip, peapod – definitely one for later – bramble... The only shortage was glasses.

'Oh, good,' said Diane, nudging open the door. 'I was hoping...' some sucker would be up to the elbows in suds. She plonked a few more on the draining board. Better make a show of doing her bit for the home front, now that –

'Your friends have left, I see,' said Jane. 'Nice of them to come all this way.'

'They're good mates.' Diane picked up a tea towel. A quick wipe round a few rims would do. 'I nearly asked them to be godparents.'

'Why didn't you?'

'Well, as Mum said, they might not stay in the area all that long.' As well as pointing out that the Hirsts' christening gift would probably run into three figures.

'You have to think ahead.' To the next eighteen birthdays and Christmases, for instance. 'We'll probably lose touch, sooner or later.'

'Don't see why. You just have to make a bit of effort – I haven't done that one yet.'

'It's okay –' Diane huffed on the glass – it would do, the peapod was guaranteed to kill all known germs '– for you dinkys. You can just drop everything. Bet you're down to London all the time.' She pushed the tea-towel inside and twisted. 'Aren't you?'

'Actually, I haven't been back. Not yet.'

'Oh.' It was a long Oh, a two-note eyes-twinkle-at-the-glass Oh. 'I don't believe I'm hearing this.' The glass winked back. 'What's happened to the friends-forever? Mates for life, you said.' Diane gave the glass another huff. 'Specially – what's she called? – Maddy.' There was nothing that wouldn't come clean if you rubbed hard enough.

'New place, new friends.' Like Simon and GF. And there was Roy, of course. But he was strictly office. 'I will go back and see them, of course. Soon as I can.'

Lifting the rim for inspection, Diane looked at Jane through the cut glass, watching shafts of light fragment off the surface and dissolve into the air.

UNDER the lamp, finger on the bell, was Jonny Wainwright.

'Jane! I heard you were coming.'

Still the same wink and toss of the head.

'Long time no see, eh?' He took her hand, took both her hands.

She'd forgotten those cracks and calluses, far more now than –

'How about a kiss for old time's sake?'

Which worked out at 2.5 seconds for each year since –

'We going in or what?' The girl pushed herself between Jonny and the door frame.

'This is Marie. Marie, meet Jane: a very old friend.'

Marie did adoration and antipathy in a quarter turn.

Jonny kept his eyes on Jane. 'You and Marie are bound to hit it off. You've a lot in common. You even look alike.'

Maybe, thought Jane, at twenty paces, but Oli would have done spot-the-difference even with the lamp switched off. Marie was the chainstore counterpart. Okay, once she might have been Marie. No need to flash that diamond solitaire in my face – I wasn't Jonny's first true love and don't think you're his last. Not when there are 240 acres in the running. Four generations of Wainwrights at Sugar Hill Farm.

She stood back to let them in. 'Go on through. Your Great-Gran's waiting.'

'YOU'RE 'ere, then.' Mrs Wainwright braced herself against the chair arms. 'I'll get me bag.'

'Jonny's just having a drink,' said Marie. 'He won't be long.'

'Hey, Marie –' from across the room '– come and hold the baby, it'll be good practice.'

Which left Jane with Mrs Wainwright and the empty cup. Not that she wanted to join the Young Farmers crowd, though she recognised a few faces from the school bus. Their clothes, hair style, make-up, piercings were indistinguishable from their metropolitan counterparts – did she count herself among these now? Impossible to place herself without comparison to this other existence she'd almost had. But there was something timeless about them, standing chattering together, while their mothers gossiped in the straight back chairs. Theirs was an exclusive club; the sole criterion for membership was to belong already.

It was their outlook, Jane decided, not their dialect, which bound them together.

'Jonny's fiancée seems a nice girl.'

'She's some use, I'll say that for her. Not like the last un. He should've 'ad more sense. In my day you didn't get two bites o' t'cherry. Not decent folks.'

'She said she'd been helping with the milking today.'

'It'll be this day, every day and twice a day, when they're wed.'

A burst of laughter came from the group of girls. A couple of years of hunt balls and hog roasts in machinery sheds, and they'd all be paired up, in a twenty-four seven partnership of mutual need.

'And a lot easier it is now than when I was a young lass just wed.'

Which was unimaginable: this face had always been a craze of furrows, skirting round hummocks of bone pushing their way out of the soil, skull breaking through skin. Decades, centuries even – she looked like she could have supplied Noah with a couple of cows and got a good price for them – spent struggling against the earth. Or – Jane peered closer – maybe the struggle was with the earth, not against it. All so the land could pass down the male line. Farmer's daughter, farmer's wife, with no expectations of a separate identity. Her achievement was to have had sons... because two cows on the Ark would have been dead meat when their udders went dry.

'We 'ad a milk round, as well. Bottles all to wash, and some came back in a right state. I did 'em in the kitchen sink, with this strong stuff med for the job. There's no wonder me hands is so bad.' Mrs Wainwright showed her raw palms, as far as the claw fingers would allow.

'They're awful! You should get Daddy to look at them,' but not this afternoon.

'Oh, I see him regular, wi' me heart. Would've done yesterday, as our Jonny were going down to t'village anyway, but it were just that young doctor on.'

'No, Daddy took Saturday surgery, as usual. It wasn't the locum.'

Mrs Wainwright shook her head. 'Her on t'desk said it were that young lad. So I said I'd wait.'

Jane smiled. Nice one, Nicola. She remembered helping Daddy with the advert. *Receptionist: suit amb prson.* That was to stop it sounding too dead-end. It wasn't actually necessary to be an ambidextrous minister of the cloth, just have *gd ppl skls*, and Nicola's were good enough. Under the blusher lurked a rhino hide well able to deflect abuse when demands for immediate appointments were refused, leaving Dr. Challis more venerated than – oh, God, the thought wouldn't be suppressed. When had she first suspected? Was it while she was drawing up her short-list or when the second-choice place was offered? When had she realised she couldn't risk it?

She looked across. There he was, cornered by a guest edging a sleeve over a wrist. *I'm sure it's nothing, Doctor, but...* She should go across, rescue him. Why hadn't she got some excuses ready? Because she needed to explain.

'He knows about them anyway,' said Mrs Wainwright. 'He's tried me wi' all sorts of different receipts. None of them any better than the goose grease we alus used to use. Me Mam'd melt it and beat it up wi' broom flowers to mek a grand yellow ointment. We used it for all sorts – stopping an 'arness from cracking, sprucing up a beast before a show. And it were just the thing for a tight chest.'

'But what is it?' Was there another panacea waiting undiscovered, so many years after Grandma Bates's mother had wrapped slices of mouldering home-cured bacon over septic wounds and never thought to call it penicillin? Jane picked up the sandwich, two squashed slices of farmhouse white with an oozing slime of – what was inside? Oh, God, not brawn, surely? Please be some sort of pâté, or even meat paste. Anything except squashed brains in glob.

'Why, girl, it's the fat from a goose. When you were dressing one you put your finger under it so you could get it all out in one piece and lay it on top. It'd be an inch or so thick, on a good 'un.'

Jane eyed the sandwich, flattened to within a few millimetres of its existence.

'It weren't bad to get out. Not like the lights, with t'cats waiting round.'

A dollop of nameless pink hung in the air.

'You had to poke your finger behind them, along the rib cage, and out they came – shclop!'

The glob dropped to the plate.

'They thought it was a real treat.'

'Oh, yes.' Jane pushed the plate to the far side of the table. 'Like the polythene bag you sometimes get inside a chicken.'

'A goose had its feet in, an' all. Wi' t'ends sticking out. We had to scald them so t'skin peeled off. Then we med a pudding wi' t'blood and oatmeal and stitched it into t'neck, to mek them look nice and plump. They were a grand sight to see, when they were all dressed.'

Across the room, like a Hydra in self-consultation, the seated circle had its heads together. HRT tittle-tattlers, wedding-guest outfits getting a second airing, minus the fascinators.

'I expect it's all done by machine now,' said Jane. 'Like with chickens.' Just another step in the production line from incubator rack to medium/large-serves-four-to-six shelf. And somewhere in between a life had chipped its way out, with scarcely time or space to turn round before being resealed in plastic. Packed in the UK but where in hell it hatched was anyone's guess. Or would be if Anyone, herself included, took hands out of the pocket long enough to find out. It's all a case of priorities. We're only human.

Mrs Wainwright shook her head. 'Not geese. Still reared natural, they are, and the only proper seasonal bird there is. They can't be factory farmed any more now than when I was a girl. I'd be about ten when I first helped because everyone had to knuckle in. I never did like to see 'em killed, though. Mind you, if you started while they were still twitching, t'feathers came off a lot easier. But they were devils to pluck, and they were left with down all over, so they needed plucking twice. Then you had to singe them, because of the hairs.'

Before the open fire, jackets and cardigans were being pulled off and spread over chair backs. Daddy was standing by himself. At last. Because there'd never been time to talk – really talk, just the two of them. Now they might at least get a few minutes together. She could be back before Mrs Wainwright had finished telling the empty teacup the merits of a drop of meths on a tin lid against a rolled-up bit of paper with one end set alight. If only he'd look across.

'We wrapped a bit of cloth round the head to stop the blood getting on t'feathers because we kept the down and all t'best feathers without quills. Mother med all our beds and pillows, med me one when I was married. Them polystyrene duveys you have nowadays aren't a patch on a proper feather eiderdown. Jack and me still have it on the bed. I put new ticking in it a few years back. Freshened things up a treat. The feathers were still nice. I think it took about seven geese. One of them was owd Toddy. He didn't go to one of the regulars, of course. He'd be tough as owd boots.'

Jane thought of the geese near the flyover, hurrying across to an old woman with a bucket. 'I don't know how you could, after you'd had him so long. It'd be like killing a pet.'

'But owd Toddy wa'nt up to his job any more. He could be a nasty beggar, an' all, when the geese were sitting. When I was little he once bit me bottom so hard I had a big black bruise for weeks. You never knew with Toddy. Quiet as a lamb one minute, then coming at you, head down, wings out, the next. Mother had him for donkey's years.'

'But the other geese – they'd have been born about May, wouldn't they? Such short lives.'

'They had a good life. We looked after them well.'

'And then you wrung their necks.'

Mrs Wainwright shook her head. 'A goose's neck takes some pulling. Me Da used to cross the wings over the back so the head'd bend down and stick his pocket knife through the brain, just above the eyes.'

Jane screwed hers tight but the words wouldn't stop.

'Then he'd put a band round the legs and hang it up so the blood'd run into its head.'

Maybe if she leaned forward she wouldn't actually pass out.

'That's what they were bred for and they'd had canny lives. They'd never have lived at all if folk didn't eat them.' Mrs Wainwright nudged her plate into Jane's ribs. 'Go and get us some'at else, honey. I'm fair famished.'

WHEN Jane came back with a slice of christening cake, the room was full. She squeezed past Jonny. His arm was hooked loosely round Marie's neck, filling in time before he took over the land from his father, until he too was ousted by sons yet unborn. Not quite Anne Boleyn on re-release but Marie would doubtless be judged on the same successes as the old woman who scowled across at her. Methods, crops, implements, stock, even seasons, adapted to the technology of the times but did attitudes ever alter? Each of these young women flashing come-on eyes would secure her position by becoming indispensable. Jane handed Mrs Wainwright the plate.

'I could have done with a bit less icing and a bit more cake.'

Yet was it any better for job juggling urban women? Who'd be first to seek a shoulder to cry what's the point? Though you'd get as much comfort leaning against a barbed wire fence as one of those stock-proof shoulders. Shortcomings would get short shrift from any of those self-sufficient multi-skillers. With her well-stocked freezer, her active breadmaker and her accounts finger on the mouse, she'd push her man to ever greater hard-work-never-killed-anyone efforts, day and night.

'I might've known a lass like you wouldn't think to cut me a bit of Wensleydale to go wi' t'fruitcake.'

Jane looked at the unforgiving lines on Mrs Wainwright's face and wondered if, like old Toddy, Mr Wainwright had ever failed to be up to his job.

THREE cups of tea later, Marie held out a coney fur.

'We're going now, Granny.'

Jane watched Mrs Wainwright stab a hatpin through felt and curls and heave herself from the chair. Was it as much of an effort for the old crone to heave herself out of the past? Oh, God, now she was offering her a bony cheek. Jane closed her eyes. *Kiss Grandma goodbye...* Grandma Bates, cheeks stuffed out with cotton wool, slab-cold flesh that moved under unsuspecting adolescent lips, sucking away the blood-heat, taking an eternity to creep back into place. *Show some respect, Jane.* She leaned forward and her lips met a layer of powder and rouge, cuddle warm and smelling of lily of the valley.

'It's been a real treat talking to you, honey. It's not every young lass'd have patience to listen to an old woman jabbering on.' And though Mrs Wainwright squeezed her hand till flesh turned white, Jane couldn't help but smile back.

Especially when she noticed they were followed out by the woman who'd been talking to Daddy. Because now there was an empty chair at the little table just for two. And a text message. Oli – at last.

It was from Roy. *Now ur a paidup membr of the godmothr clan, u can upgrade fiesta 2 a pumpkin–get waving.* Jane smiled again, kept it there for Daddy. Where was he?

She scoured the remaining faces, not so much a sea now as a smallish lake, like Coniston where they'd stayed that summer... They'd walked along it, the two of them, while Mum and Di looked round the gift shops, and he'd told her about Donald Campbell. How his achievements were never enough. And Daddy had gazed across the water where Bluebird had disintegrated into the depths, out of sight.

She might as well try Oli again. Her phone was dead. All those sodding photos, and her charger left behind at the flat. She pressed her cup and saucer on top of the tongue sandwich and squashed it into the plate, rattling the other empty cup. Not that anyone noticed. Snub-nosed Jane, sitting at the little table waiting to begin a let's-pretend tea party, and everyone else had gone out to play.

SHE would carry a few plates into the kitchen and then she'd go. On second thoughts, seeing the heaps piled up round the sink again – someone dumps the odd dish and instead of running away with the nearest dirty spoon they breed like rabbits – she was damned if she was going to start washing up again. The old cow could jump over the moon.

Yet there was no getting away from her. Her mother hovered in every room, watching every move, listening to every word, reading every thought. Dishing out guilt by the ladleful. It'd probably been drip-fed in the breastmilk. Jane nudged some dirty glasses along to make room for the plates. Her mother wouldn't expect her to wash them, wouldn't want Jane to spoil the selfless toiling into the small hours until every trace of celebration had been obliterated.

So she would. But would her mother be counting on this? After an eternity of Jane-trying-to-please, she wasn't any better at not trying to. She'd just do a few plates. Get it half right.

She flipped open the bin, scraped in flan crusts, pastry crumbs, scrunched up paper napkins. One was still folded, image only slightly crumpled. A stork on the uplift, *Baby's Christening* stamped in silver. They would be collected up, those that could be ironed, and stashed away for the next grandchild. Almost as good as first time round. Whosever's... The stork looked back knowingly, tight-beaked. Jane screwed it up and shoved it into the leftovers. She picked up the bag of rubbish and headed for the back door.

She'd forgotten how dark it was in the country. She steeled herself to edge along the path, groped for the dustbin lid. The hollow thud absorbed into the gloom was all too familiar. Except, she'd forgotten there were stars. A billion trillion miles away, twinkling specks of must-be-something-more. Distant village lights paled under the silence. Standing alone under the heavens she was the only person there ever was or ever would be.

UNDER the scullery sink, stashed inside a bag-for-life, was a miserful of carriers. She pulled one out and turned to the door. It wasn't quite shut. She'd left it letting the cold dampness into the kitchen: that latch always was a bit iffy. She was reaching to push it further open when –

'I see Jane's here, brazen as you like.'

Jane moved nearer the gap.

'You don't have to tell me why she left home so sudden. There's only one reason why a girl like that gets thrown out. And her all set to go to college as well.'

'But no-one really bothers about that sort of thing anymore, do they?'

'Judith would. Talk about tight-gusseted. All those airs and graces – the Bateses may have farmed a hundred and fifty acres but half of it was no better than rough grazing. And farming's not owning. She always did think she was a cut above, but she'd never have amounted to much if she hadn't landed the doctor. Took her long enough. No-one believed she'd ever get him to the altar.'

Jane frowned at the suspect latch. This wasn't the version she'd grown up with.

'But holding off did the trick in the end, and you can bet your life those two girls were brought up with their knickers sewn to their vests as well.'

Not so, you old bat. That particular ribbon-strapped garment had spent most of its adolescence stuffed in the bottom of her school bag, especially on games afternoons. As for those regulation knickers, Queen Victoria's bloomers didn't cover it. Voluminous enough for Jonny Wainwright to get his hand in, and more...

'But her father would have fixed all that up for her, him being a doctor and that.'

'You know what these girls are like. Probably daren't let on till it was too late.'

No, she probably wouldn't have dared. It'd been bad enough, five years on, telling them she was an estate agent.

'She always was a bit wet behind the ears. That cock and bull story about her going abroad –'

'DSO. They all do that nowadays. Even the young royals. They don't get paid, you know.'

'Exactly. Since when did a Bates do owt for nowt? And then she was supposed to be working in London. More like she was one of those drop-outs that sit around all day long. You couldn't move for them in the Tubes when we went there last summer. "Get yourselves off your backsides and do some work," that's what Bob used to say to them. Plenty of opportunities in London. Not that they took any notice. No respect for their olders and betters. And I hear she's living with an older man. Probably one of those bankers, getting a bit on the side.'

'Oh, he's not that much older. Mid thirties, I'd put him. Nice looking chap. Mind, she's improved beyond recognition. She brought him here recently to meet her parents. I'd have thought you'd have known that, Carol.'

In the drip-damp porch, the handle wasn't the least bit surprised.

'Ah, but who knows anything about him? Where's he from? What does he do? He could be one of those pimps. She certainly looks the part, made up like a dog's dinner.'

'Judith said he's doing very well for himself. And what's more –'

Smirking under Jane's loose fingers, the handle could hardly wait. It strained its ears as the second voice was lowered.

'She told me this afternoon – in confidence so don't let it go any further – that Jane's getting married soon. The engagement's not official yet, so they're keeping it hush-hush for the moment.'

Damn. It would be all round the village by now. Not that that was what mattered. Jane frowned. Because the thought that she'd been trying to push to the back of her mind all weekend would not lie still. It tossed and turned, trying to get comfortable. She clutched her skull to keep it in but the fact had decided it wasn't going to lie there a minute longer. *I don't want to marry him.* It was out. It hovered in front of her for a moment, then swirled about the room, expanding to fill every utilitarian niche.

It wasn't that she didn't love Oliver. She swatted at the very idea as it dodged round Judith's leftover-from-summer fly-paper. Oliver was her reason for living, her very being, her life's breath. She sighed. Why couldn't everything just stay as it was? Sod it. She flung open the door.

Necks turned towards her.

'Jane, my dear,' said one of the two faces. 'We were just saying how nice it is to see you, after all this time.'

'Yes, indeed. We hardly knew you.'

'Really? You haven't changed at all.'

Three smiles hung in space.

'But you haven't brought your young man with you this time. What a shame.'

'I'm afraid he had too much work to do this weekend.'

'And what is his line of work, dear?'

'He's a – psychiatrist.'

'That's nice. We'd have liked to have been properly introduced.'

'I'm sure he'll be disappointed not to have met you. He specialises in personality disorders among post-menopausal women,' which wasn't as mind-blowing as what she'd say in the mental replay, but it took the smile off the faces of the Cheshire cats.

Jane steeled herself to out-stare them. But their glares were lost between shadowed hoods and folds of pan stick, twenty-four hour cover. Brushed-on blushes over a layer of anti-aging cream, guaranteed double action – did they use it to moisturise their parched vaginas as well? A kiss-curl, platinum blonde almost to its roots, was bobbing between the furrows on Carol's forehead. What was it all for? Did these women still welcome the straying hand under the sheet? It was unimaginable. Almost as unimaginable as – but surely his hand didn't. Not Daddy and –

'Judith! We were just saying, how well your microwave's lasted. They don't make them like that anymore, do they?'

Judith put down some plates. 'Oh, Charles is getting me a new one for Christmas, with an integral quartz grill and convection oven. I ordered it the other day. They have their limitations, of course, but useful in the hot weather when the Aga's not on.'

'They are handy, so I'm told.' Carol pushed the curl into line. 'What will you do with the old one? Not that I've really much use for one, but if it's only going to be thrown out –'

'Jane's taking it.'

Which wasn't a surprise to anyone. Apart from Jane.

'Just to tide her over.'

For all her mother knew, her kitchen might be equipped beyond the dreams of Avarice. If Avarice went in for warming up dinners for a late-home partner. How satisfying to throw it back in Mother Dear's face. But, of course, the MD would know exactly what her flat was like.

So her 'Thanks, Mum' was more about pragmatism than towing the family solidarity line. 'If you'll hang onto it till –'

'I might as well start using the new one straightaway. So you can take it now.'

'HERE, let me give you a hand.'

Jane would have smiled if she hadn't just banged her thumb on the door jamb. Reliant Rob, always there when he was needed. Or just after. Every woman's second thought.

He took the microwave from her. Jane caught the plug.

'Keep a tight hold, girl. Don't want to damage it while it's still in the coven. There's no knowing what hell-hag concoctions have been brewed in here.' He hoicked it up to get a better grip. 'Sure you want it? You might be taking on more than you bargained for.'

'I'll chance it.' She switched on the outside light and followed him down the steps.

'Feels rusty underneath,' Rob said.

'It'll be a matching accessory. My kitchen's not like Diane's. Streamlined and colour coordinated, so I've heard,' in both ears. 'You did a brilliant job there, Rob.'

His usual gratuity. He would have shrugged if the heap of scrap hadn't become so heavy. 'She wants an extension now.' Rob wedged the microwave against her bag. 'Says she feels cramped.'

The words hung on the night air. Jane tucked them in with the flex and slammed the boot.

SHE took Snow Baby from the wardrobe. As she pulled it on, her arm caught the ceiling light, making shadows leap about the room. She climbed onto the bed to reach the shade and toppled backwards into a pile of coats. The bulb glared down. Jane closed her eyes, letting herself sink into a moss of fur and fabric. Capsules of brightness floated behind her lids... Swathes of light looming across the ceiling, sliding over the picture rail, slithering from sight behind the wardrobe, behind the chest of drawers, as night after night she'd lain rabbit eyed, sucking the corner of Booboo's ear, waiting for the sweep of headlights that meant she could whisper *He's back*.

'Are you off now?'

And the room was filled with light. But it was less Gabriel's sublime radiance, more SS interrogator's spot torch.

'What on earth are you doing?' asked Diane.

Because Jane, in a double manoeuvre to avoid the overhead bulb and get to her feet, was now half buried in coats.

'Did you know,' she said, blowing her mouth free of hairs, 'some people still wear real fur?'

'So?' Diane hitched the baby further up her shoulder. 'Plenty of animals still do too.'

Jane remade contact with the carpet. Whether she'd managed it with Di was debatable. She definitely hadn't with those school friends she'd not kept up with...

Best make new mates, Goggle, Maddy had told her, *if you want to make a fresh start.*

Forget the old crowd in London, Jay, Oli had said. *This is a fresh start.*

But how many fresh starts did it take to get away from family?

Di put the baby on the coats. 'Helen's out for the count, thank God. Stephie's as high as a kite, what with today and Christmas coming up. I hope you're coming up for Christmas, by the way.'

'No way. Me here equals Christmas from hell. And I know for sure,' straight from the microwave's mouth, 'Mum feels the same.'

'Don't be daft. She loves having a houseful. She's always on at me to come over.' All the fricking time.

'Course she is. You're the one who matters. You always were.'

Diane shrugged. 'I don't suppose it's possible to think the same about any two people. Even –' the sounds drifting up from below were way above kite-flying altitude '– your children.'

'Perhaps not,' said Jane. 'But she didn't bother to try.' Or even pretend. On the bed the baby stirred. She would have done it so well, the great Madonna act. The tiny face puckered. Jane shot a deal-with-it glance at her sister.

So, the baby was whimpering again. Diane looked away. So what? It was what babies did. Just like fractious nearly-fours shrieked 'Mummy!' all the way up the stairs, even though surely he could cope with it, just for once, instead of hollering 'Di!' at twenty thousand decibels. So many demands, stretching emotions beyond snapping point. Diane screwed her eyes tight shut. Who'd said love is patient, love is kind? It must have been a man. If she put her hands over her ears the sounds would die away... as Helen snuffled back into sleep, Stephie's howls dissolved to giggles, the lounge door closed on Rob.

Had she guessed? Did Jane realise that she was a bad mother, wife, daughter, sister? Is that what was she thinking? Diane risked a glance.

'I feel I don't belong here anymore,' said Jane.

She might have known. Baby Jane was vacuum wrapped in self-pity, as usual. Waltzing in like the prodigal returned, then boogying off again. Not for Jane the millstone of mother love. Diane picked up the baby and headed for the door.

'Got it in one.'

BUT had she got everything? Jane took the car key out of her bag, which left a phone size space. It would be in the scullery, with a bit of luck. And luck was in double helpings because there was Daddy, spinning round as she opened the door, switching his phone to end-call and his mouth to smile. But it took the eyes half a minute to catch up.

'Got you alone at last,' said Jane. 'Daddy, there are things I need to explain. About why I went without telling you, why I didn't take up my place at –'

'No need, Jane.' He squeezed her arm as he strode past into the kitchen. 'That's all behind us now.'

She trailed after him. Yet another sodding fresh start.

'TAKE care,' said Mother Dear, planting a kiss.

Take care you don't get dirty. Take care over your thank you letters. Take care with those minor scales. Take care not to drop your cup, your pen, your aitches, your knickers. Take care you don't spill, slurp, sweat, slather, swear or show me up in any possible way.

The remaining guests were herded back into the sitting room. For a moment they stood there, just she and Daddy. Then it was 'Bye, Princess. Have a safe journey. I won't come out.'

As she wound down the car window to avoid ramming Festina's rear end into the stone troughs, the front window curtains parted. Two eyes appeared between the brocade and the bars of lead. For a few seconds she thought she saw a nose pressed against the glass, before creeping condensation obliterated whoever it might have been. She turned away and scraped at ice forming on the inside of the windscreen, trying to make out Oliver's face beckoning through the clear patch, already freezing over.

PITCH black unconsciousness pierced by a scream. She sat bolt upright. The baby was awake.

The bus moved on. Jane groped for the clock. Minnie Mouse's face grinned back as though it wasn't twenty past four in the morning. Oliver turned, taking most of the duvet with him.

'Sorry,' she whispered. It was quiet now. Apart from the coughing. 'Shall I get you some water?' One grunt for yes.

She couldn't find her slippers, and the kitchen tiles were freezing. The half bottle of carbonated had been in the fridge so long it was probably written into the tenancy agreement. Jane went to the cupboard where she had – definitely – put a multipack of mountain spring so au naturel that God himself could have bottled it, had pre-formed Polyethylene Terephthalate been around on the third day. So it would be a complete waste of time to check the other cupboards. Which took till twenty-five past by the clock above the sink. Oh, sod it. She filled a tumbler from the fridge and held it while Oliver propped himself up on one elbow. He took a swig and convulsed in choking.

'What the hell's this?'

Lucrezia Borgia would no doubt have rehearsed something punchier than 'We seem to be out of the still.' Something to match Oliver's death throes performance. 'Sorry. There wasn't anything else,' except a few hundred million gallons on tap, but the water pipes would have given the game away. 'That bottle's been opened so long I reckoned it would've lost all its fizz. I sort of thought –' did Renaissance bambolinas go in for silly-me giggles? '– you might not notice,' which fell a squashed tongue sandwich flatter than the H_2O.

'Like I haven't noticed I've had to do every single thing this weekend. We did agree on who did what, but I can shop as well, if you can't manage.'

'Of course I can manage!' Could easily manage to turn this into their first row. 'I can't understand where it's all gone. What've you been doing, bathing in it?'

He thumped his pillow and turned it over. 'Leave it will you?' He bunched seven eighths of the duvet round his neck. Which left her very little to play with. Even so –

'S-O-R-R-Y.' She traced the letters up his thigh. Which didn't quite cover it. She snaked a finger between his buttocks and wrote SWALK across the split – after all, there was a gulp of gas lurking somewhere – and was considering how she might slip in SIAM when she heard snoring.

ARM screening the sudden light, ears straining to follow every movement. The wardrobe door, two blasts from an aerosol. The straight pull bottom drawer and the small stiff one, top left. Clothing cloaking flesh. A creaking hinge and darkness.

Fingers reached across the bed, stroking the place where he'd lain. Palms circled the hollow, feeling the shape of him. Legs stretched out, caressing his warmth. Breasts snuggled into his sweat, belly burrowing into – flesh froze.

A footstep. A turning knob. A retraction into her own space.

Coins clinked, zip closed.

A body remaining curled up tight, even after the front door slammed.

'WHY didn't you call?'

The voice was familiar but –

'Some mate you are.'

– surely it couldn't be – 'Maddy?'

'Like who else from your wicked past has been trying to get in touch?'

'You phoned before?'

'Only belled the Big O. Still had his number from way back when. Sunday afternoon – you know I only do a.m. Monday to Fri. He said you were in such a rush to get away for your dirty weekend you forgot your charger. Didn't he give you my message?'

'Yes, of course he did. I'm sorry I didn't ring back straight away.'

'Straight away? Like, this is Wednesday. Half price drinks night at the Piccolo. Remember?'

And she did. It was as if time and space had never separated her from –

'All the usual crowd. Plus a few you've not met. You'll love them.'

'I still can't believe Ally's getting hitched. Has she thought it through?'

'If trying out every male east of Clapham for size involves mental activity as well, then yes. Though I doubt she realises she'll have to spend more than two nights in a row in the same bed. I won't be able to double let her room anymore.'

'Oh, of course.' Somehow Maddy and Mortgage didn't belong to the same library – if Mad had ever set foot in a library – never mind the same twenty-five year sentence. 'You'll have to get someone else.'

'Shortlisting Tuesday. Should have someone in by the time you come.'

'There won't be anywhere for me to sleep.'

'Sleep? This is Ally's last big fling and you want to sleep? Chill out, Goggle. There'll be a bit of floor space for you to collapse on if you can't stand the pace.'

'I'm not sure. Oliver –'

'God, I'm not hearing this. Look, it's happening this Saturday. Preloading from six. Be there!'

'It's not that I don't want –'

'We're all wearing yellow leg warmers, so get some. And, Goggle –'

'Yes?'

'It'll be great to see you again.'

'Oh – it'll be great to see you too, Mad.'

'Just like old times, eh?'

'I can't wait...'

...TO tell Oli about it. 'You'll never guess who that was.'

Not when he was frown deep in papers.

'Maddy!'

Behind his bent head, the emulsion feigned magnolia.

'She said she'd phoned you at the weekend.'

Whereas it was really only smoke-screen white –

'Oh, yes. When you were away –' with no hint of rose blush. 'It slipped my mind. I do have more important things to think about at present.' He reached for another file.

'It doesn't matter. She's been telling me all the news. Ally's getting married! Can you believe that?'

He checked the label on the spine.

'You know. Alice. You remember her. In the room next to mine. In the house. In Brixton.'

'Pass the calculator, will you, Jane. Bookcase. Second shelf.'

Up or down? 'It's on Saturday.' She switched on the calculator. 'Should be a laugh,' instead of an excuse for her teeth to start their bottom lip sliding trick.

'What should?'

'Ally's hen night.' Sliding over and over.

'An occasion to be avoided by anyone with half a brain, I'm sure.'

'I said I'd go.' Scraping into skin.

'You won't be able to have two Saturdays in a row.'

'It'll be easy to get someone to switch.' Easier than getting her teeth to stay still. 'I'm not sure if it's Tony,' where plonking herself on his desk and refusing to budge would do it, 'or Roy,' which would involve a different sort of desk-perching.

'Anyway –' he looked her full in the face '– how can you, when Simon and Sophie are coming for dinner?'

'This Saturday? Since when –'

He shook his head. 'Scatterbrain.'

'Can't we put them off?' Teeth pressed into flesh.

'Are you mad? It's vital I have Simon's backing over my shake-up plans.' He thumb-flicked the edge of the papers and twenty sheets fell into line. 'This little thing I happen to have been working on all last weekend, not that you'd know about that. You'll have to phone back and tell her you can't make it after all.'

Jane didn't move. Neither did the couple locked in a going nowhere embrace above the gas fire. They'd hung *The Kiss* together, and one of them – okay, it'd been her, as she was passing up the second nail – had said it was a symbol of their eternal devotion. Because, when he'd straightened the frame, it positively glowed with love. Yet now the golden image seemed to have no depth. Shimmering on a surface of elaborate decoration, Klimt's lovers were completely flat. How could she not have noticed the vice grip on the girl's head as the man bent over her? Or the girl's fingers, the left pulling at the hand which held her jaw, the right curled away from his skin. And all the time her lips were firmly closed.

'Make the call in the kitchen, will you?' Oliver repositioned a plastic divider. 'So I can get on.'

Jane leant against the door. Watched the kitchen clock counting out the seconds. Watched the minute hand move on. And on. She rolled a flake of loosened skin back and forth with her tongue and recognised the sick-sweet taste. Did she still have Maddy's number? Of course she did. Not in Recently Used, obviously, but she hadn't deleted it; it wasn't as though she hadn't been going to see Mad again – ridiculous thought. But ever since that time she'd found Oli looking through her texts – just checking, he'd said, that he'd sent her, scatterbrain that she was, a reminder of something that actually didn't matter anymore – her list of contacts had seemed a bit... There it was, in the memory under M for Mad, as always. M for Mentor, almost. Definitely M for –

'Mate! How're you doing?'

The voice was so faint she couldn't be sure. She pressed closer to the door.

'Just wondering...'

She eased it open a fraction.

'...how you're fixed for Saturday evening? Jane's been on at me to ask you round for a meal. And we'd both like to get to know Sophie better... That's too bad. I suppose there's no chance... No problem. How about Sunday?'

The light on her mobile dimmed.

'Great. We'll sort out a time later. See you.'

As she stared at the blank screen, the door rammed into her back. A hand reached round, taking the phone.

'Have you rung Maddy?' He licked her ear lobe, poking his tongue through the dangling hoop.

'No.' She flicked her head away. 'Nor am I. Not after what I overheard.'

'Monitoring my calls now, are you?'

She could feel his breath on her skin.

'Then you'll know I put Simon and Sophie off.'

'You've just invited them! I heard you.'

'Had your ear to the door, did you?'

She tried to turn away but he had one hand on the back of her neck.

'I hadn't put you down as a snoop. Mind you don't make a habit of it.'

Locked in his handspan her face burned.

'Whatever you thought you heard, you got completely the wrong idea.' He loosened his grip. 'I asked Simon to make it Sunday instead of Saturday, in case you're still determined to go –' he kissed her nose '– and leave me on my ownsome again.'

The seconds jolted on, click after click.

'You know everything I do is to make you happy, angel. You misunderstood, that's all. Made a silly little mistake.' He blew across her face. 'You were wrong. Admit it.'

And suddenly he was twirling her round the kitchen, faster and faster, till walls, cupboards, window, curtains reeled in a frantic kaleidoscope. Her head hit the floor. Colours clashed in a cacophony of sound and she could smell the need in his eyes and the thud of his heart filled her mouth. He tore open her flies and dragged down denim and lace. His buckle branded flesh as he bore down, the bullets studding his belt cold against her stomach, his jackboots trammelling her legs, khaki twill chafing breasts. Still she refused to speak. The lieutenant's – no, colonel's – henchmen laughed as they pinned her against the rat-infested straw. He spun the cylinder, pressing the barrel against her skull.

'Say it.'

Her suicide pill rolled out of reach. Slowly he squeezed the trigger and her mind exploded.

Yes, yes. YES.

THIS time she was prepared. A wet morning always brought out the snail lines, and a sluggishness in Festina. Jane side stepped the puddles, can of WD40 at the ready. But Festina gave her bonnet a shake and shrugged her hubcaps at the rain. And by the time she reached the roundabout there was no need for the wipers. The geese weren't bothered by a bit of mud. Or even quite a lot of it. Plothering in the muck, Grandma Bates would have said.

The line revved forward. Second in the queue. Spendal Electrics crossed in front, tailing Motorway Maintenance. Fiat Uno bumper to bumper with Dominion Oils. Seven new Peugeots in suspended transit. Tipper Hire, Say It With Flowers. A wagon of sheep, shutters open. Velvet ear tips peeping from the upper deck, trying to make sense of dissonance. Down below upturned noses gasped for air. Jane could hear their silent bleating.

IT was good to get out of the office with Christian taking up all the air. A complete WOS Boss, like Roy was always saying. Although he wasn't saying that today. Or anything else to make her laugh. It was particularly good to be out of the office on Roy's day off.

Mr Cummins, two pm, but he might be early. Waiting. She took the next right.

By now Jubilee Terrace was familiar. As was the white Mondeo, parked half way along. Five weeks ago, when she'd first noticed it, she knew she must have got the registration wrong. Especially when it was there again last week. But she'd checked at the weekend. And now she double checked. What was Daddy doing so far from home?

Further down, outside number sixty-six, another car, partially resprayed, was mounting the kerb. A man was locking the door, trying the handle, making sure. Which was a good idea in Jubilee Terrace.

Forty-eight minutes later a disappointed Mr Cummins inserted his key into the two-tone Astra. The Mondeo had gone.

TWO long evenings sulked by but Saturday afternoon was not to be put off.

Jane stood aside as Oliver closed the bedroom curtains. It wouldn't do for the neighbours, whoever they were, to glance upwards and see him in action. She tugged at the zip. Something was stopping it. What was it about her and zips? She backtracked and pulled out some yellow threads. Extra ventilation in one of the leg warmers might be a bonus. Things could get a bit hot in night clubs, she seemed to remember. She swung the bag onto the floor.

'Not there, Jane.' The metal brush snarled round her feet. 'You can see I haven't done that bit.'

'It doesn't need it. I hoovered through last night. And it's not as though we've been doing anything dirty since then.'

'We are expecting guests tomorrow. Unless you've forgotten.'

'Of course I haven't.' She picked up the bag. 'Will they be spending the whole evening in here or just doing a quick circuit of the bed?'

The brush head gagged at a corner of the rug. Serve it right for snapping at her ankles. She was the one who usually took it for walkies, not him. She watched Oliver jostle with it for several moments before he brought it to heel.

'There's something wrong with the suction.' He trammelled the snagged tufts back into shape. 'The dust bag must need changing.'

'No, it doesn't. It's half empty.' And could stay on short rations from now on, to teach it some loyalty.

'Jay.'

The bag was taken from her hand and dropped.

'This half empty mind set of yours...'

A finger and thumb clasped each elbow.

'I hope this trip to London isn't going to bring back your old insecurities.' His hands slid round her back, 'Not now you're able to face up to things,' pulling her close, 'with me beside you,' pressing her head against his shoulder. 'You know that going back is a big mistake.' Lips nuzzled hair. 'Give Maddy a call.'

'Oh, Oli...' because she'd missed the hair-nuzzling, these past two days. She rubbed her cheek against the smoothness of his shirt. Fifty percent polyester, easy to manage. 'I don't know...' why I can't have just one girls' night out without this fuss.

'Yes you do. Positive thinking, remember. These people count for nothing with you now.'

'You're right.' Fifty percent pure cotton. Strong natural fibre. 'I'm not going to let old friends influence me in any way.'

'Good girl –'

'So I shall go, as arranged. And come back tomorrow, unchanged.' Apart from a quick in and out of her little red number. 'It'll be as if I'd never gone,' especially if she could ditch the leg warmers somewhere along the way. 'You'll see.' She reached up to lips that were no longer there.

'I had thought –' he grasped the beast by its tail '– the idea of us moving in together –' wrenched out the plug '– was to spend time with each other –' lifted it by the scruff of its neck '– but you go off and enjoy yourself. I'll carry on cleaning up,' and headed for the door.

'Oliver, the lounge doesn't need hoovering.'

'You don't seem to realise how important this dinner party is for me, Jane. Or perhaps you just don't care.'

'Oh, Oli, I do.' Not about the dinner party, true, but she did care about the way he wasn't looking at her. 'I can give it another whiz round tomorrow. I'll be back in plenty of time. There's no point in doing it now; you might get it messy tonight.'

'That's hardly likely, as I'll be working all night. Maybe I'll knock off for a few minutes to make myself a sandwich.'

'I told you, I've left you a lasagne.' Had spent 58 minutes of her life making it. 'Now we've got a microwave you can soon –'

'I'm sure I can manage to heat up a ready meal. As well as put in another dustbag. As I said when you got back last weekend, please tell me if you think you have too much to do. I can take over all the housework if that's what you want.'

'Of course that's not what I want.' What she wanted was for him to take her in his arms and tell her how much – he'd love to take her to the station. 'I know how hard you work.' She took a step nearer but the brush head was between them, bristles showing. 'That's why I do things to

71

help, like cooking supper when you're late –' and talking of late – but she sensed he wasn't going to, the way his eyes closed as his mouth opened, so before he could speak she shoved in '– which makes the meals you do when your friends come round even more of a treat.'

'My friends? I see. Your friends are just those bimbos. Trying to make intelligent conversation with people like Simon and Sophie must be such a drag.'

'Of course it isn't.' She picked up her bag. 'They're my friends, too. Well, I don't really know Sophie.' Nor was she one hundred percent sure about Simon's sock size, birth sign or person he'd most like to be stuck in a lift with but right now what she really wanted to know was not – 'Have they been together long?' – but how to get between Oliver and the door.

'Long enough for her to have made a real difference to his flat. Simon's always telling me how wonderful she is.' He began scooping up the flex. 'I can see you're anxious to be off, so I'll see to –'

'Oliver! Drop it, will you! I'll change the frigging bag.'

JANE felt along the top shelf for the packet, fetched a stool for a better look. Moved things round. Lifted them down. Put them back.

She'd have to empty the old one. She unhitched the dustbag from the nozzle and set about the glued ridge along the bottom. One fingernail later she'd forced a parting but the bag tore as she tried to separate it from the seam. The sellotape took one look at the dusty surface and curled its lip. An extra fold and a couple of paperclips would have to do.

Jane raced down the communal flight of steps to the fire exit. She wedged the dustbag against her ribs with one elbow and pushed down the bar. Shallow breathing was best practice when it came to bin opening. She tried not to look but it all had to come out, through the small top opening. Bit by bit she prised it free: matted hair, tissue fragments, nail clippings, mouldering crumbs, bits of grit. With two fingers Jane completed the purging of a week's existence.

IT couldn't be that time already. She shoved the beast into the corner with its tail between its legs and swished her hands under the tap. Now the tea towel had grubby patches on it. As had her cashmere. And there wasn't time to change it. Unless Oliver –

She opened the lounge door. 'I've got to go now, Oli. In fact I'm really pushed.'

'Better get a move on then, hadn't you?' His eyes didn't shift from the screen. 'I'll see you around three tomorrow. And Jane –' He pressed caps lock.

'Yes?'

'DON'T BE LATE.'

'I won't. Promise. Love you, Oli.'

He turned back to processing words.

THE *next train to arrive at Platform Three will be...* The London train. Retracing steps. No, this time she was travelling towards the known. This time she had a return ticket.

The wind blew through the perforations in the metal bench. A pigeon fidgeted closer, head bobbing, snatching at broken crisps close to her feet. Jane kept still. Trust me, little bird. You're quite safe. It moved off, half fluttering, as bristles pushed under the seat, dragging out waste, leaving a concrete canvas crying out for fresh statements – the empty can, the stubbed cigarette: notice me. I am here.

She dropped a tissue in a nearby bin and went to meet the train.

A VACANT double. Jane slid towards the window, avoiding the sprawler opposite. Why did men think they got a complimentary double leg space?

She took up the aisle seat with her bags and spread her coat over the top to dry. Oli had been right about the fabric, even though it had cost more than real inside-out sheep's skin. She'd hesitated – was it practical? – but when he'd pulled up the furry hood and tied a bow under her chin and called her his Snow Baby, she couldn't resist. Succumbing then to ownership.

Creeping from the rusted sidings, cutting past the poles and pylons, sidling through weed-lush embankments, southbound engine trundles onwards. Passing scrap yards, ordered junk piles. Empty oil drums, clapped out cars.

The man stood up; she drew her legs in. Tossed his paper on the table. Lurched from sight: buffet? toilet?

She pushed the tabloid away so it didn't encroach on her half. Saw her fingers were smudged with ink. Which meant a one-handed manoeuvre to extract a new tissue from her bag without disturbing the Snow Baby. It was bad enough that her jumper had a grubby stain. Should she tuck it into her skirt? But Oliver said that made her look – Jane whispered the f-word to the housing estate spreading out in front of her. Council built, made to last, uniform in common brick. She stared at the misfits, the houses smothered in Artex or buried behind stone-cladding. Each one succumbed to ownership. Tenants no more, we're mortgaged now...

Over the bridge, gathering speed. Leaving the town, leaving the rain. Cloud cover fades, tempting the sun.

Gardeners out, singles and pairs. Back against back, secrets on show. Tidying up, seeking control. Dug-over beds flashed before eyes. Vegetable plots meeting the train. Solitary men paused over spades, gazing across, life going by...

Faces dissolve, carriages pass... jigsaw of sheds, barbed wire strips... swept under grass, trodden by cows... polythene bales, furrows fresh ploughed... nearby signs plunged into view focus is lost tooclosetosee...

THE whole city was spread out before her eyes. Piccadilly Circus, Westminster, Sloane Square, Shepherd's Bush. It hadn't changed. The same shabbiness, the quirkiness, the unvarying climate of wind and gloom. She felt a tremble, sensed a sudden arousal, was swept into the surging mass. Jane folded the tube map as the doors opened. And remembered to mind the gap.

Chapter Two

'DO you think I was born yesterday?'
Jane strip-searched her bag. 'I'm telling you the truth. It was in here and now it's gone. If you take me back to my friend's house, I can pay you. I'm sure there'll be someone in.'

She flicked the Honest Jane eyes to full beam. But the driver had his on the queue at the taxi rank. She offered him her name and address: he called her an effing cow and told her where she could go.

The thing to do now was stay in the toilet for the whole journey. Are you kidding? said her nasal receptors, without making a better suggestion. But it wasn't only that she now had no money. Her purse had held all her cards. The thing to do was call Maddy.

Another hand-in-the-womb grope, re-rifling bag clutter. It was useless. Useless to unzip her holdall and search under the strappy red dress, the sponge bag, the Hello Kitty nightie. Useless to slide her hand into the Sainsbury's carrier and check out the damp towel and last night's knickers. No cards, no money, no phone. Not even a pair of flat shoes.

SHE shaded her eyes and squinted through the window.

There was someone in, after all. Two people, in fact, sitting very close. Jane hammered on the door again.

'Maddy – thank God.'

It was so different from yesterday. The house was different. So quiet. Maddy was different. So –

'– I'll go up and look round the bedroom. If that's all right.'

'Suppose. As long as you don't touch anyone's stuff.' All that without moving her lips.

Jane raked among the heaps of clothes, shifted the bed, felt under cupboards. Checked the other rooms, went downstairs, did the kitchen – but not Maddy's room, spacious rear-aspect dining room with original fireplace and period French doors, or possible fifth bedroom. Not with her standing there, arms folded, nails fixed.

'No luck?'

'No. I suppose it might have dropped out in the lounge.'

Maddy shifted door frames. 'Most likely you had it nicked last night.'

'But my bag was never out of my sight. I danced round it.' Danced with it, had nearly given it her number. Seeing as the others were on the pull, even Ally. Especially Ally. 'So if I can just look in there –'

Maddy shrugged and pushed the lounge door a quarter open. There was mood music. And not unpacked yet Kelsey-Jade. An empty bottle of Bacardi. Two glasses. The ice hadn't made it past the hall.

'Can you lend me some cash? I'll pay you back next week.'

'You bringing another bottle or what?' Kelsey-Jade was stirring.

'Course I will.' Maddy closed the door. 'No problem. If you can't trust an old mate, who the frig can you?' And suddenly there was Mad again, on auto-defrost, thrusting notes into her hand, telling her she was well out of it all.

'Thanks, Mad. You've saved my life. I must go. I don't know even when the next train is. Bloody Sundays. And Oliver –'

'Sure. You get off. Give him one from me.'

THERE was a lot to be said for having your back to the engine. What had been was receding, behind her forever. Goodbye to who's-been-using-my-milk, six weeks' worth of bacon fat in the grill pan and moths flitting from the Bran Flakes no-one owned anymore. Goodbye to tearing up the toilet roll middle, chipping in another tenner and stepping over regurgitated Colonel Saunders on the front step. She definitely preferred it this way even if she couldn't see what was coming.

SHE hurried, as fast as last night's legs could be made to hurry, under street lights and, if she looked hard, a sky full of stars. She swapped her bag to her other hand. Down the road the pavement glistened with a scatter of diamonds, beckoning her on… towards the bus shelter with the front and side windows completely smashed. She picked her way through shingle and slumped against the metal frame. She pulled up Snow Baby's hood. Thought of Oli. Her arms ached. She sludged a patch clear of glass and put down her bag.

At last she was putting it down outside the door to the flat. Only one more put-down to go. Jane fumbled in her handbag, wondering whether she still had her key.

IN the hallway, the walls oozed silence.

'And by the time I got back to the station I'd missed the next one and had to wait ages. Then there was a problem with the connection.'

All around, a waterfall of not answering, cascading over the tight-lipped skirting, spattering into the close-pile carpet, squelching round her ankles without so much as an intake of breath.

She trailed after him to the kitchen. 'How's dinner coming on?' Because there was no sign of it. 'Isn't Simon coming after all? That's good, next weekend I can –'

'Of course they are coming.'

'But you haven't started cooking.'

'I haven't started? What do you mean, Jane? You're making dinner this evening.'

'But you always cook when we have people round. Always.'

'Which is why you said you'd like to do it. This once. Surely you haven't forgotten?' He flicked his eyes from the porridge pan cemented to the hob, past a trail of toast crumbs and spatters of don't-ask brown, to last night's lasagne dish wallowing in the sink with a couple of plates and the sum total of glasses necessary for the kitchen to pass as fully equipped. 'What are we having?'

'Oliver, I know nothing about this.'

'Jane.' He smiled. 'You have been in a tiz lately, with all this gallivanting about. What would you do without me to remind you about things?'

'I don't know –' what you're talking about. Her head ached.

'They'll be here eightish.' Oliver picked up the Sunday supplement and made for the lounge. 'In about half an hour.'

'We'll eat out.'

He paused. 'Sunday night?'

'We'll be able to get a table at the Blue Umbrella. I'll book one now – if I can use your phone.'

'The Blue Umbrella? Bit pricey, isn't it? Sure you can you stand it?'

'Yes, I – at least, can you pay? Till I get sorted.'

He drew breath, considering. 'I don't think so, Jane. I don't want all that on my plastic, so near to Christmas. And there's no knowing how long it will take to sort out the mess you're in.'

'Then it'll have to be the Taj. I'll run there, it'll be quicker – if you'll lend me some cash.'

He raised an eyebrow.

'Please may I borrow some money, Oliver?'

The tiny Velcro hooks slowly released their grip. Oliver extracted two, no, three, notes. Then he unzipped the side of his purse and shook the loose change onto the table.

AT least in a takeaway you weren't paying for the interior design. There was the sofa sagging under the window, the TV angled on a shelf, the unlimited edition Taj Mahal curling at the edges, the menu set into the counter.

Dupiaza, Methi, Bhuna… almost a metre of choice.

'Can I help?'

Her nose dripped onto the glass. She wiped an arm across Biryani and Rogan Josh. 'Sorry, I can't decide.' Because there wasn't time to think.

'No rush.' Because he was stuck here till midnight. Seven nights a week, and the lunchtime shifts. A second class honours, a four-figure debt and no social life. Girls came, ordered, went. Girls he'd hung around with at uni. Girls getting on with their lives.

Wisps of hair were drying into tiny curls around Jane's cheeks. He could see behind the frost-touched mask, could almost touch the soft blush skin. She pushed a stray strand under the edge of her bobble hat. He pulled it off and she shook her hair free, letting the waves tumble over her breasts as he reached out to –

'Maybe –' she pushed the strand further under her hat '– you can suggest something?' Seeing as she'd got to 117 without any integer shouting Choose Me, even before translation. Now she was on the last column. 'Should I go for a set meal, rather than individual?' She went back to the start. 'What do you think?'

He bent over the menu. 'How many is it for?'

'Four.'

'Girls night in?'

'Two couples. Does it matter?'

It didn't matter at all. His finger moved down the plastic shield to where she was pointing, almost touching at 16. Except it was 91 to her. Not that that mattered either. It was all spicy and quick. What girls wanted. Except a certain girl. The one he couldn't bring home.

'I'm after something a bit –'

'Special?'

'Yes. What would you choose?'

Nothing from this lot, that's for sure. 'You won't do better than going for the set meal.'

'What do you get with that?'

'King prawn Balti, Lamb Passanda, Chicken Tikka Rogan Josh, Chicken Korma, Mushroom Bhaji, Sag Aloo.' Just like it said in the small print. 'A real assortment.'

Jane hesitated. 'I think I'll go for four of the same. Something authentic.'

He stabbed his finger at random in the middle of the Chef's Recommendations. 'Try the house speciality.' A quid above the standard nosh. Times four. 'Saag Kulfta. It's a classic Sylheti dish.' Genuine pukka to you, darling. Whichever way up you read it.

Jane looked at the description. *Spiced balls of mince meat and saag cooked with almonds, egg and cream.* 'Is there a difference between saag and sag?'

'Only alphabetically. They're both spinach.'

Should she risk minced meat? The wall heater whirred down a haze of uncertainty. Secrets of the subcontinent.

The bell jangled above the door. A regular, after his usual doner kebab. Stick with what you know.

'I'll have Chicken Tikka Masala.' She looked at her watch. 'Do you know if the late shop's still open?'

'I CAN'T wait to see what we're having. Jane banned me from the kitchen.'

'It's quite ordinary, really.'

'Surely not.' Oliver traced his finger down the dripping neck of the Pinot Noir. 'I bet we're in for a real treat.'

She began to serve. 'It's just tikka masala.' As far as she could remember.

Oliver turned to Sophie. 'Jane's been googling all weekend to come up with this. So she tells me.'

'Just a little for me – no, I don't mean the wine.' The crystal stem of Sophie's glass twinkled. 'You can keep that coming.'

And as the hint of cream curdled into the touch of ginger crust round the rim of the dish, the collection for the bottle bank grew.

JANE negotiated the kitchen door with four plates, Simon's on top, with a picked out pile of chicken. She was stamping on the pavlova box when the door opened again. 'Why didn't you tell me Simon doesn't eat chicken?'

But it wasn't Oliver. Jane threw a tea towel over the pavlova.

'He's vegetarian,' said Sophie. 'Didn't Oli mention it? He takes the piss out of him in the pub because Si gets smoky bacon crisps.'

'I didn't realise. Sorry.'

'If he's into self denial that's his problem.'

'Thanks for bringing in the dish. Do go back in.' So she could get it onto a plate before the meringue completely collapsed.

But Sophie was at the bin, slopping leftovers onto squashed aluminium trays. 'Thank God. For a moment there I thought you were some sad domesticated bitch.' She lifted the towel and poked the piped cream. 'Do you know it's still a bit frozen?'

THE pavlova was okay by Simon.

'Sorry about the chicken,' said Jane. 'I forgot you didn't like meat.'

'It's not that I don't like it.'

She shook on another dollop of fruit flavoured red and held out the plate.

'But I can't bear to eat it, the way it's produced. Did you know that thirty or forty thousand broiler chickens are crammed together in a shed?'

The plate hovered in space.

'They spend their lives squatting on faeces and decomposing dead birds. Each one has a space no bigger than this.' He drew his finger round the place mat before Jane plonked the plate down on a glob of tikkered chicken.

'I'll have a slice of pavlova, Jane,' said Oliver. 'Seeing as you went to such trouble over it.'

The meringue broke under the blade. She scraped every last crumb onto his plate and passed it across.

'You won't drop it, will you?'

Nor would Simon. 'Chickens are pumped so full of growth promoters they can hardly move.' He stabbed his spoon into the not quite thawed base. 'They can only just find the food and water anyway. The sheds are deliberately gloomy, to stop them being aggressive.'

'No need for us to be gloomy though, is there, Si?' Sophie gave him a kick under the table.

The Pinot Noir on its own might have dulled the pain, or, coupled only with the Chardonnay, could have dilated the images from that animal welfare leaflet. But topped

83

with that cheeky little Grenache Rosé, which had made it all the way from the Antipodes, via Hong Kong for a fuel stop, to the local off-licence, setting him back less than a fiver, and Simon's inner turmoil overflowed. 'Some chickens –' he slumped forward, elbows spanning the plate of meringue '– can't support their own body weight so they die of starvation.'

'Mmm, not bad at all,' said Oliver, turning his spoon to lick the back. 'Is this one of your mother's recipes, Jane?' He dug in again. 'Jane was over there the other weekend, for her niece's christening. So she said.' He gave Sophie a knowing look. 'She's always off somewhere.'

'Oh, right,' said Sophie. The thing about knowing looks was the looked-at generally didn't get it. So what was it people asked about babies? Oh, yes, how much they weighed. She scraped the cream from the top of her meringue. The obsession with scales started at birth. Sophie sized up the next spoonful. 'How old is she?' Fifty calories, max.

'Six weeks,' said Jane. 'Or –' she was then. Now she must be – 'a bit more.' Who cared, anyway? Thirty thousand, forty thousand, who was counting?

'Chickens are only six weeks old when they're slaughtered. They still cheep.' Simon looked deep into his glass, reflecting a shedful of peeping. 'Their eyes are still blue.'

'Well, at least they're young and tender,' said Oliver. 'If we'd gone out to a restaurant, even somewhere upmarket like the Blue Umbrella, we'd no doubt have been chewing on bits of old battery hen.'

'Whereas, according to Si, we've just eaten babies. And you know what –' Sophie held up a finger while she took another mouthful of wine '– we did this play at school. About someone who ate children. At a banquet.'

'Procne,' from some part of Jane's brain as yet unsaturated. 'It's a legend from Ancient Greece. She killed her son and served him up to her husband. Because he'd done something terrible –' Jane stopped. What was it? Something way beyond leaving the toilet seat up. Anyway, 'She couldn't forgive him. When he'd eaten it the gods turned all three of them into birds.'

'Chickens, I expect,' said Oliver. 'But did the story have a happy ending? Were they free range?' He dabbed his mouth on the paper napkin. 'Not that the chicken we had in Athens was anything out of the ordinary. For real flavour, you can't beat Poulet de Brest. Now there's a pampered bird, Sophie. Perfect for a mature taste.'

'I'm not talking about some old Greek fairy tale,' said Sophie. 'This woman was a Goth.'

'Recognisable by the black leather and five kilos of base metal hanging from dubious body parts, no doubt. Like that piece at the filling station on Harcourt Road. You been there, Simon? It's worth paying 2p a litre more to –'

'Listen, you Philistine. I'm trying to raise the level of conversation here.' She leaned towards him and jabbed his chest. 'This is culture. You know, Shakespeare.'

'Okay, smartie pants. Tell us about this play.'

'Well, you can't expect me to remember every little detail after all this time.'

'Come off it,' said Oliver. 'It can't have been more than a couple of years ago.'

'A couple of thousand, more like. It had emperors and tributes in it. You know, men in skirts.'

Without – Jane peeled her bare thigh from the chair seat as she shifted position – the tights. She picked up her glass. 'What was it called?' Maybe Smartie Pants – though in that dress, it was stark staring obvious from the lack of VPL that Sophie was wearing nothing more than a thong –

could come up with that, even if she had lost the plot. And, said the glass, you haven't?

'Who cares?' Sophie shrugged. 'It's all history now. I got a B for English Lit, though. So there.'

'I'm very impressed,' said Oliver. 'Have you got any other Bs I should know abou-'

'Tamora.'

They all looked at Simon.

'The queen who ate her sons.' Simon took another swig of the rosé. Reasonably palatable but it lacked body. 'A barbarian.' Not up to Oliver's standard at all.

'Absolutely,' agreed Jane. 'It's inhuman.'

'Oh, I don't know.' Simon swished the last drops round his glass. 'It's not just primitive tribes who've gone in for cannibalism.'

'Well, it makes sense,' said Sophie. 'You know, if there's a plane crash and you're shipwrecked on a desert island, dying of starvation.'

'Or tipped over the edge by having to wind your own gramophone night after night,' said Oliver.

'What?'

'So tell us, Sophie Marston, your luxury item. Is it to be a step by step guide to Fifty Favourite Anthropophagic Feasts?' He enunciated each syllable with precision.

Proof, thought Jane, that he was knocking back the grape juice at the same rate as everyone else for once. She watched his seat edge closer to Sophie's.

'So who would you sink your teeth into first?'

'It may as well be Simon, as he'd rather starve than eat anyone else. I'd chop him into little pieces.'

'I'd see that,' said Simon, 'as an act of devotion. Eating a dead loved one so the soul can be reborn in the body of the consumer.' He upended the glass and the last trickle dribbled down the corner of his lips. 'And human flesh is supposed to be quite tasty.'

'Yes,' said Oliver. 'They say it's a bit like chicken.' He held the bottle in the general direction of Simon's glass and most of the rosé went in.

'How can you talk like that!' said Jane. 'Innocent people slaughtered to appease a piece of rock.' Without the sixth commandment in sugar pink letters all the way through.

'Human sacrifice used to be quite PC,' said Oliver. 'They're the best bits in the Bible, I believe. Like old Abraham and Abe Junior.'

'God didn't let him, though. And don't forget the missionaries.'

'Most stories of cannibals were probably just government spin to justify subduing the natives. Making Britain Great.' Oliver lined up the bottle with the other empties in a spiral along the pattern on the carpet. 'Then it could drain the colonies with a clear conscience.' Thank God that was the last of the Australian plonk.

'But cannibalism wasn't confined to the British Empire.' Simon drew his finger across the blue-skies-forever tablemat, joining blobs of spilt rosé into bigger blobs. 'It happened everywhere. I read about a Chinese officer being boiled and eaten as late as nineteen hundred and something.'

'I love Chinese,' said Sophie. 'I even had it for Christmas dinner last year. Szechuan Duck, my favourite.

'Hear that, Jane? If you'd known you could have run to a Chinese, I'm sure.' Oliver topped up her glass. 'Or would that have been going too far to please a guest?'

Jane swallowed another mouthful. 'Was it a religious ritual?'

'Not at all. He'd been sent to pacify the inhabitants of a revolting town in the south-east.'

'Let that be a warning.' Oliver's bare arm snaked across the top of Sophie's chair. 'Never turn your back on an Essex man.'

Sophie flicked her head, whisking hair across skin. 'What makes you think I'll turn my back on any man?'

Across the table, their faces merged and parted as Jane tried to change focus. 'What're you doing this Christmas?'

Sophie shrugged. 'Nothing definite, as yet.'

'Come here,' said Oliver. 'There'll be more than enough to go round. We're having a goose.'

'We're having what?'

'Goose. You'll approve of this, Simon. It's hand reared.' All the time looking at Jane. 'From a local place Jane told me about. They probably give them the last rites before they wring their necks.' Smiling straight through her. 'Though I expect Jane could warm you up a nut roast. There's no limit to what she shoves in the microwave.'

'Si's going to his parents. Sherry trifle, paper hats, God Save the Queen and Great Aunt Nellie.'

'You can still come though,' said Oliver. 'Help us pull the wishbone. We'll make it a threesome.'

'But we can't eat my geese!'

'Hardly yours, Jane. One of them's got my name on it, though, even if it is costing a small fortune. Almost two percent of my salary. Gross. It'll be worth it, though, when it's sliced up on the plate.'

'Oliver – you can't!' Tears sprang unbidden. 'You just can't!'

'For God's sake, Jane, don't start on one of your crying jags.' He picked up the remains of the raspberry dessert. 'Go and stick this in the fridge –' he thrust the plate into her hands '– before it completely dissolves to mush.'

His eyes glinted through her tears.

'Do it.'

She pushed back her chair, forcing legs to stand. Waded through the swirling whirlpool carpet, across the stepping stone cracks in the hall to the kitchen doorway, where her limbs gave way. The pavlova glided down on white glazed wing-tips, wheeling and circling in the currents of air, skimming the sparkling lake, until it cut through the frozen surface, spattering her legs with blood-streaked splinters of ice.

'LACK of oxygen is the main cause. That's when you get the bad smell. Whereas oxidation gives it the aroma of sherry, so it's difficult for the inexperienced –' he smiled at Sophie '– to spot the difference between a good one that's gone off and one that's simply cheap and nasty.' Oliver gave the empty Grenache Rosé a half turn so its label faced the other way.

'Maybe so,' said Sophie. 'But you only get those brown bits if you stick your corkscrew in too far.'

'S'not what it means, Soph,' said Simon. 'It'sh a reaction between –' he hiccoughed '– the wine and something in the wood. Corking's all down to luck.'

'Or using something a tad more technologically advanced than a wooden bung.' Oliver hesitated. Was it worth opening the Chablais Premier Crus when everyone was so plastered? It would last him several pleasant evenings although those vinyl stoppers were a sod to get back in the bottle.

'So, you'd replace a renewable, biodegradabable product –' and the extra syllables merely served to emphasise Simon's point '– the only thing that keeps an ancient shytsem of agriculture going in one of the mosht environmentally sensitive parts of Europe – with yet more plastic?'

'I've heard that sheep grazing on the acorns produce a very good lean meat,' said Oliver. 'The lambs are just right for the Portuguese Christmas market.'

'But is it better than goose?' asked Sophie.

'Never mind farmed geese! Did you know –' Simon hiccoughed again '– there are only a hundred pairs of

Splanish Imperial Eagles left in Iberia? If the cork forests become uneconic the whole bloody area will degenerate into desert.'

Oliver shrugged. 'That's democracy for you. The wishes of the majority. Who don't want their tipple to let them down.' He fingered the neck of the Chablais.

'You two,' said Sophie. 'What're you like? Go for bottles with screw tops and there's no problem, is there?' She smiled at Oliver.

Oliver smiled back. It would definitely be a waste.

She tapped her glass. 'Keep the lubrication coming.'

He slipped the Premier Crus beside the table leg and reached for a bottle of Asti.

Sophie eyed him through her glass. 'We had this at my sister's wedding.'

'Your sister?' Oliver raised an eyebrow. 'Don't tell me there's another one like you at home.'

'Soph shunique,' said Simon, stretching his hand across the table towards hers.

'That –' she kept both hands on the stem '– is just where you're wrong. Everyone has a double. It was in a magazine I was reading last week.'

'Ah, yes. Your doppelganger,' said Oliver.

'No, idiot. I'm not talking spooks and made-up stuff like that. This is true.' Sophie put down the glass. 'I'll show you. I tore the bit out because they called me in before I'd finished the quiz. It tells you how to recognise your double.'

'Don't you just look?' asked Jane.

Sophie shook her head. 'This is your spiritual double: your soul mate. Just a sec…' She churned through her bag, lifting out her mobile phone and a wodge of tissues. 'It's in here somewhere.' Somewhere under her purse, some lip gloss, a bent nail file. Screwed-up wrappers, a Barclays ballpoint, till receipts, body spray. A metal case with Mona

Lisa in a kiss-me-quick hat on the lid. Still there was more. Sophie frowned. Something was caught. She tugged out a key fob and half the lining.

Oliver disentangled a link caught in the threads. 'What's this?' He poked a finger through the key ring, letting the plastic mascot dangle.

'It's my lucky Black Madonna.' Sophie tried to snatch it back but Oliver bobbed it away. 'I've seen the real one, when I was in Barcelona. You queue up to kiss it.'

'Whereabouts?'

'Anywhere you like. Si knows all about it. I got him a Black Madonna can opener with a lid magnet. Tell them, Si.'

'S'at Monsherrat,' said Simon. 'Brought back from the Crusades.'

'And what's the little key off?' Oliver waggled it just out of reach. 'A chastity belt?'

'Why do you suppose I gave him a can opener?' She toyed with the cradle from the bubbly. 'But maybe –' slanting a glance '– those Middle Age knights needed a bit of heavy metal to turn them on. So they could rise to the challenge.' Sophie threaded her finger between strands of wire. 'I bet Maid Marion found a way round it, anyway. What do you think made those men so merry?' She looked at Simon, frowning as he rummaged through the heap. 'A girl can always make adjustments –' she looked back to Oliver '– to be accommodating.' She slotted the cradle over the neck of the empty Pinot Noir.

Something rolled away from the heap, as far as a bent cardboard tube in a plain wrapper could roll. Sophie picked it up. Upending the bottle so the cradle dangled from the rim, she angled the tube through the mesh into the glass neck. She squashed the bent end so the middle of the tube broke through the paper. The tampon poked out as the bottle rose and fell.

A few drops of Pinot Noir trickled down Sophie's wrist and onto the tablecloth.

Jane was past caring. 'Looks like it's that time of the month for Maid Marion.' She'd put the cloth to soak in the morning. Something biological would shift the stain.

'You mean,' said Sophie, 'Laid Marion.'

Jane collapsed in giggles. Simon was concentrating on holding his breath between hiccoughs. Whereas Oliver –

Sophie put down the bottle. Bloody men. Everything always had to be on their terms. The Madonna lay untouched on the cloth. God, what a prig. Bet it's twice a week with the lights out with him. She glanced at Jane, wiping her eyes. All that missionary talk. Don't suppose she knows any different.

Through the blur Jane followed Oliver's gaze to the dark red stain. Blinked and saw the reason why. Why he knew her cycle better than she did. Insisted on its chemical regulation. Why he left the room if a box of her "personal stuff" dropped out of the shopping.

Sophie was shoving things back in her bag. 'I've remembered where it is now.' She began unzipping a side compartment. 'I'll have it out in half a sec,' as snagged paper jammed teeth. She shot another look at Oliver. 'Three minutes, max.' Including the foreplay.

Intraveno veritas. Seeping under her skin, answers Jane didn't want to know to questions she'd never thought to ask. Why some of the time – five twenty-eighths of the time – he slept, dormouse-curled, on the very edge, refusing to be stroked. Why his towel was space-placed from hers, an inch of chrome marking the boundary. Why he'd shrugged off the lost-along-the-way virginity. Saving himself till he was sure uncharted straits had been thoroughly skippered.

'Got it!' Sophie pulled the crumpled sheet from the bag, 'You'll enjoy doing this with me, Oli,' and set about smoothing it out. 'Soul Mate Test, Question One. *You start touching up your makeup in public. Does he (a) look over his shoulder to see if any of his mates are watching, (b) sidle round behind you so he can ogle at himself in your mirror, (c) down his pint and wander off to chat up that blonde bimbo perched on a barstool?'*

Sophie gave Oliver a nudge. God, it was like flogging a dead Honda. 'I can see –' digging in the bag again '– I'll have to put it to the test.' She flicked back her hair, flicked open the Mona Lisa mirror case. Uncapped her lipstick, swivelled up the crimson stick. Guided it to parted lips.

Jane watched Oliver watching the build-up of colour. Sophie smiled at him through the tilted mirror, while on the other side of the lid the Giaconda looked at Jane, the enigmatic lips drooping in an unfamiliar glower as her world turned upside down.

'What if,' said Simon, 'he tells her she's beautiful, with or without the slap?'

Sophie snapped the mirror shut. 'Not one of the options, Si.'

She angled the paper away from him. Oliver bent nearer.

'It tells you what to look for, so you know how close you are.'

'Why don't you read it out, Oliver?' said Jane. If you can focus past her cleavage.

'I'd rather see what's underneath.'

Sophie flipped over the page. '*The art of cooking your goose.*' Sophie's eyes edged sideways. 'Interested?'

'You bet.'

She frowned. 'Oh, this is really weird.'

Yes, thought Jane, it's called a recipe.

'It's from –' Sophie squinted '– *The Fourteenth Book of Natural Magick.*'

'Nigella's latest best seller,' said Oliver.

'Idiot. It's sixteenth century.'

'One of her earlier books then. But are all the ingredients still available at Sainsbury's Local?'

'Probably. Because it's actually even older than the guy who wrote it. Listen. *A little before our times* – see – *a Goose was wont to be brought to the table of the King of Arragon, that was* – this is gross – *roasted alive, as I have heard by old men of credit.*'

'And they say the debt culture is a modern curse.'

'Roasted alive?' said Jane. 'That's horrible.'

'This from the girl who tucked into Lobster Thermidor on her birthday.'

'You said I'd enjoy it.'

'And so you did. Have you ever had it, Sophie? I always ask for a hen: wide tail and red coral. Delicious. Jane licked up every last mouthful. Like she always does.'

'You ordered it.' Jane threaded the corner of the tablecloth between her fingers. 'You said it would be a special treat.'

'If animals could talk,' said Simon, 'you'd know how the lobshter felt about it.'

Sophie shook her head. 'She wouldn't have been able to understand it.'

'Not being fluent in Lobster,' said Oliver.

'I mean because underwater everything's distorted,' said Sophie. 'You know, that glugging sound you get in your ears.'

'Do shellfish have ears?'

'And it would be splashing like crazy, wanting out.'

'Typical female. As soon as things start hotting up –'

'They tie the claws.' Simon clenched his fingers round the stem of the glass.

'At least they'll feel at home in the salty water,' said Oliver. 'Unless they're watching their sodium intake. Jane fusses about my cholesterol level.' His eyes flicked over her. 'Don't you, angel?'

'Not as much as you do.'

'Which is why goose is such a good choice,' said Oliver. 'You don't know what you're missing, Sophie. Spend Christmas Day with me.'

'Me as in us?' asked Jane.

'Not if you're cooking it like this.' Sophie tapped the paper. 'It may be okay for lobsters, but a live goose is –'

'Feathered?' said Oliver. 'Funny how the more covered animals are, the more we drool over them. If that'd been a recipe for cooking something hairier they'd have been burning them in the streets. The mags, that is, not the mogs. Main course kitten, medium rare and mewing.'

'Oliver!'

'Stop screeching, Jane.' But the eyes were on Sophie. 'You know I'm only teasing. There's no way I could barbecue a little pussy. Immobilising the paws might leave you scarred for life. Even a goose might struggle while being tied up.' He leaned nearer. 'Could give you a long hard suck.'

'In your dreams, Oliver. You don't get to tie up the bird.' Sophie rustled the paper. 'Listen and you might learn something new. *Make a fire about him, not too narrow, lest the smoke choke him, or the fire should roast him too soon, nor yet too wide, lest he escape unroasted.* Then it says,' she scanned down, '*When he begins to roast, he will walk about, and cannot get forth for the fire stops him.*'

'Not truly free range, then.'

'Stop laughing. This is gross. And not because he's feathery, because it says, before you light the fire, *Pull all the feathers from his body, leaving his head and his neck.* So there.'

'Oh, God!' Simon pushed back his chair, knocking over an almost full bottle of Glorioso Crianza.

'Simon – bloody hell!'

Sophie's dress was soaked. With an open palm, Oliver slapped his napkin over her midriff and began to rub. Sophie lifted off his hand. Oliver held up the sodden napkin, then let it slop onto the table, spattering their too close faces.

But maybe Jane wasn't seeing right. Because he couldn't really be edging a finger between Sophie's breasts, scooping up a drip, bearing it to his outstretched tongue –

Sophie pushed back her chair. 'I'll go and get cleaned up.'

'Take it off. You can borrow one of Jane's.'

'It's okay.'

'Go on, I'd like to see you in something of hers.'

'I'll get you a towel,' said Jane.

'No, don't come. I'm sure I can find what I want.'

Which left the three of them.

'God, I feel ill,' said Simon.

'You've got to chill out at the weekend,' said Oliver. 'All too soon it's Monday morning.'

'I think it is already,' said Jane. Because her watch would never lie. And surely this was her watch, even though the face was strangely blank. So, that must be her wrist. And, hanging over the edge of the table, was a hand. A hand with black ants crawling over it, and midnight eyes impaling her.

'Gotta go.' Simon stood up, then sat down again. 'Might have to phone in sick. Thank God's not much on.'

'Glad you're so relaxed about the Crowther meeting.' Oliver spun the toppled bottle. 'Thought there was a bit of doubt about clinching that. Still, I'm sure when he sees your final breakdown...'

'S'gonna be tricky.' Simon looked his empty glass full in the eye. 'But godda bidda time left to figgle the jigures. Godill Thursday.'

Oliver stood the bottle up. 'Didn't you get the message? I told Kate to be sure to let you know. Crowther's secretary phoned to rearrange for tomorrow.'

Simon shook his head. 'Snot possible.' Shook it over and over. 'Can't expect me – snot fair.' He stopped shaking and allowed the contents to settle. 'When did he phone?'

'Must have been…' Oliver blew out slowly, making the candle flame flicker '… early last week.'

The mood music played on.

'Early last week? Why the hell didn't you tell me yourself – Christ, Oli, you know this is my big chance to show Harry –'

'And you will. I'm counting on it.'

He moved the glass before Simon collapsed over the table, submitting to an emotional outpouring that the fate of thirty thousand broilers, a handful of Iberian eagles and a solitary ploated goose had failed to evoke.

'You'd better order a taxi.' Above the moving slit, Oliver's eyes were lead-shot.

Jane tried to open her mouth. Electrical impulses bounced round the room. The only recognisable sound was the cocking of his eyes.

His mouth was moving – 'Use my phone. It's in the kitchen' – but she scarcely heard it above the sound of the eyes.

If only she could think, make sense of it… could form real words, could part her lips and let them out. If only she could escape from those eyes.

SHE reached the kitchen door.

There was Sophie, kneeling on the floor, buttocks in the air, leaning forward on reptile arms. There was Sophie, bending over the spilt pavlova, head down in the cream and raspberries and pieces of broken meringue.

Jane, hand glued to the door, was unable to move. Yet that other hand, which happened to have come along, slid along the worktop, stretched out one beckoning finger. As the phone came towards her, a single file of black ants marched over her wrist and back into position around the edge of the watch face. Measuring the time it took for the vinyl tiles to be licked clean.

SHE put the phone on the table. Oliver picked it up. Wiped the case on a corner of the cloth. Checked his balance. All the time looking at her. Her heartbeats were being sucked from her, through bone cage and flesh, through plaster and brick into a cavity of unknowingness. She stood there unbreathing, might have stood there forever but for a low slow mew that rose from the table and yowled round the walls, slicing the quadraphonic silence, filling the vacuum of being.

Oliver pushed back his chair and left the room. She sat down and put her arm round Simon.

'He knew. He knew and he didn't tell me.' Raising his head he searched her face. 'Why didn't he tell me, Jane?'

'Well, he's been really busy lately. He works so hard, never has a spare moment.'

'I work hard.'

'I'm sure you do.'

'I do it for Soph. Everything I do's for Soph.'

'She's a lucky girl.'

'Soph's a wonderful girl. Gorgeous. When we're out together, all the guys look. Have you seen the way they look?' He leaned nearer. 'You know what, Jane? I trust Soph. Completely.'

His face was so close she couldn't have focussed, even without half a cellarful sloshing behind each cornea.

'You gotta trust people, haven't you, Jane?'

'I don't think –' Can't think. Won't think. 'Oliver would've thought Kate could be trusted to give you the message. It is her job.'

'Sodding Kate. Stupid sodding bitch. Sits filing her sodding nails the whole sodding day.' He paused. 'You wouldn't catch Soph sitting round gawping at her fingers.'

Not at that moment, certainly, even had the bathroom door been unlocked. Not with two of them jabbing at the back of her throat.

'THE taxi will be here in five – well, this is all very cosy.'

Jane tried to shift Simon's head. He clutched at her strap, exposing a nipple as she pushed him away.

'Simon's had –' she yanked back his little finger '– a bit too much' and tried to laugh. Tried to shove her breast back in line.

Oliver reached between them and nipped out the candle. 'I'm sure he has.'

The smoke seethed upwards in a long slow column.

THERE was
    the shrill chattering,
      sense battering,
        wall stumbling,
          stair clattering,
            lift jamming,
              door slamming,
                brain shattering
                  of their going.

BUT he would be back.

So what? They'd have one hell of a row – and, God knows, there were a few things she'd like to tell him – then tomorrow it would all be forgotten.

Except Oliver didn't do rows.

Too late to creep under the sheets, eyes tight shut. Ridiculous to hide in the bathroom. But she could put the tablecloth to soak. That wouldn't be hiding.

She slopped the cloth into the tub, turned the taps on full. Felt the urge to pee.

She dropped the seat and sat down, wriggling knickers over knees, scraping them down her right calf with her foot. In the bath the cloth glugged. That's all she needed, an overflowing bath. She stumbled across, skirt hitched up round her thighs, knickers dragging round one ankle. She dislodged the cloth from the plughole, turned off the cold. Reached for the hot.

It was then when it happened.

It was then when the bathroom door slammed shut and the bolt rammed home. Then when her legs were pushed against the mock mahogany panel. When the knotted cotton mat began to slip back, taking her feet, while her body lurched in a spine-wrenching forward slash to the half-tiled cracked tile tactile smoothness of cold fired clay. Her forehead pressed against ceramic white, neck wrenched back. Her hands pushed against the tiles, fingers forced back, bloodless tips merging with tin-glazed terracotta while condensation trickled down the channels of grout.

A sudden splaying, skin scraping skin, easing the gap. A blunt stabbing, flesh rubbing flesh, forcing the gap. Three tiles down and seven across, the Cutty Sark carved its way across the shockwaves. Six inches by six of acetate, scarred by abrasive cleansing, steam swirling round her swollen mainsail in a cloud of bewilderment.

My ship sailed from China with a cargo of tea... one small finger stretched sideways, scratching the furled top edge of the plastic transfer... *all laden with presents for you and...* the ring finger followed, groping at nothing... filling her head with the nothingness, numbing her senses to all except the lotus strains of Sirens, hidden in amorphous swathes far, far below, in a liquid world of tablecloths and flowing wine... *just imagine my bliss...* and all the while on board Odysseus stuck to his allotted six inches above the splashback.

Lapped by a scalding torrent, the cloth bulged and scuppered... *when I found myself...* lashed to a mast of oak, Jane arched and buckled... *swaying...* in rhythmic limbo, back and forth, *like this*, in and out, *like this... like this...* steam swirling round, choking her, the words choking her, *like this, like this,* gulping them down *like this like this* watching the stain seep from the wing-clipped cloth of drowning Sirens.

Water crept up the sides, beckoning, and her feet rooted in dry earth... if she could return to the sea... be cocooned by water, safe in the womb, finding a voice from once upon a time... *There's a ship sails away At the close of each day Sails away to the land of dreams...* rocked in Mother's arms, *rolled up tight in a little white sheet, till you can't see those bare little feet...* shedding splayed legs and gaping labia, plunging scale-tailed into the waves, cutting through the red pollution that scared men into domination.

Mummy snuggles up tight... Four tiles along from the clipper, under a leaden sky, the crew of the *Endeavour* braced itself for an imminent downpour. *Daddy whispers goodnight...*

Jane's hair was yanked back. The cloth freed itself from the plughole. Above the draining vortex, the flagship *Victory* fired a double slotted broadside as the tap ran cold.

SIX thirty eight. Proof beyond all reasonable doubt. She had slept.

She tried to swallow. Tried to focus beyond the line of dust along the waste pipe behind the sink, to raise her eyes above the trail of slime where the basin rested on the pedestal. Tried to straighten a leg.

There was a sound. A room-reverberating, soul-wrenching, sense-smashing insignificant rattle. From the other side of the door.

She rolled onto her knees and began jamming the already jammed towels, pushing the acid yellow velour towel further under the bottom of the door and the deep-dyed mustard towel between the hinges on the right and the gold fringed embroidered towel along the length of the left hand edge, where there was no more space but the jamming must go on.

Above her fingers the handle began to move, so quietly she could hear the spring creaking, so slowly she could feel the coil whirling. The bolt wasn't drawn across. The fingers that had last drawn that bolt were embedded forever in the brass. She could not have drawn that bolt across, not if the door were being pounded by all sixteen frenzied hooves of the apocalyptic stallions. Not even if –

'Jane.'

The handle returned to horizontal.

She was aware of breathing. She could smell breath. Could feel it against the nape of her neck, feel it through the hardwood panel, feel it through three towels' thickness, knew he was at her level. Knew he was setting something down, down so gently, on the carpet. There on a posy of rosebuds, grubby and faded and trodden into their sackcloth bed, something was being set down.

'I've brought you a cup of tea.'

A cup of tea. Her tongue throbbed, filling the dried up mouth. She was gagging for it, just as he'd known all along. Nothing like a cup of tea for putting things into perspective. You'll look back on this and laugh. She almost laughed now. If she could have made any sound she would have laughed.

The voice wasn't hers. '...won't be in today... a sickness bug... I'm sure she'll soon get over it... I'll be in touch... yes, I'll tell her.' And he laughed.

WHEN she pulled open the door, there would be no-one there.

Already it had been daylight for ever.

Still she waited. There was no sun.

The towels were pulled out, one by one, and smoothed, each in turn, and folded, separately, and hung over the rail and over the radiator and over the side of the – Don't think about it. Just do it.

Nestling in the woollen rosebuds was her favourite mug, the china one with the picnicking teddy bears. The tea was cold, a skin already forming.

THERE was a tea bag on the draining board, a milk bottle seal on the worktop. Jane tipped out the mug of tea. Brown splashes flecked the sink and trickled down the stainless steel, merging with globs of yellow spattering the bottom, as the smell of tannin was swallowed by the stench of uric acid.

SHE must get away. The thing was – where to go? She spread out the map. It wasn't like that other time, the leaving. To find herself, the note had said, that other time.

She'd found herself bewildered and broke. Her hand hovered over the ignition key. She would have gone straight back, that other time. Back to tears and recriminations and promises and forgiveness, just how she'd imagined it. For them to be sorry. Without question. A mother wouldn't have to ask. The light on Festina's dashboard glowed amber. Her mother would know.

Di would've told her mother, that other time, that she didn't know anything. She could stay with Di for a few days, while she made plans. The engine stalled. Damp. Only to be expected... extracting every last detail, pretending not to gloat. I told you so. There were some things you could depend on.

Like Maddy. When she'd lost it, that other time, Maddy had snatched her from the subway. Stopped her from going back. A squirt of WD40 would do it. She shook the can. Trust Maddy. The nozzle frothed. An amalgam of secret formula hydrocarbons dribbled down the blue letters. No-one must know.

Anywhere would do. She sprayed around the plugs. It always worked. As long as it was far away. As long as no-one knew.

The pedal was through the floor. Concentrate on breathing. Three thousand revs. Things weren't so bad. It wasn't like that other time. Fumes filled her nostrils. Broke and bewildered, she remembered it well. Could almost hum the tune. Whereas now she had – a few random items in a holdall and an empty handbag. Everything that proved she existed had gone.

She must get on. The thing was – what to do? How to make time pass, get through the day. The needle on the gauge hovered over the quarter way line. Get through life. Get it over with.

She could go into the office. Tell them she was better. I feel much better, thank you. Quite my normal self. Everyone would look at her. Everyone would know.

Didn't she have a client that morning? Jubilee Terrace. Miss Harley. Was it at eleven? Maybe Mrs Harlow. Maybe half past eleven. Had she put her appointments diary in the holdall? There was nothing she recognised inside. Not the nailbrush or the back brush or the dustpan and brush. Not the mock alpaca reinforced with nylon or the irreversible polyester gilet. Not the solitary trainer with its stained inner sole and laces still in last night's knots.

She'd be there at eleven. Ms Harlot could please herself.

IT was his car. Coming towards her, taking all the road. There were no white lines, nothing to mark the boundary which shouldn't be crossed. Jane pulled into the side. Through Festina's mirror the tail lights of the white Mondeo glowed red as it took the corner into Mafeking Avenue.

There was room outside number sixty-six but Jane backed into the other free space, the one outside twenty-eight.

Ten minutes later a hatchback parked next to the For Sale sign. A woman got out, tried the door, rang the bell. Jane could have told her it didn't work. Across the road a ginger tom rubbed a paw behind its ear. Someone trudged past with a trolley, pushing leaflets into boxes. The high, the low, the tightly sprung, they all got one. Even shut up sixty-six. The woman pressed the bell again.

There was a short gust. Down the terrace, the flap-trapped flyers gave a Tex-Mex wave. One broke free, blew into the road. As she drove off Ms H narrowly missed the opportunity to get complimentary chilli gravy on a standard portion of tortilla chips.

Under a 2 and a screw-loose 8, a letter box snapped its jaws. The leaflet was being taken in. And so, a few moments later, was Jane.

'THANK you for agreeing to take part. Market research is vital for monitoring trends in customer requirements. By taking part in this anonymous survey you are ensuring that you, the householder, get the goods and services you really need or want.' Jane paused. 'It'll only take a few minutes.'

She moved a Brio engine from the armchair in front of the window and sat down. The train set was scattered on the floor, track in pieces, carriages in a pile. A sofa with loose covers stretched along the wall opposite the sealed-up fireplace. It sank several inches as the woman sat down, despite her smug size 6 frame.

'What do you want to ask me?'

Jane opened the folder she'd grabbed from the car seat. 'First of all... the type of property is –?'

'Type? Oh, you want to know if I'm attached?'

'Yes.' Got it in one.

'It's a terraced house. Didn't you notice?'

'That was just the $64 question.' Jane smiled. 'You know, the easy one.'

'Is there a prize? Do I get put in a draw for taking part?'

'Yes. If you give me your name and phone –'

'I thought you said it was anonymous.'

'Oh, it is. Absolutely. The draw's optional. Entirely –' there seemed to be a small child crouched behind the far arm of the sofa '– up to you.' Very different from sweetie-pants Stephanie. And yet there was something –

'What else do you want to know?'

A felt-tip squeaked into the silence. The boy was scribbling on a folded newspaper. Round and round in overlapping circles, smaller and smaller.

'Which daily paper do you take?'

'I don't bother with papers. That's just one somebody left here.' She nodded towards the scrawling child. 'I'm not really the Independent type.'

No, I don't suppose you are, thought Jane. Though I might have realised he was, on the side. At home, the broadsheet had been down to her mother. Jane used to collect it from the box when she was scarcely older than the child now stuffing the paper under a cushion. He scuttled along the floor and tried to bury his face in the woman's lap.

'Don't pretend you're a sleepy head.' She stroked his hair. 'What's the next question?'

'Number of bedrooms?'

'Two.' The woman arched her neck to see the question page and frowned.

Jane shoved it to the bottom. Because the Up Your Street letterhead was enough to make anyone frown. The next sheet was an e-mail, bandied around the office the previous week. Subject: Clips from Council complaint letters. *I am writing on behalf of my cupboards.* Three days ago it had seemed quite funny... *I request permission to remove my drawers in the kitchen...*when Roy read it out. *Our floor is damp. We already have one child and would like another. Please send someone round to do something about it...*

'How many are there living in the house?'

She lifted the child onto her knee. 'Just me and Chas.' He pawed her face.

Jane looked away. And saw a tie, thrown over the back of an armchair. A tie with a sunflower half a centimetre off bang in the middle. A sunflower from a length of silk brought home from fabric printing class and cut to shape, edges pinned, sewn during the evening news. Through earthquakes, war and famine, the stitches never faltered. As good as shop bought. Better. They'd all agreed the seepage of orange into ultramarine was barely noticeable. Anyway, as Di had said, it made it a bit unique.

'I don't seem to have told you anything important yet,' said the woman. 'You know, like what's my favourite washing powder. I always get the bio. Next door tends to give it the once-over.' She tapped the side of her nose. 'Always poking it in where it's not wanted.'

Jane looked at her folder. *I want to complain about my neighbour.*

'Or what sort of coffee I buy. I drink loads. Not own brand, either. I need more than that to get me going first thing.'

Every morning at 6am his power tool wakes me up. It's all getting too much for me.

'Would you like one?' Without waiting for an answer, the woman went out, Chas yapping at her heels.

Jane picked up the tie. Traced the edge of the sunflower, weeping into the ultramarine in a barely noticeable way. Just a bit unique.

'Or would you rather have a cup of –'

Jane dropped the tie – 'I've got to go' – and pushed past into the dark hallway.

EYES winced against the light. The beam moved away, sweeping the interior, and back over her face. Beached on the recumbent seat, Jane shrank into the vinyl, pulling Snow Baby to her throat. Cold crawled over her skin. Someone was rasping at the handle. Someone or something. Festina shook. Through a blur of condensation, another shape reared at the passenger side and banged on the glass.

'Open the door!'

It was the only way out. Or in. Not an eyelid flickered to shield her from the unseen.

'Police! Open up!'

Driven by a drilled compliance greater than conjured fear, Jane elbowed herself upright, knees drawn up to her chest. She fumbled for the lock and waited for them to take charge.

'You all right, luv?'

Yes. She tried again. 'Yes.' But surely, exposed as she was by the weak bulb above the windscreen, he must see...

He thrust his face into hers. 'Sleeping it off, are we?'

Pickled egg lingered as he backed away.

'Squeaky clean,' he told his companion.

Disappointment filled the air, drowning all vestiges of egg. Or vinegar.

'Would you step outside the car please, madam.'

They stood block-bodied while she dragged herself out.

'Are you the owner of this vehicle?'

'Yes.'

'Could you tell me the registration number, please?'

She couldn't. Nor could she show them her driving licence, the certificate of insurance or a valid MOT print-off. They took her name. She gave them yesterday's address. It was all she had. Not a problem, they told her. Any time in the next seven days would do.

No hurry, no sweat. No tears. The patrol car revved away, lights disappearing, smell dispersing, sound dissolving, into the far beyond.

ASTRONOMICALLY speaking, it was nearly two months until the shortest day. And the longest night. But what did six and a bit weeks count in an existence amounting to zilch?

It was getting light. Everywhere ordinary people would be stirring, planning another ordinary day, moving on. But she had to go back.

Already she was nearing the field between the carriageways. But travelling towards the town, she could see no further than the fence at the top of the steep roadside verge. The offside wheels skirted across the perimeter line, scrunching puddles, one by one. She edged Festina onto the slope, until the view was blocked. Jane wound down the window.

A phalanx of glinting spears bristled before her, a thousand rime-swathed stems, every blade distinct. Each one mattered. The intensity of individuality made the grass seem very close. She stretched out one finger to touch a frozen stalk but the tilt of the car put it out of reach. Motionless, the sparkling crystals beckoned.

The bottom of the door jabbed into the bank side. A car swerved past, screeching, blasting, flashing. Jane switched on her hazard lights to ward off the rest of humanity and clambered out.

The embankment was difficult to climb. Grass ground to mud under her feet, caking her shoes, her knees, her hands, as she struggled to the fence. The field was hung with patches of fog. She screwed up her eyes.

But the geese were nowhere to be seen.

It was too early. The wooden ark, its roof jutting out above the mist, was shut up. Jane picked at damp slime on the top rail, jamming her nails with compacted moss until they hurt. She checked again, looked as far as she could see, but there was nothing. She might as well go back.

A clink of metal. Jane looked beyond the top of the field where, before the carriageways joined, there was a house and some outbuildings. A figure was coming through the stackyard gate. Jane waited. The figure put down a bucket near the ark and dropped the hatch.

The geese didn't emerge.

The figure – and Jane could see now it was a woman, with spikes of white hair escaping from a woolly hat and a sagging chest bulking out the khaki trench coat – kicked over a trough. She righted it with the side of her welly and began to pour something in. Jane could hear the ricochet of grain against galvanised steel, could make out a rising cloud of dust.

From the hut nothing stirred.

The woman moved to the stackyard fence, where she leaned over to retrieve a spade leaning against the other side. She raised it above an old tin bath and brought it down with a splintering crack.

It was then that the first beak appeared, swaying from side to side, testing the air.

Out they came, crouch-bodied, stiff legs slithering down the slatted ramp. Twelve snake necks unfolded in succession. Tails bobbing in counterpoint, the geese thrust forward their breasts and raised their wings in a fan dance. Newborn sunlight played upon uncovered plumage. It stretched out in layers, from dense clusters along the bone to the spreading arch of flight feathers. Jane wanted to cry out. Take off, geese. Don't stay, growing fat and lazy. Time is running out. Pair by pair, wings retracted to the quilted warmth. Wings, Mrs Wainwright had told her, that would, like as not, have the end quills clipped across the shaft.

The birds trod towards the tin bath. Beaks thrust skywards with every swallow, so she could follow each gulp down the vertical necks. Leaving a wake of watery droppings they padded to the trough.

Food eaten, they withdrew as one. A huge bulk of shadow, pierced by narrow slits of brightness, stayed with them as they paced the field. Joined to their feet by long dark stalks, the shadow cloud stretched far in front, now alongside, now behind, but would not leave them.

Led by the shadow, they moved towards her. Jane kept very still. On they came, an undulating mass of complaint. They stopped a metre or so from the fence and straightened up, silent now, staring. Jane was glad they weren't afraid. And that the fence was between them. Especially when the biggest one, the one with grey wingtips, came right up to the rail. Was this one a gander and all the others – geese? Not a breeding flock, of course, but just the luck of the chromosome. Why did the male have a specific name when the females didn't?

He viewed her sideways on. The feathers on his neck were coarse, fused like the scales of some primeval reptile.

As he turned his head she caught a flash of translucent sunlight through his oval nostril. His eye was perfectly round, set in a ring of tiny feathers. Between unblinking orange lids, it burned deep cobalt.

The others, losing interest, began to move off. The gander – she was sure it must be a gander – hurried after them. Slithering over the trampled grass on leather skates, toes turned in, he pushed through the flock to take the lead. Without them, he could not be first. He needed them. The females didn't require a specific label: they were the species, the source of new life. Although none of these geese would live long enough to lay an egg.

Jane became aware of the old woman watching. But she wasn't looking at Jane. One of the geese was huddled apart from the others, head low to the ground. It didn't move away as the woman approached, but allowed itself to be scooped up. She gathered it to her chest, wrapping her arms round it. Nuzzling the throat feathers with a free finger, she carried the goose to the stackyard, head bent over it and lips moving as she went.

The rest of the flock was at the far side of the field, surveying the cars already queuing at the roundabout. Were they seeking out Festina? Not this morning, faithful guardians. This morning she had to go the other way. Jane lifted her arms from the top rail. Underneath, the Snow Baby sleeves were matted with slime.

SHE cleared a patch of windscreen with her cuff. If she kept her neck craned, she'd be able to spot him driving off. She'd thought he'd be long gone; he always had a session at the gym before work on Tuesdays. It was Tuesday, wasn't it? Two days since.

A front door slammed. The wrong door. Would he never go? She turned on the radio. The station came and went. She was fiddling with the retuning button, had summoned up a steady crackle, when there was a tap at the window. Jane pressed volume control, kept her finger on till the car was filled with noise enough to scrape every nerve, rasp bone against bone, grate her brain to brawn, loud enough to stifle –

'Hiya!' followed by a rap at the side window.

Jane wiped her sleeve across the glass. There, with tangerine lips hammocked across an upturned purple collar, was Sophie. Jane got out.

'I thought it was you. Si said Oli would've already left. Says he always goes – oh-my-God!'

Jane looked where Sophie looked. Down the front of the Snow Baby, past the knees of the denims to the tops of her trainers. Except that there'd been a complete merger of Wranglers and Reeboks. Even as she stood there, clods of mud and grass were dropping onto the pavement.

'So, what have you been up to?'

The easy thing would've been to tell her to mind her own. To get back in the car and settle for a hundred and twenty decibels of hysteria. To lock the nosy cow out of her life. Yet, there was Sophie, less than half a metre away. An infinitesimal space that held the briefest acquaintance, little affinity, absolutely no rapport. Yet there she was. Another human being. Another female.

Jane gave a laugh. 'Oh, I just popped down to the allotment.' She tried the laugh again. 'Silly me, forgot my wellies.'

'I didn't realise people still had them,' said Sophie. 'My Grandad had three. Grew those really tall things. You know.'

'Sunflowers?'

'God, no,' said Sophie. 'He only grew things you could eat.'

'Like carrots.' Jane gave the laugh another go. 'Or –' even funnier '– parsnips.' It was becoming more normal, at least as normal as laughs can be when root vegetables are under discussion.

Sophie shook her head. 'Leeks. He put cardboard tubes over them. Won loads of cups. I used to Blutak his prize tickets inside my Barbie house.'

'I had Sindy. My mother disapproved of anything American.'

'No plastic Ken for you, then. Did Sindy have a boyfriend?'

'Not in our house. Bumps on the chest were enough for Mum. My sister used to paint them with Smarties. She'd start sucking a red one, then dab on nipples.'

'Then I bet she put it back in her mouth to finish it off.'

Now the laugh had had a bit of practice, there was no holding it. Jane watched the two bodies as they rocked together. Noticed the purple wool blend was now frowning at the laughing white fur, fake that it was. Wondered if it would go on laughing, till the concrete buildings all around were crumbled dust and the purple fibres rotted into forgottenness and all that was left was an acrylic pelt skinned from a being that never was.

'Oy!' followed by a thud between the shoulder blades. 'Crawl back in your hole, you drunken slag.'

With a no hesitation, 'Fuck off, tosser,' knee-in-the-groin, Sophie latched a purple arm through the grubby white and steered it clear of the back-slapper doubled over the kerb.

Purple Mix took Snow Baby across the road and down the street. Their snapshot reflections flicked into a B movie as they passed the windows of the ground floor flats. All illusion.

Now someone was counting in her head, clocking up the number of times the mud-caked toes rose, left, right, and dropped away, in counter step to the scuff-resistant black leather that clicked, right, left, on every other concrete slab. Up the stairway went the feet, past Heather's doorway, up, up, till they could go no further.

'If it's not here,' said Sophie, 'I'm totally messed up.' She pulled her arm from Jane's. 'Have you got your key?'

The bump in Snow Baby's pocket bulged and writhed. The pocket mouth gawked, crying out to be frisked. But the unlinked arm stayed rigid in its slime-smeared sleeve. Sophie, who'd passed the point when she would be, even for her, more than a teeny bit late for work, put a finger to the bell.

SO there they were, in the hall, the three of them, and Sophie was giving her dippy me and the missing mobile lament another run, when the smoke alarm went off. So then they were in the kitchen. Where Oliver was tearing the least charred bits off the rashers, ouching as he burnt his fingers, and Sophie, all the while professing she didn't do breakfast, was smothering soft white rolls with HP. And when three plates and three steaming mugs were put on the table, there didn't seem anything to say except –

'Mmm, these sarnies are simply –' and Sophie kissed the air.

As well as, three bread buns apiece later, kissing Oliver.

'Oli –' she waved her phone '– you're a star.'

Pressing down the door handle with one knee, Sophie pulled at the Yale lever.

'The damp makes it swell.' Oliver reached forward. 'It needs a jerk to open it.'

'I knew I could rely on you.' She poked him in the chest with the phone. 'Must go.'

As must Jane. But Oliver is between her and the door. By now the black leather boots will have reached the bottom of the stairs, scuff free. He leans against the door. Jane is trapped, with no certificate of insurance. The catch bangs home.

'Excuse me,' she says to the Yale. It nestles against his shoulder, its brassy gleam dulled by overlapping layers of fingerprints. Hers and his, touching.

'Let me pass.'

'Are you going into work? I phoned in yesterday. Said you weren't up to it. I'll call them again. You look as though another day's rest would do you good.'

And there was something else she needed.

'You've been overdoing it lately. I've noticed how you keep getting things mixed up, out of proportion. Imagining things.'

The test, that was it. But wasn't the MOT all held online now? The insurance certificate would be in the desk, though. She turned and walked into the lounge. As easy as that. But her driving licence was in the bedside chest.

The bed had been made. Below her pillow the cover was turned back. She was so very tired. But she had a more pressing urge. She should have poured that second mug of coffee down the sink. Or over his head.

She got as far as the – When is a door not a door? When it's open enough to reveal strands of gold fringe dangling in a puddle on the floor. When there's sufficient gap to expose a dark stain seeping up from the hem. When a micro millimetre slit is way too much to show the towel humped over the bath. When it's a jarring, gaping jaw to hell.

Back in the bedroom, she pressed the door shut, seeing the key for the first time, though it must always have been there, jammed in the lock. On the chest of drawers, among the make-up and mismatched earrings, was a plastic bottle with a pink lid, just as she'd left it. And in the top right hand drawer, under her driving licence, there'd be a metal nail file.

By the time she'd jabbed off paint and dribbled in enough baby oil to get the key to turn, the need to pee was thigh scrunching. She clenched fists, curled toes, contracted every muscle in her body. Wild-eyed the room, flicking from the crumpled receipt on the floor at his side of the bed, to the loose change piled on a twenty pound note torn down to the arch of the Queen's left eyebrow, to yesterday's shirt with the cuffs still fastened, a half-inside-out sock and a size 9 Berluti boot, tipped on its side. The other was by the wardrobe, standing straight, laces loose, tongue out. Ready.

The urge was overwhelming. She unbuttoned her Levis and squatted. A shudder ran through her body, down her arms, right to her fingertips.

HE was on his knees before her. 'Got yourself sorted?'

Jane pulled Snow Baby's zip up to her chin.

He put the brush in the dustpan and stood up. 'All set to tackle the awkward clients, not to mention Christian? That's my girl.'

'I'm not going into work.'

'Then where –?'

'The police station.' She opened the front door. 'I've something to report.'

SHE'D call at the filling station first. Jane straightened the heap on the passenger seat. Sandwiched between her driving licence and the insurance certificate, was a twenty pound note with a tear down to the arch of the Queen's left eyebrow.

HER mother must be out. Even the garden looked shut up. The clods on the raised beds reminded her of the fresh filled, flesh filled mounds under the shadow of the church tower. Was it only nine days since the christening party had sidled round them, searching for a better backdrop? Hardly any time at all, a blink of an eye in God's grand scheme. And in that instant when the immaculate lids had flicked over the all-seeing eyes, the world had changed. Yet here nothing was different. It was all as reassuringly cheerless as it ever was.

'YOU'VE bought a lot of stuff, Mum.'

'It's the AGM this evening. I'll set it all out in the sitting room. The forecast's for it to get colder.'

'Why isn't it at the church hall?'

'We haven't had it there for years. Shows how long it is since you've been around.'

'I was here a few days ago! The weekend before –'

'That was different. You can imagine my surprise to come home and find you sitting in the drive.'

'I thought you might be at a class.'

'Floral Artistry's the only one running.' Judith took the kettle to the sink. 'Getting enough people to join's always been a problem. And now Mrs Sugden's passed on, and Penny Fletcher hardly goes out and...'

Water spattered from the rim of the kettle.

'A lot of the younger women are at work, of course.'

Which is where, smirked the tiles behind a cold film of mist, we'd have expected you to be.

'So you don't go to fabric printing class any more?'

'As I said, there's just flower arranging this year. I only go to make up the numbers.' Judith took some chrysanthemums from the window ledge. 'The woman who takes it can't teach me anything.'

'Daddy's tie was really distinctive. I bet no-one else ever did one like it.'

Judith sniffed the top of the vase. 'Has no idea at all.'

'You'd recognise it anywhere.'

'And some people simply won't listen.' Holding back the stems, Judith tilted the vase.

'Does he still wear it?'

The stink of decay rose from the sink.

'Who?'

The kettle had switched off.

'Mum, shall I make the tea? There's something I need to tell you.'

'I DON'T know why you won't believe me.' Jane lifted out the spoon, felt the apostle's face against her thumb. Once upon a time there must have been a full set. She licked it dry and put it down beside the cup. Milky rings subsided to a solitary drifting bubble. Her finger wandered into the bowl of the spoon. 'Shall I go through it again?' She pressed down and the handle began to rotate. 'I know it's a lot to take in.' The apostle's face was stolid.

'You have always regarded me as ancient, Jane, so no doubt you now also assume I am becoming feeble minded, but I can assure you there's nothing wrong with my understanding.'

'Of course I don't think that.' Jane relaxed the pressure slightly. The spoon shifted an inch or so across the table. 'But it's obvious that this woman – that Daddy –' The back of St Thomas's head hit the side of the mug. 'You must believe me.'

'The only thing that's obvious is your skewed perception. You always did have more imagination than was good for you.' Judith pushed her cup across the table. 'I'll have a fill-up. No more milk. You put far too much in the first time.'

'Mum, he was there.' She lifted off the cosy. 'I saw him.'

'And try not to slop it over the edge this time.'

Jane gripped the saucer in both hands and put it down in front of her mother. 'I know it's hard.' Dare she reach out to those shoulders? 'But you've got to accept it.' Not an actual hug, of course. 'He can't spend all day at the surgery, can he?'

'No.' Judith shrugged off the arm. 'He'll be through his morning appointments now, unless he's come up against an awkward patient. One so blinkered by their own misinformed opinion that they imagine a problem when there isn't one.'

'But after surgery's finished –'

'He'll be making his house calls. Which is precisely what he would be doing when you saw him the other day.'

'It was too far from home for that.'

'You seem to forget he's an independent practitioner with a large rural area to cover. And your father's always made a point of letting old patients remain with him if they move house. Those that wish to.'

'This woman was young.'

'You deliberately misunderstand. By old I did not necessarily mean –'

'I saw him twice!'

'You've always put your father on a pedestal, Jane. I'm afraid I must inform you that even he sometimes fails to cure the sick with a single visit.' She took another sip and grimaced. 'You can't get anything right, can you?'

'Do you want me to answer?' Because the phone had started ringing

'Just pass it.'

Half rising, Jane lifted the receiver from the wall and stretched across. The cable writhed along the table, knocking over her mug.

'Yes, speaking... No, it's fine, I'm not doing anything important at the moment.'

Jane went for the dishcloth.

'By all means come along. New faces are always welcome... No, call me madam chairman, please. I've no time for all that political correctness nonsense.'

Began to mop up.

'Well, someone's got to do it and the members keep electing me… Yes, my husband is the doctor here. You have? That's very sensible…'

Dabbed at her Levis with the wet dishcloth.

'Not at all. When you've lived in the village as long as we have…'

Carried the sopping cloth to the sink.

'Sorry, I didn't hear…'

Tiptoed back to the table. St Thomas was lying face down.

'Seven o'clock. We like to start on time, get the formalities out of the way before we have supper. No, there's no need to bring anything. I'm told I put on a good spread… oh, have you? People are really much too kind. Until this evening.'

The receiver was passed across. Jane could hear the disconnected tone before it was back in its cradle.

'Well, Jane,' pulling on rubber gloves, 'you might be at a loose end, but I am not.'

Judith emptied the kettle over the dishcloth and wrung it out.

'People in the village look to me to maintain certain standards.'

It lay on the draining board in a screwed up lump.

'I've wasted so much time listening to your ridiculous fancies, I'm now rather pushed.'

So pushed in fact that she didn't pause to pull off the rubber gloves as Jane kissed the air somewhere near the maternal cheek.

SHE'D tell Di about it. There should be enough fuel left for that, though the twenty note had probably passed through several hands already. Di was family: she ought to know. The tear from the edge to the Queen's eyebrow could be a lot worse by now. The matriarchal smile might

121

already be severed. God, she hadn't even cancelled her cards yet. Her head ached. But Oliver would already have sorted – She felt sick.

Miles passed, hours. Or maybe moments. Her brain clicked back to manual. This was the wrong way. She turned off the blower. She felt hot, really hot, though she could see her breath, could see nothing beyond it, could hear nothing but the pounding in her head. Her legs were jelly, her feet in spasm against the pedals. She was so very tired and it was such a long way. Wherever she was heading.

SHE wasn't meant to be here. Unguided, Festina had plodded home and was eyeing up an empty space opposite the flat. To switch off, just for a few minutes... The gearstick found reverse.

If only she'd gone back from a different angle. She should get out and check the damage. Leave a note under the wipers. Or just leave. Instead of sitting there. Finger by finger she unlocked her grip, peeling skin from moulded plastic, while the driving mirror screamed for her to look. Her focus shifted from flushed cheeks to racy green Porsche, back and forth, till the face fragmented into unremembrance whilst the car behind thrust closer, its alarm more hysterical, its flashing lights more indecisive, the black cat dangling down its windscreen more familiar. Where had she seen it before?

Jane tried to drag it to the forefront, squeeze it round the block that filled her skull. She could sense its coming, that familiar thing, could hear its footsteps. Could feel its breath on her neck as the door opened and the cracks between the paving slabs leapt towards her.

THE pavement dropped away. Far below the city crawled. Grit dug into hands and knees as she shuffled back from the edge. The roofing felt was secured by an unending line of nails, trammelled by goblin hoof prints where the hammer had missed.

She got to her feet. She could see no other buildings, nothing except this flat roof. In the distance something moved, something she couldn't make out, darting this way and that, unencumbered by arms or legs or head. She picked her way between broken bricks and bits of concrete, stepping over sawn-off pipes and smashed panes. An empty cement bag swept over the rubble and danced alongside. She quickened her pace to keep up. The bag flung itself over the side, flapping and rising briefly before being swallowed downwards. Squatting low, she gripped the roof edge and peered over. As the bag fell away from her it did not seem to get any smaller, so when it reached the ground it swathed the buildings and traffic and people in a thick blanket. She drew back.

Wind tossed, she walked on.

She clambered over fallen girders, fighting her way through the forest of scaffolding springing up all around. Tangles of rope, knotted and rotting, swung from the riveted skeletons, scraping her skin, paring off shreds of dead iron oxide. Tatters of storm-ripped plastic spread tendrils over her face, wormed up her nostrils, slithered into her mouth. She clawed them away. The heat was closing in, burning the earth where she trod, blistering the sand that stretched before her over a vast and desolate plain. There was nothing around her, nothing behind, nothing ahead.

Scorch soled, she walked on.

A grey wisp of smoke sliced the sky. Along the cold baked earth unseen spokes spanned inwards from the rim of fire that was no more. Their tips glowed under the severed sky, forming a central ring of orange. Fanning out from this seething wreath, the spokes bulged into mounds that squirmed and thrashed before her. She stumbled into one and her foot upturned a heap of ash, stirring up choking flecks that filled her eyes. She blinked away dry tears. There before her was a circle of charred bodies.

Twelve long necks thrust inwards. Twelve beaks almost touched. From each mouth a swollen tongue lolled bleeding. From each lid, a cobalt eye stared pleading.

She knelt down. Tried to lift a body. It fell to dust in her arms. The wilderness shattered with a single scream.

'SHH. Everything's all right.'

She opened her eyes. An electric fan whirred from the chest of drawers. One foot was tethered in a knot of blanket at the bottom of the bed. She could not move.

He clutched her so tightly her limbs locked. 'You're safe now.' Caressed her so tenderly her skin crawled. 'I'm not letting you out of my sight again.'

SHE was suspended between sleeping and consciousness. Time no longer counted. She became aware as always, in that second when the ticking held its breath. She poked an arm from the covers and groped space, stretching down till she could feel dents in the carpet where the feet had stood. But Minnie Mouse was not there.

The alarm was switched off from the other side of the bed, the side she had her back to. And alongside her back must be another. Two backs, lying in parallel. One was the back she had learnt well, had nuzzled its wisp of dark curls below the nape and kissed its chicken pox scar under the right shoulder blade. The other she scarcely knew at all, had never fingered its contours or tasted its softness or circled the mole hidden under folds of flesh when she lay on her left side.

She must get out of this bed. She lifted the head that was on her pillow, began to move it across and gave up. The head hit ninety millimetres of foam with a room-shaking thud. This was the hangover to out-hang all hangovers. The hangover from an evening of unutterable indulgence, an evening so incredible she couldn't remember anything about at all.

Oliver swore as he caught the clock with his toe. Minnie's tick rose a semitone as she tipped over. The flat white face would be gazing up at him, saucy pink bow flopping playfully over painted eyelashes, two pert whiskers twitching from the button nose, two glossy ears reflecting naked limbs. He stooped and righted the face. Her tick subsided to a squeak as she settled to her new position. Minnie was at his side of the bed now.

'Stay where you are,' he told her. 'I've time to bring you some breakfast before I go. Bought you some Sugar Puffs for a treat.'

Jane pulled the duvet over her eyes but even through 10.5 togs she could see him, watching.

OLIVER wedged the tray next to her pillow and pulled her up onto one elbow. There was a brim full bowl of porridge topped with a dollop of golden syrup.

'I've put some hot chocolate on the floor and brought you the paracetamols. Shall I get a couple out before I go?'

The syrup smiled a swirl of sickly yellow.

'You're shivering.' He tucked the duvet round her shoulders. 'I've brought you something easy to get down. I thought your throat might be a bit sore. You've obviously picked up something. You can have Sugar Puffs tomorrow. It'll be something to look forward to.'

SHE placed the packet in the middle of her pillow. It would be her revenge.

She tested the side of the mug. Too hot. As she shifted position the packet rolled into the bowl. She lifted it and

125

licked porridge off the corner. Then she dipped her finger into the syrup and sucked it clean. She finished the bowl, even scraped up the blob that had slopped onto the pillow. She reached for the tablets.

For the relief of pain. Jane opened the box. Two foil backed sheets of blisters, four burst. Which left – Her brain refused. Probably not enough. If she botched it, they'd say she'd only been attention-seeking. Oliver. And her mother.

She hitched herself up on both elbows, held one of the sheets of capsules. Smooth-coated, shaped to slip down in one swallow. Her thumb and forefinger closed round one of the bubbles. Easy. Like it said on the packet. Then they'd be sorry.

If only she could be sure.

She let it slip from her hand. Tried to get up. The bowl clattered onto the floor. Her elbows gave way and she sank into the pillow, whimpering.

I HATE him, hate him, hate him.

Had she said that aloud? The walls weren't thick enough to block out the sobs. Whoever was crying, it wasn't her.

Jane caught Xanthe's arm before she ducked back into the cubicle.

'Whatever's the matter?'

Xanthe wiped her hand across her nose. 'Nothing.'

'Might help to talk about it.'

Xanthe hesitated, then flung herself against Jane's chest. For several minutes they clung together, swaying.

Moistless eyes swayed back through the pitted mirror above the washbasin. She hadn't seen that face since she'd slapped on another layer while a foil tray of chicken tikka masala tried to keep warm under the folds of the Sunday paper. Her cheeks were pale, but then she had been laid up for a couple of days, and, yes, her lower lids were a bit puffy but the tinge of purple was nothing a dab of pan stick wouldn't cover. Otherwise she was just the same. Same old Jane.

'This isn't like me, is it?' Xanthe gave a smile and sniffed.

Neither of them seemed to have a tissue, but, surprisingly for a Friday morning, there was still half a toilet roll on top of the cistern. By the time the cardboard tube was bare, Jane had learned every detail.

IT was the little things she noticed most. All just the same. The piles in the red wire in-tray and the blue wire out-tray were just as high. Apart for a new wodge of papers on her desk, it was as if the past few days hadn't happened. Jane dumped them in the blue tray. Switched on the computer. The dust on the screen showed up more on certain colours. Cloud highlighting sunset in reverse. Like everything else from now on.

Because there weren't any green teabags with pineapple left, though Xanthe would definitely get another box in her lunch break, would Jane mind having ordinary just this once?

Amazing that she felt a nudge of disappointment. That such a little thing should matter, that anything should matter. The film of dust obscured more dark blue than pale. Quite amazing.

Xanthe stood threading toilet roll through her fingers. Flecks wafted into the air, settling on the Picasso mouse mat, specking the disjointed face of the Weeping Woman. Ordinary, Jane told her, would be fine. She clicked Log-in as Christian approached.

'You're back, then.'

Jane looked down to check. Yes, she was back. All visible body parts in their place. Everything back to normal. Oliver had told her as much that morning.

'Last week's action forecast on my desk ASAP,' said Christian, jabbing *La Femme Malheureuse* in the eye with two emphatic fingers. 'Get too far behind with your forward planning and you're fucked, sweetie.'

And Incorrect User Name to you too. With no forward planning whatsoever, the Incorrect User managed to scrawl a diagonal SODOF in the dust before she hit the top corner of the screen. Jane wiped her fingertip across the action forecast sheet and went to help Xanthe make the tea.

'ONCE it's boiled,' said Xanthe, hand on switch, 'it won't stay down unless you hold it.'

Jane took the lid off the teapot and peered inside. As she gave the pot a shake, just in case, the door handle was rammed into her back.

'Nice and strong this morning, sweetie. See if you can make the spoon stand straight up today.'

Wedged behind the door, Jane could feel eyes crawling over skin. Not her skin, thank God.

'And don't fob me off with bloody digestives,' said Christian. 'I'm sure you can get hold of a couple of ginger nuts, if you set your mind to it.' He closed the door. 'Ah, I see things are a bit squashed in here.'

Two guesses where he was looking.

'Bit of a tight fit, know what I mean.'

It was the melons not in the fruit bowl all over again. This time with Xanthe on the squinching end. Thank God. Jane frowned. Yeah, thanks a lot, God. Where were you last Sunday night? Don't give me that Day of Rest claptrap, you're just doing the easy stuff. Easy to time it so my back was turned. Easy for me to keep it turned, leaving Xanthe cringing. As if it mattered anymore. She turned round.

'I would have thought there'd be enough room in here for three.' Would have thought, after all that had happened, she'd be able to raise one eyebrow. Instead of just looking – she could do pointed as well – at his bulging gut. Saw chicken-flesh unrolling as Diane heaved off stained underpants. What was Christian, after all, but Uncle George with a dribbling crux?

'You watch your lip.'

'Oh, come on, Christian, it's only a bit of fun.' Like Uncle George's it's-in-there-somewhere dangling over a Charlie Chaplin moustache. 'So you're always telling us.' Which she could have followed with an elbow where his ribs might be, if Christian had sufficient skeletal structure to support them. Instead she concentrated on the vein on his temple. Counted the throbs as blood struggled up from his pants.

'Course it is. We're one big happy family here.' He nodded at the door. 'Mustn't hold you girls up any longer. We've all got things to do.'

Xanthe flattened herself against the worktop and Jane against the wall opposite as he went out. Behind the closing door Jane flashed a victory V to Xanthe. Three dots and a –

'Dash it all,' as the handle got in another jab, this time to her stomach. 'I'd forget my head if it wasn't screwed on.' Christian pulled an A4 sheet from his pocket. 'Code of conduct reminder, hot off the press. Something for you lot to cast your peepers over while you're swilling your mugs.'

He scanned the wall space, or what would have been space without the notices. Every A4 sheet drooped from a blob of Blutak. Only the poster was blessed with a blob in each top corner. Christian pulled one off and stuck up the code of conduct over War Office advice on keeping the home fires burning. Or maybe – the print was too faded to be certain – it was instructions for beacon lighting if the Armada sailed into view.

The poster's loose corner flopped over frilly suspenders. It had been up so long the wearer must by now have a bus pass tucked into her G-string along with the ten shilling note. Poster Girl was bent double, looking between her legs. Buttocks reared from a froth – or whatever the collective name for it was – of ostrich feathers. Stocking seams followed splayed legs in a giant A which began the caption.

'*All I want is somewhere to bury my head,*' said Christian, wedging the poster against the wall with his elbow while he peeled off the second blob and slid it behind Poster Girl's buttocks. He pressed hard, swivelling his thumb back and forth.

'There,' he said, stepping back. 'Up to everyone's satisfaction, eh, girls?'

Xanthe focussed two fingers on the kettle switch. Jane tossed teabags into the pot. Seven, eight, nine... Christian sauntered out, whistling.

The water kept on boiling.

Wet strands of hair clung to Xanthe's forehead. Still she held down the switch. Dampness seeped into what air was left in the room. The poster peeled itself from the wall. Lay on the floor, legs in the air, just asking for it.

'Shall we?'

'You bet.'

And when Roy put his head round the door to ask if Xanthe was making the tea or what, he found the two of them sitting cross-legged on the floor, showering confetti shreds over each other's head and laughing like there was no this afternoon.

IF only there was no tonight. Crossing the street, Jane peered up. Grey slats of curtain edged the blackness that was the bedroom. He wasn't back.

Friday so it must be mince. A day like any other day. Everything back to normal, like he'd said it would be. She should be racing round, pulling pans, grabbing plates. Filling the silence.

Because tonight – he'd said it twice – everything would be back to normal. Well, she'd be in the bedroom first. With the door locked.

She shook a crust from the bread bag. Green spores were already visible. He could be back any minute. No time, she told her stomach walls, to even think of opening the cupboard...

She pulled the ring pull. Sauce slithered down the label, smothered her hand, slopped to the floor. Dribbled down her chin as she tipped the last beans into her mouth. She ran a finger round the inside, stretching down as far as she could reach. A well of painless red spouted between her fingers, washing over tomato sludge. So much blood. She sucked it clean, again and again. The more she licked, the more it bled, and still her shrunken stomach griped for more.

Surely that was a footstep, coming up the stairs?

She shut the bedroom door. Reached for the key that wasn't there.

Surely that was a rattle, at the front door?

She pressed the bedroom door against its frame. Spread hands across the surface, feeling the undulations of twelve thousand years of patched up paint. She neared an ear; the panels blurred before her, grey in the greyness of the room.

In the world beyond the window headlights passed, casting her face in profile. Jane pressed the ear closer. Shadow features stretched beyond her one all-seeing eye. Hag nose, witch chin, edged in a mountainscape of sparkling white that came and went and came again, light years from traffic, town and mediocrity.

She stared at the micrometer contours of the paintwork, trying to make sense of the humps and hollows. She made out faces, backs and claws, bared teeth and sneak-thief eyes. With twitching nose and curling lip, the creatures of the underdoor skulked out from splits and cracks within the panels. Pressed hard, her ear picked up the pad of paws, the echo thud of distant hooves. She closed her eyes.

Squeezed them shut, till formless blobs suspended in her mind broke free and floated through the cosmos of her lids. The beat of pounding feet came louder. The blobs grew frenzied, leapt and bounded through the blackness, colliding in a burst of rainbow dots while thunder rumbled round. Lightening zigged and zagged, broke into a craze of squiggles: waving limbs and come-on eyes that beckoned through a swirling spirit breath of blue. Follow, follow, into the realm of Underdoor, to nestle safe, surcease of sorrow, within the folds of licked clean fur.

Clack.

The clunk of metal on metal.

Nothing more.

She stands wide eyed. Gradually the room reassembles. Raindrops patter down the window. Her feet make contact with the floor. Stereophonic drumming from Heather's flat dissolves to fade out.

Jane slides down the bedroom wall, legs bent, arms wrapped, as the evening paper boy's whistle reverberates down the stairwell.

NINETEEN forty two. Jane creeps into the hall. Picks up the *Advertiser* from the mat and takes it to the bedroom. Drags the chest of drawers across the door.

She flicks through the paper, listening. *Household equipment... Unwanted gifts...* Down below Heather's tuned into comedy. *Watch and swap...* When will he turn up? *Lonely hearts...* Canned laughter seeps through the joists. The worst part... *Forthcoming events...* is the wondering when.

TWENTY-FIVE past ten. Jane finds a pack of processed cheddar in the fridge. Bites open polythene, peels off slices, pushes them in her mouth. Pauses between swallows to listen. Outside, shouting youths. She fills the kettle. Somewhere, the yawl of an alarm. She clicks the off switch before the kettle starts singing.

QUARTER to twelve, or thereabouts. Jane checks the front door. She even checks the bathroom window. Which is quite an ordinary window, the sort of window you'd find in any bathroom, one you wouldn't give a second glance to. The shower over the bath doesn't get a glance at all. She wrings her hands under the basin tap and reaches for her toothbrush.

MINNIE, back in her usual place, held her breath. The two percent of Jane that was awake jabbed snooze. As she turned over, humping the duvet round her shoulders, her flesh brushed against his sleeping back.

She reaches out a finger, begins to trace across the skin. First, draw heart, then insert inscription. JC = O… Her finger freezes mid-oval.

So, he'd sneaked in while she was asleep. Jane eased her legs over the edge of the mattress and slid onto the floor. Crouched low, she fumbled in the heap and began pulling on yesterday's clothes.

And then it hit her, struck her so she sat stock still, the right leg of her tights round her ankle, the left gathered up in her hands. Oliver couldn't have come in after she'd gone to bed. Not when she'd moved the front door catch to deadlock. He must have been there all the time.

USELESS to ignore him. For three days she'd pretended he wasn't there, but he ignored the ignoring, insisted on the sharing of the same living space. But not the same sleeping space. Come the witching hour, or earlier if there was nothing on TV, he'd head to the bedroom and she'd pass on the other side to the lounge. Though he should try sleeping jammed between the arms of the two-seater, legs tucked under a square of fringed tartan with only the grubby little Snow Baby coat for warmth. So unfair. She should say something.

'I said,' he said, 'your sister phoned.'

Although that would involve speaking –

'We had quite a long chat actually.'

– he needed telling.

'I told her you'd phone back.'

Jane shrugged. What did she care... about the particulars of that quite long chat?

SHE wasn't sure when four-year-olds should be put to sleep. Half past eight should cover it. But it was Rob who answered.

'One of those evening classes. Another of my dear ma-in-law's suggestions.'

'Not flower arranging, I hope?'

'More arranging body parts. Dreamed up by some Aussie bloke. Devised his own technique, strictly girls only. Like to know the details?'

'Not particularly.'

'Apparently they finish the session lying on the floor together. Di takes along a mat specially.'

'Sounds relaxing.'

'If only. For a couple of days after, she's on at me about slumping. It's a kick in the shin, or worse, if I sit cross-legged. Any day now I'll be barred from the armchair.'

'Make the most of this evening then. Slouch across the sofa –' with all four paws crossed.

'You must be joking. I've just read Mog's sodding

134

Christmas three times through and I've got the dishwasher to load yet. Then it'll be time for the baby's next feed.'

How –?

'There's a row of expresso bottles in the fridge door. It's the mammary equivalent of giving blood. Course, a fun-loving girl like you wouldn't know about such things. Far better things to do with –'

'I'll let you get on, Rob. Tell Di I phoned.'

'Hey, don't go without me asking how you are, or she'll have my guts for garters.'

'I'm fine. But I really must –'

'Got over your bad turn?'

'Bad turn?'

'Di was telling me, after whozit – Oliver – rang to say you'd been laid up, sky-high temperature, hallucinating and such.'

'It was nothing. A slight chill, that's all.'

'He said you'd been off work for a while.'

'Not long. Though I've a mountain of paperwork to catch up on, so I'll ring off now, leave you to your dirty dishes. Good talking to you, Rob.' About as good as it gets.

'HI, Jane,' said Tony, opening the office door – 'I've beaten you this morning' – and stepping in front of her.

'There was a bit of a hold-up. The road was completely stopped off just before the flyover.'

'Accident?'

Jane caught the door before it banged into her face. 'Geese on the road.'

'An oil spillage, you mean? For a moment I thought you said geese.'

'I did. Though there was only one, actually. It'd got out of the field. Blocked both lanes.'

'Must have been a hell of a big goose.'

'It was wandering about so everyone had to stop. Two or three people got out and shooed it up the grass verge. It kept poking its neck through the rails in different places but couldn't get through. A man tried to get hold of it but it started hissing at him.'

'He turned chicken, eh? Ducked out of it. I've heard geese can be nasty, go in for fow– lay off!' as Jane jabbed him in the back.

'It was because it was frightened.'

'Bet everybody was revving their engines like crazy.' That being the only method known to urban man of coaxing straying livestock back to the fold.

'People were very sensible, actually – just sat watching. I think everyone was willing it to get back where it had come from.' Everyone except her.

'Nobody blowing their horns?' For what other fallback was there if a foot through the floor didn't do it?

'Well, not at first.'

Only after the left lane was streaming past once more and the right lane cars in front had moved on. Only after momentary communing with another life-form had dissolved to irritation. But no amount of hooting would shift the girl in the Fiesta, as she watched the old woman gather up her wayward goose, until it was back in its enclosure.

'I TOLD her it would peck. It's all right with ducks, as long as you keep your palm flat. Just throw the bread, I told her, but would she listen? Mind you, she's cock-a-hoop about it now, with that ginormous bandage on her hand. It actually only got one finger but you know what a drama queen Stephie is. Anyway, let's hope she's learnt to keep her distance, next time we go to the park.'

'There was a goose on the road when I was going to work this morning. All the traffic had to stop for it.'

'Pity someone didn't run it over. I've no idea why anyone keeps them.'

'They're for Christmas, so Oliver said.' Because, one way or another, he always had to have his say.

'Yes, he said he'd ordered a goose. Can't think why. I bet they're really fatty. Won't it be a faff to roast?'

'Don't know –' whether she had a single opinion that wasn't regurgitated Oliver.

'Well, he needs telling. Thank God Mum always has turkey. Though it's bad enough eating that up for the rest of the time we're there.'

At last, a way in. 'You're going to stay over Christmas?' Because Diane had to be told.

'Of course. They'd have it on their own if one of us didn't bother to go.'

'Actually, it was because of Daddy that I went to see Mum –'

'Besides, I wouldn't want the mess of cooking a big turkey. Last time I did a bird in the oven, you know, basting it, the full works, it took Rob the whole afternoon to clean it. Thank God for microwaves. Have you tried doing a chicken in yours yet? Mum's old one – is it still going?'

'Yes. I went to see her because –'

'Which?'

'What?'

'Yes, you've done a chicken or yes, it's still working? Though it must be working if you've done a chicken. Unless it's packed up since. I wouldn't be surprised. It's probably leaking all sorts of noxious waves into the atmosphere. You can get a new one for a few quid, if you go to the right place.'

'I really only use it for warming stuff up. I did try cooking a chicken but Ol– I wasn't keen on it, lying there all soggy in watery grease.'

'You need a poultry spike. Like an upside down mushroom, only bigger. You stick the stalk inside the chicken, so when it's cooking all the juices run out into the tray. The meat's always tender. You must get one – in fact, I've got a spare one. I'll send you it.'

'Honestly, Di, there's no need to bother. But, talking of Mum, when I went to –'

'No problem. You'll wonder how you managed without it. I'm surprised Mum didn't let you in on the big secret when she gave you the microwave.'

'Talking of Mum –'

'Oh, God, no. I can't believe it.'

'So you know! I bet she said I was making it up but it's all true. Talk about refusing to listen.'

'She's woken up now.'

'Thank God she has. But you'll only have heard her version.'

'You'll have to speak up. She's bawling her head off.'

Jane frowned. If her mother was actually there, sobbing into the cushion tassels, Di sounded, even for Di, a tad uncaring.

'It's so frustrating –' having to shout down the phone. 'I went specially to see her about it. She didn't believe it.'

'I'm not surprised, after all this time,' said Diane. 'So that's what this call is about, to make sure I knew you'd dragged yourself away from your little love nest to visit her. Like I don't go just about every other fricking week. Trust you to expect Brownie points for doing what any normal daughter has to do. Look, Helen's screaming the place down. I'll have to go.'

'No, wait! I've got to tell you why I went to see Mum.'

'For God's sake, leave it, will you, or we'll end up saying things best left unsaid. I'll send you the spike anyway. It's only taking up cupboard space. And I'll ring you sometime – only don't ever mention your fricking visit again, okay? It's all right, sweetheart, Mummy's coming.'

SHE didn't linger there a moment longer than necessary, ever. Yet when Jane came out the bathroom, swathed neck to ankle in her crimson bathrobe – as if she would take a bath again, ever – it was always the same. The main light would be off, covers drawn back from both pillows, onyx lamp glowing on the bedside chest.

And he would be sitting on the bottom of the duvet, about to take off his socks. Always about to take off his sodding socks.

Close to her side of the bed, Jane tugged at the double knotted belt, snagging a fingernail on a loop of towelling. She caught it again when she pulled off the robe. There must be a file somewhere in the top drawer.

Head bent over the nail as she rounded the edge, she glanced across. He was still perched at the end on the bed, pulling the second sock ever longer, the wool heel catching on barbs of rough skin. Although he faced the wardrobe, he was looking at her.

Grating metal cut into flesh. As did those sideways eyes. She pulled the robe back on. Wrapped it across, overlapping every inch of nightdress. She would sleep on the sofa again. Except, of course, she wouldn't. And she couldn't stand another night of staring into darkness. She'd keep the robe on, well wrapped round. Pull up the hood.

Climbing into Grandmother's bed, Goldilocks tucked her cotton armour round the basket of goodies and switched off the light.

SHE realised it wasn't ideal, but people often had to settle for less, especially in that price bracket. No, Jane was afraid they had nothing else on Victoria Embankment at the moment, but he'd be the first to know if – Christian snatched the receiver out of her hand...

'...to tell you it's your lucky day. I overheard my colleague say there was nothing else in your preferred location, Mist-' He shot a question mark at Jane.

She mouthed *hate you* through sweet-smile lips.

'-aken, I'm pleased to say,' because lack of understanding had never given Christian cause to falter mid-flow, 'since it's not half an hour ago since I took instructions on a property in Jubilee Terrace.'

He stretched across to one of the pigeon-holes and pulled out the particulars, which happened to be of an end terrace with loft conversion in Gladstone Street, but near enough. 'Practically within spitting distance of the Embankment and so quiet you'd think you were in the heart of suburbia, yet all the charm of a period townhouse... No, no significantly detrimental alterations. One or two tasteful improvements, but plenty of scope for the discerning buyer to put his own individual mark on the property... Well, nearish, but not so you'd notice, taking into account the prevailing wind. Trust me, it's an absolute gem. Your good lady will fall in love with it as soon... Even better. It's a perfect bachelor pad. I can see you in it right now –'

– although, of course, it was Jane who was to see him, at his convenience, which would be –?

'Only Wednesday or Friday afternoons? That could be difficult,' with the receiver wedged between her chin and collar bone, leaving Christian ample expanse of tilted neck to snort down. 'I'm checking my diary...' holding it so Christian couldn't see.

'Shove some stuff up, for shit's sake,' accompanied by a spray of spittle sufficient to penetrate the left side sternocleidomastoid muscle itself.

'I'm looking,' said Jane through shielded lids, 'at early in the new year –'

Christian grabbed the diary and flicked back to the present, jabbing his pen so pointedly on the coming Friday that the nib created three new stations on the Metropolitan line on the inside back cover.

Jane pencilled in Mr Kendrew for 2.30 and put down the phone. The blonde in the sliding dress on Christian's ballpoint flashed her assets as he underlined the time, twice.

'What the hell are you playing at, Jane? That place has been on the books for so long the original mugshot was done with a box Brownie. And don't give me that time of the month claptrap. You bloody women are all the same. First Xanthe tells me to stuff the job, then you make a cock-up like this.'

'Xanthe's leaving?'

'Good riddance, I say. That sassy bitch can't go fast enough for me. And you've been as bad, this past week or so. You'd better change your attitude PDQ, my girl. And you can start by making a killing on Friday.'

HE needn't think she would pay any attention. It might be the biggest hoot since the sliced white landed butterside up when Murphy was trying to make a point, but she wasn't having any of it. Even though – especially though – he couldn't wait for her to see who was in it. Oliver tried to pass her the DVD case.

Jane bunched her hands into her Levis so only the pocket linings separated knuckles. She parted her thighs, just enough, so the case fell to the floor. Then, mindful of making a permanent bulge in the denim, she mooched across to the bookcase.

Three rows of rigid spines, exactly in line. She began pushing every third book away from the edge of the top shelf. Behind her, the armchair with the broken castor scraped a furrow through the carpet. Jane pushed back books on the middle shelf. Two back, miss one. The crack of plastic, a hiss of annoyance. A double hiss as the chair, yanked back, ran over a hump that might or might not be attached to the end of his leg. He'd been right about the film so far.

'Everything's ready.'

The cushion on the sofa was being patted. Jane's hand hovered over the hardbacks on the bottom row. Volumes one to four of *Art for the Uninformed*. She tilted her head. It began with Adam. It would. Her fingers sidestepped to the next book. Corot to Epstein. That would do. Jane pulled it out, leaving Escher-Kandinsky jutting over the edge.

She studied the picture on the dust jacket. It looked modern, but surely people didn't go in for all that religious stuff nowadays? Yet this was a totally different view of the crucifixion. Okay, there was Jesus, centre stage, but his unnailed hands almost touched the top of the canvas. His was no earth-bound cross but a plunging sword piercing the cosmos. Far below the soaring arms was a grounded boat. The figure wading beside it was an insignificant little man – or could it be a woman? Could it, with those sagging britches, be Jane herself, face upturned towards the light as Christ looked down? Only as the insignificant being in the picture could she see the Saviour's face. Unscarred and unsecured, God-as-Man surveyed his creation.

Oliver stretched out his arm, finger on the start button. 'I can't wait to see what's going to happen.'

Escher-Kandinsky succumbed to gravity, slumping across empty space. Jane headed for the pushed aside armchair, volume 2 clutched to her chest.

'Hold on a sec.' He pressed pause.

She held on, eyes on the book jacket.

Oliver shoved the armchair to its usual place, the three castors and the stump each slotting into its niche. 'Look, I've put it back exactly as it was.'

She kept her eyes on the upside down cover.

'Everything as normal.'

How wrong he was. From her angle, everything was different. The image of the Saviour had been turned on its head. Now it was she, not Christ, who looked down on the scene. Sea had become sky. Sun-soaked clouds descended into foam, choking in the sulphurous lava flow which spewed from a fissure in the belly of the earth. And it was towards this festering navel that the crucifix plummeted from blackness that once was heaven. The insignificant being in baggy trousers stared blank-faced at the emptiness ahead, her world flipped.

And all the while, Oliver chuckled.

Jane scanned the inside page. *Cover illustration: Salvador Dali: Christ of St John of the Cross.* Dali, she supposed, must be towards the end. She closed the book facedown and started at the back. Virgin pages clung together as they fell away from the moving thumb. Degas's rose-blushed dancers, teetering on points in a flicker of rehearsals, metamorphosed into elephants prancing on needle tips, impressions of reality succumbing to the surrealism of the subconscious. She creased the page flat.

It showed a series of sketches of the same reclining figure, female, naked. Nothing out of the ordinary – except that the torso was pierced with drawers. She read the title. Read it aloud, as if to make better sense. *'The Anthropomorphic Cabinet.'*

'Is that the Steve Bell cartoon?' Oliver glanced across from the film.

Jane held up the book to block him out.

'Oh, I thought you must be looking at the paper. What's that you've got?'

She lowered it so he couldn't see. Bent over it, hair falling forward onto Cabinet Woman's curls as they tumbled into the open top drawer, while she searched inside for – what? More than a missing sock. And no-one hunting car keys would raise a hand against all comers. This was a secret search. Her innermost desires were for her alone. If only, thought Jane, she knew what they were.

'WHAT are you thinking of,' said Roy, 'putting in all this overtime?' Hooking his thumb under the collar he slung his coat over his shoulder and sidled up to Jane's desk. 'Everyone else has gone.'

Without glancing up from the screen, Jane flashed what couldn't, even to the most dexterous of straw-clutchers, be classed as a smile.

'I've noticed,' he said, 'you've been staying on a lot recently.'

Jane, eyes on the text, highlighted the last phrase.

'Instead of dashing off to cook a meal. You know, one of your famous mince dinners.'

Jane did a cut and paste.

'But now,' fingering Jane's in-tray, 'you seem to work late every night,' hopscotching between the edge and the pile of info, 'and I was wondering,' straightening the top sheet, 'if you and Oliver have had a tiff?'

'No.'

'Oh, right. I just wondered –' fingers walked the rim of the red in-tray '– because for a long time –' and jumped across to the blue out-tray '– in fact from the moment I first saw you I thought –'

'What a bloody sight!' as the door from the back office whammed into his back.

Claire stood in the doorway, scowling round the room, black bin bag to heel.

'And a very good evening to you too, Claire.'

'It might be for you, lad.' She bent over to pick up some balls of paper and a chocolate wrapper that had missed the bin. 'My heart sinks whenever I come into this room.'

'You and me both, Claire,' said Jane. 'Just be thankful you haven't been stuck here,' give or take a few appointments to view, 'since eight thirty this morning.' All a complete waste of time.

'There's not a lot for me to be thankful about.' Claire peeled back the wrapper and prodded an uneaten bit of Mars bar with her rubber glove. 'Not with my feet. This bunion's giving me gyp.' She raised her left foot, just a little, revealing a fur-trimmed slipper.

Jane caught Roy's eye and smiled. Just a little.

'You may well laugh,' said Claire, emptying the bin into the black bag, 'but these'll be your feet in a few years. Lasses have always worn daft shoes and they always will. Never mind how they fit so long as they're in fashion.' She nudged the bin against the desk with the natty little court shoe on her right foot. 'Well, make the most of it and enjoy yourself while you still can.' Claire scraped the wrapper against her bottom teeth, threw the paper into the bin and clop-padded to the far side of the office.

'She's got a point,' said Roy.

'Maybe I'll come in my Granny slippers tomorrow.'

'You'd look great whatever you wore. But what I meant was how about –'

With difficulty – because the mouse definitely needed some attention – Jane hit shut down.

Please wait while...

'– we call in for a drink before you go home?'

The screen went black.

'That'll do me for tonight,' said Claire, twisting the neck of the bin bag.

Roy turned and frowned as she pushed behind him to the back door.

Jane snatched up her bag and made for the front door, leaving the stand-by light glowing red and Snow Baby rubbing shoulders with Claire's synthetic sheepskin in the cloakroom.

'Well, I'm game, even if she's not. We can fit in a quick one before my bus.'

Roy looked at the clock. 'Sometimes it's best not to rush things.'

'Two ticks to get this on and I'm all yours.'

'Maybe –' he watched the second hand going round in circles '– it wasn't such a good idea after all.'

But Claire was already forcing her foot into the shoe.

'HEY, wait!'

Jane stopped. What now?

Steps echoed up the stairwell.

She turned. Pulled her lips into the right shape. Not that she needed to, seeing as the last security bulb had called it a day.

'There you are at last. I've been listening out for you.'

It was only Heather, bless her second class socks.

'Thought I'd take it in. Save you the bother of picking it up.'

Jane took the brown paper parcel, made the right noises, continued up.

'It's such a nuisance, having to go to the sorting office specially.' The words pea-shootered off Jane's back as she took the steps two at a time. 'Shall I hold it while you open up?'

'No, it's okay, I can manage the door,' even if she couldn't shake off a twelve-miles-a-day postie.

'Folk are always excited, getting a parcel.' She peered round Jane's shoulder as the door edged back from the lock. 'Can't wait to see what's inside.'

Apart from a rabid dog on the wrong side of the letter box? But –

'Oliver not back yet? It'll not be much fun, opening it on your own. I'll come in for a bit, shall I? I've nothing else on.'

'No.'

Heather's nose didn't shift from the gap.

'It's a Christmas present so I'm not opening it yet.' Jane eased the key from the lock. 'Thanks again for taking it in.'

And the door was shut before Heather could get any prominent body part a centimetre nearer. Jane leant against it, eyes closed. Time stood still. Or maybe it was just getting on with life, somewhere else. Down below Heather's audio system started up. So it couldn't be her, knocking.

Jane straightened. Time had decided to show up after all and was demanding to be let in.

'Hi, Jane. How you doing?' And Sophie was in the hall, unwrapping a chunk of scarf and shaking her hair free, followed by Simon, muttering something about needing to see Oliver.

'He's not here.'

But she could hear him in the stairwell, marked the crescendo of moulded sole on sixteen concrete slabs.

'Look at me!'

Jane looked at the back of Sophie's head before the hall mirror. Oliver stood in the doorway listening to Simon, letting out what heat there was.

'Talk about windswept!'

Jane watched the reflection boosting hair, puckering lips, tilting cheeks this way and that. Saw herself, smaller and less focussed, behind Sophie's left shoulder. Or was it her right shoulder? Because everything was the wrong way round in a mirror. You never saw your own face as it really was. She shrugged. Immaculate Sophie and insubstantial Jane were nothing more than reflected light. Or was it refracted? She was unsure. Diffused maybe.

The Sophie image raised a pencilled eyebrow and glanced at the Jane who was not really there.

'Let's leave them to it.' Sophie gave her other self a smile and turned from the glass. 'This corn's killing me.'

SOPHIE kicked her shoes off under the kitchen table. 'Si's got something major to discuss with Oli. You know what I'm on about.'

Jane hesitated. The kettle began to hum.

'You're bound to back Oli, but you haven't heard Simon's side, have you?'

'No.'

Behind the once transparent gauge, the water was becoming agitated.

'I can't help feeling he's not being on the level. Si doesn't believe that, says Oli's a good mate. But I'll tell you what I think.'

Steam seethed through the spout, into the air.

'Oliver isn't to be trusted. Not a hundred percent.'

Bubbles overstepped the maximum line, forcing up the lid.

'Si thinks the sun shines out of his backside, but I think he's a bit too good to be true. There, I've said it. You've got to say what you think, haven't you?'

Auto switch clicked in. 'Black or white?'

'Whatever,' said Sophie.

The steam subsided.

There was none of the usual I will if you will palaver with Sophie. So the biscuits stayed unopened on the worktop.

By the time Sophie had downed her coffee, they'd done Christmas shopping, which Jane hadn't; Indian Head Massage, which neither of them had; Salsa dancing, which they both had, once; and that new shade from L'Oreal. Jane hadn't tried it.

'I can see that. Have you ever done blonde? No – I don't suppose you have.' Sophie pulled out another chair and swung her legs onto it. Leaning forward, she adjusted a wedge of padding between the little toe and the fourth, then prodded the corn just hard enough to check it still hurt.

Jane scarcely touched her coffee. Just had the necessary three mouthfuls, so the teddy painted on the inside was no longer drowning in caffeine.

Sophie wouldn't have another. 'Otherwise I'll need to stop off on the way home.'

If you ever go, thought the bear. It stretched its front paws up towards the inner rim, one eye looking at Sophie over its shoulder. Perhaps it was waving. Below the surface those furry legs must be turning own brand instant to cappuccino, to stop itself going under.

'If we ever go,' said Sophie. She readjusted her legs. 'Si doesn't like to eat late.'

'Who'll be doing the cooking tonight?' said Jane. Damn. Brain in neutral. Now Sophie might feel obliged to mouth the reciprocal question.

'Si can phone for a pizza.' That was supper sorted. Which is more than seemed to be the case here so Cellophane Jane needn't feel smug. Sophie could well remember what the little poser had dished up the other week. And tried to pass it off as home cooking. Most likely did the domestic goddess thing all the time with nerdy Oliver. That recipe book placed so obviously between cooker and sink was all part of the charade. She strolled across and swilled out her mug, glancing at the book. Just as she'd thought – not a pesto stain in sight. Pristine, apart from a few splashes of water.

Jane was making serious eye contact with the sculling bear, as it tried to get a pawhold on the side of the mug.

Sophie picked up the dishcloth to dab the dust jacket. 'Oh!' She jabbed the picture. 'I've done him!'

Jane looked up. She'd leant over the book last night, following every detail of Dali's *Christ of St John of the Cross* on the front cover, while she listened out for the filling cistern and the creak of the bedroom door.

Sophie traced her finger down the shaft of the cross. 'Don't you just absolutely adore him?'

Above the coffee the thrashing bear gasped. Had it missed something here? Had Sophie fitted in baptism into the bosom of Christ between present buying and the platinum rinse?

'You know –' Sophie tapped the cover '– Dali.' She carried the book to the table. 'You wouldn't believe what old Doggy – Mr Sheehan, bless his tits-high Y-fronts – used to say about him. He didn't rate any of the Surrealists, but specially not Dali because I picked him for my dissertation.'

'This was at uni?'

'God, no. I did an art foundation course. Well, started it. I decided if I was going to get seriously into debt I'd have something in the wardrobe to show for it. How about you?'

'I didn't think I was cut out for student life either.'

'Didn't Oli say something about you going to medical school?'

Jane's hand tightened round her mug. How dare he? She'd never told anyone else, not even Maddy. She twisted the mug round. The bear changed sides. How much had he told her? The teddies picnicking round the outside of the mug were licking their paws.

'Or rather –' Sophie flipped open the book '– something about you not going.'

The Saviour had turned his back on the whole scenario. Left her to the bears. Jane turned their smug faces away. What else had he told her? Sculling Bear's one eye glinted. She tilted the mug and swished coffee across its face. While Christ of St John contemplated mock formica, the upturned snout went under for the third time.

Coffee slopped onto the open book. Sophie grabbed the dishcloth. That was twice in the space of forever. She wished Si would get a move on. 'Just as well,' tossing the dishcloth out of sight, 'it's not the real thing, eh?' But she had to admit Jane was taking it well. Just sitting there, staring at the picture. Still, Dali grabbed you like that sometimes. She'd told Doggy Breath as much.

Where had she seen it before? That clock face. Jane tried to think. No, it wasn't a clock. It was a watch. Of course. A watch on a worktop. Lying there, in that same detached way. Not slumped over the edge like this one, though. Her eyes moved round the painting. Two more watches, one hanging from the branch of a dead tree, one draped over a bodiless head. A sleeping man, tongue drooling. Maybe Dali himself, drifting in the dream-sodden black hole of his own fabrication.

'You could get those floppy watches all over Barcelona,' said Sophie. 'The gift shops were full of them. They're clocks really, but with a pretend winding bit on the top so they looked like this.'

Of course they did. These were pocket watches. The one wafting in and out of consciousness – the one on the worktop, that night, when the world flipped – had its winder at the side, next to the three. Except – Jane frowned – the three wasn't there. There were no numbers. Or pointers. The face was completely blank.

'It's so obvious,' said Sophie, 'but the thing is, Dali did them first. That's what genius is – getting in there before anyone else, like Tracey Emin's bed. Bet this painting made him loads of money. It's called – Don't tell me –' Sophie drummed her fingers on the picture, between the largest watch and the floating head.

The sleeping man slept on, despite – Jane shuddered – those black ants close by, massed on the back of a gold watch. As Sophie's fingers drummed, the ants began to stir…

'*The Persistence of Memory*!' The fingers stopped.

The ants settled. All except one.

The renegade ant was crawling over the edge of the watch, crawling along the worktop, crawling towards her, over her fingers and along the back of her hand, onto the blank face of her watch. As it settled next to the winding screw, the rest of the ants left the golden circle and marched in line towards her outstretched hand while Sophie crouched on the floor, buttocks in the air, licking raspberry pavlova off the tiles.

Jane was fixed in time, unable to move, unable to shift her hand from the oncoming blackness. It was that night all over again. All of it. The persistence of memory. There was nothing she could do to stop it happening again. And again.

'GOD, I thought it would never end.' Without taking the packet out of her bag, Sophie split the wrapper with her nail.

'Aw, Soph, you know I had to sort things out.' Simon rubbed the windscreen. 'I think it's on the outside.' He turned the blower on full. 'Should have scraped it really.'

'Haven't you done enough scraping tonight?'

'It's not like that. Oli's a mate.'

'If you say so.' She adjusted direction control while her other hand tore back the wrapper, just enough.

'Soph, we need it on the screen.'

'I'll breathe on it.' She eased off her shoes and rolled one foot over the can of de-icer. That frigging corn. She'd have a go at it when they got home. Face to the side window, she churned another biscuit to mush. Thank God they were finally on their way. Still, she supposed it was worth spending five centuries with a frenzo like Jane if he'd got this thing sorted. Because this past week her hair straighteners had been more fun than Si. He'd make up for it at Christmas, though. She'd make sure of that. Besides, she wouldn't have missed making Jane open that parcel for anything. Not when she saw Oli's face when he came into the kitchen.

'Maybe I should stop and give it a squirt with the de-icer.' Simon's nose was almost touching the glass. 'Is it down there somewhere?'

'Can't see it. Oh, don't stop, Si. There won't be any traffic. Not at this time.'

'Sorry, I know it's late. You must be tired.'

'And frozen.' She lifted her feet into the stream of hot air. 'It was Arctic in their flat.' The trouble was the blasting heat made her corn hurt more. 'Not surprising the ice maiden needs something to get her going.' Or maybe it was the start of a chilblain. 'Talk about phallic.' Something was definitely throbbing.

'That plastic cone thing? What was it?'

'She said she was going to stick it up a chicken's arse. Still –' she gave Simon's thigh a squeeze '– whatever turns you on, eh?' and fumbled for the last biscuit.

THE keys shot off the passenger seat onto the rubber mat. Jane rammed Festina into reverse and careered back down Jubilee Terrace, straining to see.

153

But it wasn't a Mondeo after all.

There was a space behind a Renault. She checked the clock. Subtracted an hour. She was only in control of the minutes now. And didn't need a reminder that summer was well and truly over. She switched off the lights and let the engine tick over. Festina had taken a bit of coaxing this morning. If her battery went flat she'd be totally out of sync with the rest of humanity.

A man got out of the Renault. Non-metallic grey, had seen better days. Jane turned off the ignition.

HE didn't offer to help like some of them did, didn't come breathing down her neck. Didn't put his hand over hers to ease the spring. You were always on dodgy ground with lone males. Situation, as Christian was forever telling her, was everything.

'If you'll just bear with me...' But the back door key refused to budge. 'Sorry about this.'

She flashed upturned lips at the fireplace. Mr Kendrew was standing in front of the grate. Completely cheerless. On the whole, Jane decided, you didn't miss a great deal by avoiding eye contact.

'It's easier to do it from the outside,' she said. 'I'll pop out the front and along the street to the back yard. Why don't you have a good look round the kitchen, maybe get some ideas for revamping it. Although those pot sinks are making a real comeback now.'

'It doesn't matter.' Mr Kendrew cleared his throat. 'I've seen enough.'

'Oh, right. This place does need a lot doing to it.' Jane opened the kitchen door and stood back to let him through. 'Sorry you've had a wasted journey but do stay on our books.' She followed the brown suit down the passage, with the sharp right turn after the dining room. 'We have new properties coming onto the market all the time.'

Another turn, to the left, would take them past the sitting room to the front door.

The brown suit stopped. 'We haven't been upstairs yet.'

'THE master bedroom is nice and light, with the two windows. You've a good view of the other side of the street, when it's not foggy. There's a useful double socket by the built-in cupboard – do feel free to look inside, you'll be surprised how spacious it is – as well as separate switches for the wall lights, which are included in the asking price.' Though why the old crone who'd slept under them for the past nine centuries had taken the shades with her to the nursing home was anyone's guess.

Mr Kendrew looked blank.

Jane waved an arm. 'The switches are down there, on the skirting board.' At each side of the crop of lichen black-spotting the wall, demonstrating not only was there indeed space for a double bed, but within this stinking place, clung with cold, cold seeping through the floor, cold creeping up the walls, there was life. Here, in this God-defected room, something considered it worth making the effort to exist.

'It's deep in these old houses, isn't it? You'll notice the same quality skirting along the passage – that's the airing cupboard on our left – and here in the second bedroom.' Except where the fireplace had been ripped out and the gap above the lino had been plugged with a length of two by one. 'A good-sized single room, but could easily accommodate a double.' As long as both sharers got out of bed at the same side. 'It looks out onto the backyard, so it's nice and quiet.'

Jane turned from the window, to find she'd been talking to herself. Where'd he got to? She looked down the passageway, both ways, and saw a glimmer of light from the front bedroom.

She pushed open the door. One stark bulb on the wall light bracket glared through dust. So he'd found one of the switches on the skirting, after all. And hadn't bothered to turn it off again. How like a man. Jane went across and bent over the socket.

The door yowled, swinging shut.

She turned. There against the wall, between the hinges and the corner, stood Mr Kendrew, flies unzipped. No doubt looking straight at her, if she'd caught his eye. But Jane could only look at –

– the door, swinging open.

'I did knock.'

And in came a woman, now walking towards her.

'I saw you pull up and I thought, that's that girl who came to see me the other week.' The woman held out a folder. 'You left this behind. Chas spotted it, soon as you'd gone, didn't you, poppet?'

Chas, having done a quick recce of the surprisingly spacious built-in cupboard, was running a little red engine along the quality skirting.

'I said to Chas, if we find that lady's book, we can take it round for her.'

'Mummy...'

'You'd hidden it under my bed, hadn't you, you little monkey?'

'Mummy –' The boy pulled at her skirt.

'And you've been drawing on it. Just on the front, though.' She rubbed her sleeve over purple scrawls on the cover.

'Mummy! What dat man do?'

'What man?'

Chas pulled the edge of the door. Slowly it creaked back. And there was Mr Kendrew, shoving his chicken spike back into its plain brown wrapper.

CHAS steered the toy engine down the banister, chattering all the way. 'Dat man sowing his willy, wa'n't he, Mummy?'

'Yes. He was very naughty.'

'Naughty little tinker. He want a smack bottom, don't he, Mummy?'

'Very possibly.'

She looked at Jane and laughed. Jane laughed too, three dread seconds dissolved by the opening of a door.

Chas had disappeared into the front room. 'He's a nosy little so and so,' said his mother. 'Mind you, I wouldn't mind a quick look in the kitchen, see how it compares with mine. I bet it's still got one of those old ranges, hasn't it?'

'No, there's –'

But she was already down the passage. Jane went into the front room to check the street.

'Look what Tas got.' Chas opened his hand. 'What is it?'

Outside the grey Renault had completed a nine-point turn and was scuttling away between the two rows of parked cars.

'A moth.'

'Oh – it comed to bits.'

'It's all right, it's dead. Put it on here.' Jane held out the folder. 'Then you can see it properly.'

The boy poked it until it completely disintegrated and the fragments of dust wafted over the edge.

'I dwawed dat,' said Chas, pointing to the purple lines. 'Dat house.'

'Is it your house?'

'No, it a house in de book. Mummy said not open it, but he did. I sawed him.'

'Who?' The word hung in the air.

'He said Tas naughty to dwaw on de book.'

'Who said?' She could hear her voice rising.

'Dis your book?'

'Yes. Who said you shouldn't draw on it?'

'You cross wiv Tas?'

'No, I'm not cross with you, Chas. But tell me –'

'He cross. He say Tas wants a smack bottom. But Tas don't.'

'Tell me who was cross.' She grasped his shoulders and pulled him to face her. His mouth was speckled with paint from the engine. Say it. She could have shaken him. Shaken off all those flecks of red. Say it, will you? Say the D word.

He wriggled from her grasp and ran to his mother standing in the doorway.

They couldn't get out of the house quick enough. Any of them.

Chas's mother hurried him away without a backward glance. But he'd already forgotten the strange lady.

'It was a big willy, wa'n't it, Mummy?'

'Not especially.' Because everything was comparative.

EACH one weighed exactly 2.2 kg, so there was nothing to choose between them. As long it didn't have one of those squashy little bags inside, she didn't care. She wanted a main course, not a digestive history. Not that they'd be its own giblets, Simon had told her. It was one of the things she'd learned, that night. When they'd been plucked – those that had any feathers left – and gutted, bags were stuffed in randomly. Dead flesh, with another creature's heart frozen inside.

IT was almost thawed. She scratched at the clingfilm for a loose edge.

'Ah, chicken.'

So Oliver must have come in.

She peeled clingfilm from the polystyrene tray. Blood-tinged water leaked onto the worktop.

'If we economise now we can really live it up at Christmas.' He came closer. 'I'm going to make this one your best ever.' Oliver prodded flesh through loose plastic. 'Do you want me to bone it like the one I did a while ago? I remember you liked my fennel and apricot concoction. As soon as I've showered, I can stuff it.'

Now, she decided, was as good a time as any. Jane put the chicken spike on the worktop. Because Diane was sure to ask, if – when, now they were Best Friends – she rang again.

'For God's sake, Jay, it'll be pretty tasteless if you just stick it in the microwave.'

There were other places. Except they all involved contact. Talking – restricted to absolute essentials – she'd had to accept as necessary. Touching was a step too near.

'Still, I suppose it'll be quicker. And we'll appreciate Christmas dinner all the more.'

She stared at the label. *2.2kg*. He watched her staring. *Packed in the UK*. All the time watching. *Contains giblets*. She'd picked the wrong one.

'Free range goose. Mmm, I can hardly wait.'

She peeled clingfilm from the legs.

'Soon I'll be going to select the one we're having. There are three or four that should be the right size. Allowing for a bit more growth before it's time for the chop.'

She peeled clingfilm from the breast. Watched the slow return of skin, pocked with holes where once had sprouted feathers.

'Of course, you can't be absolutely sure of the weight until the birds are plucked and dressed.'

She screwed the clingfilm into a ball. Blood wept over her hand.

'But you know better than me how well they're fattening up individually. You must come with me. Point out the one you like best. The final choice will be down to you.'

The ball bounced against her foot as it went over the edge.

No.

The word swelled in her mouth, forced its way through sealed lips, scraped the air as it bounded and rebounded across the miles, to the outskirts of the town where the ring road met the flyover in a triangle of green.

Oliver was shedding his jacket, draping it over a chair, humping out the recipe book, thumbing to the index. Behind her back the silence laughed out loud. She spun round.

'No!'

Oliver continued scanning the columns.

'Are you listening?' She moved beside him, said it in his ear. 'Have I made it clear enough? I am not coming.'

Bypassing Quiches, and any more Qs there might be, he traced his finger down the next column. *Ragout... Raspberry parfait...*

'Yes you are.'

Ratatouille... Redcurrant coulis... He skimmed down. *Rhubarb crumble... Rice noodle roll...*

The finger slowed, jabbing each entry.

Roasted chicken, Roasted duck, Roasted – R, R, ARE

'Aren't!'

'I thought you'd jump at the chance. You used to go on about them such a lot. Your geese.' His finger moved down the S column. 'Not a bad selection, as stuffing goes. Here's one specially to accompany roast goose. Hazelnut with brandy and tarragon. Sounds perfect for Christmas. I could give it a practice run tonight. See what you think – before we commit ourselves. Of course, I'll have to make a smaller quantity for that.' He nodded at the chicken. 'Geese are big, aren't they? Do you think we'll have to break the breast bone to get it in the oven?'

'Oliver –'

'Don't suppose we'll have any hazelnuts, though.'

'I don't want you to do this.'

'Okay. If it's going to upset you, I won't.

Jane searched his face. 'Do you mean it?'

'Of course.' The face was smiling. 'No problem. We'll have something else.' He looked along the shelf. 'How about peanuts?'

'Oliver!' She stared at her fingertips, the whorls picked out in blood. 'I don't want you to get a goose.'

'Not get one? But I've put down a deposit, quite a hefty one.' The words filtered through fixed smile lips. 'You've no idea of the price you have to pay for a goose now.'

'I'll cover it. Only cancel the order. Please.'

'You'll make it up to me? In full?'

She looked at supper, nestling in preformed plastic. Headless, footless. 'Yes.' Laid out on its made-to-measure bed. 'Whatever it costs.'

He moved closer. 'Promise?'

She could feel his breath on her neck. Milk-white bone protruded from the torn skin at the end of each purple thigh. 'If you promise too.'

A hand clamped her shoulder. She braced herself on the edge of the worktop as one finger kneaded the loose skin on her collar bone, where once had sprouted feathers. A second hand slithered inside the front of her skirt as he pressed himself against her. Over the pock-marked parson's nose Jane and Oliver made their vows.

SHE heard the bolt being slid across. One of the stunted shaft-stubbed wings fell back with a slow-motion flap as she lifted the chicken to the sink. Oliver would be stepping into the shower. She prodded at icy globules of fat plugging the entrance to the cavity. The inside was rigid. Now he'd be adjusting the control, the hotter the better even if it meant reduced flow. It was all about compromise.

She could hear him whistling, could feel his hand clamped on her shoulder. She turned the tap on full.

Water flooded over the carcass, sparking a cry from the bathroom. Hot enough? She turned off the tap.

'Don't,' Diane had said, 'stick it up the obvious place.' The plastic cone had to go in at the neck end. 'So the juices can drain away.'

The neck seemed endless, a thick bumpy tube with a secret lining of slime. She began to roll it down the spike. It slithered off at the first attempt and needed coaxing. Then the spike slid in easily until it reached the breastbone. Jane pressed with her full force and the whole body slammed down onto the spike, completely engulfing it. A corner of the bag of gore poked out between splayed legs. In the bathroom Oliver resumed his whistling. The wings flopped down in final acceptance that they were never born to fly. What did it matter? It was just dead flesh. Inside, another heart was still frozen at its core.

Jane pulled a polythene bag over it all and closed the microwave door.

SUPPER was cleared away. Oliver had pronounced the chicken, when mixed with basmati rice and smothered in stir-fry, not bad at all. Had finished the lot, in fact. He'd quite fancied rice, seeing as he'd missed out the other day when she'd made all that risotto and Harry had whisked him off for a pub meal after work. He'd been looking out a pan when Jane had told him to leave it all to her. She would, she'd said, need to be able to give a full report to Diane.

It wasn't that she'd completely run out. There'd been a few grains rolling around at the bottom of the packet. She'd have put it on the shopping list, if she still bothered about such things. Not that she'd wanted rice. And definitely not

162

any of the chicken. But she'd supposed she should make something else for him. She was sort of committed, now.

Not jacket potato, though. Not with the chicken still waltzing round. And it hadn't been worth putting the oven on, not just for him. Not pasta, either. That would have meant making a sauce and she couldn't be bothered. Not just for him. Which had left the risotto. She'd remembered she'd shoved it in the fridge the day after and there it was still, lurking at the back under a soggy tray of tuna steaks. Jane had taken out the bowl and sniffed it.

Fished out yellowing prawns, a few bits of brown-edged sweetcorn, the odd grey pea. Scraped the rest into a sieve. A kettle of water tipped over and it would pass for freshly boiled.

Besides, it would have been a waste to bin it. Her mother would have approved such thrift. Although she'd warned Jane that leftover rice could be risky. That and getting into the back seat on a first date. Something about being thoroughly heated. Oh, yes – *Never dish it up lukewarm, Jane.* Well, the microwave would take care of it. Heating things up was what it did best after all. Not cooking. Because when the bell pinged, the meat wasn't done. The chicken and the rice bowl had to swap places several times before a two-pronged fork could be jabbed into the breast. Which would have to do. And Jane decided, as the number of chicken-radiating rice-warming-cooling-warming-again times clocked up, that there was nothing quick about making a meal in the microwave. Yet another thing that wasn't as wonderful as other women made out.

SHE let him refill her glass, again. Anything to get through the night as mindlessly as possible. She felt hollow inside. Whereas he must be pretty stuffed, all that meat he'd eaten. Not to mention the rice. He was eager to please.

He even picked up the art book and spread it out between them on the sofa, so the cover overlapped their thighs.

'What really fires you up?' He turned the pages, brushing against the top of her trouser leg. 'Tell me when I'm in the right place.'

'Oh!'

His hand stopped. But now she was uncertain. Something wasn't quite right.

'Not your usual portrayal of naked flesh,' said Oliver. 'That's got to be the most un-erotic nude ever. God, she looks like your mother.'

It did a bit. But it was probably just the hairstyle. Because you'd never catch Judith floating above a golden pedestal, eye to beak with a great hovering bird.

'It's Dali's wife. He painted her a lot.'

'She looks a right old bag. Looks like she's just pulled it out of the lake by its throat. What's it supposed to be about?'

Jane looked at the caption. '*Leda Atomica*, 1949. Oh. I thought his wife was called Gala.'

'Leda? That's from Greek mythology, isn't it? Leda and the swan. You must know the old story. Zeus looks down from the top of his mountain, spies Leda bathing in a stream and naturally wants to give her one. She's having none of it, so he changes into a swan and they start romping around together. There are different versions of what happens next.'

And three guesses how it would end.

'One of them says he took her off guard, but personally I go for her being up for it after all that frisking. Look on it as foreplay with feathers.' Oliver was closing the book. 'Ready to turn in yet?'

Jane jammed her hand between the pages. 'I'll show you some of his other pictures, the more famous ones.' She flipped onto another page. 'Oh, yes. Sophie told me about this one the other night.'

'Sophie did? Let's see.'

'You might have come across it before. It's *The Persistence of Memory*.'

Except it wasn't. The soft watches were there but everything around was breaking up. The tree had been sliced. One watch dangled from a detached branch. Another hurtled into space in a rain of missiles, for the table had been diced into bricks and bullets, some drifting under and over the sleeping head, others penetrating the brain itself.

'*Disintegration of the Persistence of Memory*,' said Oliver, finger on the small print. 'It's a later interpretation. I suppose he was trying to show that you remember things differently from how they actually were. Or –' as she didn't look convinced '– that you soon forget about what's happened anyway, so don't make a big thing of it.'

Still she frowned. He scanned the text.

'Apparently it was Dali's way of perceiving things so he had them in his power. He says, *I used my paranoiac-critical method to analyse the world... A brilliant inspiration* – not your average modest sort of guy, is he? – *shows me that I have an unusual weapon at my disposal... I can penetrate to the mysteries of the real in a moment... Mine the ecstasy! I cry*.' He snapped the book shut. 'Bedtime, Jane.'

HE stands in the doorway. She sits on the bed.

Softly, softly, he glides across and kneels beside her, dipping his head into the stream, nuzzling her feet with his wet beak. Trapped at the edge of the pool, she dabbles a toe.

Wings enfold her, flight-feathers nudging up the lace-edged hem, wing-tips stroking buttocks. His head nestles in her lap. She feels the warmth against her skin, can see the downy tufts curling over his neck, could stretch out her hand to stroke the smooth feathers. Atomic Judith floats naked above her golden pedestal, ringed hand steering the serpent head, smiling down the maternal blessing. Her fingers waver.

Suddenly he thrusts his head between her thighs, forcing her legs apart. He snacks at her crotch, sinking teeth into flesh. There is nothing she can do to stop it. There is nothing to do but accept it, give in to the wave of nausea that engulfs her –

'I'm going to throw up!'

And he was gone.

Jane clutched her knees to her chest. Rocked back and forth, listening to Oliver in the bathroom, retching. She slunk between the sheets and tucked the covers round herself as tightly as she could.

He crossed, none too steadily, to his side of the bed. 'God, I feel awful.'

One out of two, then. Because Jane had a smile on her lips and her lids were so tightly closed that she must surely be in dreamland.

SHE lay not daring to move, not daring even to breathe those times Oliver lurched upright to scuttle out the door until at last, shivering and stinking, he sank into a lathered sleep.

Inch by inch Jane removed her body from the bed and tiptoed towards the bathroom. The stench was bad. Even the mirror was splattered, so the figure coming towards her was peppered with the contents of Oliver's stomach. There was a low rumbling. The figure froze on the glass. A thud, a creak of floorboard. Jane turned and fled.

SHE had the road to herself. She pulled up next to the little field and wound down the window. Everything was still. In the distance the house and outbuildings were in darkness. There was a rustling in the long grass near the fence, a disappearing into the ditch. A fox maybe? No matter. Across the field the ark was battened down. Inside, the geese slept safe, pagan hearts beating through the aeons of darkness, certain of the light. When all the time the days were shortening.

SHE drove on. The sky was getting lighter though it was still early. Give or take an hour. And she was still the only thing on the road. Apart from the hump of brown. She saw it in the headlights, feathers spattered with blood. Already crows were tearing at the flesh, eyeing her approach, waiting till the last moment before they carried away their great bodies with laboured flapping. She swerved to avoid it, skidded off the road. The verge saved her from the gutter. She leaned over the steering wheel, shaking. Remembering. Another car, spanning another body.

'No sense in wasting it,' her mother had said, pulling up. 'Go on, Jane.'

And Jane had gone, trail legged.

Her mother wound down the window. 'Get on with it.'

Get on and get it over with. Jane ran with gasping breaths, praying for something to come past and flatten it into the tarmac.

Hesitated, fingers hovering. Judith honked. Jane grasped the horny legs, recoiling as the limp toes slowly moved. When she lifted up the body its wings sprawled, feather-tips stretched out too wide for flight. The ruff of feathers fanned out in an iridescence of turquoise and russet. She ran back, dodging an oncoming car, the half open beak pecking against her leg, dark red drops following her all the way.

THE car came towards her, shrieking past, somewhere to go. She must move off this narrow road. But most of all she must – She pulled into the next gateway. Stumbled over rime-crusted ruts to the five-bar gate. The sneck was frozen across. *Always climb gates at the hinge end, Jane.* She stepped onto the second rail and swung her leg over.

She crouched near the hedge. *Never wee into the wind, Jane.* But here there was only stillness. Steam rose from the gush as it flooded across the soil. She watched it stream away, trickling into the stubble, and Oliver's mouth round her crotch and the hanging droplets turning ice in the cold daylight. She began to pluck some grass and stung her fingers. *Check for thorns before you wipe, Jane.* But here there were only nettles and the dried-up river bed fingering its way to the stubble and Oliver sinking his teeth into her flesh and she powerless to stop it.

She reached out and grasped a handful. Back and forth she rubbed, pressing the leaves against her until her skin convulsed and her labia screamed out loud. She stood up, hands tugging at the trouser zip, cart-track wandering along to the farm. The house all in darkness, the buildings bolted up, and the zip biting, Oliver tucked into his side of the bed and a dozen geese snuggled up together. The metal stud slotted home. Jane reversed onto the road and headed back to the flat.

THE day passed unmemorably. And the evening. The night could be a different ball game, as Di might have said, if she were here. Jane wished she was here. Di, or anyone else. Anyone except her.

She lay flat on her back. Di had recommended it from her course. It's far better, she'd said, than tossing around, wishing it was morning.

Forget all that tosh about sinking into the depths. The mattress is there to support you. Don't fight against it, Jano.

Follow this technique, Di had told her, and it would change her life like nothing else. It was important – Dr Alexander had stressed this on several, maybe even consecutive, pages – to keep your body completely aligned. Forget what's going on around you and think about maintaining a perfect match.

Jane's breasts sprawled across her ribcage, lolling away from Oliver's cupped hands in absolute unison. He traced a path round the nearest areola and began kneading the nipple, while the other struggled to keep up.

He hadn't, Jane decided, got the hang of this at all. Symmetrical thinking was called for. It was vital to avoid crossing the legs. She kept her limbs parallel, palms flat on the bed, heels supported in imperceptible depressions, letting the mattress take the strain. When he ran his hand down the side of one leg, neither flinched.

Oliver wormed his fingers between the jam of firm flesh.

Concentrate on the place where bone meets bone.

Jane concentrated, while Oliver pushed his hand inside her thighs.

By focussing your mind you can create your own space.

Jane focussed her mind.

Think about increasing that space.

The gap widened.

Detach yourself completely from your body parts.

And there they lay. Two femurs, angled at forty-five degrees. Disconnected knee-caps, twin tibias detaching down the bed, tiny fragments of shattered metatarsals calcifying into dust. Some distance away, separate and spineless, a pelvis lies exposed. Between hip and leg bones nothing remains. The carcass has been picked clean long ago. Even the most crow-eyed of all crows could not fail to be disappointed.

'Good God, Jane!' Oliver flung back the covers for a proper look.

Slowly the bones began to re-member.

'You've got these lumps.'

Tendons and ligaments strained to make the connection.

'Some sort of rash.'

Sensations were rekindled.

'You must have picked up something.'

Sinews pulled together. The imago raised itself from its hollow scrape, forgetting all about keeping its elbows symmetrical.

Oliver stood up. 'You need to get to the doctor's with that, Jane. Or maybe even a clinic. ASAP.'

Jane was still in the centre of the bed. Spreading across into his half. Oliver headed for the door, tomorrow's boxers tucked under his arm.

She heard the lounge door bang. Jane nudged his pillow onto the floor and pulled her own into the middle. Tucked the duvet round. She felt tired. Well, a lot of unmemorable things had happened since she got up this morning. She snuggled into sleep-thoughts of soft-feathered geese in the arks and rock-hard ruts in the gateway. Of warm bodies nestled together and frost-touched blades of grass meeting the furrow's edge. The rising breath curls of down, the rigid barbs of a thousand nettles. England's green and pleasant land. Jane closed her eyes and didn't mind at all.

WHO would take it on? Christian's gaze rested on the top of Jane's head. Who else, for God's sake, was taking notes?

'And, finally –' Christian paused, mouth at the ready '– something that'll really make you take notice.'

Tony looked at Roy, but Roy was looking at Jane, as she flicked over to the third page of her hundred sheet pad, narrow feint, no margin.

'Up Your Street is poised on the edge of a great opportunity.'

Jane slid her pencil across the sheet, point pivoted on the edge.

'And just what, you're asking yourselves, has your wily old boss managed to pull off this time?' Christian took another swig of coffee and spat it back into the mug. Stone cold. He wiped his hand across his mouth. 'Keep your eyes glued to these lips, because what you're about to hear will stop you in your tracks.'

The pencil began its return journey.

'We – that is, Up Yours – are about to enter uncharted territory.'

The pencil, in seven league boots, crossed line after line of latitude without pausing for a directional check.

'You lot are going to lift your sights to new horizons.'

Christian did a quick eye sweep. Tony was staring out the window, at the brick wall opposite. Roy looked completely glassed over. Secondary double glazing without the uPVC frames, that one. Whereas Jane was still bent over her pad, recording every last detail. Totally focussed.

Shifting the pad round, Jane squinted at it from another angle.

'I'm telling you, this is the big one. A totally new venture but nothing to panic about so long as we stick to the guidelines.'

She tilted her head. Funny how every design followed the same spiralling path, keeping within the imaginary margin while ignoring the rules.

'The time has come for Up Yours to go that extra mile.'

Roy looked at his watch, for the fifth time in the past minute. Not that he could have told you the time. Or why Jane had been so offhand lately. He slumped further down his chair.

'But you must be wetting yourselves, wondering what it's all about. Let me put you in the picture.'

If she added a couple of dots, the circle in the centre of the swirls could pass for Christian with Medusa hair extensions, all set to party.

'Up Your Street is branching out, destined for the bright lights. We've been approached out of the blue, to be sole vendors for what I can only describe as a prestigious property, in – wait for it – the country. Opportunities don't get much more unique than that.'

Jane considered the latest meandering, virtually identical to the others.

'We'll be scratching the surface of a completely different market. A better class of clientele altogether.'

Roy picked at a scab. If only he knew what she felt, deep down.

'First thoughts, then. Let's hear it from the floor.'

The floor didn't blink as the dried up blood clot landed. It had seen worse.

Roy studied the patch of new skin. He should come straight out with it, ask her directly.

Christian drummed his fingers on the desktop. 'C'mon, let's have some gut reaction.'

Roy hesitated. Maybe he should wait till she brought it up first.

'Tony.' Christian jabbed a finger. 'You start.'

'I must say it sounds a bit risky to me, Christian. We're not really placed to get to grips with that corner of the market. Maybe this calls for a re-think –'

'I'm not shifting on this one.' Christian shuffled his left buttock along the desk, away from the laminated corner. This lily-livered reaction was just what he'd expected. At least he'd be able to count on Jane. Still scribbling, the little swot. 'Like they say, a fate's a cumplee when it's in the

bag. Bridges well and truly burned. It's a case of –' getting
it the right way round when you were '– crossing the –'

'Rubicon?' asked Tony.

Christian scowled. 'Crossing,' he repeated, 'the I's and
dotting the T's. Or versy vice.'

Jane had finished filling in all the loops and was
wondering whether to block in the space at the bottom
with her name. Just in shadow writing.

'Otherwise, it's set in stone. And I'm looking for
someone to carry it off. I'm looking at – Jane.'

As was Tony. Jane was shading the diagonal across the
N when she became aware that all eyes were on her. A lot
of eyes, anyway. Roy's were watching blood well from the
patch of new skin.

'Gobsmacked, eh? Enough said. A nod's as good as a
wink to a blind monkey.' Or was it a donkey? 'Anyway –'
Christian nodded '– I refuse to take no for an answer.'

'HAVE you done anything about it yet? If you won't
make an appointment, then I will.' Oliver picked up his
phone.

'No, it's all right.' Because, of course, it was. She only
remembered about the long-gone rash at bedtime. He,
presumably, thought about it every sixth second. 'I'll do it
in the bedroom. It's a bit personal.'

Even so, she spoke her name loudly. Spelled it out. And
listened for the sole-trudge towards the sofa. She moved
her pillow to the middle of the bed. Checked her balance.
It was looking very healthy. One-way conversations, she'd
found, came at little cost. She heard the click of the lounge
light and smiled.

'HELLO, Daddy,' with just enough upward lip
movement.

He looked surprised, though presumably Nicola would have rung through to tell him. So he was faking it.

'It's lovely to see you, Jane.'

Like he'd probably faked it all her life. She drew her chair closer, leaned her elbows on his desk. Looked into his eyes.

'Just give me two ticks.' He scrolled down the screen.

She glanced round. The room seemed smaller than when she was a child. Not just four coats of magnolia smaller, and not just the room, but the doctor's desk, the doctor's chair. The doctor.

When had this awareness of perspective begun? Maybe at that first interview, dismissed as nerves, only to niggle away through sorting accommodation, applying for a loan, checking the reading list, digging his old trunk out of the loft... *Your father took that when he trained, and look where he is now. You think you can follow in his footsteps.* Always to follow. *Well, we'll see, shall we?* See with cornea scraping clarity that she couldn't risk it. Couldn't risk overtaking him. Couldn't do that to darling Daddy.

'All done with now.' He clicked on a couple of crosses at the top corner. 'It's been a long day.'

He half attempted to cover a yawn. A pretty good yawn, in fact. She only just caught the whiff of artificiality wafting through the fingers.

'Are you on your way home?' he asked. 'Or perhaps you're going somewhere else?'

'Are you?'

'No evening calls nowadays.' He gathered some loose papers into a pile.

'But you still make home visits.' Careful. Speed still kills. 'You sound as if you're putting in as much time at work as ever.' And confrontation clams. 'Poor Daddy Dimkins. You should be taking things easier, at your age.'

'Good grief, Jane, I'm not quite ready for the box. There's life in the old dog yet.'

His laugh was hollow enough for her to slide in with him and still leave space to jump either way.

'I'm sure there is.' She could just leave it at that. Give him a big kiss and tell him he was the best Daddy in the world. Even now, she wasn't committed.

Nicola buzzed through. If there was nothing else she'd be off.

'Well, Jane,' squaring the pile into shape, 'it's been lovely to see you, but I really need to be making tracks as well.'

'I'll follow you, shall I? Then we can have a nice chat.'

'Better not, Princess. Your mother's got one of her meetings later on. Organising the over-sixties' Christmas party. So we'll be having a scratch meal and then it'll be –' He smiled. 'Well, you know what it'll be like.'

And this time she leapt in with him and together they wallowed, splashing the smile all over their faces.

He stood up. He was leaving. And she didn't want to be left. There'd always been Daddy. Even when there was Oliver, there'd still been Daddy, deep down. And now –

He took his jacket from the back of the chair. Holding it up, he patted one of the pockets. Before he could reach for the other, Jane grabbed the hem.

'You won't get far without your car key. If I find it first you've got to stay till –' she glanced at the clock '– half past.' She twirled the jacket, trying to twist the loop round his finger.

She dived her hand into a pocket, maybe the same one he'd checked, but maybe the one holding the key. Yes, she could feel it, the smooth stub of wood. She pulled it out.

But it wasn't the school trip souvenir she'd given him all those years ago. This was no princess of the forest, or even a common or garden dryad in a pilfered tiara. It wasn't even a key fob.

Charles took back his jacket. 'Must belong to one of my little clients.' He slid in an arm. 'They usually bring something along for a bit of reassurance.'

The little red engine lay on her palm. She could see tooth marks where the paint had been gnawed away.

He took it from her, put it on his desk between the dish of Smarties and the *Super Patient* stickers. 'Some little tyke'll be back for that sooner or later, I expect.' He pulled out his keys. 'We can walk to the car park together, then we'll have to go our separate ways.'

He jangled them in front of her. Still on the same fob. The same slice of dead wood, the eyes still bulging, the grinning mouth as wide. But where the golden crown had been there was only a blob of hardened glue.

He unlocked the Mondeo from twenty metres. 'I'm afraid I'll have to love you and leave you, Jane.' A kiss on the cheek and he was gone.

Jane stood for a moment before putting her hand into her own coat pocket. There were her keys. And rubbing up against them was a little red engine with half the wood laid bare.

THE problem was, she thought the world centred round herself. It was, said Christian, a scientific fact. Which was why a woman couldn't read a map. Couldn't focus on the overall view like a man. Which must be why she was lost.

Yellowing strands of sellotape peeled away as Jane spread out the map over the steering column. The top corner hung on by less than half a mile. It was only the north east of town, the bit where their flat was. She tore it off and tossed it to the floor. She ran a finger along the last familiar road, followed it to a frayed crease where it disappeared.

The windscreen had misted over. Jane wiped away a circle of condensation. There was a T-junction ahead, a sign for one anyway. A sharp right would take her somewhere. It was a geographical fact. She gave the windscreen another rub, so she could focus on the overall view.

If the extensive panorama seemed a trifle bleak, put it down to the time of year. Come spring, when young love's fancy turns to DIY and the blossoming wisteria just about covers the crack in the supporting wall, Stobb End – charmingly situated off the beaten track – might appeal to a discerning purchaser seeking an ideal renovation opportunity to give full rein to his creativity. Or hers. Jane went upstairs to measure up.

The back bedroom had a small window under the T-fall roof. She pulled at the curtain and her fingers went through the fabric. The glass was thick and distorted. She managed to loosen the catch but the sash wouldn't slide down. Jane ran her hand along the frame. She could feel an edge of paper sticking up between the slats of wood. Piece by piece she prised it out, flakes of bygone news clogging fingernails.

A bluebottle batted half-heartedly against the glass, considering its options. Find a way out and soak up a few hours of weak sunlight before nightfall? Hang around the window and end up trussed in that web in the top corner?

Your best bet, Jane told it, would be to crawl back into whichever dark hole you've crept out of and wait for better times.

The bluebottle buzzed away. Thanks for sorting out my life.

No problem.

The top window still wouldn't budge. Jane pushed up against the bottom frame till her thumbs ached. Suddenly it gave, jarring her wrist as it jammed again. There was an uneven gap, just a few centimetres at the right hand side and a few less at the left. Not enough to see out.

Unless you were a bluebottle. It appeared from nowhere and gave the panes another go before finding the opening. Jane crouched down and peered through the gap. The air was crisp, fresher than the dank room. She took deep breaths, feeling the chill in her chest. She didn't know where the bluebottle had gone but she was going to follow it.

ONLY a stackyard and a bit of a rough grazing – read that as pony paddock – because the ploughed field to the right was part of another farm now. Near the hedge a baler lay on its side, rye grass sprouting between the metal plates. Jane headed for the paddock, past some large curved spikes jutting out from the thistles, past a trailer with a flat tyre.

The gate was propped shut with barbed wire round each post. *Always climb gates at the hinge end, Jane.* It probably didn't matter much when the gate was off its hinges. Not as much as it mattered about her charcoal wool trousers with lycra. She looked at them, saw Oliver looking too, swirling them round on the hanger, running his hand over her bottom when she'd tried them on...

She put her foot on the second rail and straddled the top bar. She could see for miles, could see a flock of geese rising up into the sky. Somewhere down there, over the hill, there must be a lake. She'd be failing in her duty – Christian was forever harping on about what a good selling feature water was – to check it out later.

There was some old harness hanging in the shed. Mrs Wainwright would have been able to tell her what it was for. That an' all t'other owd bits o' junk. She looked through a stash of tools in the corner: rakes, shovels, pitchforks, a long-handled brush, a metal tube – a double metal tube – sticking out of a hessian sack. She tipped it out. Weren't shotguns supposed to be kept under lock and key? Most likely it had seized up long ago. She put it back in the bag and arranged the tools over it, just in case. Something ran along the far wall and disappeared behind a heap of sacks. She prodded one with her foot and a sluggish trickle of mouldy wheat spewed from a hole near the bottom. The whole place reeked of horse. Could be another selling point.

The stepping-stone path must lead to the privy so there was no need to go and see. She pushed open the door. There were a few broken plant pots, an upturned hanging basket, and a rusting tin of Jeyes Fluid. The wooden shelf on the knee-high wall must be the actual toilet, so there was no need to look.

She lifted the cover. Three holes, one big, one middle-sized, one small. Did Ma, Pa and Baby all sit down together? The Three Bears' chairs with comfort slots. Though the stench would have been – her mouth twitched – unbearable. La véritable essence de – what was the French for bear? She could almost see it on the page of the textbook. If she closed her eyes – the stink became more intense. Definitely in need of a few squirts of air freshener before she showed anyone round. The smell in the lean-to was pleasant in comparison. Owd 'orse preferable to eau d'ours. But she doubted you could get it in a can.

She turned away and caught the last gleam of sun, a glob of golden syrup sinking into skimmed milk sky. Goldilocks skipped out, closing the door behind her.

'NOW Jane's been to Stobb End to measure up –' Christian stopped. 'You a hundred percent about these dimensions?'

Jane shrugged. 'If you don't trust me...'

'It's those sonar watzits I don't trust. You can't beat the old way of doing it. I never go anywhere without my thingy.' He patted his trouser pocket. 'Always spot on. Inches as well, if you turn it over.' He looked at Jane's print-off again. 'Upstairs doesn't seem to square up with the ground floor at all.'

'They do things differently in the country,' she said. 'It's all the in-breeding.'

'Well, make sure you put "approx" after each one. And remember it's a cottage. Even if they're four storeys with a pink marble jacuzzi and a crazy golf course out the back, they're all cottages.'

'All?' asked Tony. 'Have we been given instructions for others? If so, I'd –'

'Not as we speak. But you can bet your bottom dollar Up Your Street's going to break into the country big-time.'

'But,' said Tony, 'country properties and Up Your Street – it's not right.'

'Don't give me all that soul-searching ethical claptrap. This is no time for morals. Not when Carver Hogg has a board along South Parade. Treading on our toes good and proper. The sooner the whole world sees an Up Your Street sign in the back of beyond the better.'

Tony shook his head. 'It would be totally wrong.'

'For God's sake, you saw last month's figures. Up Your Street is up against the wall. If this doesn't take off you could well be selling fries next year, my lad, not frigging houses.'

'That's why we've got to get it right,' said Tony. 'The name, I mean. Up Your Street's too urban. It doesn't evoke images of a country idyll.'

'You might have a point there. Okay –' Christian jabbed his finger at nobody in particular. 'Brainstorm me.'

'Actually,' said Tony. 'I've been mulling it over. What it needs is something that links with Up Your Street. So I thought: Down Your Way.'

'Didn't that used to be on the radio? I remember my mother –' but only vaguely. 'No matter. Water over the bridge now.'

'Which would be a good thing to have on the board. We need an image, like Carver Hogg's pigs in clover. It grabs you more than words alone. That's something else I want to talk to you about –' went on Tony '– like a babbling brook, you can see it, can't you? Dabbling ducks, splashing frogs, weeping willows...'

'Rising damp?' said Roy.

'Okay, how about a country road, winding into the distance. The W of Way could become a valley between two hills.'

'Only if they put the board upside down.'

'Don't knock it,' said Christian. 'Winding road. I like it. Free spirits and all that.'

'Like the Romantics,' said Tony. 'You know, Shelley and co. Did them for A level. *Hail to thee –*'

'*Hail to thee, blind spirit,*' said Christian. 'You weren't the only one who went to school, lad. Still remember it.'

'Hard to forget a groping spook.' Roy looked at Jane. 'Make sure you put it in the particulars,' he said to the side of her head. 'A period feature.'

'And Keats,' said Tony. '*Ode to a nightingale.*'

'At three hundred percent ARP,' said Roy. 'Or was that *Owed to a shark*, one of his maritime rhymes?'

'You're thinking of Coleridge,' said Tony. '*The Ancient Mariner*. I did them all for A level. That wasn't about birds in the countryside, though.'

'Course it was,' said Roy. 'When did you last see an albatross in an urban garden? Have you noticed any albatrosses round the nuts in Jubilee Terrace recently, Jane?'

'Number 66,' she told her left thumbnail, 'doesn't run to a bird table.'

'Course it doesn't,' said Christian. 'We're not talking starling shit now. We're selling the good life. Joe Average doesn't know what he wants but he's ready to over-extend to get it. It's the dream he's buying into.'

'It shows soul,' said Tony, 'like a poet.'

Christian nodded. 'That's it. Go on.'

'Well – it's about understanding the meaning of life, like a philosopher, and...' Christian still seemed to be listening '...the simple tastes of a ...' Full eye contact as well. '...hermit. And, er...' He turned to the others. 'What else do you need to live in the country?'

'A four-wheel drive?' said Roy, trying to catch Jane's eye. She was staring into space. He didn't seem to be able to make her laugh any more. Probably hadn't even been listening. Lost in her own little world.

Which was, Jane decided, a very lonely place to be. There would be no reliving the weekly boss-baiting, no clink of glasses as they giggled over the Friday night Rioca. Nothing to look forward to beyond another microwarm supper on separate knees.

Emptiness clogged the air. It permeated the walls that enclosed her, seeped into the skin of any who approached. She could smell it searing the insides of those around her as they backed away, struggling to gasp some meaning to their existence. Yet no matter how much she longed to be charred to oblivion, her lungs kept inflating, her heart kept beating. Life was unstoppable. Even though there was no point to it at all.

SHE could, should make an effort. Could make a proper meal, cook something special. Cook something.

She turned off the main road. There was a mini supermarket somewhere among the parked-up drives. Meadow Rise, Meadlands, Badger Nook. She threaded her way through.

The shop had two aisles. Jane did them both. What to get? It didn't do fresh. What did he like? That chicken dish with apricots – no, not chicken. What did she like? She no longer knew.

SHE tried 'Hi!' a couple of times in the stairwell. It would probably pass for normal without the echo.

She positioned a smile and pushed back the lounge door, just a shove too much, so the actual performance 'Hi!' was stifled by wood thumping plaster.

'You need have no concerns on that score, Harry.'

She pussy-trod in front of him.

'I'm sure Simon will do a great job.'

Held up the melting bag.

'In the end.'

Upped the smile.

'Actually, I did offer. I'm all for team work, you and me both.'

Jane gave the bag a shake. The smile was stretching so far it almost reached her eyes. Oliver scowled into the phone.

'The thing is, he prefers to go it alone.'

Crystals of ice slid down the polythene onto her foot. His eyes blowtorched the patch of wall under the picture frame, where paint was beginning to flake.

'Simon knows how important, how absolutely vital –' enunciating the words with a ruler-straight double line '– this contract is,' most likely in red ink, 'so he's going to give it all he's got, and more. I know I would, given the chance.' Blotted spotless.

The droplets joined into a pool. Jane watched it slide over the edge of the leather. Turning her back on Klimt's varnished lovers, cement-rooted on their pedestal of eternal summer, she slunk out.

PERHAPS he hadn't heard, so she'd better go and see. He was standing in the same place, still holding the phone.

'It's ready.'

'I'm waiting for a call.'

'Bring your phone with you.' Couldn't he see the superhuman effort she was making?

She'd even dug out the china dish, with *Golden Wedding Congratulations* on opposite sides in non-microwavable gold. She could warm the plates anyway. Quick Start times three should do it.

'It's ready to eat,' without a cooling blow. Shame he didn't return the smile, as she'd almost run out. 'And there's your call.'

Oliver looked at the keypad and swore.

'Do you want me to leave –' the room, the flat, the country?

'No. It's fine.' He switched off. 'Sorry,' to the space between her left collarbone and her earring. 'I've got to go out.'

The microwave pinged. There were the two plates, sandwiched together, lukewarm and empty. Jane pulled the congratulatory dish nearer and reached for a fork. It wasn't until she'd eaten almost half that she noticed his phone on the worktop.

HAD he forgotten his key as well?

By the time she got to the hall, the hammering had slowed to rhythmic thuds, a drum beat driving the galley ever closer. The door chain hung loose. Below deck the slaves were unshackled, unprepared for attack. Jane opened the door.

Simon fell into the hall, fists pounding air. 'Where is he?' He pushed past her, flinging back doors as he charged from hall to kitchen, lounge, bedroom, bathroom, back to hall. 'Where the hell is he?'

She shrugged. 'Out.'

Claws dug into bone as he seized hold. His eyes were craters of madness.

'Tell me.' Her head rocked. 'Tell me, you sodding cow.'

Her head snapped back. 'I don't know,' she cried to the ceiling light.

He let go. Jane's head jolted forward, teeth stabbing tongue.

'Gone into hiding, has he?' The craters belched sulphur.

'He didn't say –'

'I bet he didn't, the double crossing piece of shit. Hasn't even the guts to answer his sodding phone.'

'He was waiting for a call.'

'I bet he was. And I sodding well know who from, so you can drop the Little Miss Innocence. Don't pretend you don't know exactly what's going on.'

'There's nothing going on. You're imagining it.'

Like she was imagining the taste in her mouth.

'He's sold me down the river.'

'Oliver wouldn't do that.' She felt slightly sick.

'You must be the most calculating little poser ever – or you're so green you're not even born.'

'All I know is Oliver would never...' But, try as she might, the words could not elbow their way past her swollen tongue. She dabbed at it, looked at her bloody finger.

'God, Jane. Did I do that?' He reached out his hand.

She pushed him back. 'Don't touch me!'

'I'm sorry. It's all his fault. The bastard –'

'Get out!' She pushed him again. And again, forcing him into the hall, knocking him against the mirror, shoving him out the door. She shut it with a bang. The mirror trembled in its frame. In the kitchen Oliver's phone began to ring.

No name, just a number. She took the call.

'It's Mrs Appleby, about the order. Just to let him know we're starting them the Thursday before Christmas, so they'll be available from the Friday. So if he wants to call in and collect any time over the weekend, that'll be fine. Bye for now.'

'Wait a minute. Could you just clarify –' what you're talking about.

'The order for the goose. He put down a £10 deposit.'

'No, he cancelled it last week. I was there when he phoned.'

'That's right, dear. It's all here in the book. He called round next day, to say he wanted a bigger one now. I remember the gentleman well. Said there'd been a bit of a misunderstanding, but he'd sorted it out. He needs to come in good time if he wants to get the pick. You'll be sure to tell him, won't you?'

SHE'D be sure all right. Tell him exactly, just as soon as he came back. There again, she might as well say it now – the kitchen wall was becoming a good listener. Which is more than she'd been. Even though Simon was the only one who understood about Oliver. The only one who would understand about the geese. She needed to tell Simon.

Where did he live? She rifled through Oliver's box files, tipped out his briefcase, strew his piles of papers across the floor. Came across a small hinged case, with a lipstick holder at the bottom.

She had the address. But would Simon let her in? She fingered the picture on the case. She'd seen it before, that sepia smile under the kiss-me-quick hat. Seen that knowing look.

Jane paused under the hall light to dig out her keys. She was about to drop the Mona Lisa case into her handbag when a flash of fake gold reflected from the wall mirror. She pulled the lipstick from its holder and began to write.

AS soon as her finger pressed the bell, the door was flung open.

'Oh, it's you.' He glared at her.

The craters had narrowed to boreholes.

'What do you want?'

Which was merely a different slant on scary.

'I've brought this back.'

The little case was passed from her hands to his, was laid flat on his palm with the inlaid picture looking up. He raised it to his lips and doused the Giaconda with kisses. Which all went to show, thought Jane, as she followed him through a doorway, that those hats really do work.

He sat on the edge of the bed, cradling the case, swaying back and forth with a strange and ceaseless whine.

'Simon!' She shook him. 'Stop it!' His head lolled. 'Simon – look at me!' She saw the pinpricks drowning. Reached out to pat his shoulder and he sank into her lap, burrowing his face into her rainbow skirt. Arms enfolding, she began to rock.

'She's left me, Jane.' The words heaved out in sobs. 'She's gone.'

'Ssh,' as she stroked his hair, running her fingers over the soft curls, nuzzling her cheek against his fur, clutching him close, Jane and Booboo, safe from the outside world, away from everything horrid. 'Ssh,' and she began to hum, smothering the words.

My ship sailed from... not coming back...*with a cargo of...* lost my job...*all laden with presents for...* taken all her sodding stuff...*brought me a fan...* the scheming bitch *...just imagine...* he's done it...*when I found myself...* got what he wanted...*like this, like this,* like he always does *like this like this likethis...*

SHE woke up cold. No wonder – Oliver had all the duvet, not just pulled over to his side, but tucked round him. She was completely uncovered; completely naked, in fact. That little reconciliation scene must have gone better than planned. Thank God she couldn't remember anything about it.

So they were back together, back to where they'd been before – she mustn't think about it. She lay very still, concentrating on not thinking. If this was meditation she'd opt for a three hour multi-choice any day. Although choice was no longer an option. But he needn't think he'd won. Whatever might have happened last night – had happened; she could hardly move her thighs – was as meaningless as any other life function, from emptying bins to bowels: necessary but inconsequential, depending on which side of the God-almighty Phallus you were on. It was just as her mother had told her, when the soaking high school knickers meant The Talk could be put off no longer. Coldness, she'd said, had its uses. Jane reached for the duvet.

She stopped. Something was wrong. Something about the shape of the darkness, the pulse of the silence. But most of all it was the smell, the slight scarcely perceptible smell, that was wrong. She strained to inhale it, till her nostrils could detect nothing except the wrongness. She didn't belong in this room. Or this bed.

Breath held, she slid out, dragged back the curtain to let in the breaking dawn. A patch of light striped the duvet, mottling shadows across the heap as it rose and fell.

There were clothes strewn about the floor and some of them must be hers. She found enough, pulled them on in some sort of order. Footwear appeared to be down fifty percent so she'd have to hobble to the car – no, there was a heel sticking out from under the bed. Her bag was here, thank God, but where was her coat? More to the point, where were her knickers?

It was just light enough to see they were nowhere. There was, however, a lacy thong draped over the radiator alongside the bed. So he'd been wrong. The scheming bitch hadn't taken all her sodding stuff. Leaning against the bottom of the mattress, Jane stretched across the hunched duvet, caught a lace edge, began moving back. A hand sprang out and grabbed the thong. She tried to let go but her thumb had latched into the elastic which twisted tighter as the hand pulled. The duvet reared and tossed. A face thrust from it, inches from her own, eyes a torchblow away, lips within spitting distance. The thong was wrenched free and disappeared. She left Simon whimpering undercover, cradling ten square centimetres of nylon froth.

JANE closed the door. She turned. Oliver was standing there, wet from the shower.

Where –?

Unvoiced, it frisked through the air, dancing under the hall light, bouncing off the hall mirror, trickling down Oliver's spotless hide onto the hall floor.

No mitigating hangover, no conscience fixing. Blouse unbuttoned, skirt half-zipped, she watches pools of accusation gather at his shriven feet. She looks away, into the mirror. Framed on the wall, lipstick words on silvered glass. *Fucking doubleXXer* writ large across her face.

And moving through the mirror clear, shadows of the world appear, while the Lady weaves her fingers through her folds of coloured swirls. For little other care hath she, searching the winding road where he will ride beside the river eddy whirls.

From the bank and from the river he flashed into the crystal mirror. Whirlwind haired and tousle-eyed, she picked him out as on he rode, dazzling through the barley. Blowsy lipped, she bade him come, brazen-greaved and bold. Unfettered legs stepped close to see, slung from his blazoned baldric, the mighty silver bugle hung.

Bridle bells ring merrily as nearer she goes. She reaches out to touch his burnished spur; round she reels, shadows spinning, smashed against the mirror. The crack of glass from side to side: her chain unloosed and floating wide. Back she leant, and so he trode.

Burned like one burning flame together, the broad stream bore her far away. She spun three maelstroms round the room, consumed the helmet and the plume, she spawned the water lily bloom, as he rode on to Camelot.

'NOT exactly mind-blowing. Is that the best you can do?'

'Believe me,' said Jane, 'that's as good as you're going to get, from me.'

'I would've thought,' said Christian, 'it was simple enough, even for a woman. Up your bloody country. That's only three words, for God's sake.'

'Perhaps we should get in a professional,' said Roy. Because he wasn't going to start explaining crowdsourcing to Christian. Not with Jane within elbow reach.

'Good God,' said Christian. 'There's no need to pay someone. You have a go. I don't suppose you can do any worse.' He tossed a wedge of A4 along the table. 'You as well, Tony. You can stop sulking because we rubbished your idea. You're not paid to do negative.' The sheets dominoed over the table and lay motionless, backs covered, completely blank.

'None of you –' he stabbed at each in turn '– are going anywhere until you come up with something. All that's needed –' he sat down '– is a bit of lateral thinking,' swung his legs onto the desk, 'I know you can do it,' and crossed them.

A bit of lateral thinking, Tony might have thought, if he'd been paid to do negative, was all that would have been needed to connect Up Your Street to Down Your

Way. Instead he wrote *UP YOUR COUNTRY* across the middle of the paper, and glanced at the other two. Jane was gnawing her pen. Roy had lined up *U R C O* under the *U P Y O* at the start of his top row. Lateral beyond the call of duty.

Just what, thought Christian, was Roy up to, folding and tearing the paper into squares? Waste of time, far quicker to screw it up. He should know. He gave his feet a sideways shift. Which didn't help the view. Or the cramp.

Roy sorted the pieces. Thirteen letters, almost a doubly bad hand of Scrabble. No Es or As, and two Ys. Everything as awkward as could be. Especially her. And he was a straightforward plain speaking sort of guy. Perhaps he should try a different approach. He shuffled the squares into a laterally challenged circle and began selecting. *POUT PUNT RUNT ROOT COOT*, half a dictionary of four-letter words. *COURT* took five, but this was about more than merely scoring. He might manage *OUTPOUR*, but couldn't spell out his real feelings, however hard he frowned.

Just what, thought Jane, was Roy up to, whizzing letters about like a Ouija board in overdrive? She clicked her biro out and in. Absolutely pointless.

After his third try, Tony decided to give each word a sheet to itself. Laid one above the other, it seemed to cover every possibility. Or did it? He rearranged them side by side. Jane moved the one encroaching on her space a quarter turn.

Landscape to portrait, Tony realised, put a different perspective on things. 'The board needs a picture. I suggested it when we first talked about going rural, remember?'

'A mountain stream, wasn't it?' said Jane.

'We're after Miss Marple not bleeding Heidi.' Christian got to his feet, 'The vicar on his bike not cows with bells on,' and found he couldn't straighten up. 'Now a stream

191

through the village green is a different kettle of fish. Throwing bread for the ducks and watzits eating out of the hand of an old –'

'Trout,' said Roy.

'No,' said Jane, leaning across. 'Not possible.' Not when there was only one T.

'Course not,' said Christian. 'Too slimy by half. I mean those other things – beady eyes, sharp teeth, swim about hunting for food. There was a film about them.'

'Not –' Tony hesitated '– great white sharks?'

Letters changed places. *TONY U PRUC*. Because vowel availability was limited.

'I'm not talking teeth,' said Christian. 'I want to offer the ladies something they can dream of stroking.'

Roy and Jane snatched at letters. Roy came up *PONY*.

Jane shook her head. 'Not aquatic.' She shuffled squares. 'There – *COYPU*.'

'Foreign upstarts,' said Christian. 'And they've got bristly hair. Not like our native thingies, small and furry.'

Except *UP YOUR COUNTRY* didn't do furry. *CURRY* was the best Jane could manage. English, near enough. After all, the *Cat and Fiddle* back home had transmogrified into the *Bengal Tiger*. She looked at her watch. It was a long time since lunch.

It was, decided Roy, one of those now or never moments that only happen a couple of times a week. He added POT and, underneath, *U ON*. The question mark was in his look.

It was tempting. The wholemeal bap with lettuce was a distant rumble. But she could see in his eyes that the Curry Pot would be more than a space filler. Her finger hovered over one of the *Y*s. But *YOYO* was all she was able to do.

Christian was having second thoughts. 'Maybe we should steer away from water – all this knicker twisting over flood plains. Stick to solid ground, fields of sheep.'

'Or cottage gardens,' said Tony. 'Roses round the door, orchards in spring – hey, I've just thought of something brilliant.'

Roy spotted the snag straightaway. There was a tribe, wasn't there, that didn't have a word for yes – except it had probably died out. He drew down *OUT OR* – he'd have to improvise – *YN*.

Either way, thought Jane, it was a set meal for two. Maybe she could start to move on. But not a candle-lit table behind plush velvet. She wasn't ready for that.

'How about replacing the O in Country with a bright yellow sun?' said Tony. 'And instead of all the letters in the last syllable – tell me if this isn't a great idea – there could be a giant T, sort of like a tree.'

'It isn't a great idea, Tony.' Whereas a curry for two with plastic forks might be. All she had to do was move down those three squares. It could be fun. It was ages since she had an Indian takeaway – oh, God. Tikka masala. Picked-out chicken, squashed foil trays, smashed pavlova... hands braced against the tiles, six little ships battling through steam – *NO!*

And then there was one. Tony, arranging squares below the gibbet arm of a geometric oak, pushed *TRY* aside. Which left only – he counted them twice – seven. He didn't notice *ROY* screwed up on the floor under Jane's chair.

'I THOUGHT we'd eat out. Go to the Blue Umbrella, for a treat.' He ran his fingers through her hair. 'I like it all tousled like this.'

The fingers traced down the back of her neck. She felt again the crawling convulsion of scissor point jabbed into nape and she powerless in her high chair, wisps of baby curls dropping down her collar.

'Then I thought, it's such a cold night, let's snuggle up on the sofa with a pizza. It'll be here –' Oliver checked his watch '– in ten minutes. Just time for you to slip into something comfier.'

Her phone rang before she'd even taken off her coat.

'You okay, Jano?'

'Why shouldn't I be?'

'Well, you being ill and that.'

'It was nothing.'

'I thought you were about to croak, the way Oliver was going on. Quite sweet really, like he was about to lose his most prized possession. Anyway –' and now it was undiluted Di '– as you are better you could've got in touch. It's so like you to not bother. So I'm just checking – you are coming to Mum's for Christmas, aren't you? She was wondering if you'd have to spend part of it at his parents. Rob thought that, our first Christmas together, till I put him right. Where's Oliver from, anyway?'

Jane couldn't speak. Because, it suddenly struck her, she didn't know.

'We were trying to place his accent, but he hasn't really got one, has he? He must have moved around a lot. Maybe his Mum and Dad split up when he was little?'

Jane frowned. Oliver never had parents. *I didn't exist before there was you, Jay.* End of conversation.

'I'll tell her it's definite, then.'

'The thing is,' said Jane, 'I don't know how much time I'll have off from work...' though it could be 24/7, the way her sales record had been lately.

'Well, you'll get the bank holidays at least. So we'll see you on Christmas Eve. We're hoping to get there in decent time, though I'll never get Stephie to bed, what with Auntie Jane coming as well as Santa. Hang on a mo. I'll fetch her and she can tell you about the playgroup nativity. I was on duty there this morning, glueing cotton wool onto lambs' ears. The kids are rehearsing non-stop. Stephie'll want you to guess what part she's playing.'

'Actually, we've got a pizza delivery in a couple of minutes.'

'So what happened to home cooking? Or is this supposed to be a treat?'

Jane could hear background bleating. 'Yes, that's what it is. A special treat.' The bleating became more insistent.

'Coming, darling,' Jane called, and switched off her phone.

She still hadn't got her anorak off – the frigging zip had stuck again – when Oliver poked his head round the door, grinning like he was possessed by all the cats between Derbyshire and Wales.

'I heard you call – darling.'

Somewhere someone had a finger on the bell.

'That'll be the pizza. Don't be long.'

Tell that to the anorak. Jane stopped tugging at the zip. Would things have turned out differently if she'd kept it on, that other time, instead of going into reverse mermaid? Maybe that was the surreal existence, and what she was floundering through now was reality. She looked in the mirror – *I like it all tousled* – scraped her hair back, secured it with a rubber band three times round. Which was real – the face in the glass or the one she could never actually see? Had that been the beginning of the end or the end of the beginning – no, worse than that, it was the middle of the middle. Her life was going to go on much the same. She scrunched her neck to focus on the zip pull. *YKK*. Which more or less said it all.

'Don't let it spoil, darling,' he called. 'This packaging won't hold the heat much longer. And, guess what? I ordered extra topping.'

Grasping each side of the collar, she ripped the zip from its stitches and kicked the anorak under the bed. Tomorrow, Snow Baby would be demoted to everyday.

JANE pulled her collar closer.

'Do you think it's damp?'

She shrugged. 'We do advise an independent survey, Mr Elliot.' Or you could ask the fungus on the back wall.

His wife came to the top of the cellar steps. 'Phwaw, it doesn't half stink down here.'

So it was good to get out into the fine drizzle. They'd inspected the hedge along the paddock and were rooting about in the stackyard. Mr Elliot seemed more interested in the tipped-over baler than the bit of God's earth under its rusting side. Maybe he was after scrap metal not Bricks and M? Jane dabbed her dripping nose on a dirty sleeve. The fake fur stuck out in damp clumps, Snow Baby turned to slush.

Now Mrs Elliot was at it, too, trampling down the thistles for a better look at the thing with the curved spikes, whatever it was. Mr Elliot had his eye – more than his eye – on the old trailer.

'I must point out that when we show clients round it's on an understanding –' that they don't knock seven bells out of the junk that's lying about. Okay, the tyre was already flat, but even so –

'There's nowt wrong with that,' and to prove his point he gave it another kick. 'Bit of air and that could be on the road. See –' and now it was the towbar's turn for some wellie '– the wood's sound enough. That trailer could carry half a ton, easy.'

Or, thought Jane, a dozen fat geese. Easy.

THE final flight. Jane hesitates. *For goodness, sake, Jane, just keep putting one foot in front of the other.* She can do that. This is Jane, climbing the stairs, step after piss-stained step. Now Jane is slotting her key in the lock, crossing the hall, pushing open the door. The hero, centre spotlight, stands by the table, freeze framed. Life at the Flat, an everyday story of deceit and disillusion. Handsome Rugged Hero looks up. Another episode is about to begin.

As usual, HRH gets the opening line.

'How you doing?'

'Okay.' You could have toasted a crumpet on her smile. Okay? She should be Bafta-nominated.

'There's a parcel for me.' He fingered a jiffy bag. 'Heather's just brought it up.'

'That was nice of her.'

Oliver flipped the packet address-side down on the table and began peeling back the flap. 'She's a nice woman, really. Do anything to help.' He poked his fingers inside.

'Salt of the earth,' the interfering old bag. 'Though don't you think at times she oversteps...' the recommended daily allowance? Because, from the colour of Oliver's face, either his cholesterol level was greater than his IQ or he was competing for air space with the moth batting the light shade. Even the jiffy bag had opened to full gape as it spilled its goodies onto the table.

He held them up by the elastic. 'Are these – yours?'

His look was disbelief but she wasn't taken in. She could deny ownership, of course. There must be thousands of pairs in this style. Hundreds this size. Dozens, possibly, with caked up crotches, crusty with desire gone cold. But how many actually came post-paid, with what looked like a compliments slip, which was now having its third reading?

'You know, of course –' nevertheless he made it into a question '– where these are from?'

M&S was always a safe bet, but she doubted even St Michael could get her out of this one. Anyway, why bother? Was he going to turn her out and cough up the full rent till the lease was up just because someone had pulled off the old knickers-through-the-post gag? Or pack his bags and drive off into the sunset – if his Tom Tom could find it without a postcode – which would leave her... a bit scuppered, financially. The prospect of sleeping rough didn't seem so appealing five years on. And it was December, for God's sake. So really, she told the errant knickers, she was stuck here till spring.

Always got some excuse ready, haven't you? sneered the knickers, as they dangled from Oliver's thumb.

'So,' he said, 'what have you got to say about this?'

Presumably asking who sent them was the stock response. Better coming clean. She unhooked them from his thumb. 'I'll put them in the laundry bin.'

IF he had any sense of decency – the floss snapped as she forced it between her incisors – he'd have taken himself off to the sofa for the night. She barred her foaming teeth to the mirror. It wasn't scary, not really. Only – he was totally unpredictable. She couldn't rely on him. At least – she spat into the basin – the toothpaste had a flip top.

There he was, perched on the end of the bed, naked from the socks up. And there they were, lying on the top of the bed, though she'd pushed them to the bottom of the laundry bin. He wasn't going to let them – or it – rest. He'd switched the main light off and lit the lamp at her side. Just like he used to. She checked her nightie was buttoned to the chin, pulled down a sleeve that had dared to expose an inch of lower arm. She gave her hair a swift once-round. *A hundred strokes a night, Jane.* She chewed her lip. *That's the way to stimulate the blood vessels and keep the skin healthy.* It didn't much matter, not if she was about to be scalped.

As she pushed the brush back in the drawer she sneaked a glimpse in the mirror. He was still on the end of the bed, hunched over, head resting in his palm. The *Thinker* lost in suburbia. Maybe wondering whether or not to sleep in his socks. Except – she squinted at the reflection – he wasn't thinking. Not about hosiery anyway. The cupped head was slightly turned, so from the corner of his eye he could see her. Could, she realised, see right through. She was stripped bare, betrayed by the bedside lamp. The polyester nightie had become a veil of finest gossamer over shimmering flesh.

Under a thousand Arabian stars the sultan stirred. The maiden's breasts quivered, blood swelled. She throbbed with the heat of his wanting. One by one she made her way down the row of buttons, slipped her shoulders bare. Nipples pushed forward through the falling cloth. The glass darkened before her. In the smouldering Levantine night the eyes of the wazir's daughter burned.

Forget pure bristle scratching skin; this was flesh on flesh, each stroke sucking her further in.

Ninety-nine did it for her.

'Enough,' cried Scheherazade.

But it was a good few hours till dawn and he wasn't going to be fobbed off, not tonight, not the next thousand nights. He threw her back, pinning her down.

She groped a hand across the duvet and found the knickers, thrust them in his face – *that's the way* – shoved them up his nose – *to stimulate the blood vessels.*

'Why don't we leave them on the bedpost as a memento? So –' nothing short of beheading could stop her now '– while I'm waiting for you, I can remember…' She felt his grip slacken. 'Don't worry, I'd never tweet on you. Not the full details, anyway. And I promise I'd only do it on a Friday –' He slid off the bed '– after three.'

She wondered if he'd be very cold on the sofa, or just cold. She fingered the paperback on her bedside chest. Reached across to turn out the lamp. The next chapter would have to wait for another night.

Chapter Three

'ANY joy yesterday?'

Jane smelt his breath before she felt it on the back of her neck.

'That last couple –' Christian flicked back a page '– the Elliots.'

'Afraid not,' which wasn't strictly true, because Mr E had made her day when he'd pointed out the trailer's potential.

'You have followed it up?'

'Of course –' she hadn't. Not yet. She needed to do a lot more planning. And give that trailer a thorough inspection. Just as well it looked set to be fine all day.

'You haven't –' Christian tapped her diary '– made a note of this afternoon's clients. Always get the name down in black and white. I tell you lot till I'm blue in the face: it's the personal touch that makes all the difference. Get the name in, every other sentence. A touch of familiarity works wonders, girl. There you are, longing to get matey with – let's say, for instance, me. *Mr* – you begin, then you look at me and blank out. What are you going to say next?'

'Berk,' said Jane. 'That's what I'd call you, Christian, because I'd remember. However, to keep you happy, I'll write it in. See.'

'Burke, eh? Let's hope he is one.'

His breath was coming at her now in huffs that would have made the Big Bad Wolf's mother proud.

'Now we've got up a few boards round the area –' though, he had to admit, just to himself mind, only one property actually on their books, bony Fido '– it would be nice to have a sold sign,' or maybe three or four, which could easily be arranged. He'd give Chalky a call, show Joe Public that Up Your C was getting a foothold on the flora and fawns, and all those other furry creatures. 'Hey, Jane, it would be even better if –' he could hardly wait to hear what he was going to say '– your client was Mr Hare!'

Jane cupped her hands round her nose. Having Christian nearby was enough to up the insurance premiums on any timber frame residence.

'Burke and Hare.' He pulled out his hankie. 'You must have heard of them.'

'Of course. They sold bodies for dissection in Victorian times.' In the days when females didn't have the option of studying medicine. Or not studying it.

'Not,' Christian wiped his eyes, 'that you'll find many body snatchers around nowadays.' He stuffed most of his hankie back in his pocket.

Don't be too sure, Christian. There could be one within wheezing distance of you right now.

BURKE and Hare had it easy. Snatching live bodies was going to be trickier. Those beaks looked seriously scary. And how was she actually going to pick them up? Jane thought of the old woman carrying the goose, lying calmly in her arms. Maybe it was used to being handled. It was obvious, even from a distance, that the woman cared about it, like a favourite pet. Except people don't eat their pets. That time Gareth Holden took the class rabbit home at the end of term and didn't bring it back in January didn't count. Well, this Christmas holiday would be different. The Elliots weren't the only ones about to relocate.

SHE was getting more familiar with the roads. Just as well. Next week – she hadn't decided on the actual day yet – she'd be doing it in the dark. She turned into Stobb End and drove past the house, keeping to the ruts where the track to the stackyard was worn down at each side. She could hear grass scraping Festina's undercarriage.

Leaving the engine ticking over, Jane lifted the five bar gate far enough to release the sneck. She pushed against it and squeezed through the gap. She'd have to trample down the grass to open it fully. The slouch calf boots saved her from the worst of the nettles, but after a few minutes she realised it was pointless. Even if she managed to push the gate back, there was no way she could persuade Festina – what, in these tyres? – to trek to the trailer.

And no way, as she waded knee-deep through thistles, the trailer was going to make it across to the gate. Not without clearing a path through the grass… Hadn't she seen an old scythe somewhere?

There it was, in the lean-to shed, between an upturned metal bucket and a rake in serious need of orthodontic treatment. She fingered the blade. It wouldn't, Grandma Bates would have said, cut through butter. She wasn't even sure how to use it. Which hand went on which of the little poles sticking out from the main shaft?

That was it, left on top, to act as fulcrum, right arm straight, supplying the power. Swing back and sweep forwards… Swing back and sweep – not too far, don't – swing back and sweep – want to amputate – a leg, not that – swing back and sweep – this blade would make – much impression – even through grass… it was easy to get… into the rhythm… and out of breath… going to be much… too hard unless… she found some way… of sharpening the…

swing back and – clank. A wave of pain shot up her arm as the point jabbed through the side of the bucket.

It took some dexterous hand-foot coordination, plus a good bit of brute force, to free the scythe. Jane laid it on the floor, then sank beside it. It was either sit on the dirty straw or drop down dead. She'd have to get in some practice before G-day. Never mind the bucket, she'd badly jarred her wrist. She stretched out a foot and prodded the damaged metal. *There's an 'ole in my bucket*, a fairly big one. *With what shall I mend it, dear Lisa...* Plenty of straw around, though she'd never quite understood what Lisa had in mind. Well, he could stuff it, could dear Henry.

But the song wouldn't go away. Straw too long, axe too blunt... *with a stone, dear Henry, dear Henry...* That was it. Not a common or garden stone, of course. She'd have to buy one. Unless – who said a bucket with a hole in was no use? By standing on it she could reach along the high shelf that was just asking to be looted.

She found not only a baton-shaped whetstone, still rounded in the middle, but a grease-gun and a can of 3-in-1, both of which might come in handy. That bucket hadn't been as busy for many a month. But not as busy as she was going to be. Mr Burke would need to book a second viewing. It might even be necessary to give a slot to Mr Lepus Europaeus.

'I KNOW you were expecting more. I've tried my best,' said Roy. 'Sorry, it's difficult to hear,' when being nudged further and further from the earpiece. 'Mr Morrison can complete in three weeks but I must warn you he's seen another – no, I haven't forgotten the original asking price, but surely you're not going to let this slip –' Roy struggled to keep hold of the receiver '– for five thous-'.

'And the thing is,' Christian told the phone, 'you can't get away from the position. We've tried to avoid school chucking out times, but all those needles and spent spliffs, to say nothing of the con– no, the property wasn't overvalued, we're not that sort of business. Quite the opposite. You have my personal assurance that all my staff are experts in the field. Although I must confess, hand on heart, none comes more highly qualified than yours truly. You've only got to look at the letters after my name...' which, gazing across to the plate glass which separated the office from the outside world, he never tired of doing. There they were, fanned along the top, back to front and going in the wrong direction, but definitely upper case.

'I'm sure there's nothing I can tell an astute lady like yourself about the present fluidity of the global economy.' Christian flicked a tongue over his bottom lip. 'The market for properties in such locations – damn me, the beauty of borstals was that the little devils were under lock and key – has almost dried up.' Where the hell was Xanthe with the bloody coffee? He'd give her a right bollocking when – oh, of course, she'd done a bunk. One of the rats deserting... 'A sink school, there's no getting away from it.' Or them. Bloody women.

'Well, dear lady, if you insist, I'm a hundred and ten percent certain –' ignoring Roy's frantic headshaking '– we could hold out.'

He glanced at the message Roy had just scribbled.

'What's that?' – throwing his voice at the front window – 'Excuse me one moment, madam, I've just had an urgent message from my colleague.'

He winked at Roy.

'It definitely looks like the buyer might be having second thoughts. The guy's got his eye on a place in quieter parts though we might still be able to swing it, if we act now. Just say the word, I'm all ears –' but the one he heard sent his earlobe crimson.

'Look, cards on the table: if you can meet the buyer half way on this...' he'd send Jane out for some of those chocolate digestives, 'I'll call it a done deal,' and stick the bloody kettle on himself. He put down the phone.

'Christian, this two and a half grand –'

'Peanuts. I could see right away it was the only way to clinch it. When you've been in this business as long as I have –'

'But,' said Roy, 'you've scuppered it.'

'Well, unscupper it, lad. Otherwise –' he poked a finger up his right nostril '– you can kiss your commission on its pretty arse.'

'I'm telling you, I can't get any more.' Roy pointed to the post-it note. 'You saw what I wrote.'

'Sure. Oldest trick in the book. It's knowing when to play it that marks the men from the boys.' Christian worked his finger round and round. 'Teach you to focus on the hot buyers in future. I don't need to remind you –' he pulled out his finger and examined it '– we've got the bogey of recession hanging over us.' He flicked the finger in no particular direction. 'And,' picking up the post-it note, 'you don't need to tell your grandmother how to suck her watzit, lad.'

He pressed the note against Roy's forehead, 'Now where the hell's Jane?' and moved off.

Where she was, Roy realised, was right beside him. He didn't need to look. He could feel her fingers unpeeling the post-it note, could smell her softness, hear the whisper of her breathing, taste the sweetness of – what was it? He opened his eyes.

'I thought you needed this.' She pushed the mug towards him.

'Thank you.' He took a gulp of hot liquid and spluttered.

'Sip it slowly.'

Roy stared at the shards of vegetation floating on a sea of yellow. If his lips were sewn together he wouldn't be able to sip it slowly enough.

'What the – what is it?'

'Chamomile flower tea. I added some valerian leaves and lavender as well. Shall I stay while you drink it or would you rather be left alone?'

If she went he could tip it in the pot on the window ledge. He'd heard spider plants were practically impossible to kill. Anyway, what did one dangling-in-the-way bit of shrubbery matter in the grand scheme... or, come to that, a bucketful of this God-awful mixture? He'd happily spend the rest of his days – and nights – chomping meadow grass if she was there beside him. He pulled the client chair round to his side of the desk and patted the hollow in its padded seat.

'Lovely,' he said, taking what he hoped would pass for a sip.

'I've been using it for a while now. It's meant to be calming.' A rather overstated claim. 'There's more in my desk if you need a refill.'

'No, this'll do fine. I'll make it last.' And she was smiling at him in that Jane way, the way he hadn't seen for quite a while. But lately she seemed to have regained some of that old sparkle. He didn't know what'd been wrong these past few weeks – if he thought for a moment that the Oilrag had done anything he'd show him what for. He'd – he looked away, towards the flaking edges of the lettering on the plate glass. 'You must think I'm completely spineless.'

'I don't think the WosBoss would recognise a vertebrate if he tripped over one.' She unscrunched the post-it note. *This man's after something better.* She smoothed it out and pressed it on his name badge. 'He certainly doesn't appreciate your capabilities.'

'Capabilities? Oh, sure. Just about capable of scraping enough commission to get me through to the end of each lousy month.'

She'd never seen him so miserable. 'Do I detect the slightest trace of job dissatisfaction here?' Not that she'd really looked at him lately.

'I'm not exactly contributing to the general happiness of mankind, am I? Not even to my own. This job – the whole lousy business... When I get home, I'm straight into the shower, trying to get rid of every trace of the grubby little day, and I watch all the dirt swirling down the drain, and I feel one day I'll be sucked down with it, so there's nothing of the real me left. Have you ever done that, Jane? Have you ever watched part of yourself going down the plughole?'

She didn't answer.

'Sometimes...' he lifted the mug and put it down, watched the broken petals circling '...when I'm shaving, staring into the mirror, I ask myself: Who is this idiot? And I think, if I keep on scraping away the layers of skin, I'll find the real me underneath. Then I start to draw blood and I daren't carry on, in case there's nothing there after all – that this charade that's my life is all there is.'

She picked up the mug, threading her fingers inside the handle. For one terrible moment he thought she was going to tell him he'd feel better after a nice cup of tea.

She took a gulp. He could hear the liquid going down her throat.

'That accounts for it, then.'

'What?'

'The little bits of tissue you sometimes have stuck to your face in the mornings.'

And he knew she understood. He reached for the mug. The level had dropped but the valerian leaves still floated. He reckoned when the tea was drunk the future would be spelled out on the bottom of the mug. There they sat, sipping tea, his hand cupped round hers, taking turns drinking from the same side. Two futures mingled together, computers on screen save, phones silent, and not a hot buyer in sight.

IT would do. She put the whetstone in her coat pocket and hitched the scythe over her shoulder. It was, Jane thought, one-man-went-to-mow gone pc. Well, she didn't need a man or, for that matter, a pooch.

Thirty minutes and half a dozen blisters later her second thoughts kicked in. It wasn't that she hadn't developed a good swing, or that she hadn't got the hang of sharpening. It was just taking too long. Leaning against the handle, she looked at what she'd done and what there was still to do. At this rate she'd be on till Christmas. Which would be twelve roasting dishes too late.

'Caught you slacking, eh?'

Jane spun round.

'You've taken on a lot there.' The man striding nearer nodded at the paddock, then at her. 'You're from that estate agent's, aren't you? Saw you here a couple of weeks ago. I see you're dressed for it today, though.' Her wellies got one nod between them. 'Smartening the place up a bit, are you?'

'Yes,' so get lost. Unless – 'all this junk –' he wasn't the only one who could use his head to make a point '– needs shifting somewhere less conspicuous. But I'm afraid I can't.' She gave a helpless sigh. This wasn't the moment to spout equality. 'If only I had a strong man to help me,' because under that Army surplus greatcoat must lurk muscles fit to wield the scythe he was bound to have hanging in his own cartshed. One woman, one man and his nodding-dog tic would get a path cleared in time.

But the head under the flat cap was now shaking. 'Take for ever, with that old scythe.'

Well, she hadn't got forever, so he could get out of her way. She resumed her grass attack with such frenzy the man took several steps back.

'What it needs,' he said, 'is a few turns with a grass cutter.'

She stopped, mid-slash. 'And have you –?'

'Sure. Could yoke it up now, if you like. Course, you understand, I don't do owt for nowt.'

Course you don't, thought understanding Jane. No-one ever does.

THE vehicle close behind was making the most of the five hundred yards from the roundabout to the forty sign. Jane pressed Festina's hazard button and began to mount the verge. Moving across was always dodgy. But this wasn't what made her chest stutter, throat quiver, arms tingle to the end of her fingers. She reached the fence at the top of the embankment. Was she in time?

She was having to leave the office ever earlier to keep up with the shortening days. Scanning the field, she could make out two stragglers. She watched them go towards the ark, bodies looming and fading in the passing headlights, floating over a twilight swathe of time dissolved into space.

She moved further along, stumbling over rough sods, slick with damp. Too late she grabbed at a rail. A trumpet horn, a catcall from the line of cars. Struggling to get up, her foot squelched out of her shoe and into mud. She parted the grass to find it, revealing a narrow track running down to the fence. There was a pawmark in the mud. Jane crouched down for a closer look.

She could make out the imprints of the pads, two close, the second pair further apart, and – she waited for the next flash-past of light – a strange shaped indent at the back. No claw marks but it looked much like a dog print. Most likely the collie she'd sometimes heard barking in the stackyard by the house. And yet... She frowned as she tried to recall the book she'd done for a Brownie badge. BRITISH WILD ANIMAL TRACK'S by Jane Louise Challis. With the errant apostrophe ringed by her mother in red biro. *Perhaps this will make you less careless in future, Jane.* Too narrow, even for a bitch.

She flattened more grass, peering at the flickering ground, found another print, not as big, not as clear as the first, but the back pad was a regular shape, smaller too. She pictured the page: the diagram with the differences between hind and fore feet clearly labelled; the creature with the crosshatch crayoning of orange-red fur, stopping just short of the tail-tip; the description copied from the library book in best joined-up writing. *Common on farmland and woods but also in towns. Usually nocturnal. Catches small mammals, birds and poultry.* Remembered looking the last word up in her junior dictionary.

The laggards had gone. Already the old woman was opening the stackyard gate. Bedtime, sleepyheads. She might as well go. Nothing to be seen in the far-off gleam of sodium light, nothing to be heard over the rumble of traffic.

The old woman was halfway to the ark. Another minute and the door of the pop-hole would be raised, the geese fastened in, tucked up safe for another night. Or would they? Jane screwed up her eyes. A pale blur moved along the far fence. She couldn't be certain, there wasn't time to be certain. She shouted over the traffic's rumble, waved her arms through the far-off sodium gleam.

The old woman plodded on. Forgetting she'd lost a shoe, Jane stepped onto the fence. Her nylon sole slipped off wood slime, sending her forward, chin smashing onto the top rail, teeth sinking through flesh. Swallowing blood, she leant against the fence, shaking. Spitting blood. She should be in that line of foot-down drivers, set on nothing more than a full stomach and an empty mind.

A low grey, slow grey shape slunk past below her face. A flash of white glinted in a headlight. She heaved herself up, two feet quaking on the second rail, two hands clutching on the top. Swinging one leg over, Jane straddled the fence. She cast a haloed relay of shadows so huge they almost touched the ark, before they dominoed towards the distant fence, longer and longer, but never long enough to catch whatever it was that was out there. If there was anything out there.

Jane strained to see, strained so hard the gasping breath, the throbbing lip, the roaring cars ebbed into far beyond. So when it came, the calling, it rang out ten thousand miles.

Come by.

Now she could see it, as clear as the east wind in the dead of night. A bolt of grey, sweeping the perimeter of the field, arcing over grey rigs, arrowing past grey rails, sinking to earth by the far fence, grey ears silhouetted against grey grass.

Steady away.

Inching now, ears alert, nose skimming rough blade-spikes, raised haunches shuffling over belly-flattened turf. The goose rises, neck snorkelling, beaming ark-wards.

That'll do.

Paws halt. Goose waddles up the ramp. Catch slides home. From between hind legs a tail emerges, white tip waving all the way back to stackyard, kennel and a bowl of scraps.

'HOW about we crack open a bottle of wine?'

'Looks like you already have.'

Oliver poured her a glass – 'See what you think of this' – and refilled his own.

Jane ignored the outstretched arm. Just like he was ignoring her bloody lip. 'I need to change my shoes.' Or hadn't he noticed?

'Good God.' He was looking at her feet. 'Are you telling me you've spent another day showing people round that old farmstead? I can't believe there's so much interest in it.'

Why not? Christian could. Every time.

'Good God.' Now he was looking at the kitchen floor. 'I've washed these tiles.'

There would no doubt be, she thought, a third cry of anguish to the great domestic skivvy in the sky, assuming Oliver accepted the possibility of a female deity, if only as a sidekick. After all, there could be times, during eternity, when angel cake palled and the less saintly inmates, those who'd only scraped in on a second interview, could murder a plate of spag bol. Well, if that was what he fancied tonight – as a foil to the pricey looking vino – he'd have to defrost the mince himself.

'And hoovered up for you. Came home early, specially. Good God.' He'd shut his eyes. All the better to imagine the trail of mud there must certainly be across the hall. 'Surely you could've taken –' He smiled, took her bag from her shoulder. 'Forget it. What's a bit of mud, after all?'

Without a proper soil analysis – squashing down the back of each heel with the opposite toe, she kicked off the shoes and a fair bit of roadside verge – she'd guess it was ninety-five percent solid clay.

'Aren't you going to ask –' nudging the shoes into a corner with the side of his foot '– what we're celebrating?'

Apart from surviving another day? Jane took her phone from her pocket and headed for the lounge. 'Must just check my messages.'

Which wasn't strictly true. There was only the one. From Roy. *Xmas fair @ town field tue-fri.not xacly alton twrs but cud b fun.u up 4 it?* And an image of a carousel. Not from a poster, though. She'd seen that picture before somewhere. Probably the National Gallery. She leaned back into the armchair. Her mouth was really hurting and she felt a bit woozy. She closed her eyes. Not the National. Tate Britain. Who was it by? She was sure it began with a G. It was a strange painting, something to do with the unstoppability of the First World War and people being made to – a hand was grasping her ankle, lifting it from the floor, forcing it down.

She opened her eyes to see Oliver kneeling before her, lowering her foot into the bowl from the sink. Jane cried out as her sole skimmed near-boiling water. She struggled to rise but he had hold of the other foot, had them both over the bowl, one hand gripping the back of her ankles, the other rolling up her trouser legs.

'Stop it, Oliver,' but the more she tried to pull free the more firmly he held her.

'This,' as he squirted in Fairy liquid, 'is a special occasion. It's exactly,' he said, swishing up a froth of bubbles with the washing-up mop, 'thirty-nine weeks since we met,' swirling it round, 'which means,' splashing the water round her ankles, 'it's our three quarters anniversary. Let's make it a night to remember.'

'Stop it, will you! Let go of my feet.'

He slid his hand underneath. 'This is only the start.'

He tickled her soles as she squirmed and writhed.

'You're loving it really.'

He circled a finger over one instep.

'Round and round the garden, like a teddy bear.'

He stepped the finger onto the top of her foot, 'one step,' onto her shin, 'two steps,' up the rolled-up trouser leg.

Grasping the chair arms, Jane wrenched both feet free. She scooped her toes under the rim of the bowl and tossed it into the air, sloshing scalding water over the carpet, over the towel, but mostly over Oliver's bulging crotch.

EVERYWHERE dripped damp. What she should have done, looking at the heaps clogging the way between gate and trailer, was to have raked away the grass as soon as it had been mown. Jane dug her wellie under a sodden swathe and tried to lift it. Two fat black slugs lay underneath. She let the grass drop.

It wasn't far, striding over the slippery heaps, from A to B, or rather, half-stumbling – she must remember that dip in the ground – from G to T. She was pretty sure, now she could get the gate open, that the car would make it to the trailer, if she took it steady. But would Festina manage to pull the extra weight back? If she did a trial run, because she'd never yoked anything onto a tow bar before, it would help flatten the grass. At least now there was a path through. It would have been harder if – She cried out at a sudden movement beside her.

Something rose from the long grass, slow-flapping the air, black claws bent above her face, black beak dangling flesh, black eye meeting hers unflinching. Jane ducked down, shielding her head from its ponderous wings. When she looked, it was perched on a fence-post, all tucked in, watching.

The man with the mower had evidently gone as far as the trailer, then raised the blade – she could see the track left by the tractor wheels through the uncut grass – before going back. Leaving, Jane realised, no turning area for her car. Which meant – and the crow had obviously realised this too, cocking its head on one side as it considered the problem – she would have to reverse all the way from the gate.

Are you kidding? The crow ran its beak along a flight feather while it mulled the matter over. In the dark? Giving itself a shake, the crow sank head into breast and closed its eyes, while all around the dampness dripped.

'HEY, Jay –' as she let herself into the flat '– definition of an evergreen: a tree that keeps its needles all year round, except at Christmas.'

She scrunched numb toes. How could last night's scalding flesh be so cold?

'Of course,' Oliver continued, 'it's the central heating that does it.'

The left foot felt particularly numb, wet even.

'I googled a list of varieties claiming not to shed needles. If it's to be trusted.'

It was a pity she had to keep her wellies hidden in the car.

'Nordman Fir is the best performer.'

But it was essential to keep up the city girl image of wouldn't-know-what-to-call-a-spade.

'In an arid microclimate, that is.'

Instead of bringing them in to dry out by the radiator.

'It's reckoned to stand the atmosphere for twenty-one days before it starts to drop.'

She kicked off her shoes. All she wanted was to sit down with a cup of tea.

'As long as you keep it moist by spraying the tips.'

One sock was definitely a darker colour round the edges.

'So I thought,' he was smiling now, 'we'd go artificial this year.'

If she smiled back – the sole was completely sodden – maybe he'd shift out the way.

The drone followed her into the kitchen. 'Some of them – kettle's just boiled – are really good now.'

She unscrewed the top off the semi-skimmed and sniffed it.

'It isn't just the appearance, it's the fragrance.'

There was a definite pong. Not the milk, though.

'I don't know exactly what it is… you know, when you're walking through a pine forest, that particular scent.'

More like dirty wellies shut in the boot for a week.

'The best thing about it,' he decided, 'is everything around takes on that same smell.'

She'd have to change her socks. But not until she'd finished her tea. She slumped into a chair, pulling the other one nearer with her feet and resting them on the bar. Her legs ached, ached with wellie trudging, ached with grass trampling, ached with doubt that she'd ever get the trailer shifted. But most of all they ached with longing to put them on the seat of his chair.

'Yes, they've certainly come a long way. Not like they used to be, like a cluster of bottle brushes.'

Jane frowned. She wasn't sure what the collective term was, but cluster didn't sound right for bottle brushes. A cluster of crows, maybe? No – what was it Grandma Bates used to say? *If you see crows, they're rooks; if you see a rook it's a crow.* Crows, even hooded ones, didn't hang about in gangs. She took another sip of tea. Not like geese. Which, as everyone knew, came in gaggles. But only when they were grounded. When they took off they became a skein. She cupped her mug in both hands and leaned back. She only had to get that trailer hitched, and then –

'Are you listening, Jane?'

She opened her eyes and sat up. 'Course I am. Bottle

brushes. I'll put them on the shopping list.' If she ever started keeping one again.

'That's what trees used to look like. Don't you remember?'

Well, actually – no. She frowned again. Christmas would always be Christmas as she'd known it, with the old fir tree dug up from the garden and fairy lights plugged into the light socket on Christmas Eve. A magical time, a can't-wait-for, yearned-for time of never more. Was it possible to share a Christmas, never mind a life, with someone with whose tinsel experiences were so unlike her own?

Someone who was grinning all over his little-boy face. 'I know you're dying to see,' tapping the enormous box she'd failed to notice, 'what's inside.'

Jane stared. Her mother could have wrapped up all the family presents, including the recycled ones put aside for second cousins in case they dropped in, with the amount of jolly holly paper he'd used.

'Come on, open it.'

'What, now?' Before Santa had eaten the left-out mince-pie?

'Of course. You must be itching to rip that paper off.'

Impossible to stop the tickle of anticipation in her throat. But she couldn't do it. Not until she found scissors and snipped along five metres of sellotape and folded each peeled-off sheet. Oliver was watching with eyes all aglow, and possibly a handful of chestnuts roasting on the open radiator, as though he didn't know what lay inside. Which was, like all parcels, no matter how drossed up with ribbons and bows, a disappointment to the adult heart.

'There'll be an instruction leaflet somewhere.'

In case it's not wrist wrenchingly obvious that the top shaft pushes into the bottom tube.

'I'll have it up in a jiffy.'

Plug into plughole, male into female.

'Then we can spend all tomorrow evening doing it.'

As if decorated fibre optic trees were, like the Wainwrights' pedigree Ayrshire calves, produced in any other way than artificially.

'Perhaps you could make it back a bit sooner than you have been. You'll have to the night after, anyway, so you've time to get yourself dolled up. You know we have to be seated by half seven, don't you? Anyway –' resuming the all-weather smile '– I've seen the perfect baubles. Crimson and burnished gold are this year's colours, according to the gurus. Anything else looks tacky.'

Jane had returned to her chair, had her feet up on his.

'There.' He stood back, unaware of the dark stain spreading over the surface of the seat. 'What do you think?'

'I'VE just finished putting the tree up,' said Diane. 'Stephie insisted. Apparently everyone else at playgroup's had theirs up for weeks. Don't let on to Mum though. You know what a stickler she is for tradition. As if there isn't enough to do on Christmas Eve without that. Mind you, I can't say it was a bind this year. Talk about plan ahead. Did I tell you what happened last January?'

'No,' said Jane.

'Rob had a brainwave, you won't believe it. You know how it's sort of exciting putting up the tree, so you hang on every bauble and trinket you've got – ssh, Stephie, you can see I'm on the phone – then on Twelfth Night the prospect of packing up all those bits and bobs is such a pain you leave it for another couple of weeks – Stephie, go back into the lounge, or it's bed now. Well, Rob got hold of this ginormous box – shut the door nicely, please – and lifted the whole thing in, decorations, the lot. So last night, a trip to the shed and hey presto! One ready trimmed tree. Just shows, Christmas doesn't have to be a nightmare, does it?'

'No,' said Jane. She supposed not.

'Take yesterday morning. All the Mums had sherry and mince pies after playgroup. I took Mr Kipling, didn't want to look stingy, and made sure I had a Waitrose – homemade ones can be dodgy. So why bother? I've told Mum, a couple of trolley loads from M&S would save you a week's work. But she'll just carry on doing what she does best.' Which was, and Di's sigh huffed across the miles, to delegate. So, no prizes for guessing who'd end up elbow deep in pastry the minute the four of them got there.

'It'll be good having you there for Christmas, Jano. Just like old times, eh? You never know, *Gone with the Wind* might be on again. Remember how you always cry in that bit where Scarlet O'Hara beats the horse to death, then gets out of the buggy and runs the last bit home, only to find her Pa's gone doolally and, surprise, surprise, isn't going to make everything all right, after all. I wouldn't mind watching it again. The ending's a bit of a cop-out, though. All that t*omorrow is another day* stuff.' When everyone knew tomorrow would be Boxing Day with nothing more look forward to than cold turkey.

'Anyway, have you settled it with Oliver when you're coming – Stephie, is everything all right in there? – because it sounds to me you need to get organised instead of swanning around enjoying yourself. Listen, I'll have to ring off. Everything's too quiet in there – don't want to go in and find Stephie's strangled Helen, do I?'

'No,' said Jane. She supposed not. Whereas –

'Anyway, it's been great chatting to you. Let Mum know as soon as poss. In fact, decide as soon as I ring off.'

What Jane decided was that the silence which followed was the best thing she'd heard all evening.

'HAVE you had any thoughts about it, yet?'

'What?' Jane quadruple clicked the mouse. Why was it taking so long to connect?

'The fair,' said Roy. 'As it's only on for four nights I was wondering...' why it's so difficult to talk to you, when two days ago everything seemed –

'Brilliant.' Jane stuck her tongue out at the blank screen. Might as well deal with something else. All this time she wasn't putting in at the office was mounting up. She turned to Roy. 'I hadn't forgotten,' not entirely. What was it? Oh, yes, 'the picture. Thanks. Loved it.'

'Wait till you see your screen saver.' He took control of the mouse. 'There. It's called *Merry-go-round*. By Mark –'

'Gertler.' She remembered now. 'So you've seen it as well.' She smiled at him. 'I'm right, aren't I? It's at the Tate?'

'Sure,' he said. Only there were Tates all over the place, weren't there? Better come clean. 'Actually, I just came across it when I was browsing.'

'Oh.' She took back the mouse.

'About the fair –'

Tony staggered in clutching a cardboard box held together with string. He dumped it on Jane's desk. 'Christian's just had me dig this out the loft. Reckons it'll bring in clients. Look at my shirt.' He spat on his fingers and rubbed at the marks. 'Got a viewing in twenty minutes. So I'll leave it with you two.'

They looked at the box, looked at each other and dived in.

Roy untangled a knot of hairless tinsel. 'I bet you the last place this was hung was the Ark. Though actually,' he said, pulling out an odd-shaped pad with a patterned cover, 'my Mum's still got some of these. I think they came from my Nan's.'

'So has mine!' Jane snatched it from him. 'We used to call them lying lions.' She stood the pad up, flat edge on the desk and outlined a paw, head and body. Roy found another in the box and slithered it up to hers till the noses touched.

Jane picked hers up and fanned out the folded sides of card, opening out a tissue paper bell. 'It never turned out as good as you imagined.' She secured the edges with paper clips and held it up.

'Would you –' looking him full in the face '– describe this as tacky?'

'Afraid so.'

'Good.' Jane fixed it to the top of the notice board with a drawing pin, above the A3 print of the *Merry-go-round* which had materialised overnight.

'Ding-dong,' said Roy. He shifted the box to one side. 'Getting back to the fair, how about tomorrow night?'

'Oliver's got a work event. Brailsfords is a supplier for some big-shot company that's having its annual Congratulations Evening, handing out the usual awards. Cliff Richard'll be belting it out, added nausea. The feeder firms are all expected to send a rep.'

'So you're free. Great. What time shall I pick you up? Unless you'd rather meet at –'

'There's an obligatory guest. Glamour purposes only. It's a strictly non-speaking part. Black tie and regulation bimbo: it's on the invite.'

'You'll be bored out of your mind. Aren't there agencies for that sort of thing? He could hire a designer chav for the evening.'

'I wouldn't like to let him down,' because the lion couchant wasn't the only one who could do a bit of lying.

'Well, how about tonight? The forecast says it'll stay fine, I've checked.'

So had she.

'So,' he smiled, 'let's make the most of it.'

Which is exactly what she intended to do. 'Tonight...' was scheduled for a recce of the embankment round the fence '...we're putting up the decorations. Oliver's buying some baubles to hang on the tree.'

Just give him half a chance, thought Roy as he slumped back to his desk, and he'd have the Oilrag's balls strung up, good and proper.

OLIVER marched in, shirt tail barely covering his essentials, as Jane was unclipping the cereal packet.

'You should have woken me,' he said. 'Shift your chair in a bit, will you, so I can get past.' He began sifting through the washing on the radiator. 'There isn't a dry pair of pants anywhere.'

Which wasn't strictly true. When she'd unloaded the machine she'd made sure her stuff was spread out, bunching his along to make room.

'Unless some's fallen behind...' Oliver leaned to slide his hand between wall and radiator, shirt tail wagging over his buttocks.

Jane put a couple of handfuls back into the packet. His gyrating backside with the waggling underhang was enough to put even Snap and Crackle off their Krispies. She folded over the top and pressed open the bulldog clip to reseal the packet. And yet there it was, snapped onto the hem of his shirt, joining the dilly-dangle between his legs as he stomped out.

Head tilted, she poured on the milk. She could just make out, above the pinging rice, the creak of the laundry bin lid in the bathroom. She couldn't be certain, as she crunched her first mouthful, if he was doing a sniff test on yesterday's Y-fronts. But she laid an odds-on bet with Pop that he was.

THERE was a good chance, he'd told her, as he'd tried to land a good-bye kiss somewhere near her cheek, that he'd make some useful contacts that night. So she wouldn't be late, would she? And he'd said please.

She checked the clock. He had asked nicely. She should really go straight back to be ready on time. But Festina was already mounting the grass. A double line of cars flashed by as Jane leaned against the open boot, pulling on her wellies.

She walked back along the verge, to where the fence flanked the roundabout. She'd spotted an overgrown gateway there, dating back to the Pre-ring-road era in the Hitch-your-equus period. The gate would be fastened, of course, maybe a padlock or, fingers crossed, just tied twice round with baler twine. What she hadn't reckoned on were the six-inch nails. Bent ends stuck out at random, a hedgehog on a bad hair day. Twisted heads winked at her in the flash-past lights. They'd be dealable with, just. But the ones knocked home – she ran her fingertips over the wood to check out the telltale circles –would be what done-the-course Tony would call a challenge. Or, for a girl who had to muster positive thinking from below scratch, a facer with a capital F.

JANE pulled out into the gap. She could just about do it, even though he'd already be double bowing his shoe laces. Whereas she, she realised, was still in her wellies. Fifty yards on, the lights at the Frisky Filly said go. Forget the shower, another under-armpit layer of Surely Not and a good sloshing of Camel Number 2 behind the ears would do. Keep everyone out of sniffing range. Especially him.

Thirty yards ahead, the come-on glow. Now he'd be perched on the armchair, alternating between scanning the Which Car section and watch scowling. Ten more yards and she'd be through. He could well be edging towards silent seething.

Ahead green ducked to amber. Jane put her foot down. You can do it, Festina. And she would have done, easy peas–

The door in front slammed. Jane watched the driver go to the back of his Toyota and bend over, though she was confident such a very little bump mightn't have caused much damage. Confident-ish. She found reverse, she would give him a few inches. It was the least she could do. She eased the clutch. Her wellie slipped, caught the right side pedal and the horn behind was a wolf howling at the moon for all the good it did.

Toyota man realised he'd got off lightly. Which was more than he would do if he missed the kids' bedtime story for the fourth night in a row.

As the lights changed Jane saw his scratched bumper bar disappear into someone else's night. Leaving just the one to face.

They got out of their vehicles and came together where Festina's rear was on intimate terms with the snout of his Cortina. Stretching behind them, a single file pack of four-wheelers bayed and flashed. Should she go for It-wasn't-my-fault-you-must've-moved-forward or Little Miss Helpless? You could usually tell by looking at the eyes. She looked. She knew those eyes.

Had known them a lot madder. In fact, as he looked from Jane, in her mud-caked wellies, to his cracked bumper, with her tow bar somehow jammed underneath, the creases of skin upturned and Simon began to laugh. On the hilarity scale she wouldn't have put it above three and a half, but it beat road rage.

'Any suggestions,' he said, pulling her in close as the driver behind took his chance and nipped past on the wrong side of the road, 'as to how we're going to dislodge your tow bar from my bumper?'

'ANYWAY,' putting a Coke – because, she said, she was driving. 'Is that what you call it?' – on the beer mat in front of her, 'where were you off to in such a rush?'

'To –' she lifted her glass and took a gulp. The frisky filly on the beer mat winked at her as she prepared to clear a gate. 'B&Q. Wasn't sure what time they closed. I need some tools.'

'Urgent, is it? Don't tell me, the tank's burst and, even as we speak, water's swirling round his arse. Over his bloody head, with a bit of luck.' He sipped his pint, watching her over the rim. When he put it down the horse on his mat sidled nearer to hers. 'What is it with him? He's got you well and truly hooked.'

She shook her head. The Coke tasted good. Tasted of more than Coke. She didn't care. 'You're thinking of me hooking you back there.' Oh, God. That had come out all wrong. She took another mouthful. Good job she didn't care. Perhaps he didn't remember six nights ago anyway. Wasn't six seconds the memory span of the average guy? Though whether he'd been merely average she couldn't recall. Anyway – 'I mean Festina – my Fiesta – before you got her unhitched from your –' what was it? 'Cortina.'

'Colin? He's been in tighter spots.'

Jane laughed. Just like Simon, to give his a name as well. She drained her glass and put it on the mat. Under the translucent base the little horse kicked her heels.

'How about another?' He put his finger and thumb over the two rims so the glasses clinked. 'Have you time?'

She smirfed. As far as time went, she was seriously in the red. Even so, like the clockless tower of Pisa, she might not have the time but she had got – She inclined her head towards the beer mat, and the frisky filly winked right back.

IN the car park, a good while later – 'No point in leaving till the traffic's died down' – Simon opened the tool box in his boot.

The claw hammer he handed her was a far clout from the chisel-ended thing Oliver had bought to nail up the Klimt. Even that, she remembered, had been too much for him. As she'd bandaged his bleeding thumb, she'd tried to make a joke about it not being called a pein hammer for nothing. Afterwards, while it was still throbbing and sticking out like it was – she'd made a joke about that, too – he'd laid her down in front of *The Kiss* and –

'You shouldn't be made to do that,' said Simon. 'The vendors should see to any repairs. Shouldn't be down to you.' He rummaged in the bottom of the box. 'I think there're a few nails in here.'

'I don't need any nails. I want the hammer to pull some out.'

'Right. These pincers might come in handy then.' He was, she decided, a useful guy to have around. 'I take it they're not very big nails?'

'Biggish.' She stretched a full handspan, then drew her forefinger in a bit. She didn't want to exaggerate. Not being a man.

A slightly longer 'Right.' He paused. 'Might be easier to knock them completely in. So they don't show.'

She shook her head. Typical DIYer, after all. 'There are two bits of wood nailed together that shouldn't be.'

'Right...' A four syllable right. He picked out a hacksaw. 'What needs doing exactly?'

'Oh, you know, this and that. I can't really explain.' And then she realised she could. If anyone would understand about the geese it was Simon. He'd be all for it. Entirely as a hypothetical notion, of course. He might even – this was pure conjecture, obviously – want to help lift the presumably sleeping birds from the ark and take them to some imaginary lake '...where I'd be able, in theory, to set them free.'

Silence. Finally, 'You couldn't do it.'

'Well, getting the trailer into the field might be a bit tricky.' Just like a man to play hunt-the-snag. She was beginning to wish she hadn't said anything.

'It wouldn't be right.'

Not right? It was sanctioned from above. If God hadn't meant her to rescue the geese, he wouldn't have told Festina's last owner to have a tow bar fitted.

'Even supposing you could get them out of the ark – I'll come back to that later – you couldn't uproot them from all they've ever known and dump them somewhere totally alien.'

'Alien? Geese and water? I think not.'

'Do you suppose,' wagging the hacksaw at her, 'they've ever seen water?'

'Well, they go for a drink. There's a white sink by the stackyard fence. I've seen the old woman filling it up. She does seem to look after them well. I'm not saying they don't have a happy life, but it's not going to last much longer –'

'Happy life? That's the biggest contradiction in terms there is. And the biggest con ever.'

He slammed the boot shut. Through the back window Jane could see letters zigzagging across the windscreen. Back to front but unmistakable. Soph Si. Linked by a line of cut-out hearts, black against the car park lamp.

'The longer I'm on this planet the more I realise how pointless everything is. You grab at happiness, but you can't hold onto it.'

Together they stared through Colin's back window.

'Even when you finally find it, you're not really happy, because all the time you're shit scared you'll lose it.'

Soph, Si. Si, Soph. And in between a pair of shall-we-shan't-we furry dice, hanging motionless.

'And you will. It's the only thing you can be certain of. That and death.'

As a philosophy of life she couldn't see it having mass appeal. Jane hoped he wasn't going to get all morose again. Like at the dinner party – dear God, don't think about then. Like that time back at his flat – but she didn't want to think about then, either. In front of her Soph and Si danced backwards over the shatterproof glass.

'If you believe that,' she said to the letters above the steering wheel, 'you haven't really known true happiness, not yet.'

'And you have?' The hacksaw blade glinted red as a car squealed out of the Frisky Filly.

She glanced at him but his eyes were fixed on the windscreen.

'Think you're happy now, do you?'

Was he talking to her or to turnabout Soph?

'You'll find out, just you wait. Slag.'

Jane cringed but the four letters didn't flinch from their side of the windscreen.

'Oh, God.' He leaned on his arms against the back window, clutching the hacksaw. 'I didn't mean it. I'm sorry, so sorry...' His knuckles whitened on the handle.

'Oh, Simon, please don't get upset.' Jane frowned. Sawing through the nails might turn out to be the easiest way. She reached out, patting his shoulder... 'It's all right...' stroking his hair '...she understands...' uncurling limp fingers '... she knows you didn't mean it...' sliding the hacksaw away '...everything's going to be all right.'

Except she could hardly leave him like this. One over-the-limit driver – because she supposed she must be, the state he was in – was more than enough. But, after what happened before – and try as she might, she couldn't get it out of her head, now she'd seen him again – she daren't risk frisking him. Not here. Even if he didn't remember. He was, as she didn't need to keep reminding herself, a man, after all. So, of course, his car keys would be in his trouser pocket. Which one? He'd held the hacksaw in his left hand. She circled her arm round his body – careful not to touch – slid her hand in the left side pocket and removed the giveaway bulge.

She left him disarmed, crying on Colin's shoulder. Hacksaw in one hand, hammer and pincers in the other, Jane went to her car. He'd be able to bus it home, eventually, and he'd have a spare set there. She could post the others on. Of course, she thought as she stowed the tools alongside her wellies, she'd have to get these back to him as well, sometime, somehow... She shut the boot and ran her hand over the tow bar. Her only concern now was whether bumping into Simon had impaired Festina's ability to take a trailer.

SHE checked the control. Of course. He'd switched the heating off – though the idiot had somehow switched the water on instead – because he'd thought they'd both be out. Fully expected it – there were the allotted togs laid out on the bed.

Seamed stockings and suspenders – *feel good and you'll look good* – no-frills thong – *lace and rosebuds spoil the line* – up and away bra – *you could do with that extra boost* – black silk clutch bag – *which doesn't mean hold it like it's going to get away* – satin wrap – *loose, remember, not like a scarf...* but no dress.

Funny, that. He wouldn't have let her choose. It would have to be the drop-dead red. Yes, there were the matching five-inch heels paired up on the floor. Well, they were going straight back in the wardrobe, for a start.

She shoved them in the corner, pushed in her skirts so they didn't get trapped in the door – and noticed the empty hanger. For goodness sake, had he decided what little there was of the red dead-drop must be ironed for tonight's Big Event?

But it wasn't in the kitchen, or the lounge, or anywhere. Funny times two. Jane sighed. She wandered to the window, fingered the edge of the open curtain. The west side of town stretched before her, suburbia dozing in front of unwavering gas-lit coals, finger on the remote. The whole area a subdued glow of smugness – apart from the psychedelic pinwheel to the left. What was it? Of course. That must be Town Field. She hadn't realised she could see it from here. Nor how much she wanted to be there.

TEN thousand bulbs flashed before her. Did they make the stars pale – or was it her kaleidoscope eyes?

Six again... twirling round in the Cup and Saucer, stuffing her mouth with candy floss, squealing for Daddy to knock off a coconut...

Jane ducked between a hotdog stall and the rifle range as a moving wall of adolescents raucoused past. Yeah, we think we own the place, you got a problem with that?

No, no problem, not at sixteen... loose-haired with Jonny on the Corkscrew, willing him to bag a pink elephant, snuggling close as the waltzer dipped and spinned...

And there it was, loud and brash and next along. A lad and his girl stopped next to the hotdog bin, swapped bites of sausage in a bun, kissed across the pile of trash. Jane drew back, stepping over cables and a pile of dog shit, into an indigo twilight of shadows. Head down, she picked her way behind the rifle range, round the generator, back to the lights, the noise, the crowd. Couples waited by the waltzer, for the next dance.

She found an empty car on the far side and spread out in the middle of the horseshoe bench. Don't even think about sitting here, any of you. The bar came down and she relaxed. Safe. Sit back and enjoy. Too late she remembered about keeping her head tucked in. Gripping tight, she pushed against the bar, trying to inch her body down the seat. Any second now her head would snap off and be sucked into orbit in a billion watt galaxy of naked bulbs. She managed to reduce the pain level to semi-agony by scrunching her neck into her shoulders. Understood why tortoises outlived humanoids.

'Watcha.'

Jane opened her eyes to a tight-zipped bulge of denim. Below, seafarer legs splayed hers. She was impressed. God, he wasn't even holding on. One hand was signalling to a giggle of twelve-pass-as-eighteens in another car. The other was held out, flat. Too late to remember to put some loose change – who was she kidding, pound coins – in a pocket. She fumbled in her bag, steadied her purse against her chest to undo the clasp.

'How much?' She had to shout it twice.

He looked at her open-mouthed as the Wrigley's stretched and slackened to the beat.

'Two tokens,' with the appropriate number of fingers thrust up. So she wasn't in any doubt.

It was difficult to explain, over the music, that she was tokenless, his attention being four cars away, and his in-her-face crotch straining to join it. It wasn't possible to back away. Already the car's steel rim was totally embedded in the base of her skull. A millennium or so hence, when her skeleton was unearthed from Town Field to make way for the Mars-Venus interchange, archaeology boffins would wonder what barbaric ritual had caused such mutilation.

He was bending over her. 'You gorrem or what?'

The rim was almost through the bone. Jane offered him a note. She couldn't see its colour under the flashing lights but he seemed, as he stuck it into his back pocket, satisfied. More than satisfied – before moving on to the next car, he gave hers a lusty shove and she was flung into the void.

Why did she feel like this? Six years ago she would've – Six years. It might as well be sixty. Forget that nonsense about being old when palaeontologists look young. Old was wanting to throw up after one go on the waltzers. The air hung with diesel fumes, burger grease, lager breath. This wasn't how it used to be... was it? Getting oil on her new suede jacket climbing out of the Dragon, Jonny in a fight with a local gang... Was nothing ever as good as you remembered it? Squabbling with Di over the dodgem driving seat, held fast by her mother to have her face lick-wiped, Daddy taking Di on the Octopus and not her...

Well, she was old enough now. Too old. Go home now and in an hour she could be tucked up in bed. Feigning sleep before he got in. Sod him, she was going to see it all now she'd come this far. She'd walk the full length of the fair, then back to where she'd parked Festina. And hope she still had four wheels.

Surely she could recapture the magic. You just had to pretend to believe in it, like fairyland and democracy. It was all a glitzy facade – especially the galloping horses. So they still had them, those wonderful, glittering galloping horses. And she could still remember...

Blue Peter scrolled in gold letters on a band of navy round his neck, midnight eyes ringed with gold, a bright blue bridle with golden snaffle and golden bit. How scarey they'd looked, those grinning teeth, like Grandma Bates's in the Steradent. But he'd kept quite still while Daddy lifted her onto his back. She'd patted his neck, was reaching out to touch his ear-tips, when the music started. With a toss of his head he'd sprung forward and she was sliding, sliding off the red saddle – but Daddy held her round the waist. And then she was riding, really riding. Blue Peter tossed his head and rolled his eyes and galloped and galloped...

Jane watched them pass, in rows of three, rising and falling, too fast to make out names, too fast to see if he was among them. The pace was slackening. The inside horses were still a blur, those in the middle obscured, but the outriders were clear enough. Black Beauty, Merlin, Prancer, Foxy Lady... the next name hidden under a clinging arm. Jane glanced at the rider, waited for them to pass again to be sure.

Yes, it was Xanthe, with her boyfriend's arms around her. It would be nice to catch up, meet her fellah. Next time round Xanthe looked out at the crowd and saw her. Leaping in slow motion, the horses did another circuit. Xanthe smiled and waved, nudged her partner. He looked across, then turned away so fast he banged his head against the pole. Jane moved off before the horses came to rest. Wear a hard hat next time, why don't you?

She kicked an empty beer can out of her way. She'd seen enough here for one night. She stopped under the lights of the Octopus to find her car keys. More than enough. Far above her, rigid arms flayed the sky, capsule cages open to the stars. Xanthe and Roy. So what? She felt fine, not the least bit nauseous. Not any more. Though the cutey-girly way Xanthe was straddling that saddle was enough to make anyone – Without warning it came, from the highest car, smothering her hair and face, slithering down her back, splashing over her coat and shoes, slurping into her open bag. Those around backed away.

Jane wiped hands across face, snorting to clear the airway, spitting away the sour, stinking taste. She blinked through matted lashes, rubbed her eyes, shook her head. Globs of slime spattered down. She reached up to touch. Her hair was thick with gunge. No need to waft her fingers under her nose – She looked for an unfouled patch of coat and wiped them in the fur before dipping into her bag. Her hand plunged into still-warm sludge.

AWAY from the fairground, wind spiked flesh. Jane shuddered. She couldn't put up her collar, not when her hands touched sticky fur. However cold she was, she couldn't bear it near her neck a moment longer. She unzipped it, shook it off, held it at arm's length, one finger snecked under the top of the hood. No way was this coat going back to the flat. To the left of the path lay the canal. And the end of the road for Spew Baby. She swung back her arm and flung it.

There was no splash. Jane trod over clumps of grass and peered down. There it was, Oliver's darling, selected, groomed and petted, now marooned on a custard skin of mouldering water. Which wasn't enough. It had to go under. Jane scoured the bank side for a branch.

How it fought to stay afloat, balloon arms rising to scull the water, hump back swelling, writhing, creeping away from her. She stretched out further. Her foot slipped. Down the bank she went, grabbing at tufts and roots, managing to stop only a hand's dip from the water. The branch drifted out of reach, towards the coat. Jane could still see flecks of white, a moonlight trace of time past. Could, she was sure, make out the imperceptible rise and fall of fur as it embraced the wreath of forked twigs. Although – Jane screwed her eyes as clouds obscured the moon – it was less Ophelia, more Swamp Babe.

Back on the tow path she picked up her bag. Somewhere in this pouch of soup were her keys. Taking a big gulp, she tipped it up and managed to lift clear keys, phone and purse before she ran out of breath. Sod everything else. She kicked the bag over the side of the canal and got back to her car just as the first icy drops began to fall.

SHE shivered under the spray – it didn't even make it to watering can standard if you wanted anything warmer than tepid – and knew a shower wouldn't be enough. Not to be really clean. Not when there was a tank of hot water going to waste. Except – she hadn't run a bath, hadn't even touched the taps, since.

As she was rinsing off the fourth lot of shampoo, she noticed she was ankle deep in water and froth and God knows what else. Turning off the flow didn't help. She stretched a toe towards the plug hole and drew back. What it needed was something to poke it free. Not that she could see, from where she was standing, anything apart from, in the mug on the wash basin –

She did only mean to use the handle, except that, when the last couple of lumps had been prodded down, the metal grille could do with a good brush round. She gave the bristles a shake and replaced it, as far away from her own as two mug-sharers could get.

The bath was empty but there was a layer of scum round the bottom. As well as over her feet. And all that hot water just begging...

She wouldn't put the plug in, of course, just swill some water round. A few seconds and it would be done, and maybe she'd manage to get dried before she turned into a block of ice.

There. The tap was on. Scalding her feet. She turned on the other tap and swished hot and cold together, splashing water up her legs, stooping down to swirl the warmth over hands and arms and breasts. She reached for the plug.

So peaceful lying there, lapping water over her skin, dissolving every trace of desecration. Maybe, if she lay there long enough, she would dissolve as well... skin, flesh, bones, liquefied... every trace of her existence obliterated.

She slid her head further down the bath side, letting the water wash over closed eyelids... hair flowing free, face fragmented under a watery veil... her hands drifted away from her, palms upwards, unresisting... to float forever... slipping further, water rippling over mouth... nose... far away the sea gurgling... waves rolling breaking crashing pounding through her head – outside her head. Dear God!

She sat up, spluttering and spitting, groping for the towel. Oliver was back.

IDIOT. She'd been so set on peeling off these filthy clothes she hadn't brought in any clean ones or even her robe. She looked at the screwed up heap. No way could she put them on – God, he'd have the door down any second – but no way could she face him like this, stripped... of power. Twice idiot, to have trusted in unemotional detachment overcoming emotional dominance. These past few weeks, in the tunnels of her mind which surpassed physicality, she'd felt secure. But tonight, as ice burned through skin and sinew, she'd regained awareness of her body, had gained a new awareness as frozen memory liquefied in the bone-aching warmth of the bath. That bolted door now marked her sanctuary. And behind the door was Oliver.

Except – it wasn't that door. The noise was too far off. She edged it open.

The banging was coming from the front door. He must've forgotten his key. Time to dash into the bedroom, pull on pants, bra, jeans – She stopped. A few layers of blended fibres weren't going to be enough. She needed to be armed with plausibility not processed cotton. Keep it simple. She'd been ill. The heap on the bathroom floor was proof enough. Oh, God – the bath. Changing into nightie and robe, but keeping her knickers, Jane pulled out the plug, skip-jumped over the sick pile and made it to the front door – pausing only, on a sudden inspiration, to grab the seven-clove garlic bulb from the kitchen and stuff the whole lot in her mouth – less than twenty seconds after the hammering finally stopped.

As a backup for the sick-story, the garlic being minced in her molars was above and beyond. She'd been gathered into his arms and rocked to and fro several times before her eyes and throat cleared sufficiently for her to realise that the head nestling on her shoulder wasn't Oliver's.

'Thank God, thank God,' over and over.

Finally he drew back, smiled at her, eyes welling. Strange how she seemed to have this effect on Simon.

'I thought, when I found it, by the side of the towpath – your organiser thing, it was all soggy, what with the rain, and I'd been cursing you, leaving me stranded like that, so I chucked it in the canal – and then I saw it, floating there.'

He latched his arms round her again and kissed the top of her head, while her hair weeped silently onto her robe.

'I broke off a branch to get it and when it was just your coat I didn't know whether to laugh or cry,' and even now he was doing both. 'I looked around and found your bag at the edge of the water, caught on a root or something. I'd have just thought it'd been snatched – it was empty, apart from a load of gunge from the canal – if it hadn't been for the coat. I knew it was yours, there couldn't be two like that. But I didn't know – daren't think – what had happened.'

He hugged her closer, so her nose squashed into his collar. She smelled the Simon smell and it was good. A moment later it was obliterated by garlic.

'I searched the car park, running round like crazy, and this bloke asked if everything was okay –'

She breathed garlic, exuded garlic from every pore...

'– and he gave me a lift into town, and I ran all the way here, just in case –'

...could feel garlic seeping into his fleece, through his shirt...

'– and when I saw the lights were on, I had to find out –'

...creeping under his skin...

'– I had to know.'

He locked his hands onto her shoulders and pushed her back, searching her face.

Blinking garlic tears, she stared back, watching a trickle slow-rolling down his cheek. *Thine eyes, sweet lady, have infected mine.* Why had she thought of that?

'It was then I realised,' he was saying, 'after all this time...'

It was ages ago, since she'd learnt the part. As the understudy. What was the next line –

'It's so hard, to put it into words –'

– the one before that speech from twisting Richard, declaring adoration –

'– to tell you how much you mean to me –'

– manipulating truth –

'– because it was your connection with him that stopped me seeing how wonderful you are –'

– oozing more schmaltz than Double Gloucester long past its expiry date.

'You're amazing, so beautiful. Absolutely gorgeous. When I look into your eyes...'

...*sweet lady*... And she remembered. '*Would they were basilisks, to strike thee dead!*' Loud and clear, like it never was in Year 12, waiting wing-clipped in case Lady Anne didn't make it through the first night.

The shrink of pain made Jane look away. She opened her mouth to speak – say something nice to him, for goodness sake, before he starts crying again – then shut it. Closed it tightly, trapping venom breath, scorching throat and tongue, while he unwithered.

He even smiled. 'Oh, Jane, you're so funny.' Pulled her close again.

At last she could unclamp her mouth, exhaling into his fleece, nestling into the fur. She could have stayed there all night, sight and smell and taste shut out, wallowing in the wrap of unconditional Simon arms, the only sound two drumming hearts – and the single slam of the outside security door. Which could be any number of nameless residents.

'Maybe you should –'

But he already had his hands on the latch. He left without a backwards glance, which was just as well because, as the flat door opened once more, the basilisk eyes were sparking and the lolling tongue belched putrefaction into the air.

THERE she was, at her desk, unscarred and undefiled – what the hell was wrong with him last night? He'd come in – surely he must have passed Simon on the stairs – with a Pure New Wool smile, and was into his side of the bed, pyjama cased, in seven minutes flat. Leaving her with nothing more to worry about than whether to bother cleaning her teeth again after she'd crunched the last Polo.

Across the room, Roy was overly engrossed in his What's-not-selling-this-week file. Unless he was chatting to you know who. Jane sighed. It all left a nasty taste in her mouth. She stuck her tongue out in front of the screen. There wasn't enough reflection to see the depth of furriness.

Christian stomped in, banged some sheets on Roy's desk – 'You seen these bloody sales figures?' – and would have noticed if he'd been on Facebook. 'You going sit on your backside the whole day?'

'I've got a valuation later on this afternoon, Temperance Row. You know, behind the Frisky Filly. Used to be the Old Grey Mare, till it had a facelift.'

Christian nodded. 'Tony took instructions for one there last Tuesday. He'll beat you to it if you don't buck your ideas up. He's got a slot there this evening. Best time to view it; they reckon Temperance Row's got more graffiti per square inch than anywhere in town. Don't recommend you include that in the particulars. Or that you leave your car anywhere near. Best bet's to park at the pub. And what about you, girl?' as he moved across, 'You not bloody well switched on yet?' and banged another pile on *La Malheureuse*.

'Actually –' she addressed him mouth to mouth but last night's seven-clove garlic wasn't a match for Christian's standard CO_2 cocktail '– I'm just on my way out.'

'Don't tell me, another Stobb End viewing. You set up some pick-your-own-sheep knocking shop there, or what?'

'What?' seemed to cover it, especially as Tony had just come in with three mugs in his hands. Not that that saved him from the sheet-banging, full in the chest.

'And there'd better,' restomping his footsteps, 'be some decent bloody biscuits today,' followed by a reference, not even borderline pc, to Xanthe as he went out.

'He's not the only one,' said Tony, trying to soak up coffee from his shirt with the sales figures, 'who wishes she hadn't left. How come this has ended up my job, anyway?'

'Because,' said Jane, coming over to take the mug with most left in, 'you do it so well.'

'Jeez, Jane!' Tony took a step back. 'What've you been eating?'

'Sorry.' She shielded her mouth. 'It's from last night. A kind of safeguard.'

'What from – vampires?'

'And other fiends.' She sneaked a glance but Roy was engrossed in memorising two rows of figures that didn't add up. Sod him, was he deliberately not noticing she was ignoring him?

She plonked down the mug and began opening and shutting every drawer in her desk. Several times. Not a flicker, not even when Tony put the second mug on his desk. Ungrateful sod. She click-clacked to the radiator – nice one, wearing these hard heel boots – raised her mug, 'Cheers, Tony,' and flashed him a likely smile.

Tony, sandwich child between sisters, made for the kitchen. He'd seen looks like that before. Would sooner, even knowing there was nothing more than a broken Malted Milk in the tin, face Christian than a spike-eyed female at any time of the month.

As soon as Tony stepped over the metal strip separating polypropylene pile from cracked linoleum, Jane was at her desk, shuffling papers. As soon as Tony closed the door behind him, Roy was at her desk, taking the papers out of her hands.

'About last night –' he said.

She picked up another handful from the blue tray.

'– when you saw me with Xanthe.'

She banged them into some sort of shape.

'It wasn't like it looked.'

Septagonal would do, or was it hept – she was never sure.

'You've got the wrong idea –'

She began stapling the heap together –

'– about what was going on –'

– thumping the stapler again and again, because odd sheets kept falling away, refusing to stay in line.

'Please, Jane.' Roy stilled her hand with his and slid the stapler away. 'Let me explain.'

'There's nothing to explain,' and if Tony had thought her previous smile fearsome, this one would have left his mouth too dry to finish the lick-stick joining of the two sides of the malted cow. 'It's no concern of mine,' pulling out her hand, 'what you get up to.'

'But if you'll just listen a minute –'

She shook her head – this wasn't the moment for practising the one-eyebrow uplift – saying, 'I have appointments to keep, even if you haven't.' Cue for haughty retreat. Which was somewhat spoiled by the seven-sided pile going along too. Taking the mug with it.

The smash and Jane's accompanying 'Oh!' caused Tony, half way up the stairs, to slosh Christian's coffee over the plate of fused biscuit.

The problem was that her blouse had managed to get itself stapled into the heap of papers. Added to which Jane, prising up one of the metal ends, broke a nail. Leaving only nine for scratching out eyes. But after Roy had steered her into a chair and knelt before her, unpicking the necessary staples, it seemed a lot less problematic. And when he'd brought his coffee across and handed it to her, it was no problem at all to share it with him. An activity which, she reflected, with a most unscary smile, was becoming a bit of a habit. By the time backstairs Tony had squashed the two halves of Malted Milk together again, there was very little of the cow visible.

Leaving Christian's office, to the sound of something thumping the back of the door, Tony found the only signs of occupancy in the front office were a cheat's attempt at origami and several fragments of London 2012 pottery on the floor. He put the stapled sheets on Jane's desk – they looked important – and the pieces, after a second's hesitation, in the bin. The mug, he decided, would take more than a bit of spit to mend, even though, petty cash being as empty as the biscuit tin, someone would have to do without in future. And, watching Jane and Roy cross the street side by side, he had a pretty good idea who it would be.

IT wouldn't have been every young man's first choice. Not when he was trying to impress a certain female, now striding ahead over the rough sods. Even if he'd been able to keep up with her – Roy gave a sideways leap as a long-haul container lorry passed within inches – there wasn't enough room on the grass verge to walk alongside. He caught up as she waited at the roundabout.

'The trick is,' said Jane, 'to watch for those lights.' She pointed to the exit on the right. 'Come a bit nearer the edge and you'll see them. As soon as they change you've got half a second flat between the cars going through on red and the others setting off on red and amber. Got it?'

She didn't wait for him to reply but sprinted across pretty nimbly, considering what she had on her feet. Hells bells, the last pair of wellies he'd owned had had frog faces and his name felt-tipped inside.

'Look,' she said. 'This is why I brought you here.'

He looked. The most interesting thing, and it was scraping zero on the zilch to zillion spectrum, was the old farmhouse at the top of this field. Had they been given instructions on it? This was Jane like she was when she'd first joined Up Yours, so keen, so naïve. So pretty. She'd walked through the door that morning and he'd noticed the candle blossom across the street, where the horse chestnut peeped from behind the public bogs, and the spring sunshine making it through *God IZ dAd* scrawled across the outside of the window, dazzling him so that even after Christian had steered her upstairs, hand hovering over her so-pattable bum, he could still see those eyes, so eager... so determined.

She was rattling the gate. 'Those nails – what do you reckon?'

'Well –' He paused. 'Mid to late twentieth century, I should say. Rarely seen in this condition.' Okay, it wasn't that funny but he reckoned it didn't deserve such a look.

'They're not as rusty as you think.'

'Right.' So those daggers weren't targeted at him.

Jane was scraping a key along one of the nails. 'See. Still solid underneath. And there are so many of them. They'd all need sawing through. You can't think of a better way, can you, to get the gate open?'

'Well – no. But that's the point, isn't it? It's meant to be sealed off. I'm surprised they didn't rip this hedge out and put up a post and rail fence when they built the flyover. I suppose they knew no-one in their right mind would think of using this gate. I don't see how anyone could. There's no way in from the roundabout, it's a high verge all along.' Which only intensified the look. If black could get blacker.

Following her along the narrow verge bordering the side of the field was even harder than going, but it was worth it when she stopped. So these were the famous geese.

'Aren't they wonderful?' she said. 'Have you ever seen anything more wonderful?' For one moment those eyes flicked towards him, and he had to admit he never had.

He'd intended to take her arm across the road, but her sudden spurt left him hanging onto her elbow as a van skimmed past, and Jane laughing as he caught his breath. Still, it would be his turn next, when she discovered she couldn't get into the car. And then they'd have a laugh together when he pulled out the key she'd dropped by the gate. But it wouldn't be the last, he was certain, because from now on it was – very odd that she was unlocking the boot, though he could feel the key through his pocket lining, so he double checked, because you could never be really sure, when it came to Jane. And as she drove them back to the office he wondered what the hell all that had been about.

IT was all so strange. No face-to-face confrontation; he seemed to be avoiding eye contact entirely. Asked if she'd had a good day, said he'd bought a couple of ready meals but would she mind warming them up as he had a lot to do.

He didn't even come in to investigate the explosion. Jane opened the microwave door and took out the plastic tray. She scraped out the food still clinging to it – God, you'd have thought he'd have chosen something else for a change, not that there was much mince in evidence – and shoved the next tray onto the spattered turntable, remembering this time to stab the plastic lid. Several times. Five minutes, it said on the cardboard sleeve, in a standard microwave. Better give it seven.

Ignoring the serving suggestion picture, Jane tipped it out on top of the other – they should put the white sauce layer at the bottom if they wanted it to look anything like lasagne – because these individual portions were always hamster-size. Which was why, after taking the minced-up mush through to Oliver, she was going to have the Two Portion Paella she'd picked up all to herself.

BREAKFAST, however, was almost companionable. She watched his lips form syllables which were no doubt getting together to make words, sentences, paragraphs – did people talk in paragraphs? Probably, if the other person – let's call her the listener – didn't do a bit of syllable making in response. His lips had got stuck on a semi-colon; it definitely wasn't a full stop because they were slightly parted, so Jane could see the tips of his incisors. She thought of him squeezing the glo-white paste along his toothbrush. Maybe even flipping shut the top, to keep out germs. She smiled and the semi-colon reinvented itself as a smiley face, and there they sat, all smiles together. Oh, well, she'd heard it took fewer muscles than frowning. But when he placed his lips on hers, and pushed them out and in, she found it took no muscles at all to be absolutely unmoved.

SHE stared at the screen. An email from Roy. *How about we get together for a nibble at lunchtime?* No need to look across.

'Post here yet?' Tony's head and a good portion of neck appeared round the inner door.

Jane glanced towards the letter box. 'There's something on the mat, but it's probably –'

'Only the Free Press,' which he picked up anyway.

Jane's cursor hovered over the options boxes. Tony leaned against the radiator. The cursor lined itself up to Reply.

Tony turned another page. 'Hey, mate, isn't that that girl I saw you with last night?'

Roy looked at him. So did Jane.

'In the Frisky Filly.'

As the punch-line it didn't do it for either of them.

'I was going to come over –'

Roy made for the paper, but Jane snatched it first. She laid the double spread Gossip Page across her keyboard, glanced over the photos, settled on the biggest. Under *Celebration of Region's Talent*, in the *audience of five hundred enthralled guests*, close-up near the bottom right, sat Oliver, in mid-clap, and draped on his left, head turned for the full camera shot, Sophie in – 'My frigging dress!' Her little red number. There was no mistaking it. It was there in black and white.

Tony, leaning over Jane's shoulder, was stabbing Sophie's smiling face with his finger. Which made Jane think she'd quite misjudged him.

'It's definitely the same girl, he said. 'I remember her – face.'

Definitely Sophie. Sophie, filling her place. Filling her dress a damn sight more than she ever did.

'I thought I saw you earlier, when I parked. Couldn't be sure, had to dash off to meet a client. Then when I saw you later on, inside, you were getting on really well. More than really well, really.' He found the undivided attention a bit unnerving, but rather pleasant. 'Which is why I decided not to break it up.' And he beamed at Roy. But it soon became clear he was as likely to get a *Thanks, mate* as he was to receive the asking-price from his client, the lighting on Temperance Row being almost as stark as Jane's eyes. Tony suddenly remembered urgent things to do.

'Jane –'

– ignored him. She tore out the photo and took it to the notice board. There was one spare drawing pin, which surely would do, but no, Jane had to extract the two holding up the picture Roy had put up the other day. She pushed them in, not at each top corner, but both low down, towards the bottom right. Sophie certainly got around. Not only the Troikarena with Oliver, but a not-so-dry run at the Frisky Filly with Roy the same night. Ha, ha, that Supersnoop Tony was there too. Uncle Tom Cobbley as well, she shouldn't wonder.

As she turned, Gertler's going-nowhere horses snickered at her from the floor. Don't forget, they snorted, Roy'd been at the fair with Xanthe the night before that. Sophie wasn't the only one to get around. She ground her heel into the picture. Not so sodding merry now.

Roy glared at his PC. Playing up as usual. Sod all women. Any slip-ups, however small, stored in the memory till the end of time and you never knew when they'd be brought up. But you could be damn sure they would.

Back at her desktop, Jane was scowling. Would she allow an unknown user to make changes? Yet another bloody stupid question. Oozing useless information yet still couldn't think for themselves. Bloody men. Life would be a whole lot simpler without them. She scrolled down. Somehow Roy's email had been deleted.

NO-ONE must see. Jane ducked down low as a car jammed on its brakes at the lights, though it could have gone through. It wasn't as though there was any other traffic about, at this ungodly hour. Probably been drinking, daren't risk a lurking cop car – oh, God, she hoped not. Incapable in charge of a hacksaw was probably thirty-days-without-the-option worse than being four times over the limit. Because there wasn't much evidence of hacking, even though she'd been at it for the last twenty minutes.

She leaned back against the gatepost and shivered. Now that she'd stopped sawing she could feel cold sweat clamming viscose to skin. She tugged her anorak zip the final half inch. Impossible to pretend fibre padding was as warm as polar bear fur, even when it was fake. Impossible not to remember that first time, when he'd fastened it up to her chin, kissing her nose, so the Snow Baby melted in his arms. She wrapped her own around herself, leaning forward on her haunches, rocking. Thought of him, curled up at his side of the bed, maybe stretching out a leg into the coolness at her side, maybe dreaming of her... or of Her? Two-timing, snug bastard, lying in the warmth, lying through his teeth, lying about Her. About Them.

She straightened her spine. She might as well give up. She whammed back against the gatepost. Sod him – she banged her shoulders against the post – sod her – banged again – sod the banging nails – and again – her own stupidity – her own feebleness – her ow-h! She fell back at the last bang as the post broke off.

Scrambling to her feet, Jane could see where it had rotted at ground level. The other must be the same, even though it was still standing, hanging onto the leaning gate by buckled hinges. Yes, when she shoved it, hard, it moved, would have gone over if she hadn't grabbed the falling gate. Working her hands along the top rail, forcing the gate towards her as she moved along to the first post, she managed – and if she'd thought sawing was hard this was time for a rethink, if she'd had any energy left for brain graft – to bring it into line.

By the time Jane had collected enough stones to shore up the post, there was more traffic about. She couldn't risk being discovered either way: messing with the gate or missing without a good conduct pass. Or even a good excuse.

SHE put her weight behind the door as she eased the key. One short bang was best. With a bit of luck he'd just turn over and go on sleeping. She fumbled with her anorak zip. God, she was cold, so cold she hoped he had been spread across the bed, as long as he'd rolled back to his own half. But what the heck, she could sleep on the fridge floor, she was so tired. And was, she admitted to the twenty-seven aspects of Jane in the wall mirror, feeling decidedly smug. The nailed gate problem had solved itself. She sparkled at the crazed glass. Behind her smile, fifty-four blue-steel eyes sparkled back.

He spun her round. 'Where the hell have you been?'

Followed by a sub-zero unbreathing hour-crawling nanosecond long enough for her bones to fossilise as her life ground to ashes before her. So, this was it. His vice grip would snap collarbone and shoulder blades, go on to shatter tibia, fibula, femur, sacrum, sternum, take out the lumbar vertebrae one by one until she crumpled into the carpet, her amoeba-existence seeping through the floorboards, drip-feeding the culture spots of algae under Heather's reindeer skin rug. So what? Let him. Let him smash her skull against the wall, swing her neck until it snapped, shake her till her eardrums burst – She heard the geese cry out as, one by one, their necks were pulled. With open eyes she saw them hanging, wide-beaked and silent. No longer could she feel fingers piercing bone. His hands were not on her flesh but theirs. She felt nothing except the death-screw of twisted skin and feathers...

'Dear God, Jane!' as she gagged and rasped and writhed.

'Dear God, Jane!' as his arms slid round her, keeping her from buckling, getting her to the bedroom. He laid her down, tucking her legs under the covers.

'Ssh,' stroking her hair, 'it's all right, I've got you safe,' kissing her brow, 'everything's going to be all right,' sliding his arms round stiffened shoulders, 'I've been neglecting you lately,' rocking the rigid body. 'So busy at work, this CPF deal – which, I now dare say it, is as good as in the bag. I know you'll be as thrilled about it as I am. I've done it, Jane, made Harry realise once and for all he can't do without me,' and he wrapped her cold-cast torso in a mine-forever hug. 'He's asked us over, Friday night, special invite. You know – Elaine and Harry request the company.'

Of Oliver and corpse.

'Just the pair of us, like we're always going to be, from now on.'

Except, of course, she wasn't. A corpse had that sure and certain hope there was a chance, however slight, of something better to come.

I'm no angel... he took her hand and kissed the fingers in turn.

Was she hearing right? Was he finally going to come clean, ask forgiveness? Was this to be a Fresh Start?

He cleared his throat and said it over, so she was sure. 'I know, angel,' rubbing the back of her hand against his cheek, 'that things have been a bit difficult these past few weeks.'

He lowered the hand and gave her the Intent Look, full face. One of his eyes, the right one, only to her it was his left – the usual problem: people saw things differently – was bloodshot in one corner. She was trying to decide which corner, give it a corresponding compass direction from their opposing viewpoints, while he was, stutteringly for Oliver, going on about her misconstrued perception of reality – well, anyone would stutter over that – since her unfortunate breakdown. Did she realise, by the way, her recovery was down to him? Which made her wonder not only whether SSW was opposite to NNE, but was the annual direct debit to the AA value for money? Maybe it was SWW?

'From now on, things are going to be different. Let's call it a fresh start, shall we?' The bloodshot eye winked. 'I think we should both take a few days off over Christmas, have some quality time together. We could drive over to your parents –' he gave the finger-kissing another shot '– and show off your ring.'

His tongue circled her left-hand third-along, like it had done once before, an aeon ago.

'It's about time we got round to getting one. It'd be a daily reminder of our commitment, if nothing else.'

He squeezed hard, crushing her fingers together.

'Your choice entirely, angel, though a solitaire's obviously the best investment. Platinum's the only metal worth considering, of course. Over a lifetime it won't pick up as many marks and any surface scratches can easily be polished over so they don't show.'

Released from his grip, her fingers remained fused, encircled by a band of drained flesh.

'Apparently they use a ninety-five percent alloy in jewellery, because of its inertness.'

The hand lay on the sheet, disconnected from any part of her.

'See, I've been looking into it, even though I've had so much on. Some people mistake it for silver, but it's obvious to anyone with any nous that it's whiter. In fact, I bet there's nothing you can tell me about it I don't know already.'

Platinum? Pt to its friends. Probably not. Jane watched the colour return to her fingers. Group 10 on the curling periodic table, pinned behind the shelf of test-tube racks and round-bottomed flasks, their round bottoms firmly wedged in ring-necked tripods. Corrosion resistant. Dense and ductile. Atomic number – what was it? She frowned. She used to know.

Oliver smoothed her brow. 'Don't fret, angel.'

Precious and malleable.

'We're going to be fine, trust me.'

So much she'd once been sure of.

'The two of us together, always.'

Now she wasn't certain of anything. Except that, just by the by, she should leave that litre bottle of Martini, if she happened to come across it behind the bread bin. That at least had been made perfectly clear.

'SO that's definite, is it? I don't want to drag us all on a thirty mile detour if you're going to be out clubbing,' or whatever someone who had a life did with it. Diane pulled the door shut at the sound of movement from the lounge. 'You still there, Jane?'

Jane opened one eye to check. 'Yes.' Still there.

'And you'll be in?'

'Yes.' Still in bed, the way she was feeling. 'That is – well, it's not going to be that late, is it?' She checked the time. God, she should be on her way to work by now. 'Won't Stephie be –' even more of a crabby, demanding little sod than usual?

'Oh, she can sleep in tomorrow. She's had so many late nights lately, another's not going to matter. Besides, she's dying to see her Auntie Jane. Did I tell you she's got a pressie list as long as your arm? Not exactly sure what time it'll be, depends on how long it takes him. I couldn't believe it when he said he had a job in your area today. He's just on a call-out then we're setting off.'

'It's still a long way out of your way. Surely Rob'll just want to get home after he's finished work?'

'Oh, Rob won't mind.' Diane reached across to grab hold of the door handle. 'And I can't wait to see your little love nest.' The telephone flex stretched out its curls along the radiator shelf, past the vase of two dozen guaranteed seven days with their lingering aroma of 24-hour petrol and lads-night-out, and across the door frame.

'It's very ordinary.'

'Novelty wearing off a bit, is it? Wait till you're married, then you'll see – yes, Stephie, I know you can't open the door. Talking of which, when are you actually getting engaged? Mum didn't know, said she hadn't heard from you. I think you might ring her every once in a while now you've stopped pretending to be a dropout. Me too, for that matter. Anyway, I told her, it's bound to be Christmas – don't do that, Stephie, you'll mark the paintwork – so we'll see it when you come over.'

'Speak up a bit.' Diane pressed a hand over her left ear and the receiver closer to her right. She was damned if she was going to pay whatever it was a minute to phone a mobile just for silence.

'Have you got one yet? I wish I'd bought mine together. You know, engagement and wedding as a matching pair.' Instead of ending up with two that were somehow never quite right together. 'It's best to choose one in good time, it's bound to need altering. And even if you don't go in for a companion set, get nine carat, same as wedding rings. Otherwise – for goodness sake, Stephie, will you stop scratching the door – they'll rub up against each other and the harder one'll wear out the other one out – oh, you're a little mouse, are you? You've got to know what you want because men never have a clue, do they?'

'Oliver was saying something about platinum,' though she couldn't remember exactly what, or when. Had it just been this morning? Less than two hours of sleep ago. Jane stretched a leg into his half, but it was already cold.

'Platinum? God, you might as well get stainless steel. Don't let him talk you into something you don't want – eek, eek, who's a good little mouse? – it's so dull, so spiritless. Did I tell you about this taster day I went on last Saturday – I might do the class next term – all about achieving inner watzit through these seven windows to the soul – Stephie, stop kicking the fricking door –'

Diane flung it open, yanking the flex to breaking point, and twenty-four nameless blooms hit the dust on the parquet floor.

Jane clicked end call and pulled the duvet over her head.

IT could be worse. Heather Sings the Beatles was, Jane reckoned, at no more than volume 7. Well, it was only half past nine... God, she must get up. It was an effort, but yesterday's clothes were back on, yesterday's makeup touched up. She couldn't face breakfast. Opening the curtains was going to be bad enough. She nudged them back and squinted at the day.

It was overhung with grey. Decidedly murky. She pulled them as far as they would go; maybe the rail just needed dusting. She might even get round to that, though why should she bother or why – was Oliver crossing the road? Because it was him, wasn't it? She peered into the street. Overhung with grey, decidedly murky, definitely Oliver.

Jane stood listening. Despite overplay to the point of driving out every infestation in the block, from the silverfish in the kitchen cupboards to the rats round the wheelie bins, Heather still hadn't got the words off pat.

But when she did chip in no-one within a fifty yard radius could deny her enthusiasm. *Roll up, roll up for the Mystery Tour...* Jane heard the front door bang.

'Jane? You still here?'

...hoping to mmm you away... She heard the bedroom door open –

'Jane?'

– but couldn't see him. Not when she was crouched down in the narrow space between his side of the bed and the window. He seemed to be smoothing the sheets. If he was making it – there was a first time for everything – he'd be round this side any moment. And maybe want to know what she was doing there. She couldn't think of a reason, not even the real one.

An opening drawer. Crouched here sound is everything... *Day after day,* Heather in full warble alone on the hill... *the man with the foolish grin* whistling along and Jane keeping perfectly still. *Nobody wants* – a short blast from the doorbell – *to know him...* another from an aerosol... *he never gives a–* longer ringing, held on through the second squirt and Heather's ten bar *nanswer...*

Something hits the floor and footsteps fade out. Jane watches the deodorant can slow-roll towards her as Heather picks up on *clou-d, the man of a thousand voices talking perfectly l-ou-d-* drowning out the words from the hall.

Strange how even footsteps are recognisable. Those coming into the bedroom weren't Oliver's. At least, the first ones weren't.

'I thought you were making coffee.' The voice was only slightly familiar. But unmistakable.

'Kettle's on, but I thought I'd come and show you, in case you don't know where to put it.'

Behind the bed, Jane cringed. God, that man deserved a knee in the groin. And Sophie was just the girl to give it to him. Although it sounded like she was pushing him towards the door.

'Kitchen. Strong and black, two sweeteners.'

'It'll be the best you've ever had.'

His voice shimmered across the room and glinted on the edge of the deodorant can inches before Jane's nose.

'And you won't need sweeteners, I promise.'

The sole-sweat smell of fifty former tenants drifted up from the carpet and Heather hummed the next line.

'Out.'

Jane heard the door close. And another one open. Muffled rustling, metal wrenched along metal, then nothing beyond the next track seeping up into her groaning knees. She lifted the right one and stretched it back, knocking into something behind. She froze, leg held midair, but the only sound was the twanging of *Blue Jay Way*. She lowered her leg. Heather never did join in the first bit. Jane shuffled forwards and tried easing the left leg. Which only made her elbows ache more. She stretched her neck, found she could just see round the edge of the bed to the open wardrobe.

Saw Sophie standing in front of the door mirror, holding up the polka dot print which Oliver had chosen last summer. It brought out, he'd told her, the colour of her eyes. Now one shoulder slid from the dangling hanger as Sophie considered it from all angles before wrinkling her nose and stuffing it back on the rail. Jane shrank back as the wardrobe door closed and, right on cue, the bedroom door opened.

'Hey,' pushing it shut with his foot, 'look what I've found. Better than coffee, eh?'

The sheet hanging over the side of the bed rose slightly, brushing Jane's ear, as the mattress dipped. Oh, God, he must be sitting on the bed. And any moment, the way the duvet was being patted –

'Come on, or do you enjoy it more standing up?'

257

– they'd both be on it. Both be at it. It would be almost funny if her knees didn't hurt so much, if Heather wasn't giving the chorus full voice. She couldn't bear it much longer. Still... *please don't be long please don't you be very long...* going on his current form...

'I thought,' said Sophie, 'they couldn't spare you for more than half an hour. You were so insistent I came at ten. As if I hadn't got better things to do than traipse round here with that tacky dress. I've got plenty on myself, you know.'

'That can be easily remedied,' accompanied by more bed patting. 'Come on, Sophie, sit down and let's talk about some of those better things we could be doing right now.'

The mattress dipped. For God's sake, couldn't he skip the chat-up, such as it was, and just get on with it? Before her kneecaps disintegrated.

Glass clinked glass.

'Careful,' said Sophie, 'or you'll spill it.'

Don't, thought the ruckled sheet, even think about answering that.

'Do you always manage to fit half a bottle in a glass?'

Which Oliver couldn't let pass. Jane winced at the sheet. It looked as though it might throw up at any moment.

'And don't think I'm getting the bus back, either. Do you know this stuff –'

'Is thirty percent proof? Don't worry, a spot of vigorous exercise and my head'll be clear as a bell.' He tapped the side of his glass.

Which, the sheet couldn't help observing, fell a bit flat, as illustrative sound effects go. Still, it was nice to think he'd given his guest the one without the hairline crack.

'– has 192 calories. An ordinary glass, that is. Whereas this one's bloody enormous.'

'Oh, babe, you bet –'

The sheet sagged a couple of inches as Sophie stood up. 'Thanks for the drink. Forget the lift, I've just remembered something I need to do this side of town.'

This time, the same door did the opening and closing. Those old proverbs didn't get it right every time. Just as well, for the next second a half empty glass hit the jammed shut wardrobe, accompanied by a single short expletive. Which only confirmed the sheet's opinion that Oliver was a man of words rather than action.

JANE staggered to semi-upright. Those pockmarks on her knees could well be permanent. As was the patch where martini had trickled down melamine and soaked into the carpet. And the bit of fabric sticking out from the door was decidedly damp. When Jane opened it the polka dot print slid to the floor. She reached for the hanger, which had got itself tangled with the one holding, not only her old denim dress, but the red hot number, straps slung over the hook. So, it was back.

She unlooped it from the hanger and sniffed the side edges of the bodice. The cow hadn't even washed it. Not that he need think she was ever going to wear it again, but even so... She stretched out the skirt. There was a pale stain down the front. No doubt about it: this was a Monica Lewinsky moment, if ever there was one.

SHE dumped the two dresses over the back of a kitchen chair and checked her phone for the time. It was a bit late now to ring in sick. No missed calls. Maybe nobody had noticed she wasn't there. Surely Roy... Not even a message. Well, she'd make damn sure he noticed her as soon as she got in. Jane picked up her stuff, cupping bag under armpit and wedging a couple of folders between chin and shoulder as she opened the front door.

And in strode Sophie, stepping over the scattering papers as she swept across the hall into the kitchen.

She sat down. 'We might as well finish this off.' Sophie tapped the martini bottle in front of her. 'Where are the glasses?'

Well, we did keep a pair of brandy snifters in here for everyday, but, guess what, they're a pair no longer. 'I could get some from the lounge.'

'Don't bother.' Sophie picked up two mugs from the draining board. They were a bit stained, especially the one with the teddy bear inside it, but she'd make sure Jane got that one. 'These'll do.'

Sophie filled them up to the brim and slid one across the table, skirting round an opened packet of chocolate coated peanuts. Jane sat down.

Sophie lifted her mug. Oliver's mug, to be precise.

'Za vashy, zoo dryee.' Sophie took a sip. 'It's the Russian equivalent of bottoms up. One of the things this guy from Murmansk taught me. You know any good toasts?'

'Only Cheerio.'

'Here's another. Bread, eggs and syrup – that's French toast.' Sophie smiled. 'You know, you might well have pulled it off, if I hadn't seen you through the wardrobe mirror. That dress with the spots on, by the by, is okay except for the neckline.'

Jane picked up her mug and didn't put it down again until the bear was safe from drowning.

'Okay, I know I don't really need to ask but –' Sophie put down her mug '– it was a set-up, wasn't it? You and him, in it together.'

The only thing to do, when you'd no idea what was going on, was to keep sipping.

'Not letting on, eh?' Sophie twirled the mug round, watching Jane through narrow eyes. 'You're a bit of a doodah, aren't you? A dark horse.' A trickle of martini skirted round a brown teardrop congealed on the side of the mug, where Oliver had dribbled his morning coffee. 'There's a lot more to you than you let on.'

Behind her mug, the dark horse wasn't letting on at all.

'Besides,' Sophie yanked out a bit of the polka dot dress from under the seething red, 'spots make you look fat. Don't you think?'

'Maybe.' Had she had an opinion about spots since she was fifteen? 'Actually, if you really want to know, Oliver said –'

'For God's sake, tell me!'

'Well, as far as I can remember, he said it looked good. Especially –' Jane drained her mug '– the neckline.'

'Stop going on about the frigging dress, will you? You know what I'm talking about. Where was it leading, a threesome? Or –' Sophie's eyes narrowed '– something altogether more dodgy? There again, maybe –' she scratched at the side of the mug '– he wasn't in on it at all. That's it, isn't it?' Sophie flicked the brown teardrop into the air. 'I should have suspected something funny was going on when he came round with that.' She nodded at the red number, blushing coyly on the back of the chair. 'All that twaddle about you laid up with a migraine. As if you'd send him round with a dress like that, for God's sake.'

The dress squirmed self-consciously.

'I honestly thought – call me innocent if you like – he was just playing away, so, as it sounded like a good night…'

The red number, innocent that it was, shrugged, making no attempt to hide its stain.

'Fell for it like a sucker, didn't I? The way he told it, sounded like it was him lined up for a gong, instead of us just being in the audience. The food was top notch, though

– show me a crème brûlée and I'm anybody's.' She nodded at the dress. 'I expect it'll wash out. That biological stuff works every time.' Sophie sloshed martini into both mugs, holding the bottle up to drain.

As the last drip hung from the neck, Jane had a feeling there was something she ought to remember. The drip gave up the struggle. As it dropped into Oliver's mug, she said, 'I think there are some olibs in the cupboard.' Because it seemed easier to go along with the drip, now sloshed with the rest of the martini in Oliver's mug.

'Olibs?'

'Mmm, green olibs.' Easy peasy to pretend. She'd been drunk enough times to know how to be. The hard thing was being Jane. Because she hadn't ever been Jane, not for real. 'Somewhere in here...' She managed to extricate the jar without knocking over anything else, though she had a couple of goes with the soy sauce bottle, for Sophie's benefit. Had Jane actually existed outside the fabrication of others? She took off the lid and plonked the jar on the table.

Sophie shook her head. 'No sticks.'

'It's true,' said Jane, poking a finger into the jar, 'that you appear to be sticklickly challenged. Completely lacking in pointy things. In fact, anyone would agree you're absolutely stickless.'

'Speak for yourself,' said Sophie. Because the silly cow just didn't know how to take it. Whereas – God, how many had she had the other night? Not just with Oli, but before that, with that other guy... 'Hey, I picked this up the other night.' Sophie rummaged in her bag and took out a cocktail parasol. 'There's a little horse on each panel, so when you open and shut it they go up and down like one of those oldy worldy rides. And when you twirl it round – like this – their tails fly out.'

'What does it say?' asked Jane.

'It doesn't neigh, if that's what you mean.' Or have flashing lights, for God's sake. 'It was only stuck in a drink. You know that theme pub opposite the tip. The sign on the ladies is Fillies, and the gents is –'

'There, on their necks.' Jane stretched across to pick up a biro from the worktop and pointed at the parasol. 'Little medallions with letters on.'

'Oh, that.' Sophie laughed. 'It's supposed to spell out my name as the horses go round. He wrote them on – this well fit guy I was with. Six horses, so it should have worked out.'

Jane was concentrating hard... lining up the nib for some serious olive stabbing, working out what was going on... or, more to the point – she jabbed the pen straight down – what had been going on, the other night. She jabbed again, determined to make no allowances whatsoever for refraction.

'I met him in the car park. Thought he was nicking Simon's precious Cortina, because his key could unlock it. Funny that.' Sophie twirled the parasol. 'He spelt it with an F, the idiot, so he put an X in the last space. That's what he was like.'

Liquid slopped from jar to table as Jane skewered an olive.

'I couldn't stay for more than a couple, of course, because of this Oliver thing.' Sophie wiped up the puddle with the hem of the drop dead red. 'I thought of not showing up, but I'm not that sort of girl.'

'Have an olib.' Jane dunked it, still impaled, in Sophie's mug.

Sophie pulled out the biro and dropped it on the table. 'Is it stoned?'

'Absolutely.'

'I really only like them stuffed.'

Jane reached for the packet of peanuts and shook a few out. 'Feel free –' she flicked one towards Sophie '– to stuff your own,' hitting her mug with a ping.

Sophie pushed the mug away. 'I've had enough.' She stood up.

'Don't go without this.' Jane spun the parasol round. 'You never know when it'll come in handy.' If you forget your name, for instance.

'Keep it,' said Sophie. 'I'm off to the real fair tonight.'

'Have fun.' The stick snapped as Jane stabbed the parasol's point into the peanut.

'I intend to.' And without blowing so much as an X, out breezed Sofie.

Jane squashed the galloping horses into the bottom of Oliver's half empty mug, prodding them with the broken stick until the letters were nothing but mush.

THE grey morning had become greyer. By the time Jane crossed the road, two black coffees later, large flakes were falling. Someone had upended a ready meal on the edge of Festina's roof but it was snowing too fast to do anything other than get in the car. Snow was settling on the bonnet as she joined the main road. Good. Enjoy the fair, Sophie.

She stopped smirfing when Festina's back end skidded across where the white lines would have been if you could see anything in this blizzard, even with the wipers on fast speed, spreading a sludge of Oriental spices and European additives across the glass. There was such a ridge of saffron mush at the bottom of the windscreen, the wipers could no longer manage a full sweep. At least there wasn't much traffic about. As far as she could see.

She eased down the brake pedal as she approached the roundabout. The side window was too snow-spattered to see through. She wound it down a few inches. Snow pelted her face and into the car. The field was a haze of driving snow; the top of her anorak sleeve was coated white. Just the kind of weather that would have shown Snow Baby up in her true colours. Jane began winding up the window. The handle creaked and scraped, taking so much effort she almost missed the haze of whiteness moving across the blur that once was field. She forced the window down again and peered out.

White on white. Was it a mirage? How could you tell? The pupils let in as much as they considered necessary, the rods and cones could be relied on to do their double act but as soon as the brain got involved, things went haywire. Not satisfied with mere image-flipping, it had this compulsion to fill in the blind spots with whatever came to mind. Which made your perception as skewed as everyone else's. And your life as screwed up. Her life, it seemed, could not be unscrewed.

She shrugged, and the snow wrinkled along the folds of her sleeve. Other lives, at least, were fixable. For what came to mind, seeing those flecks of could-be orange, was geese. Was it an illusion of bodiless beaks and feet, or the after-image of compacted vindaloo? The geese were, after all, just as likely to be tucked up safely in the ark. There again, were they really anywhere, as visual entities, when no-one could see them? Apparently the unheard tree makes no sound as it falls. So does one life depend on another to recognise its existence for it to exist at all?

Was it impossible to be an independent being? Impossible to shake off the shackles of individual pre-determined devices and desires, never mind the collective done and not done thought-word-deed transgressions since man first chipped breasts and vulval lips into a lump of rock and called her god?

Jane looked into the grey-shroud sky, greyness closing in and the nowhere sun a nano-speck further away than yesterday. Newton might as well have tossed the apple on the compost heap, for all the chance of her escaping the domination of a certain dark energy. Eve had it sussed. Freedom was as unrealistic as any other abstraction in this concrete world. But, if the universe was expanding faster than the speed of light, was it asking too much to want a bit of space?

Chapter Four

'IS it snowing?'

Jane eyed him narrowly. Tony, she decided, didn't do sarcastic.

'Just a bit.' She felt the radiator, to check it was worth draping her socks over the top and lining up her shoes underneath. She considered hanging her trousers over it as well; Tony probably wouldn't notice. Roy would. And Christian.

Right, she'd managed to get here, so where was everyone? Roy, for instance. Not that she was interested. She rubbed her soles on the back of her legs. 'Where's Roy?'

'He's around somewhere. Come on, send.' He quadruple clicked the mouse. 'I'll literally be two seconds.' He shook the mouse and banged it on the mat a couple of times. 'Roy said you wouldn't mind.'

Very generous of him. She scowled as he began poking the underside. 'Tony, you're rattling my mouse.'

'Is this one of those you unscrew to clean it?'

Jane cupped her hand over his and forced it down. 'Stop fiddling with my mouse's private parts, will you?'

'Oi, Jane! You're dripping all over my papers.' He looked up at her. 'Hey, what do you look like? Your face is all blotchy, your hair's stuck to your scalp and –'

'You know your problem, Tony?' She leaned over and switched off the computer. 'You've just crashed.'

'Oh.' That was all. No that-took-me-half-an-hour-to-write-you-bitch.

'Sorry, Tony.'

Not even an if-looks-could-kill look.

'You can swear at me if it'll make you feel better,' she said, because it would definitely make her feel better. She tried a laugh. He didn't move. Which made her want to shake him. Instead she patted his shoulder. 'I really am sorry,' because she was. 'It was unforgivable.' Not that he need think she didn't expect to be forgiven, preferably within the next three minutes.

What, thought Tony, was she after? Such wheedling brought back not-distant-enough recollections of parent bamboozling, concocting false alibis – for which he always ended up getting the rap – or, at the least, supplying a 4am taxi-service for sisters on the loose. And there was nothing, he well knew, more ungrateful, more unpredictable. More illogical. How, for instance, did Jane think that sliding her arm round his shoulder was going to make him feel better? Aside from losing the Balkowski-MacBride details, snow melting down the back of his neck wasn't adding one iota to the joy of being here. He knew the place Life had allotted him. And wished he was there right now. Instead, her hold on him inexplicably tightened – he could feel the dampness seeping through his jumper – so there was no chance of fleeing to the back office. Especially now she was rubbing her head against his – her hair dripped down the front of his shirt – somehow completely unaware that Roy had just walked in and was standing behind her desk.

'Hi there, mate,' said Tony. If only she would get her face out of his hair. 'How're you doing?'

'I think I've fixed your problem.' Roy drummed his fingers along the top of Jane's computer. 'Don't tell me this one's out of action now.'

'No, Jane switched it off. Sort of accidentally.'

'And you've been very sweet about it,' said Jane, moving her head slightly so she could, if she opened her eyes, see Roy's face. If she happened to want to. 'Dear Tony, always so dependable.'

Dear Tony squirmed. At least, thank God, she'd lifted up her head now. 'Well, I'll get back to it then.' Except he couldn't. 'Got quite a bit to do.'

The arm continued its hold.

'Glad someone has,' said Roy. He moved to his own desk and began paper shuffling.

Which made the Tony-clinch a bit pointless.

'I'll have mine black today, please, Tony,' she called after him but the door to the back office had already shut.

'You've missed coffee,' said Roy.

She was occupied with the usual tussle with the anorak zip. Maybe, if she didn't force it too much... 'My zip seems to have...' he'd come over and help. She glanced across as he reached for another heap and the pull slid down. '... come unstuck.'

He screwed up his eyes when she began shaking the coat right next to his desk. He could feel water spattering his face, could smell her nearness... Roy and Jane, standing close in the shower, Jane and Roy, within a skin-touch, breath on breath... The damp edge of the coat caught his nose with an upwards lick, and flicked his cheek with its flapping ears, and a stub-tailed terrier straight from the stream shook itself over him. Billy Bones with his rabbit-sharp nose and a black patch over one eye, Billy and Roy, romping together through summer days he'd thought would never end...

Jane caught a finger in the neck loop and trailed the anorak through the door.

Idiot to believe things went on for ever. Roy watched the handle go down and back up, then – did it begin to go down again? He couldn't be sure. Idiot to believe things could ever be different.

In the passage, Jane's hand hesitated on the handle. Then she turned to the row of hooks along the wall between the back office and the toilet, making Tony's guaranteed 100% waterproof share a peg with Christian's mock Barber so her coat could have one all to itself at the end. It was soaked through. She spread out the sleeves, hitching one cuff behind the framed instructions in the event of fire. The other she tried to drape across the next coat along, the two-tone parka, but it kept dropping back.

She rubbed the mirror above the wash basin, moving her head to the place where the mottled glass managed a reflection. And moved it back. She unearthed the pot of Swirling Smoke eye shadow which brought out, the girl in Boots had assured her and did she know there was a fantastic offer on if she bought two, the colour of her eyes. She smeared some on the left eyelid. Not today it didn't. Maybe she should have got the half-price Carmine Tinge as a stand-by for mornings like this. She'd just dipped in, to match up the second lid as best she could in the dingy passage, when she heard a creaking noise. Finger loaded, she watched the door handle go down.

The door opened just enough for Roy's head to appear.

'There's someone asking for you. Looks like he's come all the way from Tibet specially,' he said, unaware of the smudge of smoke swirling down his jumper as she followed him into the front office.

'Sorry,' said Jane. 'I don't think I know you.' Because she didn't, not at first.

'These Yetis,' muttered Roy, shaking his head. 'They all look the same.' He reshuffled the paper pile, feeling a certain satisfaction when the stranger shook down his hood and brushed off his sleeves within spattering distance of Jane. The feeling didn't last. She was giving the newcomer a way too big smile. As the guy was only covered in snow and half frozen to death, for God's sake, she seemed unnecessarily concerned.

'Let me help you off with your coat. Has it gone through? You must have been out in it for ages.'

Apparently, despite standing over half an hour, no bus had showed up.

'Wouldn't your car start –' Jane stopped. 'You don't have a spare key, then.'

Simon shook his head. 'Sophie's still got it.'

Roy flinched, although he was out of spattering range.

'So,' said Simon, 'I've come round here to get mine back. I nearly came round to the flat. But I remembered last time.'

Jane remembered too. Standing in the hall, snuggled into Simon's chest, breathing garlic into his camel fleece... She held it now at arm's length, ice cold and stiff with snow.

'I could,' she said, 'put it on the radiator.' But it wouldn't do any good. Might as well admit it. 'The thing is, I seem to have temporarily mislaid your key. It must have dropped out of my pocket somewhere.'

Roy, giving the papers a third sorting, could have told her exactly where. If she'd asked. If she was even aware he was in the room. But no, she was too busy telling this jerk how sorry she was, how she was sure it would turn up. He banged the papers together. Not unless he could get her to frisk him it wouldn't.

'In the meantime,' she was saying, 'I can take you anywhere you want to go. Just say and I'm all yours,' and she was so smiling at the jerk she didn't notice Roy opening the passage door.

He looked along the coats. There was her anorak, at the end of the row, one sleeve stuffed behind the Fire and/or Nuclear Attack directions. *All employees should ensure they are familiar...* She never seemed to wear that white furry thing anymore. Maybe she'd ditched it. She'd said the Oilrag had bought it for her; maybe this was leading up to ditching him. The other sleeve, he noticed, was tucked into the pocket of his parka. He pushed it further in. Why was it taking her so long? Most women chucked out what they didn't want without a second thought.

He took the key from his trouser pocket. If he slipped it into the anorak pocket, there'd be no need for her to go. He held the key in his hand, wondering, when Jane came in. She reached up for her coat.

'Surely you're not going out?'

For a moment the anorak resisted, clinging on to the parka with one arm and the glass-fronted notice with the other.

'You can't show anyone round in this. Or are mortgages available on igloos now?'

Something about frozen assets flipped into mind, and out again. 'I'm just giving him a lift.'

The left sleeve slid out of Roy's pocket.

'I lost his car key – I just happened to have it. It's a –' bit complicated '– Cortina, so I hope he can get a replacement.'

The right sleeve dropped, bringing the correct safety procedure down with it.

'But maybe it's not possible –' to get past you without having to ask. Jane stepped over the cracked glass. 'Excuse me.'

Roy opened the door and stood back, making a little bow as she went past. He watched her take Festina's keys from her bag and shake them in front of the jerk's stupid smiling face as she asked him where he'd like her to take him.

So, this loser, now steadying Jane through the snow, was the one sexy Sophie had dumped. Not surprising: that girl could have anyone she cared to flash her eyes at.

Or any other body part. But what did the jerk want with Jane? Bloody stupid question. Why did she go for these bastards, instead of someone who appreciated her inner beauty? God, he'd be writing poetry next. There must be loads of words that rhymed with Jane, like pain... and – Roy smiled – scatterbrain. And... but he could only think of plain, which she definitely wasn't. Not in the same way as Sophie wasn't, of course. He smiled again. It had been quite a night – well, evening: they'd said goodbyes, and such, outside the Frisky Filly, though he sort of thought she wouldn't have taken much persuading, because abstain didn't rhyme with Soph at all. Maybe another time... like tonight. If it kept on snowing, the obvious thing to do would be skip the fair and settle for a cosy night in.

He stuck his head out the front door. There was no sign of it stopping. Or of Jane and the jerk, not even their footprints. So there was no way of knowing which way they'd gone.

SIMON didn't want to call round at Sophie's, though, yes, he did know it was her day off. Forget the spare key, he told Jane. He needed to go to Brailsfords.

'Some unfinished business?'

'Something like that.'

Jane waited in the car while Simon went in. She wound down the window and tried to catch a snowflake with her tongue. It was all so beautiful, even here, behind the office and next door's restaurant. Everything smothered in a hush of white. A half-grown cat was picking its way along a wall, brushing snow off with its tail. It leapt down onto a wheelie-bin, slithering into a splat of soft meringue. Another leap and it was scrambling among formless mounds below the bin, then, nose set, tail held high, it step-trod round the corner without a backwards glance. Somewhere there was the sound of shattering glass.

Next moment Simon came into view, leaving craters as he ran, bringing the winter wonderland into the car with him. Some of it anyway.

He slammed the door, grinning. 'Let's go.' A tyre spun – 'Shove her into reverse, then ease off' – and Festina kept her grip.

So by the time Oliver had recovered sufficiently to pick up the brick from his desk and go to the window, what was left of it, all there was to see was Jane's car zigzagging out of the car park.

THE place was a mess. How could it have got so bad in just a few weeks? Just a few weeks, from wall-to-wall bliss to – what was it now? Dystopia? Except it wasn't. Dystopia came clean, none of this posturing as paradise. Whereas their existence together – it could hardly be called a relationship – was all pretence. And no-one was striving more to promote the romance than Oliver. In many ways he was more attentive – more affectionate, given half the chance – than before. Before, it had – so it seemed now – been all down to her. Faking it every time. Had the balance of power – back in Before, she hadn't realised there was a balance of power – shifted? Di would be able to tell. God, she must tidy up before her sister got here.

She began picking up things from the floor. Apart from Then, apart from that one night, he'd been caring and considerate, on the whole. So maybe, when he hadn't been, it had been her fault. Maybe Then was all her fault. She pushed back the sofa. Checking to see what's underneath was the sort of thing Di would think of doing. Jane tried not to. Had tried to block Then out so deliberately that it hardly existed in remembrance, like a dream which was reality for a few moments on waking, before slipping away from conscious thought. Unless now was the dream.

From the patch of crumbs and dust something glinted. She picked up it up. Did memory exist in dreams? Because she could remember yanking off this bit of frippery, flinging it across the floor. Remembered when he'd first fastened the locket round her neck.

She heard his key in the latch.

Now the chain was broken. But inside the heart – she prised it open – there was still his smiling face. And next to it, herself looking back...

The locket snapped shut as her wrist was seized in a vice grip. He spun her round, twisting her hand back till the fingers unfurled.

'What was all that about?'

The locket slid to the floor.

'What the hell did you think you were playing at?'

Had he let go? Her hand could be severed, lying bloodless alongside the locket. Or maybe he still held it. She couldn't feel anything, couldn't shift her gaze to see. Her eyes were transfixed by his – not both of his, not at this distance, but engulfed in one shimmering cyclopsian orb, azure as a cloudless summer sky... and out of it, swooping towards her, a microscopic pin prick on great black wings, slow-flapping unflinchingly nearer –

'Auntie Jane!' and Stephie was whirling into the room with Di – 'The front door was wide open' – behind her followed by Rob – 'You didn't tell me it was on the third floor' – lugging a Moses basket and an armful of bags.

In the blink of an eye the crow was gone.

'SO, this is it.' All, thought Di, much as she'd expected. She'd seen it all before.

Jane was seeing it for the first time. But it wasn't just the dirt on the worktop, knife scored and branded with burnt-pan rings; it wasn't the unidentifiable khakiness oozing under the dropped hinge door of the end off-the-wall cupboard; nor was it the curled edge summer-of-love photos, leaving snail trails of sagging Blutak above the socks on the radiator, or even –

'What's this, Auntie Jane?' for, scooped from under the radiator, behind where the tap was weeping brown water through a knotted handkerchief, was – 'A furry ring! Is it a bracelet for a hamster?' Stephie held out her palm. 'Can I take it home for Humbert?'

'Don't be silly.' Di said. 'It's nothing but a greasy old ring-pull with dust stuck to it. It's anyone's guess how long it's been there.'

But Jane knew exactly. She looked across the lino pattern of black and yellow tiles, no different today – if you ignored the change of surface grime – than when they'd first moved in. Only a layer of dirt separating now from long before, when he'd challenged her to a game of forfeit draughts. They'd lined up their chosen cans, savoury facing sweet. And when, with the loss of T-shirt and jeans, she'd nobbled his baked beans with sausages and one of his chopped tomatoes, and he'd taken her pineapple rings, pear halves and all her fruit salad in natural juice, so she was down to her peach-skin, he finally made it to the far wall and declared the white wine sauce king. One by one he took the rest of her pieces, before peeling back the lid and smearing sauce –

'Stephie, don't lick it off! Let me wipe your hand.'

But Stephie, pausing only to hang the ring-pull on the oven timer's knob, raced out.

Okay, she'd let things slide recently – Jane muttered something about busy at work – but had it, any of it, ever been anything other than tacky?

'And to think,' said Di, 'you were always the tidy one. Careful, Stephie!' as the door slammed back, as far as the 300mm wide cupboard jutting from an eleven-inch wall would allow.

Stephie's face glowed as she came back in. 'Mummy, isn't this the superest house ever!' and for a last brief moment it sparkled magic. 'Oh, and Daddy said to tell you Helen's poohed on the carpet.'

YET while Di was telling Rob he should have brought the changing mat up, like she'd told him, and he was telling her he couldn't have carried another sodding thing, as he'd told her, the carpet leasers exchanged, if not exactly smiles, then looks bordering on camaraderie.

'You didn't,' Oliver hissed, but not viperishly, 'tell me they were coming.'

'I didn't, no.'

Then Oliver surprised everyone by fetching a bowl of soapy water, kitchen roll and a bottle of Dettol Jane didn't even know they had. And somehow, because Di was busy working on the carpet and Rob was busy dealing with the dirty nappy and Jane made herself busy searching for another plastic carrier – an aroma like that needed to be double wrapped, before committal to the communal bins; even rats have standards – Oliver ended up holding the baby. Which surprised everyone even more.

'Tell you what mate,' Rob said, when they were sitting down, three squashed onto the sofa, Oliver with his arms full in the armchair, 'you've either had a lot of practice or else you're a natural. Don't you agree, girls?'

Which definitely would have led to an exchange of looks, if Jane hadn't been so determinedly avoiding her sister's eye. It only needed Stephie to climb on Oliver's knee and he'd be in the running for first prize in any shaved Jesus look-alike contest this side of the Atlantic. A dress rehearsal for the second coming laid on especially for the entertainment of the guests. As host, Oliver could not be faulted.

So it didn't surprise anyone when Di started on about the 'imminent engagement,' for which, she said, a strategic plan was necessary. It was so easy, she said, to end up dissatisfied.

Thus the gold versus platinum got another airing and even Rob chipped in when it looked like the smarmer was winning Di round. Otherwise, he was pretty sure, she'd be wanting an upgrade. On the ring at the very least. Rob tapped his watch. It wasn't, he decided, even worth asking if they'd got Sky.

Jane was almost glad when Stephie stood up, demanding a drink.

'IS this where you sit, Auntie Jane? 'Cos the chair's a bit wobbly.'

'No. I usually sit on this one near the radiator,' which sounded like a straw-grasp at luxury in the shabbiness of life, the universe and whatever else it was that had once mattered.

Stephie changed seats. 'Oh, I know why. It's because you can see the fridge door, isn't it?'

They said it took someone else to point out your blessings.

'But –' Stephie paused.

Jane waited. There was always a but.

'– why haven't you got any maghetti lettuce?'

So that was it. The answer could have been staring her in the face all this time.

'If only you had some,' Stephie said, 'I could've shown you now. What a pity...'

...it wasn't possible for the Ultimate Question and the Ultimate Answer to be known in the same universe.

'Mummy's got some on her fridge.'

Or even in the same kitchen.

'So has Kayleigh's Mummy, my bestest friend. So has Willow's Mummy. So has Destiny's Mummy, who's got the key to the big cupboard at playgroup.'

All these women who had the answer. But did it make them happy? Wasn't it better not to know, to go on believing what you had was as near paradise as you were going to get, short of being six feet under? Or was living next door to Nirvana no more satisfying than shacking up at number 2b Inferno Way?

'I wish you'd got some!' Stephie kicked the table leg. 'It's not fair!'

Once you'd become so caught up in passion to abandon all reason, nothing was ever enough. Whatever you had –

'Thank you' (because Auntie Jane was scowling) 'for my drink but –'

– you wanted more.

'– can't I have a biscuit as well?'

The door slammed a non-resounding 'No!' as Diane came in and the edge of the wall cupboard notched up its forty-third hit that week. 'It'll spoil your meal.' She glanced round the room and gave Jane her one-raised-eyebrow party piece. 'What're you planning on doing?'

What was she planning on doing? Jane mouthed the words. Maybe this was the Ultimate Question. She was just letting things drift along, no matter how bad they were, instead of doing anything –

'About supper?' Di said, because up-market Jano – that was a laugh, the state of this flat, she couldn't wait to tell her mother – probably didn't call it tea any more. 'Stephie gets a bit grouchy if we eat late.'

Of course. They expected to be fed. 'Sorry, I've just got in from work. I intended to shop at lunchtime but it's been one of those days...' One of those days that started with inflicting criminal damage on a defenceless gate, progressed to a restricted view performance of Partner Trying to Pull before a martini breakfast with the prima donna, followed by playing getaway driver to the lovelorn ex – what exactly had Simon been doing at Brailsfords? Just one of those days, when a wintersworth of weather decides to get it all over with at once '...what with the snow and everything.'

'It doesn't matter.'

Thank God. They would be off soon.

'We'll just make do with whatever you've got in.'

Jane tried to remember what was inside the fridge. Decided it was, like the outside, lacking in the essentials. Not a single maghetti lettuce leaf limping around the salad drawer. There'd be no hiding the fact from Di, who was already frisking the cupboards for plates.

'Anything'll do,' said Di. 'The main thing is – I hope we can have it soon.'

'Abandon hope,' Jane announced – the only thing to do was make a joke of it – 'all ye who enter here,' and pray that Di and the Grouch would see the funny side. Because she was damned if she could. 'Should have that on the wall in letters two foot high. Because I seem to have run out of just about everything.' The accompanying laugh did its best and managed eight seconds as a solo act.

'If,' said Groucho, 'you had maghetti lettuce you could put it on the fridge. That's what Mummy does when she runs out of – those things you said, bandahopes, so she remembers to buy some more.' She finished her drink. 'What is a bandahope, Mummy?'

'It's another name for an engagement ring, sweetheart,' Di said. 'Talking of which –'

Oh, please let's not. 'I'll see what I can rustle up.' Jane opened the fridge. There must be something in here, among the accumulation of gunge-rimmed jars of jam, pesto and Chicken-two-nights-last-Thursday, that was vaguely edible. She didn't mind a coating of black spot fur, or even a suspect discharge. All it had to be was there.

'Oliver seems pretty keen. It all goes to show –' Diane looked over Jane's shoulder into the fridge '– he hasn't very high standards, has he?' and she laughed.

A couple of minutes after cue, in Jane's opinion. Not that Di had ever been so short of opinions she needed anyone else's. Or did she rely on a fridge message, in four plastic colours, to get some more in when stocks were low?

'I reckon you'll need a shovel to defrost that.'

'Let me look.' Stephie pushed her head between mother and aunt and gasped. 'Oh, Mummy! Isn't it wonderful? Auntie Jane's got her own baby snowman.' And her crossness at the lack of maghetti lettuce quite melted away.

'UNCLOLIVER...'

Stephie ran the words together in a way that didn't seem to irritate him at all. In fact, he was being totally nice. Di and Rob couldn't fail to be taken in by it. Oliver was a totally nice guy.

'...you do believe in Father Christmas, don't you?'

'Course I do. He's not going to bring you any presents if you don't believe in him, is he? Have you sent him a letter to tell him what you want?'

'Not yet. Mummy says –'

'Don't leave it too long. Otherwise he might have run out of what you want and all you'll find in your stocking on Christmas morning will be a... smelly old sock.'

'Then you'd have a pair,' Rob said. 'A useful present.' He eyed Di. 'So I'm always being told.'

'Daddy! Socks are boring. Socks are what daddies get. I want –'

'Why don't you do that letter now?' Oliver said. 'Just to make sure. Look – there's some paper and a pen on top of the desk.'

Jane smiled. Don't think you're going to get rid of her that easily, Unk.

Stephie wriggled beside him in the armchair and held out the pen. 'I'll say what to put and you write it.'

'But he won't know who it's from if I do it. Then all your presents will come here.'

'No they won't, will they, Daddy?'

'No chance,' said Rob. 'Not when there isn't a chimney. Shame that,' when the flat roof would have made such a good landing pad.

Stephie looked at the gas fire. 'Won't you get any presents?'

'Of course they will,' Di said. She didn't want these questions hanging over till tomorrow, when Stephie might start wondering about their own fire, albeit living flame with a tile surround and a mantlepiece of polished cherry, or whatever it was. The whole thing was make believe, anyway.

'But if Father Christmas can't get in, you won't get any presents.' Stephie studied his face. Uncloliver didn't look in the least bit upset. But then he'd only be getting socks, whereas – 'Poor Auntie Jane.'

'Tell you what, Stephie,' in a loud whisper. 'I'll make sure Auntie Jane gets lots of presents, in case Father Christmas doesn't manage it.'

'Lots and lots of presents?'

'Sackfuls. And one of them's going to be very special.'

'What is it?' Stephie hissed in his ear.

Hissed, Jane hoped, damply.

He put his finger to his lips. 'It's a surprise.'

Stephanie looked across at the grown-ups wedged on the sofa, her eyes sparkling like...

...big diamond solitaires. Not, thought Di, that it would be much of a surprise to see Jane flashing one around when they came over at Christmas. She could picture it now, bloody enormous and gleaming like...

...glazed skin basted in its own juices. Jane's eyes narrowed. Oozing tarragon and brandy, lying on a bed of roasted roots dripping honey. Dream on, Loliver. Your big surprise is about to backfire. A few days from now, when you go to collect your trussed up carcass, you won't be looking as smug as you are now. Sitting there, trowelling on the charm, as though he's...

...God, he was looking at her like she was – Di blushed. Something she hadn't done for a long time. That look – it made her feel... She shook herself. She would go into the kitchen, like a good milch cow. Away from that look.

'THE way I see it,' Di said, plugging the baby onto whichever teat – whether it was left or right's turn to bear the brunt had completely gone out of her head – 'Oliver's one of those guys it's better to get to know. First impressions can often be wrong, don't you think?'

The dirty knives rattled in the washing-up bowl as Jane turned the tap on full.

'Are you comfortable like that?' Jane said, without turning round. 'I could fetch you a cushion.' Except that would involve going back in the lounge.

'It's okay.' Di wangled another chair round with her feet and put them up. 'You don't mind, do you?' Not that she had any intention of removing them. But asking always gave you the upper hand. Because out of politeness – she was the guest here, for God's sake – Jane had to say...

'Feel free.' It was what visitors did, the female ones anyway. Whereas when males called round... but why had Simon come to the office? Why wait until now if he only had one set of keys? Why did it matter, when nothing mattered except –

'Christmas dinner's going to be mammoth.'

'That'll make a change,' Jane said, dunking the rest of the cutlery.

'Yes, I know it's always scoff-at-the-trough but the bird seems to get bigger every year. So I hope the two of you are staying on a few days to help eat it up, otherwise she'll be sending a load back with me.' And you can bet your life it won't be breast. 'Ooh.' She wormed a finger between lip and nipple to ease the suction grip.

'Actually, I don't think Oliver —' because it was convenient to have someone else to blame. One of the advantages of not living on your own. She'd forgotten what the others were. She lifted out another plate. It was incredible there was so much washing up after beans on rice cakes and the putting-on-the-Ritz crackers left over from That Night — maybe if they'd followed the raspberry pavlova with cheese everything would have turned out differently...'Oh, God.'

'So that's it, is it?' said Di. A bit of grease was what was needed. 'I could tell the minute I stepped through the door you two had just had a row.' Maybe there was some Vaseline in the baby bag. 'He's wanting you both to spend Christmas day with his family, is he?' Sod giving equal time at each one, 'I can see his point,' she was all for switching sides now, 'but it's important to establish a routine and stick to it.'

Jane shook her head. 'We hadn't been rowing.' She began wiping round the sink. It wasn't that bad really.

'I see.' Di gave Jane's back a knowing look. 'It happens to us all, little sis. You spend the first few months floating on air then, bit by bit, you sink back to earth, aka real life. It's obvious you're not so spaniel eyed about him now which is just as well, really. You've got your man, that's the main thing.' Though who'd have thought Jano could have landed one like him?

'It's that sort of attitude that makes things so hard for the rest of us. Getting equal treatment in the workplace, for instance.' Though to be fair to Christian, he didn't treat her any worse than he did the others. Better, in fact, if she gave him a maybe-I-will smile once in a while.

'The hardest thing for women's always been keeping hold of a guy.' Though this nipple came a pretty close second. 'So then he can keep you. Men ran a mile from in-your-crotch feminism so women ditched it.' Di had a feeling she'd taken the jar out of the bag. 'Who wants equal treatment?' It was his fault because he'd said there wouldn't be room for a load of stuff, what with his tools and such. 'Far better to have men at your beck and call.' So if she had, Rob could damn well go out and find a late-night supermarket. He would, too, otherwise he'd be in for a three-night sulk.

Jane squirted some cream cleaner onto the bottom of the washing-up bowl.

'For goodness sake,' said Di, 'stop pretending to clean that sink. Anyone can see you don't bother anymore. Playing house is okay for a while but it's not long before the novelty wears thin.' She might slacken off soon, in the daytime anyway, when she had the house to herself. 'Mind, it'll be a bit different in your own place.' Give the formula a go. 'Make sure he puts down a deposit before you get married. One of those boxes on a new estate'll do to start with, as long as you put up lap fencing.' Nothing wrong with Cow and Gate, and she could undo a couple of buttons and stick the sterilising unit in the conservatory when breast-is-best Rob came home.

'You can always build on. I've finally persuaded Rob we need a kitchen extension. And – I haven't told him yet – we might as well replace the whole lot, instead of trying to match things up. New tiles and appliances as well as units and then there's the floor to decide on. It'll be worth it in the long-run. You have to put up with a bit of upset before things end up how you want them.'

Jane pulled off a rubber glove and blew inside it.

'So,' Di unhooked the left side of her bra, 'I'm really looking forward to it.'

Jane sat down. 'That's good then. I'm glad –' someone has something to look forward to. She watched the baby latch onto the second breast with less enthusiasm.

Di shuffled down the chair. 'You don't look it.' Definitely less sensitive now. 'What's up? He's not been having a bit on the side, has he?'

Jane smirfed. Almost laughed. Because that episode this morning, when she was doing the fly on the floor bit, had been almost funny.

'So that's it,' said Di. She could read Jane like a Mills and Boon. Always could. 'Well, it's no big deal.' Not that Jano should tell him that, if she had any sense – she could make him pay for this for months, years even: there was no use-by date when it came to bringing up past wrongs – but then her four-A-level-A's sister never did have any, not the common sort anyway. Otherwise why had she jacked in her Uni place? Completely unfathomable. But then Jane always was a closed book. Whereas it was only too obvious what men were thinking about.

'They're all at it, given half the chance. It's what men do, all of them. You know, brains in their boxers. But –' Diane crossed her legs on the seat and the red dress slid off the back of the chair '– there're worse things than being unfaithful, don't you think?' Like being boring. And Oliver, she decided, would never be boring. Not with those eyes.

Jane thought. Oliver at the awards do with Sophie – had they slurped that crème brûlée together, swapping mouthfuls? They were welcome to it. It was sick-makingly sweet. The red number looked up from its crumpled heap, asking to be picked up. Jane wondered if the stain on the front had slopped straight from the spoon or done a there-and-back down Sophie's gullet first. As far as she was concerned the dress could stay where it was. Oliver could pick it up. It was what men did. All of them. And which galloping stallion would Sophie's buttocks would be squashed against tonight? She closed her eyes. She didn't have to be a mind reader to –

'Guess what!' Which must be Stephanie. So in a door-to-cupboard millisecond there would be the big bang. Welcome to the re-creation of Creation. She squeezed her lids tighter, so the blankness swarmed with colours, floating off the spectrum far from jabberwock tongues…dissolving into meaningless sounds…vibrating through the indefinable, absorbed into consciousness beyond concrete existence…

'Wake up, Auntie Jane!'

Her neck snapped back from shaken shoulders.

'It's not bedtime yet.'

Jane opened her eyes.

'I've got a new part. An importanter one.'

The familiar surroundings, the changeless background of emptiness filled with stuff.

'Guess what it is.'

Jane frowned.

'Keep up, Jay. She means the nativity play.'

Reality beyond imagination, with a tea towel round its head. A part for everyone, but it would be just her luck to pick the one Stephanie had before. 'The door knocker?'

'That's a boy's part, silly. But Joseph's got to do it gently or the Wendy House wobbles. I'm the third wise man. Mummy asked if I could be swapped.'

About time, thought Jane.

'They were rehearsing last time I was on Playgroup duty,' said Di. 'Mary's cranked up to be the star part but as far as I could see she just sits around and keeps her mouth shut even when Gabriel dumps the baby on her and flits back to heaven. Smart move that – don't be fooled by the halo and the dress, he was male, you know, though not in the play of course. Rosanna this right little madam's got that part, all because she's the blondest, though it's more straw really, and Stephie's is longer. Some of the other angels are boys, though, to make it look pc.' As in plain crazy.

'Do angels have a sex?' Jane asked.

'Do angels have sex, do angels have sex,' chanted Stephie, whizzing up and down the far wall, trailing a damp finger along the yellow paintwork.

'Every man's fantasy, I expect,' Di murmured.

Stephie examined her finger. 'What's fantasy?' It wasn't golden like she'd expected, just grubby.

'It's what you're doing in the play – dressing up. Though muggins is having to make a costume. All they've got left for the third wise man is a tatty old crown from the year dot.'

'Could be the genuine article, then.' Jane looked at the overlapping stripes running along the wall. It would take more than a wet finger to wipe out the past.

'Stephie, that was naughty,' said Di. 'The whole wall needs washing now.' Like it didn't before. So much to tell her mother.

'Look, Mummy.' Stephie picked up the fallen red dress and flicked it round her back. 'This makes a super cloak. Isn't it lovely?' She twirled round, catching the bag of chocolate coated peanuts on the worktop.

'Stephanie!' as peanuts scattered over the floor. Di fastened the front of her bra. 'Take that off. You can see it's Auntie Jane's dress.' What there was of it. She buttoned up her blouse. God, was she ever going to get into normal clothes again?

'It's okay. Take it if it's any use. It's only an old floorcloth.' Obviously. Being where it was.

'Floorcloth? Haven't you heard of microfibre mops?'

Though from the look of these tiles... 'Sounds like something from Grandma Bates's day.' Except Grandma Bates, bless the old faggot, would have said it wasn't big enough to make a decent dishcloth, never mind a –

'Floorcloth, floorcloth,' sang Stephie, trampling the dress over the spilt nuts.

'Stephie,' Di said, hitching the baby up to her shoulder and rubbing its back. 'Go and tell Daddy it's time we were going.' More than time. She looked at Jane and smiled.

Jane smiled back.

'Righty-ho,' said Stephie. 'But first,' kicking the dress to the far corner of the draughts board, 'I'm going to tell Uncloliver all about the nativity.'

'There won't be time for that,' said her mother.

But the wise man had already skipped out.

AS it happened, there would have been time, as the cheerio-for-nows took so long Stephie had to be called twice to come from the kitchen before eternity finally ended and Jane was able to close the front door.

'Thank God for that,' and they almost exchanged almost-smiles again, before he went into the lounge and she the kitchen and both doors closed.

Jane picked up the kettle. What she needed right now was – not to see the red dress slopped in the sink and a puddle on the floor next to it. Plus, now she looked, several more leading to the opposite wall, where most of the finger trail cipher had been swept into blotches of brightness. Below them was a new message, spelt out so there could be no room for doubt.

S t e P a i n e

Jane turned back to the sink and held up the dress. It was filthy, snagged and seam ripped. But the stain had disappeared.

DIANE unfastened her coat and eased it away from her neck. She wiped a little patch on her window and looked out. Vague forms along the roadside reared and shrank in the passing lights.

'Watch it!' cried Rob.

The Land Cruiser skidded towards the far verge and half way round the other way.

'What the hell was that?' He pulled on the hand brake. Doing a thirty mile plus detour on what was already a hell of a long journey – Roy rammed it into reverse – had been bloody madness in this weather and why the hell – the offside rear wheel spun – they'd had to stay so long was beyond him.

Diane turned away, flattening her palm against the window, circling the clouded glass, feeling the dampness against her skin.

'Sorry,' he said, as the front tyres found their grip and the car edged across the ridge of snow between the lanes. 'Aw, c'mon, girl –' he slapped her thigh '– don't sulk. But the days of being irresponsible are over.' He flicked his head towards the back seat.

She pressed her hand against the glass, the cold tingling up her arm. Between her outstretched fingers, a grey shape moved in the hedgeback and two laser eyes turned to look.

SHE couldn't stand that staring her in the face a moment longer. Dunking the dress in suds, Jane carried the bowl to the table. She'd just rub off the dotted lines, plus, of course, the artist's signature, what was left of it, since one of the wet patches had trickled down, wiping out the first three letters. She grasped the dress by the scruff of its neck and wrung it out. Hesitated over the remaining letters. As a name, it just might stick.

By the time Oliver put his head round the kitchen door to say he was calling it a day, Jane, red-faced and beaming, had finished the fourth wall and started on the units.

TWENTY miles on, the eyes still burned into her skull. Diane undid her seatbelt and pulled off her coat. Might as well take off her cardigan while she was at it.

'Hey, belt up, girl. The roads are still bad, even here.'

As she clunked in the seatbelt she caught sight of Rob's face. Still the same strong profile, now obscured, now bathed in silver light, a shadow kaleidoscope of unfamiliar faces as mask after mask was peeled, yet flesh and thought remained concealed.

For a moment he turned – 'That's better. It only needs some idiot to get distracted for a second and lose control' – and then his focus was back on the road...

...while she was on another ride, with that other Di and Rob, two Mondeos and two lifetimes ago. Clothes prickled skin, breasts chafed against their padding. Nipples itched. She slid out buttons, unhooked cloth, bared them to the brushed caress of passing headlamps, stripping and unstripping in their shadow wake, unseen by a hundred passing eyes. But she wanted him to notice, wanted like she never thought she'd want again.

'Steady on, girl. Show some sense – not in here, for God's sake. There's a Little Chef in a couple of miles. I'll pull in.'

He parked between a van and a saloon. 'Not very private, but I'll hold a coat up if anyone comes.' He turned to the back seat. 'Are you sure about this? Seems a pity to disturb her. How long is it since you last did it?'

'Too long...' skimming the nearest knee with her fingertips '...since we did it...' fingers creeping up his thigh '...like this.'

'Come off it, Di. What're you playing at? Have you any idea how far we've got to go yet? Besides, the kids are in the back.'

'Both fast asleep.' She leaned towards him and ran her tongue along his neck, over his earlobe, into his –

'Don't be daft!' He flicked his head away, as though from a persistent fly. 'I need to be up at six. If we ever get to bed, that is.' He turned on the ignition and pushed the wiper stick to intermittent. 'Take a look at it now.'

Slow flakes had begun to fall. She watched them spatter the glass, blocking out beyond, before the rubber blades squashed them against the bottom of the screen, over and over again.

'Anyway, we're a bit past doing it in the car, aren't we? I can't imagine what you thought it'd be like with a gear stick up your bum. Besides –' he set the wipers on continuous action '– I'm about knackered. All this overtime I'm doing so you can have that kitchen extension you want.'

Flakes were falling faster. Side by side in separate seats they watched the wiper blades struggle.

He turned towards her. 'That is what you want, isn't it, Di?'

She stared at the wipers, unseen and unheard, doing what they were programmed to do. 'Yes – course it is.' Snow was building up on the side window. The little patch she'd wiped looked out to flat whiteness. She fastened up her breasts. No way was she letting on about the nicely accumulating nest-egg from Grandma Bates. 'That's exactly what I want.' Because there were some things – plenty of things – a husband didn't need to know.

He put his hand on the ignition key, then took it off. 'Mind you, now we've stopped –' he chucked her chin '– you could nip out and bring us some burgers. I'm desperate for red meat. Baked beans on bits of cardboard – I ask you, what sort of a meal was that? Don't know why the poor sod puts up with it. All I can think is...' she must be red hot in bed. 'I could really fancy a couple of baps. Go on, girl.' He slapped Diane's knee. 'A man can die of hunger, you know.'

'If you want burgers –' Di pulled her coat over her and tucked it round her shoulders '– you can fricking well get them yourself.'

'COME on.' Oliver drew out a chair. 'Sit down at our smear-free table. It's fantastic,' he said, waving his hand round the kitchen like Christian doing a hard sell, 'to see you back to your old self. Let me pour you some juice.'

Jane lowered herself onto the seat. 'There isn't any.' Every muscle ached.

'Hey, presto.' Oliver poured her a glass and refilled his own. 'Been out to Costcutter. Early bird and all that. Almost had to wait for it to open.'

He reached for a carrier and put it on the table. 'Look. Milk, coffee – I noticed you were scraping the jar last night. Didn't get teabags, though I know we're about out. Thought we could do a supermarket shop tonight. You know, together, like we used to. But you'll never guess what I'm about to pull out next. Wait for it – Da-dah! I know how much you like them and you don't seem to have bought any for ages.'

There was no need. Not when there was still the packet from that other time he'd gambled on the free gift from Sugar Puffs being a magic bullet. She'd stuffed it at the back of a cupboard, behind the fondue set marked "boxed" on the landlord's inventory. Had half thought of mixing them in with the beans last night to make them stretch a bit further. The non-cognitive half had left them where they were.

'Tell you what, we'll both have them,' and two bowls appeared from thin air.

Or maybe he'd got them out of the end cupboard, scrub-cheeked and grinning under the fluorescent light. As was the whole kitchen. No wonder she was so tired. *A clean house is a sign of a wasted life.* Not her mother's words, for once. Which had made it all the more satisfying. But the best part, despite two split nails and the blood blister now throbbing at the end of her forefinger, had been at 3am when she'd crammed the not-so-red-now dress in the bin.

He was tipping Sugar Puffs into bowls and topping up her glass. 'This is just what you need –' he ripped the seal off the semi-skimmed with his teeth '– to give your blood sugar level a boost.' He poured half their daily calcium requirement onto each bowl.

Not a crackle. But she wasn't really in the mood for symphonic cereal. And now the smell was reaching her, the tooth-slackening sweetness of sugar soaked gluten... tiny cowrie shells swimming in a creamy warm sea, caught up in her Goldilocks spoon as she snuggled close to Daddy, wrapped in Di's old dressing gown, scrubbed clean and ready for a story of once upon a time...

He'd put down his spoon and was sliding his hand across to hers, 'Let's call today,' over hers, 'the first day of the rest of our lives,' lifting it towards his face.

She didn't pull back, though she was still holding the spoon, and the spoon was still holding a taste-try of Sugar Puffs, because you couldn't really question the logic of what he was saying. And rational thought –

'I know you know it's the way forward, angel.'

– was, after all, what marked out homo erectus, and presumably femina prona, from lower forms of life.

'It's clear to me that you cleaning the kitchen like this, wiping away that build-up of invisible germs, was your way of showing you want things back to how they were.'

He directed her fist so the spoon was in reach, not of her mouth, for Goldilocks had skipped to the next page, but of his own. He opened it, and paused.

Sleeping Beauty stared at the red spot at the end of her finger and everyone in the scullery was frozen in time.

Then Oliver's lips moved, closing, not round the bowl of the spoon, but snickering at its tip... just like Daddy used to do to get his sleepy princess to take that last spoonful...

Oliver steered the spoon towards her. Jane opened her mouth and swallowed.

'Whoops.'

He pointed to a drop of milk that hadn't made it across. It lay between them on the smear-free table, a blob of shifting whiteness under the shadow of his hand.

'I guess things never stay perfect for long. Not that anyone would really call this place perfect.'

She supposed not. Compact, unpretentious, conveniently proportioned, but even Christian wouldn't go further than bijou.

'But then –' he drew a finger across the blob '– it wouldn't be home, would it, without a few upsets. Because, let's face it, none of us is perfect either, except –' his finger circled, spreading the spilt milk into a transparency of dampness '– that's kind of perfect, isn't it?'

No, you've lost me there, Oliver.

'What I mean is, two people's imperfections sort of complement each other. So in the end –' he lifted his finger and pressed it against the tip of her nose '– they cancel each other out.' He rubbed his hand across the table. 'There. Nothing to show there was anything amiss.'

Apart from the drip on the end of her nose.

'AND what,' he asked, prodding the diary, 'do you propose doing this afternoon?'

The diary had come to realise, over the past forty-nine and a half weeks, that rhetorical questions best remain unanswered. But then it didn't need to cover its tracks like Jane.

'I've found it's good policy to leave a substantial chunk of time for Stobb End.'

And there were now only two and a half blank rectangles before Thursday, which happened to be chock-a-block with pencilled hieroglyphs.

'It's bloody well time it was off the books. This arse-brained scheme of yours for wading headfirst into the bloody country like a bull at a bloody watzit has fallen on its jacksie.' Christian banged his fist on the open page. 'It won't do, you know.'

Knowing, thought the diary, wasn't caring. Midnight 31/12 marked the end of its shift.

'And what the hell's going on on Thursday, for God's sake? All these bloody arrows – what the hell's that all about? If it's definite it should be down in black and white.'

Jane picked up the nearest pen, which happened to be blue but would do well enough, and wrote GEM under the twelve pencilled beaks and black dot eyes.

He scowled. 'GEM? What the hell's that all about?'

If he came out with that many more times she'd have it filed under FAQs. 'Oh, come off it, Christian. You and your –' she tapped him playfully on the arm. It was either that or a knee in the – 'little joke. You know full well what it's all about.'

And at the EOD it was all about what the emperor wore when his new clothes were in the wash. And her WOS Boss wasn't going to be the one to ask what ACRONYM stood for, not in a MY, or even ten million. As long as she followed it up PDQ, before Christian had time to think. Some time in the next ten minutes would do. During which time Roy came back from his first ATV. Without, from the look on his face, getting a sale, not even an OIRO.

It was only because she was intent on un-noticing Roy that she saw Christian wasn't scowling any more. Was, in fact, almost smiling as he told Roy he was pleased to see him. Which – and it would have been so nice to have exchanged what's-going-on looks with Roy – must be a first.

'Now we're all here – Jane, pop through the back and bring Tony in – we can have a get-together.'

What was this, the office party? she and Roy might have flashed to each other, back in the old days of last week. She flattened the page in her diary and started going over the G in felt tip.

'Nip and fetch Tony, Jane.'

But Jane was half way along the E.

'Roy, give Tony the wink.'

Which, less than a week ago, thought Roy, would have made Jane's eyebrows rise, both together, in that way they did when they swapped aye-aye glances, back in the old days.

'Then I'll let you all in on this little plan of mine.'

'Does it involve mugs?' said Roy. Or just the four of them? Because he might as well go through and fetch Tony and the mid-morning shot of caffeine and get it over with. Then he could get out of the office and stop not looking at Jane not looking at him.

'This,' said Christian, 'isn't the time for bloody coffee. Tony!'

Five yells later, the door opened.

'Kettle's on,' said Tony. 'I thought –' you must want it at 9.45 in case we're in liquidation at half past ten.

God give me strength, muttered Christian, elbowing the potted tinsel-tree along as he lowered himself onto the front desk. No wonder everything's fucked.

Skewered at the top of the wire trunk, the seen-it-all fairy shook her wand in no great wonderment as glitter glided down to land where once had sprouted hair.

'What we need,' said Christian, 'and I've given this a lot of thought, is something big.' He settled himself more squarely onto the desk. 'Something that'll bring the punters in. Not that anyone's saying houses aren't still selling.'

And no-one was. Not Roy, trying to decipher – not easy at ten paces – what Jane had been so intent on writing. Not Jane, putting the cap back on the felt tip, because she really needed orange to go over the pencilled beaks and – she couldn't be certain from this distance – there might still be an orange in the pen tub on Roy's desk. Not Tony, listening for the kettle – he wasn't sure, not with the door closed – because you couldn't rely on it to switch off nowadays, it might just keep on and on until it boiled dry.

'So, that's pretty much it, in a nutshell. Not bad, eh?' Christian folded his arms and beamed at them. 'Might just do the trick.'

Here and there, between the spread-combed strands, a speck of magic dust caught the light.

'Of course, there are a few fine points to be ironed out, like who's going to actually stand there all day doing it.'

Roy looked at Tony – anyway, Jane was still engrossed in whatever it was she'd been writing – but it was difficult to read anything into his expression. Apart from undiluted panic.

'I think –' Christian drummed his fingers '– it should be Jane.' He slapped his hand on the desk top. The fairy didn't move a muscle. 'Yes. Jane – board!'

She flinched. 'Well –' no more than usual, when the WOS-boss was unloading another Not Bad Plan. Which this time seemed to involve –

'Jane, standing there in full view, maybe in one of those cutesy Santa girl suits... short little skirt, with fur round her –'

'Hold it right there, Christian. No way –'

'You'll be the one holding it, sweetie, so to speak. I can see you now... high-heeled boots, thick leather belt with a big shiny buckle, cheeky little cap and a furry pom-pom dangling –'

'Christian, let's get one thing straight. Whatever you have in mind –' and she really wasn't in any doubt, just a bit hazy about one or two details, like – 'What the heck is this about?'

'Well, it's no good just sticking a board up on its own, no-one'll give it a second glance. Whereas when you're holding it, dressed, as I say, in –'

'Yes, I think we get the picture,' said Roy. He certainly did, though Tony's sights were on the door to the back room. Probably waiting to make his escape. Well, no-one was going anywhere till a few things were made clear, like – 'What's this board, where's it going to be and – why? Because I don't think that Jane should have to –'

'Because Jane,' said Jane, 'isn't.' And Roy needn't think she needed his help, though it had, she supposed, been nice of him. Nice-ish, anyway.

Christian sighed. It was a big sigh, almost desk rattling, though it was his heaving himself upright that knocked the fairy askew. Bloody women. He reached up and rammed the central spike further up its cardboard skirt.

'Shut up, you bunch of whingers, and listen. What's going to happen is...' they, the great house-buying public, were going to see Jane – okay, they'd talk about her get-up later – and read her board as they drove past – yeah, all right, she was going to have to be some place where the traffic slowed down, like... a roundabout, good idea, Tony – and then they'd drop by, or, better still, phone – because one of them, say Tony, could look into getting one of those numbers where the firm gets a cut – to make an appointment to view – no, not "or a free valuation," Tony, God knows Up Yours had enough bloody houses on the books – and then they'd be entered in the grand prize draw, free, gratis and for nothing – which might well be the case, because if the winner wished to have their name withheld who was to know any different?

'But what if,' said Tony, 'they don't?'

Christian patted his shoulder. 'You've a lot to learn about this business, lad.'

Like, thought Roy, exactly how overdrawn it is. 'Okay, if we are going ahead with this scheme – your scheme, you should get all the credit, Christian, if it's a success –' or the thirty days without the option if it's not, because, aside from the non-existent prize, 'Are you sure it wouldn't be contravening some by-law to have Jane by the side of the road in a drop dead outfit? Bit of a distraction for drivers, I'd have thought.'

'Well, one of you can keep watch for any approaching cop cars. Tony –'

'I'll do it,' said Roy. 'Tony'll be needed here to answer the phone, and deal with anyone who calls in. You could be in fancy dress, as well, mate. Maybe one of Santa's elves. You too, Christian. Fair's fair, if Jane's got to. I'd need to keep a low profile, obviously, but you could really let it all hang out. I can see you as –'

'Don't push it, lad. Anyway, we've no money to splash around on damn fool costumes.'

'Exactly,' said Jane. 'If I do this – and if I do, it's on the understanding that: a) this month's bonus will be forthcoming, unlike the previous two, and b) I wear nothing more than a Santa hat.' And, realising what she'd just said wouldn't be at all funny if she didn't catch Roy's eye, she did exactly that, because, what the heck, it all might be: c) a big laugh.

'Actually, Christian,' said Tony, 'there's no need to buy even a hat. It just so happens I have a Santa outfit.'

Which, of course, Roy couldn't let pass without flashing a glance at Jane, who, of course, was flashing right back.

'It's got everything,' Tony went on. 'The padded jacket, with a proper hood, the baggy trousers, the welly-boots, the mittens. It's even got the sack.'

'Don't put ideas into my head, lad,' said Christian, sinking back onto the desk.

'The welly-boots will probably be too big for Jane, though,' Tony was saying, mainly to the tree. 'Maybe she should deal with the phone calls and me and Roy could...'

Behind Christian's sprawling rear, the fairy smiled down. That glitter dust dotted over the glistening scalp might take some shifting. If he was even aware it was there.

'It's okay, Tony,' said Jane. 'I've got my own wellies.'

At which point all the lights went out.

'Oh, God!' shouted Tony. He flung open the back door and a corridorful of steam slapped him in the face. Almost exactly like a wet blanket.

SNOW covered everything. This wasn't just a twelve tog duvetsworth – Jane tugged at the gate – it was a twenty mattress smothering. With a minus five wind chill throwover. Any princess camping out in this permafrost would be hard pressed to feel the protruding carrot of a chancing snowman under the sheets, never mind a pea. There was nothing for it but to dig out the gateway. So it was just as well she had a shovel.

The gate was open, the shovel was back in the boot, her foot was on the accelerator – and Festina's tyres were spinning like roulette wheels trying to outdo chaos theory. Jane tried reversing. Tried pushing, kicking, swearing. Almost tried crying, except she didn't do crying anymore. Anyway tears would have solidified mid-trickle because although her fingers and toes were numb, the sweat from digging had turned to a cold clamminess that set her whole body shaking. Festina was going nowhere, but she must keep moving.

She crossed the stackyard, giving the trailer a wide berth. What use was it now? She'd never be able to tow it away from here, never mind back across the goose field with a full load. It was hopeless.

She climbed the fence and began to walk, hands bunched in pockets, eyes on the snow under, and over, her feet. So much sodding snow. She trudged on, towards the far hedge...

...where the snow piled up along it was not in the dirty sludge-heaps that lined suburban driveways but a crystallised border of curves and crevices. She stood and gazed, saw sculpted forms arm-linked to make the ramparts of the White Witch's castle. Further along, the drawbridge was raised against her. Only the top of a gatepost showed through the snowdrift. The sensible thing, of course, would be to turn back.

Eyes squinting against the glare, she followed the hedge along, searching. She wasn't, she told herself, such a dyed-in-the-polymer-fibre townie as to force her way through, but there could be... Yes, that might be a post and rail, patching up a weak spot. She stretched across, reaching sideways to steady herself on a wind-carved pillar of snow – there might well be a ditch lurking beneath – and found a handhold in a notch near its conical peak. Was this a frozen Ku Klux Klanner or some other pointy hat wearer, maybe the White Witch herself? The point broke off in her hand and she slid forward, landing on her bottom.

The ice hat had stabbed through a mound of snow and disappeared. Jane grinned as she reached for another spike to heave herself up. She'd never ditched a witch before. Or – the snow horn of an unnamed Mr Tumnus snapped off in her hand – moated a goat. She crumbled it to lumps of ice.

As she struggled to her feet, snow filled her wellies, crept up her sleeves, down her neck. She shook the hem of her coat, shook out her cuffs and collar, took hold of her scarf below the knot and shook the long ends like a two-tailed dog. What did she care about a bit of snow? No way would she get her wellies back on, even if she managed to pull them off. And what would be the point? Now her feet were flat-sharing with enough compacted snow to build an igloo, at least up to the damp course, she might as well wade into the gateway. But instead of plunging waist-deep into the snowdrift she found it was solid enough to bear her weight.

Soon she was standing on top of the gatepost, with a sun-sparkle realm spread out before her. Jane laughed out loud. The laugh was buried in a muffle of whiteness. She was on the top of the world and the world was silence. All around was frozen desert, a magical land of ice. *Always winter...* She saw the greylags before she heard them. Over the sky they flew, over the hillside, dropping from sight, down to the lake... *but never Christmas.*

Before she got as far as the lake, or as far as she thought it must be, because it always seemed to be over the next hill, she came to a wood. Not a vast drop-a-trail-of-breadcrumbs wood of leafless oaks and hazels, but a small plantation of firs which, after she climbed the fence, showered powdered snow onto sleeves and shoulders as she brushed past. There was less snow underfoot. It was also, now the sun was blocked out, colder. Here and there she crunched into fallen twigs or stubbed toes against undercover roots, sending shockwaves up her legs, though she'd have thought they'd be completely numb with cold.

She must keep moving. Never mind she didn't know where she was heading; even Robert Frost would have been hard pressed to cram all the roads not taken in this maze of tracks into twenty lines. Nor had he – looking at the footprints on the path ahead – ended up back where he'd started. Except – she tried her own foot inside one for size – these were too big to be hers.

Jane followed the tracks round another clump of trees, definitely no different from the rest. Once you'd seen one needle-case of forest you'd seen more than enough. Which was probably why, now she could see what was making the noise, that guy was chain-sawing through sapling trunks as though he had the sole Far East contract for next year's chopsticks, with a Wales-size shuttering of rainforest to go at, instead of a couple of acres of twelve day wonder-if-the-lights'll-work self-seeders.

He spotted her as he was loading trees onto a mini trailer, which was hooked behind a mini tractor, which was exactly the sort of thing –

'You need,' he nodded towards another clump of trees, 'to be up there.' He pushed a loop of rope through a hook on the trailer. 'This bit's out of bounds to the general public.'

The general public admitted it had got a bit lost. 'But as I'm here, maybe I can help.'

He coiled the rope and tossed it over his load. 'If you like.'

Jane went round to the other side of the trailer. The rope had snagged on some branches and by the time he came round to see what she was faffing about at, there was a rope-branch entanglement to rival an incest-nest of vipers.

Jane stood picking needles out of the palms of her woolly gloves while he sorted it out. Where, wondered the cactus thumb and forefinger of her left glove, was that tractor kept at night? He climbed aboard, upped the revs by a few thousand and shoved it into gear. Through the diesel fume smog he nodded for her to follow. The only way to find out, decided the similarly spiked right glove, was to do as the man said.

Four rows of trees leant against lines of wire stretched between stakes. Someone was selecting a likely one but his wife had spotted the bargain rail alongside the shed. Jane had spotted the shed alongside the bargain rail. It had double hardwood doors and the sort of padlock that would be rejected by any self-respecting Category A prison as being above its job.

She watched the husband stand every spindle-shanks sapling as vertical as a tree-for-a-tenner could be expected to go while the woman made her choice. He carried it to the bagging machine. Jane sucked back her last cloud of breath. She knew that bagger. And that bagger knew about cars. Especially ones snowfully challenged.

'WHAT she needs,' said Simon, 'is a bit of sand or some such to grip on.' He looked round the stackyard.

Jane scanned it the other way and their eyes met over the white hillock she'd last known as a baler. But she couldn't for the life of her recall seeing a bit of sand lying about. And not so much as a sprinkle of such.

'Maybe in that shed,' he said. 'No, you stay there.'

So she got back in the car and directed the blower at her feet, because there didn't seem any point in keeping the windscreen clear. Festina wasn't going anywhere.

But after Simon had wedged an armful of straw under her tyre and put his weight behind her rear, and told her driver to take it slowly, for God's sake, Festina found herself parked at the front of the house, ready to make a quick getaway. Though her driver didn't seem in much of a hurry.

Simon checked his watch. 'I'm only supposed to take half an hour for lunch,' but it didn't really matter. This netting Christmas trees job wasn't likely to be made a permanent position. And there was something a damn sight more interesting here. 'Look!'

Jane looked. The shed was full of the same old rubbish. There was the same smell of horse, and the same bits of old harness on the wall. As well as the sacks of mouldering wheat, the toothless rake, the broken down old tractor...

'Isn't she a beaut?' said Simon, wiping his sleeve across her bonnet so the red paint showed through. 'A Massey Ferguson 135. The workhorse of your average family farm in the sixties. They don't make them like this anymore. And –' he peered at the engine '– I reckon this is a Perkins. We're looking at a 45 horsepower engine here.'

Forty-five horse power, eh? Jane wrinkled her nose. No wonder it smelled so bad in here.

But all Simon could think about was – 'I guess she'll just stay here till she drops to bits. It's a crying shame. A bit of TLC and she could be purring.'

Jane grabbed his arm and never mind it was covered in half a century of dirt. 'Are you saying you can get this contraption moving?'

He might have winced at "contraption" but her face, her whole being, was so animated he knew she must be smitten as well. The old love at first sight thing. He wondered, vaguely, if she cared as much as he cared about – but he couldn't see Sophie's face clearly anymore. All he could see was Jane's eagerness, all he could feel were Jane's fingers, now gripping both sleeves, digging through fabric and flesh more ouchingly than he would have thought possible by two woolly gloves.

'Can you?' She was shaking him now, and only stopped when she saw his eyes turn from greyhound in the trap to rabbit. 'Sorry,' she laughed. 'Got a bit carried away.'

'It's okay.' He ran his hand along the bonnet, revealing a new patch of red. 'I understand.'

Jane stretched out a finger and wrote MEND ME in the dirt. And wished she hadn't bothered. Not only had some pine needles pushed their way through wool to skin, but Simon was shaking his head, saying if only... What was it about men, for God's sake? What did it matter who owned the thing?

'Because the thing is,' she heard herself saying, 'as agents, we've advised the vendor to get rid of all this.' She waved her hand around the shed. 'Told him he's more likely to sell if the place is tidied up. So –' she picked at an impaled needle through her glove '– he's getting someone in to shift the lot. ASAP.'

All that and he was still shaking his head.

'Could be worth a lot more than what he'd get for scrap. And look –' he began poking about inside the engine '– it might not need much...'

Jane looked, saw a spaghetti bolognese of leads, gaskets, pistons, hoses, carburettors, concertinas, cornettos with rusted nut topping... saw Simon was frowning. She pushed her nose, and any other body parts that might swing it, a bit – a lot – closer. 'Do show me.'

Well, for starters, because you never knew, they might as well have a go at turning her over, which involved nothing more strenuous than a key-twist with a finger and thumb – her finger and thumb, because he made her climb aboard, stretching up onto the foot plate and reaching her other leg over the gear box.

But it was what he had known all along: 'The battery's as dead as a d-' the word disappeared under the tractor with him.

Doornail? Dodo? She could see his trapper hat moving below her feet. Dream-come-true? Jane gnawed at her glove.

'Dead mouse,' he said, emerging with exactly that. 'The little beast's chewed through the wiring from the key to the solenoid.' He held the shrivelled body up by the tail for her to see.

'Is it serious?' she asked.

'No,' and he tossed it into the corner as though it wasn't going to be on the endangered species list three months after man had blown himself off the planet, and the ready supply of wire-to-the-solenoid had dried up. 'I've got some spare wire that'll do, in the boot of my car.'

Which, Jane wanted to know, was where? Still grounded at the Frisky Filly? Guilt got in a quick jab but irritation floored it with a firm left hook. 'If your car – if Colin –' be on first name terms, Christian had told her, and you're halfway there '– is still parked at the pub I can –'

'No, it's at the plantation, which is where –'

'I shouldn't be,' said Jane, 'at all surprised if you could get this – get Fergus –' she patted the cab, what was left of it, but who needs doors? '– going before tomorrow.'

He was shaking his head again – it was, Jane decided, one of his more annoying habits – but continued to tinker with the mouse's last meal.

'It really needs a couple of new terminals to clamp on. I suppose I could cut the old wire and twist on a new bit... I'd love the chance to do a proper restoration but if your client just wants to be able to shift it –'

'Oh, he does. By Wednesday if possible. In fact,' before the head could even think about re-shaking, 'Wednesday at the absolute latest. And he's not expecting anything for it. Just wants rid of it. I'm sure I can get him to hang on a day or so before it's taken away to be crushed...' and this time the head shake didn't irk. 'So, if I meet him here on Wednesday and he sees I can start it, he'll cancel the scrap man and you could take it away on Thursday.' As long as it's not too early in the morning. 'Then you can take as long as you want to do it up properly.'

'Well, I'm not sure where I could leave it. I won't be able to afford to rent my garage for much longer, unless something turns up' – like a job that pays somewhere near the minimum wage – 'and there's not much space behind where I live.'

For God's sake, there was plenty at the Frisky Filly, wasn't there? 'You could get a loan. I bet it'll be worth loads when you've done it up. It'd be a collector's item, wouldn't it?'

'Maybe. It certainly would be better to move it from this unlocked shed. It's not as though there's a dog to guard the place.'

'And when you've done it up you could sell it on, and you'd have had the satisfaction of giving a new lease of life to a fabulous –' she patted Fergus again '– piece of machinery.' As well as to twelve got-fat geese, because she might tell him about it, when it was all over. But until they were safely on the lake those birds wouldn't get a mention.

'Even some geese would be enough.'

'Even some –? Enough?' Which didn't leave much more to be said. Except for –

'Geese. They're really good watch dogs, apparently. You've heard about them saving Rome from some invading horde, haven't you?'

'That's just a fable, isn't it?'

He shrugged. 'Probably. I mean, why would they have live geese inside the city walls? They'd be on the farms.'

'And the lakes. Only –' because it was coming back to her now '– they were sacred geese, weren't they?'

He shrugged again. It seemed to be the next body movement down after the head shaking.

'Kept in the temple on Capitol Hill. The Romans were besieged there and even though they were starving to death they didn't eat the geese.'

'Or the corn,' said Simon. 'Because they must have saved some to feed them. But they wouldn't know how long for so it'd be difficult deciding how much to hold back.'

A problem indeed, agreed Jane. So did Fergus. They stood together, mulling it over, just the three of them, and – something ran across the floor between their feet and Jane gave a little scream and Simon gave her a little squeeze and told her she was a scaredy-cat.

'I suppose they've come in here for the winter,' she said, 'to eat the wheat.'

'Among other things.' He turned his attention back to the engine.

'All the more reason to get Fergus moving, don't you think?' Jane patted the bonnet again, and this time she meant it. 'Are all your tools in the boot? I could go and fetch them while you carry on checking. If you'll let me have your car key –' again. Which, she could see by his face, was asking a bit much.

Anyway, he must, he said, get back to the plantation. In case he still had a job there. He'd pick up a new battery tonight, along with some oil, because it would almost certainly need changing, and maybe two new filters, because there was bound to be sediment in the fuel lift pump, and she didn't know why he was telling her all this because she was nodding her head and saying get whatever you think it needs.

'But the thing is –' and he stopped.

And the thing was, when she'd finally tweezered it out of him, that he hadn't been paid yet. The maybe-wouldn't-be wasn't even worth a watch-check.

Nor was there much point in Jane checking out the shed. There was never an ATM around when you needed one. She opened her bag, fingered her credit card... looked at Simon through narrowed eyes. Sharing a bed – which seemed to have been totally wiped from his memory – was one thing, but sharing her PIN? That was likely to stick in his mind a darned sight longer.

'I'd go with you to get the stuff but tonight's a bit tricky,' seeing as Oliver had suggested, as he and Harry, and Harry's VW, were going to a workshop at that conference hotel not so far from Up Yours that afternoon – gosh, she must have really been listening – which would finish about fourish, but he'd like to hang on a bit after Harry beetled off, do a bit of networking, why didn't he set off to walk down to Up Yours at half five? She could make a quick getaway for once, God knows she'd put in enough overtime at that place lately. They'd stop off for a bite to eat before going home. There'd be no meal to make and clear away so how did she feel about an early... bird menu from the In Your Hand snack bar? Because there wasn't anywhere else, now that the Curry Pot had gone into liquidation. Jane frowned. No chance of jasmine rice with Roy there now. All possible combinations of spicy sauce completely dried up, just as she'd known they would all along.

'I'm sure I'm right,' said Simon. 'Water and sludge in the lift pump. Hey, don't look so serious. I can blow the muck off and wipe it with a rag, once I'm in. If only I had a screwdriver with me.'

Jane let go of her card and felt for her nail file.

He was back to head shaking again, but it was a positive shake, as shakes go. 'Too rusted up. Anyway, I'm useless without a spanner.'

Proving once and for all, thought Jane, the total erasure from memory of – 'Coo-ee!' – her one-thirty client.

Which left Simon to take the lone trek back to his tree-netting, with only the promise that she'd meet him at the cash machine outside that branch of HBOS across the road and along a bit from Up Yours and down the first, or it might be the second, side street – you can't miss it – at twenty-five to six. Or maybe it was HSBC. But be there.

ROY looked at the clock. Twenty-five past, which tallied with his computer, give or take five minutes. Might as well turn over the sign on the door. Going past Jane's desk he couldn't help noticing she'd left her diary there. Couldn't help noticing it was open.

Only one viewing, Stobb End – which was taking a hell of a long time. He frowned. You couldn't trust anyone nowadays. He scanned the page. No appointments Tuesday or Wednesday. How much longer before the closed sign on the door remained unflipped? But it should be easy to find a day for the latest mad rescue plan which, he had to admit, was by far the best idea the Chrysalid had ever come up with. Looking at his own diary, Thursday was the most likely day. Because, looking back at Jane's, that line-and-a-bit of squiggles above some initials must be doodling, a pattern of arrowheads to fill a space – except they didn't. The end three were squashed in, with the last one having to go on the line below, as though it mattered that there were – he counted them – twelve. Why twelve? Why the dots?

'Why are you looking in Jane's diary?'

It wasn't an accusing why. Tony didn't do accusing. He didn't usually do why either. Or poke his nose in.

Tony drew a finger under the arrowheads. 'She's got a real thing about geese, hasn't she?'

'What do you mean?'

'All those beaks and eyes. It's obvious.'

So was the twelveness obvious too?

'Maybe,' said Tony, 'geese come in dozens.' After all, eggs did, and which came first? 'Or maybe it's the twelve days of Christmas. Except there're only six. You know, six geese a-laying. Except a goose wouldn't lay an egg at this time of year, would it, not an ordinary egg anyway. Maybe a golden egg, or...' he put his finger on the GEM '...an egg made of diamonds or something,' and it was satisfying to see Roy's mouth drop open in sheer wonderment.

'So when you opened the box – except it wouldn't just be a half dozen box, or even a dozen, would it? That's where Jane's gone wrong. There'd be six on the sixth day, another six on the seventh, making twelve, then six more...' Tony took a sheet from Jane's in-tray and started jotting down figures.

So when he came through, coat on, Christian felt a certain satisfaction at seeing at least one employee still busy with paperwork. Which made two out of three – Tony carried a figure forward to the next column – Up Yours males ending the day well satisfied. Not that Jane had time to notice as she pushed open the door in the face of the exiting Christian. Nor did she, as she threw stuff – maybe even the same stuff, she was that frantic – in and out of her briefcase, have time to answer Roy's 'Everything okay?'

'Must go,' and her eyes so out-flashed her hands in franticness he couldn't help catching her arm and asking again.

'Yes, fine. Everything's fine. It's just – Oliver's coming to meet me – he's at the hotel.' Please God he hasn't left already. 'I've got to go.'

SO Oliver was meeting her after work... Roy looked back at the diary. Nothing in here about it. Just an ordinary Monday. Followed, after a double blank, by an enigmatic Thursday. GEM. A diamond egg... oh, God, surely they weren't getting engaged? Was he ramming the ring on her finger on Thursday? But what was going on tonight? Whatever it was, whatever that creep was forcing her to do, one thing was clear: she wasn't at all happy about it. But the question was: what? If only he knew –

'The answer,' said Tony, throwing down his pen, 'is 42.' And he'd got there a lot quicker – 7½ million years minus a quarter of an hour quicker, to be exact – than Deep Thought.

But as soon as you solve one universal problem, there's another staring you in the face. Should he drop the latch, seeing as Roy had rushed out leaving not only his coat but his briefcase as well? Or should he just cross his fingers and hope that the closed sign would be enough to deter the burglars who, these dark evenings, were probably already out with their swag bags, so they could be back home in time for supper-on-a-tray in front of the match. And, although by the office clock Tony's bus should have gone, if he legged it now, he could be doing exactly the same.

ROY set off at full pelt over the ice-rink pavement, would have run across the first junction without looking if he hadn't heard a motor. It was an old Cortina, not bearing down on him but drawn up on the wrong side of the road, ticking over in that spike-arsed way of a saloon pushed off the production line when the Greenhouse Effect was but a small crack in man's imagination. He didn't need to have seen it before to know whose it was, though the nerd drumming his fingers on the steering wheel was a bit of a giveaway. As was the hair trailing down the back of a certain anorak. Roy watched Jane take her card from the machine and turn to Simon.

For the second time in ten minutes, Roy stood open-mouthed. Jane was thrusting a fistful of twenties into the nerd's outstretched hand. Then, before the Cortina's window had squeaked a quarter the way up, she was off, racing towards him. Roy ducked into the doorway of the boarded-up Curry Pot as she skidded round the corner. Leapt back again as the Cortina swerved across the junction, spraying him with slush and muck, and headed in the opposite direction.

He watched it chug away, saw it stop behind a double decker near the top of the hill. Saw only one brake light was working. So much for sodding maintains-it-himself Simon, foot on the clutch waiting for the bus to pull out. It would be petty to report it while he was waiting for don't-you-bloody-call-me-Mrs-Mop Claire to toddle down the hill and let him in. The police wouldn't bother about such a piddling thing. Too much trouble just for a fixed penalty fine. He might as well wander up to the stop and see the old bat didn't slip. It would be warmer than standing here anyway, because the slush spray had soaked through his trousers. And his feet were wet through. Weren't there three penalty points, though?

The bus pulled away. It didn't look like anyone had got off. He took out his phone.

JANE pushed her way through the rain forest, drenched in sweat. She flattened vegetation, fingering the warm dampness beneath… *Don't be cross, Mummy. I didn't mean to…* She reached out to cuddle Booboo. Touched naked flesh. She shrank into wakefulness. Back in the real world there was a leaking hot water bottle and, worse, Oliver stirring.

'Jane – is that you?'

For a moment she was tempted to give a Sophie impression, but she didn't do slut. Not at three in the morning. Not any more.

Nor was she staying in this bed any longer. Her mother had warned her about damp sheets. Almost ranked them with the male species in the 365-things-to-steer-clear-of list. Which just about covered it, apart from the occasional Feb 29th when a girl could ask a man not to.

Maybe if she smoothly slithered out he'd settle back to sleep. Slithering a damp nightie across a damper sheet wasn't as sleep-settlingly smooth as she'd hoped. She crept out without fumbling around for her robe. When would she ever learn to leave it just so?

When did anyone – she triple flicked the spark knob – learn anything new? Holding it down with fingers crossed only hurt the fingers. Yet was there any other way? Everything you ever really knew was learnt in those first few years; then, just as reason started to kick in, it was swamped in an acne-burst of hormones. The gas flame wavered. The rest of existence – she tried swapping right for left without releasing the knob – was spent trying to forget. Or at best, put up with how things were. The flame decided it really couldn't be bothered...

A hand came over, struck the knob and held it, just long enough. Another hand unfastened buttons at her neck, a third gathered up the hem. Any moment now it would be total hands on, hands all over. Blue flames transmorphed to orange as the wet nightdress was dragged over her head. Octopus arms pulled her down with him, side by side on the rug.

'Jane...'

An orange shimmer settled in behind the grinning fire logs, keeping its distance. Instead of just getting on with it. He spread her hair over her shoulders, shaped it down her spine.

'You're shivering.'

The orange backdrop roared, showing the golden fire-surround for the base metal it was. Condensation clouded the glass. She watched a trickle of water wend down the inside, inches from her face. Didn't some great ruler – probably Tiberius, he seemed to be around when any earth-shattering non-event was taking place – have someone punished for inventing unbreakable glass?

'Lift your bum,' and Oliver pulled out the rug. 'Don't want you catching a chill.'

It was all to do with some fear of imperial gold stocks being devalued. She flinched as he wrapped the rug round her, furry side up, like a green-leaf version of Snow Baby, though the heat was blasting out now, throwing its orange gleam over the metal surround, dissolving glass from sight. Only punishment wouldn't be enough to keep the secret buried.... the hessian backing scratched at her skin. The only way to stop it chafing was not to move at all.

But, even though the Klimt lovers weren't looking, the octopus paws stayed still, if you didn't count the one straying round her shoulders. True, it was under the rug, but that, Jane decided, was preferable to sack-cloth pressed into skin. And when the rug slid down, it was rather nice to snuggle up against undemanding flesh. Almost made her want him to...

...ease the rug under them, soft side facing. Nailed over the fire, the Klimt lovers were petal-deep on their floral mat while down below Jane and Oliver snuggled in tufts of acrylic green. And never mind the patch where the baby had left its mark and a thousand other stains of six-month leasers long moved on.

'In the new year,' he said, 'we'll have to start looking for somewhere else, a place of our own.'

That would be good – what the hell was she saying? She was only staying on, staying with him, till she got sorted, till she'd turned the page on GEM day. Well, maybe till after Christmas – which made her think, and she might as well say it now, before she got too comfortable spoon-nestled in the slouch of his body.

'You promised,' and the orange was at full blaze, 'to cancel the goose.'

And so he had. Yes, later he'd re-ordered, but a different one, and when she'd thought it through, same as he had, he knew she'd see he was right. Would see in the orange glare that her pale thighs burned as red as his bronze, till it was difficult to make out whose skin was whose.

'I've asked for a bigger one, the biggest there is.' He laughed. 'Like in Dickens. You know, when Scrooge becomes a reformed character, the biggest turkey in the shop. It's what Christmas is all about, isn't it? Laying old ghosts to rest, getting together with family, pulling a few crackers...'

...slaughtering a few million birds. Which, Jane acknowledged, happened all the time. Apart from the crackers.

'The way I see it, those geese are going to be eaten by someone. You know, born to die, and aren't we all, or not be born at all –'

– and if you don't get the joke round the paper hat someone else will.

'What I've been secretly planning – you're going to love this, Jay – is taking the goose up to your parents on Christmas Eve.'

She stared through glass that wasn't there till sun-spots floated before her eyes.

'I've arranged it all with your sister.'

The retina should have been stimulated to maximum response yet everything was drifting out of grasp...

'It's time you took up your rightful position in your family. And made a niche for me too.'

...except the logs. Immovable from the preordained placing of an unknown hand, uncharred by a continual flick-switch from sub-zero to 1200 in sixty seconds, they remained as irreversibly grey as the clay they could never return to. No going back.

Even though he was telling her it was the perfect chance for him to get to know her father better – she smirfed; better luck you than me – because he'd thought that maybe

318

Charles could see his way to helping them with the deposit. Smirf times two. It was the MD who would need to be wheedled into dipping into the Challis reserves. Except – the smirf blanked – Oliver would find a way.

'I know,' he said, 'you've got that legacy from your Grandma, though not being able to get at it till you're twenty-five's a bit of a disappointment.'

As the legacy might well be, if she took what she'd overheard in the scullery on trust. It hadn't made any difference to Diane's life, as far as she could see – but did anything? It was all delusion, that stuff about the road not taken, as though you were in control in some way. It wasn't what life threw at you, it was how you dealt with it – whether you picked it up and lobbed it back or stood rooted to the spot while it floored you – that determined its rating on the agony-ecstasy fate scale. And how you dealt with it was settled the moment the first plastic-spoonful of mashed banana was prised between your not-going-to-open gums. Before you even came near a fork.

He pulled her closer. She could feel him – it – pressing against her thigh. But he wasn't trying anything else. Not yet. That was the nub: you never knew with him... *quiet as a lamb one minute, then coming at you, head down, wings out*... How, and she couldn't put off thinking about it any longer, was she going to pick up the geese? To actually, physically, scoop one up. She'd seen the old woman do it, in one swift movement. Hand round the legs, arm round the body to keep those wings down, other hand holding the neck under the head so that beak couldn't swing round. She'd seen a potter at the wheel too. Ball of mud to Grecian urn in the twinkling of an eye. Nothing to it.

Don't look at us, said the logs. We're press moulded through and through. We might look different, look like individuals, but you'll meet the six of us in fireplaces just like this all over the world. All settled in our allotted positions. All living in the same houses filled with the same stuff. All wearing the same clothes, watching the same films, listening to the same music... because there was no getting away from the fact that Heather was up and about, psyching herself up for another postie snow-trudge with a bit of Abbey Road. Not when her CD player had been plugged in directly below the rug.

Oliver smiled. 'Quite considerate of her, really,' and the hand round her shoulders began to drum... *believe me...* he turned his face towards her...*when I tell you...* she could feel his breath on her neck...*I'll never do you no harm...* They'd warned her at school about falling into the double negative trap. But not about the double hand movement as *Oh! Darling* faded on his lips. And Jane had heard Abbey Road through the floorboards too many times not to know *Octopus's Garden* was followed by *I want you...* a wet tongue wormed its way into her ear...*so bad...*

SHE didn't know how she was going to get through it. Eight thirty-five. As if by coming into work early would somehow make the day go quicker. She'd never had the whole row of coat pegs to go at. She hung her anorak on the nearest one, ready for a quick getaway tonight. Might even need to write in another appointment for this afternoon. There was already one penned in at Stobb End. And a second not written down, after dark. And if he hadn't fixed Fergus in his lunch break, she'd hold the torch at his back till he did. Or, better still, if that shotgun was still stashed behind the rakes and shovels... Not that she'd ever fired a gun but she didn't suppose you could miss at point blank range. Without Oliver's handling-a-shotgun instructions. *When you're new to it, you need to focus with both eyes for accurate depth perception.* A finger jabbed in the back would probably be enough. *It all comes down to analysing the situation correctly*. Jane went past the pegs into the cloakroom.

The seat being down was a first as well. She checked her list.

Torch. Must remember to do a Festina to Fergus switch.

Boxes. She'd managed to get six, had had to fight for them with the Happy to Help lad on the split and recycle shift.

Sacks. Could end up being more useful than the boxes, if the geese were awkward, and the more she learned about them the more she suspected they would be. It might be easier to slip a sack over each one. If only she could have a practice run. But all she could do was press on.

Rope. She'd found one hanging from the rafters.

String. She'd collected up enough laid-about bits of baler twine to tie up the sacks.

Pocket knife. Already in place, first peg along.

She could hear another coat being hung. And someone's whistle-while-you-wait outside the cloakroom door. She folded the paper up and stuffed it back in her pocket. Prised her fingers in again for a tissue. It was a few weeks now since the Up Yours budget had run to a toilet roll.

'Morning, Jane,' said Tony, and regretted adding, 'God, you look a bit rough,' as Jane doubled back into the cloakroom to slap on a bit more eye-bag cover.

So by the time she made it to her desk it was after nine. Was well after nine by the clock. Roy must have forgotten to move it back to office a.m. time. Bloody men. Her can't-rely-on-them scowl quelled Christian's enquiry into what time she thought it was. Leaving his mouth open ready to answer the phone.

'Jubilee Terrace? Ah, yes, my colleague's dealing with that property.'

So why didn't he pass the phone across?

'She's told me there's been a lot of interest in it. Not surprising at that asking price, so I'd definitely recommend an early viewing.' Christian reached for her diary. 'It happens she has a window this morning when she'd be only too happy...'

She didn't, thought Roy, look too happy – but could you be too happy? If dreams – his dreams – came true, if Jane suddenly fell into his arms... It could happen. Things weren't right between her and the Oilrag. Okay, they were still sharing a place but he was sure they weren't still sleeping together. Pretty sure, anyway. So all she had to do was walk out. It was that simple. Except nothing was that simple. Well, some things were. Being with Soph, now that was simple. No hidden agendas, just bloody good, and he had a feeling that tonight was the night she'd tick all the boxes. But once ticked, Roy reckoned it'd be time to move on.

As did the clock. It hit the radiator on the way down and landed with a double bounce on the floor. Which was more than Tony managed when he lost contact with the chair.

'What the hell –'

Jane took the phone from Christian's hand before the client got the wrong idea. Tony, she decided, could always be relied on.

He was, Tony told Christian, only trying to put it right, and it was funny because he'd noticed sometimes it was fast and at other times slow. Whereas now – he picked up the clock – at least it'd be right every twelve hours. In fact, was spot on when Jane put down the phone.

Christian watched her squash in 10.30 JubTce above 2.00 StbNd and fill the rest of Tuesday with cross-hatching. It was funny, she told him, but she really felt this Stobb End client would be the one. So, as this afternoon's appointment could well go on late, she'd take all her stuff and not call back at the office at half five. Aka – she squinted at the cracked plastic face – eleven minutes past nine.

'Well, ten thirty should just about give you enough time –' he hammered a glance at the nail on the wall to emphasise his point '– to get on a bit more slap. You might be in with a chance if you don't turn up looking like you've not slept for a week. Out clubbing all night, were you, or what?'

Which was precisely what Roy was wondering. The clubbing he didn't mind but –

'It's bloody obvious, lad,' said Christian, taking the clock from Tony as Jane went out, and tossing it into the bin, 'that little beauty's well and truly fucked.'

TWENTY to ten. Jane unzipped her makeup bag and rummaged for the concealer stick. With a bit of luck she'd get away from Jubilee Terrace in time to check on Fergus before the two o'clock client. She wiped her hand across the mirror. Just time to put on another layer –

She scowled at the pitted glass. If she moved her face from the one remaining clear patch, the brown blotches made her invisible. She shoved the concealer back in the makeup bag. Her fingers hesitated over the zip. Then she tipped the whole lot into the waste bin and reached for the soap.

'OF course, a lick of paint would make all the difference.' That and a complete refurbishment.

The Jubilee couple weren't sure.

'Do go away and think about it,' or at least go away.

Maybe, they told her, that would be best. And they had another property to go to.

You and me both, smiled Jane, as she saw them to their car. Saw them out of their parking place as well, because a white car had squeezed itself between Festina and their hatchback. A white car which didn't merit a backward glance from quick-getaway Jane, until she reversed into it.

She got out to see the damage. 'Oh, sh-ugar.' A double spoonful as she recognised the car. There was no mistaking it, even with a smashed headlight. Of all the Mondeos in all the streets – Festina took such knocks in her stride, of course. Except, as Jane crouched down to check if her bumper bar would hang on a bit longer, what was that dripping from underneath? Something that had been dripping for a while, judging by the sludge patch in the trammelled snow. What to do now? If only someone was there to deal with it, like –

Daddy, whose eyes turning to face her changed from anger to – 'Jane! Fancy bumping into you here.' He laughed, almost. 'Literally, I see. Looking in the mirror never was your strong point, I seem to remember.'

He bent to pick up a piece of plastic. 'Not much damage done really.' He fitted it in place in that way people do, as though by holding the pieces together everything could be made whole. 'It'll easily be fixed. Nothing to worry about.'

Nothing to worry about? When Festina was wetting her pants onto the ice ruts under her bonnet?

Nor was there, he was saying, any need to bother her mother with what'd happened. Or where, Jane might have added, if double-life Daddy occupied any smidgeon of her consciousness, apart from a wish that he would go away and leave her to think. Because all that mattered was – would Festina keep going till tomorrow morning?

But the more she didn't speak, the more he kept on. Wanted to know – nodding at the for sale board – if she was often up this street. Wondered if she'd noticed the Mondeo before, not that he was here often himself, of course, but he wouldn't know her car from any other battered Fiesta.

Talking of which, he could see how worried she was about it and he'd be more than happy to give her a little something so she could trade it in for a newer model. Not a word to her mother, of course. She did understand that, didn't she? Everything strictly between the two of them. Would that be any help?

Swap Festina? Jane narrowed her eyes. Trade in her best friend? No help at all. Not unless it could be done before tomorrow.

'Jane, there's something I think you should know.' He circled a finger through the dirt on Festina's boot. 'I must tell someone – and you're the only one I can trust.' He turned his eyes towards her. Eyes that were full of relief.

Was this what she'd waited for all these years? Under the finger swirls, Festina's true colours almost showed. Was this it?

'You're the only person who'll understand.'

She understood all right.

'Jane – Princess. I'll come clean.'

Spew out his conscience all over Festina's rear end? Not likely.

'No need,' she smiled. 'I know exactly what you want to tell me.'

She put her hand over his finger, guiding it over the paintwork, and wrote WASH ME.

'There. A squirt of Fairy on a shammy and no-one'll ever know.' She held up his finger and wiped it over the screen print sunflower on his tie. 'No need for a fresh tart.'

She turned and got into the car, winding down the window a few inches.

'Goodbye – Dad.'

She wound it up again and turned the key. And hoped Festina wouldn't spoil her eyes-straight-ahead departure by refusing to start.

HAD it been fixed? Jane wrinkled her nostrils. It certainly smelled fixed. The air was heavy with oil and diesel and the ambrosia stench of raring-to-go. But there was only one way to be sure. She stepped onto the foot plate.

Damn him. She turned the key again. Why had she ever thought he would – a hand reached across her knees and pushed in a knob.

'Try it now.'

Fergus rattled into life with a shudder that thrummered through the metal seat and sent a tingle up her spine. The hand stretched over again and moved a long lever that stuck out at the side of the steering wheel. Jane felt Fergus's soul roar. She caught hold of the retracting hand and planted a kiss on the knuckles. Which came as a bit of a surprise to the two o'clock client. Not to mention his wife, though exactly what she thought about it was drowned out by Fergus.

Jane pulled-to-stop, just like it said on the knob. 'Shall we,' she said, swinging her leg over the gearstick, 'start with the upstairs?'

BY the time they returned to the shed it was beginning to get dark, which hid the holes in the roof. Even so, the client had seen enough.

'No need to thank me,' said Jane, in case he was considering it. 'It's me who should say thanks. You know, earlier on, with the tractor.' She rubbed Fergus's bonnet, and didn't show any surprise when Simon appeared from the other side. Hopefully, ready to carry out two more wishes. For a start, she wanted to be shown how the hydraulics thing worked and also she needed to be –

'Quite sure you're happy for me to take this?' Simon asked.

The client nodded. 'Do whatever you like, lad. As far as I'm concerned, there's nothing here I ever want to clap eyes on again.' He waved an all-encompassing arm, though whether it included his wife, now stomping towards the car, wasn't clear.

SO that she could be absolutely certain, because it was really interesting and she'd never have known how interesting it all was without him showing her the hydraulic lift, twice, why didn't she drive Fergus across to that trailer she'd noticed along by the fence, and try it for real?

Shaking his head, Simon shouted something about waiting till tomorrow as it was nearly dark. Jane smiled and shrugged, even though he was now hollering, and shoved in the clutch.

'Don't worry, I'll take it slowly.' Lucky she remembered which way he'd said the short gearstick went for low range. Pressing down hard on the clutch pedal, she tried the long stick, moving it through an H of gears. Just like Festina, without fifth. Easy peasy. Left and forward into first – she'd take it slowly, like she'd said. No sense in running Simon over before he'd shown her how to back the trailer, not that she intended to do anything as difficult as reversing...

The tractor lurched backwards as she let out the clutch and six ten-gallon milk churns hurled themselves off the stack of pallets in a clash of aluminium meets steel. Jane wrenched the gearstick towards her, ramming it into her right knee.

It was funny that she hadn't really noticed the thing with the prongs sticking out in front before. The thing-with-the-prongs that now had four of them embedded in a hessian sack. Jane hit reverse, as well as the line of tools she sent dominoing along the back wall, to try to dislodge it. It refused to be dislodged. She juddered forwards – she was really getting the hang of these gears – and a hundredweight of wheat gushed from the bottom of the rotting sack to form a hummock in front of Fergus's nearside wheel, like a sandglass trying to clock up some extra hours before the winter solstice.

'For God's sake –' who said you couldn't get on a tractor from the right? '– knock the bloody thing out of gear.'

Though he was actually doing it himself, straddling the gearbox with his full weight on the clutch – and on her foot, sandwiched between the pedal and his Doc Marten.

'What the hell are you doing?' he yelled at her as she fumbled between his legs.

'Just feeling for the knob,' which, even without the shattered kneecap and three broken toes, she would never have found anywhere near as funny as he seemed to, especially as he lurched back on her arm when she finally got her fingers round the pull-to-stop control.

'Sorry, Jane. Are you all right?'

'Yes, fine. If you could just –'

But the steering wheel had him so firmly wedged that by the time he clambered out the tractor, her legs had lost all feeling. They crumpled under her as she got down. He slid his arms round her, swooped her off the ground and dumped her onto the pronged thing. Before she'd sorted her body parts into sitting up, he was back on the tractor and the holes in the roof were getting bigger.

'Put me down!' she screamed.

The Thing jerked ever higher. She clung to the prongs, not daring to move for fear of falling between them or rolling off the edge or – her eyes widened, though she scarcely noticed the holes were receding.

He climbed out of the cab. 'That'll teach you not to indulge in unsolicited thigh groping, though on second thoughts –' he stretched his arm towards her.

But she was already scrambling to her feet. 'This thing with the prongs –'

'The muck loader fork?'

'Yes. Would it lift –' was there a way of saying goose ark without actually using the words goose and ark? '– something like a big box, only bigger?'

'Like they use in warehouses, you mean?' he asked. 'You're thinking of a fork lift. A muck loader's for digging into –'

'So it wouldn't be any good for carrying a sort of very big box?'

'Is there one that needs shifting?' He looked round. 'In here?'

'No, it's outside,' said Jane. And, no, it wouldn't be buried under a snowdrift by now because it was in the middle of a field and anyway, this particular box happened to have a pitched roof. Yes, a bit like a dog kennel, only more so, more – 'Like a kennel-share for about a dozen,' assuming the dogs were around ten kilos with their feathers on.

'No, it wouldn't be any use.'

Of course it wouldn't. Nothing was.

'Even with a fork lift it would be touch and go, though you might manage it, with the extra reach.' He directed a final head shake at the muck loader. 'No use at all.'

Which, Jane decided, summed him up completely.

'I'LL get off, then,' said Simon. 'If there's nothing else you want me to do.'

No, there was nothing else. And she must go as well, though still he hovered, as though there wasn't a back-before-Oliver deadline to meet. Tonight of all nights, everything must appear normal.

And Simon didn't seem to think it at all out of the ordinary, kept up in fact, as she welly-sprinted to the front of the house, where their cars stood side by side, facing opposite ways. He opened Colin's door as she closed Festina's so, when he wound down the window, it would have been churlish not to do the same. He rested his elbow on the edge, as though they were a couple of farmers pulled up alongside on a country lane, collies dripping down the back of their necks, passing the time between haymaking and harvest.

'And you definitely want me to move it tomorrow? I could do it before my shift starts, if I get here early.'

'Better not make it too early. In fact, I forgot to say, just before the owner left he said it could stay a few more days. So why not leave it till next week?'

'Suits me. It'll give me time at the weekend to fill her up in daylight.' He began winding up the window. 'By the time I'd bled her I should think I used up most of the bit I brought in the can.'

He smiled through the clouding glass and mouthed bye-ee. And didn't seem to notice she was mouthing back what-d'you-mean with a parting come-back-you-sod shot at Colin's tail lights.

This mindless running back to the shed was no use, she might have thought, as she ran back to the shed. She slumped against the rear wheel, arms spread over the mudguard, catching her breath. Her head was racing. Brought a bit in a can, he'd said. Well, she could do that. She'd get some on the way home and top Fergus up when she came back later on. She flashed her torch round the shed. The can must be here because he hadn't taken it with him. So where was it? Of course. He'd have gone looking for a diesel tank and taken the can with him.

And there it was, just waiting to be filled up. Simon must have decided to leave it till daylight. No need for her to find a garage. Even if he couldn't manage it in the dark, she was sure that she could. Typical man. Full of big ideas, but when it came down to it – the tap wouldn't budge. She gripped with both hands so fingers squashed fingers. Was she trying to turn it the right way? *Lefter looser righter tighter.* So why wasn't it? She tried kicking it, shooting tremors of pain up her leg. She rubbed her knee. Was it rusted up or just frozen? She hobbled to the shed.

A minute later she was back, swinging a sledge hammer with such force that she fell backwards into the snow, knocking over the can. She struggled to her feet and reached for the can that wasn't there. Diesel gushed over her sleeves, splashing her face. Where the hell was her torch? Where, more to the point, was the can?

By the time she found it and pushed the neck under the tap, the diesel was down to a trickle. A trickle that dribbled away to nothing, even when she rattled the tap. She beat her hands, beat her head, against the side of the tank. Hollow dullness boomed into the dark and died. She ground her skull against the galvanised steel in a soul-curdling wail.

Through the night air came an answering scream. Jane looked up. Far from this dank corner, moonlight spiked the earth and cast its bloodless sparkle on the sound. Somewhere a memory stirred. She knew that call. A vixen shrieking her readiness to mate. And, across those fields and hedgerows, the dog fox would be waiting... dear God, she must get back to the flat.

HE came into the hall as she took her key from the latch.

'Hello,' ever so brightly, so there was no need for that scowl.

'What the hell's happened? And I want the truth, for once.'

'Happened? Oh, nothing much.' Because, apart from a bit of property sabotage, nothing much had. Okay, she'd duped an unwitting – and they didn't come much less witting than Simon, thank God – accomplice into aiding and abetting intended theft and abduction, but the aforementioned crimes – along, no doubt, with the contravening of a few minor traffic regulations – hadn't actually taken place. Wouldn't do for another – She glanced at her watch. It couldn't be that time already.

'Sorry I'm a bit late. ' She tried to sidestep. 'A spot of unpaid overtime. You know what Christian is.' She began to unzip her anorak – 'I'll start cooking right away' – and looked down to see why it wouldn't.

Saw caked-up mud and dark sheen patches. Smelled the unmistakable smell of diesel, seeping into the carpet, over the skirting board, into the walls. Nothing much, eh? sneered the polypropylene tufted pile. A spot of unpaid overtime? scoffed the chamfered MDF. Get out of this one, sniggered the chipped eggshell emulsion.

He would have grabbed hold of her, she was sure, would have shaken her till her bones rattled, if it hadn't been for her leper-skin of stink and filth. Maybe it was better this way. She'd go straight back out, get the can, and Fergus, filled up. Get herself filled up, because, if she did go now, there was going to be a long cold night to fill as well. She couldn't keeping the heater on and risk Festina not starting. She looked at the car key. Saw Oliver was looking too. And smiling.

'Don't tell me. You ran out of diesel.'

She nodded. Sometimes, you couldn't do better than the truth.

'I told you the fuel gauge was dodgy. It's time you scrapped that old heap.' He reached to tousle her hair, then thought better of it. 'Poor angel. I bet it's been really difficult, hasn't it?'

She nodded again.

'I'll go and run you a bath.'

Oh, God, no.

She couldn't do it. Not with him in the flat. Not even if the bolt was right across, the door wedged with towels. Not even if she tied him hand and foot beforehand. She opened the front door. The cold from the stairwell clawed her spine. What use would she be in the dead of night if she were frozen?

So – face it. He was going to watch her take a bath. It was almost certain. But what was absolutely certain was that he wouldn't get in with her, not with a layer of silt under her buttocks and a film of oil floating round her breasts... Giraffe bubbles tickling rosebud nipples, and grinning Uncle George... Uncle George, Oliver – what was the difference? Only this time her mother wouldn't be there. But there comes a moment in life when a girl realises she no longer needs her mother. Needs, in fact, to be free of her. Only that way can the vixen be sure the dog fox is fast asleep while she goes a-hunting geese.

She stuck her tongue out at the mirror and twenty-seven crazed Janes returned the gesture. She headed for the bathroom, wondering if, scrubbed up, she could introduce a bit of lashing to the bedpost as an extra precaution. Perhaps not. Oliver smiled as she pushed open the bathroom door. Stick with what you know.

SHE lay back. It was all over bar the shouting. *Oh, Jane*, as she gazed into space. *Oh, Jane*, as she traced the cracks across the plaster. *Jane – Jane* – as she followed the coastlines of a faking-it map. *Jane-Jane-Ja-ne!* She couldn't help the smug curl on her lips – where are you now, Sophie? Couldn't know at this very moment that Roy and a certain female were only a few moves behind. But a few time-stroking skin-lingering moves, nevertheless. Because a new relationship had its own pace. Whereas with oft rubbed together flesh, you not only knew exactly what would happen but exactly, give or take ten seconds, when. So as the earth moved for Oliver – and so it frigging well should after all the effort she'd put in – Jane was fixing the final line of latitude on her fantasy world.

EVEN with her eyes wide open, she could feel herself drifting. Jane bit hard into the back of her hand. Keep awake. Concentrate on the curtain gap lights moving across the ceiling, one after one after one... buttermilk fleeces wending over the hillside in a never-ending undulation. Not sheep, for God's sake. Keep your mind focussed on birds... gliding over a plaster sky... a line of ducks rising up Grandma Bates's wall, three pairs of wings stretched in going-nowhere flight... And the cat by the fireside with finger-sink fur and fiend-scratch claws, the heat smell of damp from the box on the hearth and the mew of the motherless lamb, its bloody cord weeping into the straw.

AT least this way he was dead to the world. But events had scuppered the laying out of clothes, to be at hand at 2am. Jane inched back the duvet. She daren't risk a drawer-opening. There was nothing for it but to slink naked to the bathroom and put back on the heap strewn over the floor. Just as though the last three hours had never happened.

'WHAT do you think you're doing?'
Her skin froze on the trigger.
'You can't fill that up. Not that old can.' A hand reached round and took the nozzle. 'It's against the law. Contravening all sorts of regulations, you are.'
Fine. Would he get her a non-contravening container? Surely they sold them. This was a garage, for goodness sake.
Certainly they did. He nodded at the dark kiosk. During normal opening hours. All she could do at this time

of night was fill up her car. As for the other – 'No can do,' and he laughed.

Tears, even if she could, would be wasted under this dim lighting. She giggled. '*No can do*. That's so funny.' She sidled closer. 'I'm sure a nice man like you could see your way to helping a girl all on her own. The thing is, I've just come across this old lady who's run out of fuel miles from anywhere and I know you wouldn't want it on your conscience if she died of hypothermia.' She tried to slide her hand under his. 'No-one will ever know.'

'Back off!' He yanked the nozzle away, holding it up like a pistol at dawn. 'What's your game? Look at you – covered in oil and stinking of petrol. You planning on torching this place?' He pointed the nozzle straight at her. 'Clear off, you bloody nutter, before I call the police.'

IT wasn't until Jane had put a couple of miles between herself and the nozzle waver that she realised not only had she not got a can of diesel – or even a can – but she hadn't checked Festina's water level. She didn't need the light on the dashboard to miraculously start working – which it didn't, thank God, because if every life was only granted one miracle, max, she'd hang onto hers a couple of hours longer – to know things were hotting up. Hotting up seriously, with a capital S, from the amount of Steam – or was it Smoke? – rising in front of her. Only another five or six miles to go if she put her foot down... Idiot, trying to trample time not space. Take it steady. *Festina lente*. Make haste slowly, trusty steed. I know you won't – Festina sputtered to a standstill.

Ow, as she opened the bonnet. Ow, ow, as steam scalded skin. She drew back. Even if she managed to unscrew the radiator cap, she had no water. She stood, rabbit-fixed in the headlights, fists bunched in pockets, cheeks scorched with frost, damp hair already freezing into spikes of ice. To have come so far for this.

She shivered, stirred herself to action. Turn the lights off for a start. No foolish virgin, she; she knew full well the consequences of a flat battery. She flicked a switch and all around was thick black, pitch black, stretching into silence beyond the spitter of clicking metal. Her eyes widened. Dark dissolved into moon brightness lighting verge and hedgerow. And where there was a hedge there might well be a ditch.

She crunched over the clods left by the snowplough into sink-down depths. No matter that snow overflowed the tops of her wellies. She'd have to pull them off anyway, canless as she was, and fill them from the ditch. So where was it? Nothing here but a trench of snow. She turned away and turned again. What was snow, but water that had skipped the liquid course? She scooped up a double handful.

Jane turned the ignition, over and over. Had she forced one snowball too many down Festina's throat? Sod it. Sod you. Call yourself a mate? Weren't diesel engines supposed to start in the dead of Siberian winter? Maybe it was actually colder here. You're not the only one with a frozen chassis. Jane blew into her hands. She'd give her one more try and then – what? Walk? How long would that take? Quicker, maybe, to cut across country. Could she do it? Could she keep going, step after step, snow filling each footprint, snow blanking the world till all direction was obliterated?

She blinked back tiredness, put her fingers on the key. Please, my trusty steed. Just for me. And Festina kicked up her heels and galloped into the night.

SNOW was coming down thick and fast, and where the moon had gone was anybody's guess. Festina was having trouble holding the road but, worse than that, all the snow clogging the windscreen couldn't hide the steam rising from her bonnet. Jane eased her foot off the accelerator. Her foot was barely touching the pedal. Dear God, if she went much slower she would – stop.

Jane switched off the headlights. Moonless, there was nothing beyond the splat of snowflake on glass, nothing but smoke snaking through oblivion. She ground fists against forehead. How many times was she going to have to cram snow down Festina's throat? She was so tired, she could go to sleep, right now. Could seal off sound and sight, shut out memory, cease all thought. Could – would – lie down right here, where there was neither light nor shadow, with night enveiling her from invariation… The gearstick jabbed in her side. She got out of the car.

Snowflakes were falling on the bonnet, spreading into a kaleidoscope of ice carnations. Down they came, spattering over the lattice-melt of what had gone before. More on more, through wafting steam, coming and going like lights on a ghost carousel, absorbed by the hollow gaze of wisp-breath horses harnessed in perpetual gallop, eyes dissolving till only the sockets stared out at her.

Click-clicking through the stillness, Festina cried out for water. To start the slow-fill process all again… or abandon the car and go on foot? The farmhouse wasn't that far away, would almost be visible on a sunny afternoon. At least it had stopped snowing.

She gave Festina a pat, and left her lying in the shafts. Gathering up her hooped petticoats she ran – as fast as anyone could run in wellies – towards Tara. Because there wasn't a moment to lose. Tomorrow might be another day for Miss Fiddle-de-dee, but tomorrow would be too late for the geese.

337

SHE inched towards the tractor, pawing nothingness. So there was nothing to be frightened of. That scrabbling somewhere in the depths was probably only the resident mouse. Mice, maybe. But not rats. Absolutely positively definitely not rats. It was only the cold that was making her shiver. And the smell. Undeniably animal, yet not horse like she'd once supposed. It was more like the niff of fur inside Tip's kennel, in the faraway land of Grandma Bates's farmyard.

Jane's fingers touched something solid. Something not metal. Idiot to have left the torch in Festina's boot. She felt along, sank fingers into a clog of thick stickiness that clung to skin and would not be shaken off. Spiders as well as mice. She shuddered at the thought…

…of one huge black spider running across her hand as she swept out the corners, and the chink of dragging chain as Tip trailed an arc over the earth, waiting to reclaim his kennel. A streak of moonlight shimmered through the hole in the shed roof and she could see once more, could squint at dust beams dancing where the sun sneaked into Tip's lair. She shook her Little Miss dustpan into the clouds and Tip skulked back inside, to turn round twice and lie in shadow, only his head showing. *Crouched in his kennel…* black nose resting on tucked-in legs …*like a log, with paws of silver…* black eyes closed …*sleeps the dog.* No, not asleep – black ears ready to prick at the slightest sound. Forever on guard, in the kennel opposite Grandma Bates's back door.

Forever on guard in the kennel alongside the goose field fence. Poisoned meat? Unthinkable – that twenty-four hour Tesco would have some in stock. There must be another way of stopping a dog barking…

…barking like a dog possessed, nose-diving in front of the pick-up, snapping at the wheels as Grandad Bates drove across South Pasture to take a pot-shot at rabbits alongside the beck. Grandad Bates cursing damn blasted Tip to kingdom come. Grandad Bates raising his shotgun – *Stop wowling, lass, it's not loaded* – barrel pointing straight between the eyes. *It's just to scare him off.* And Tip had cowered, had skulked home, tail between his legs, to the back of his kennel.

Jane dragged the double doors open. Moonlight streamed in. Yes, there was the shotgun, tucked away behind the forks and shovels. She wiped her hand along its length, wiped a cobweb down her anorak. What did she care about spiders now? With the butt tucked into her armpit she stepped onto the footplate.

HEADLIGHTS, Jane decided, weren't a lot of use when reversing. Still, as long as she got Fergus somewhere near she'd be able to drag the trailer into position. Except there was something between somewhere-near and Fergus's back tyre, something that couldn't be nudged out of the way. All that increasing the revs was doing was gobbling up precious fuel.

She tucked the gun between the tractor seat and the hydraulics lever and climbed down. Gave the something a kick. Would have given it another if the first hadn't sent shock waves up her leg. Proving, once and for all, that she wasn't completely numb from the waist down.

She bent over and poked at the snow. What was there lurking underneath? More to the point, was it movable? She rubbed a patch clear, revealing a heap of tubes, long and thin like scaffolding pipes. So like them, in fact, that that must be what they were. She tried to pick one up but the whole lot were frozen together. No matter. A few nifty moves with his front loader and Fergus would soon have them shifted.

Back in the cab, she shunted the tractor round and pulled back the control stick. Prongs lowered, Fergus advanced. The stack of pipes scattered in all directions. Damn. Now she'd have to move them by hand. She raised the muck loader till it was just clear of the heap, then climbed down and tried to pick up three at once. The pipes splayed out and fell from her grasp, one spearing the ground. Jane pulled it out of the snow and noticed its end was damaged. The ground must be permafrost hard to have flattened it like that. She tossed it to the side and bent for another.

Several pipes later her tossing was becoming decidedly haphazard. The ninth pipe struck the edge of the muck loader before it landed, right in the way. She picked it up and saw this one had a squashed end as well. No, not squashed. She felt its thinness between finger and thumb. Machine-pressed. For jamming between bricks, she supposed. She straightened to throw it and caught her forehead on one of the loader spikes.

Glaring at the spike didn't stop the warm trickle down her brow. She wiped her eye, drew a finger across the dark stain on the back of her hand. Not exactly a river of blood, but certainly an above average mountain stream. She turned her scowl on the scaffolding pipe. Turned it back again. And smiled. It could have been a whole vampire's breakfast cascading down her cheek for all she cared. Please – she drum-majored the tube so she held the open end – let it fit.

Ten minutes later each of Fergus's prongs was sporting a two metre nail extension that the royal manicurist to Vlad the Impaler might have been proud of.

SPIKES leading the way, Fergus trammelled the frozen ruts along the lane without so much as a slither. Nothing was going to stand in his way.

NOW he'd got the first couple of buttons undone, Roy was confident the film on Sophie's DVD wasn't the only thing heading for denouement. A dead cert.

EXCEPT that – could you believe it? – someone had abandoned a car right in the middle of the road. What an idiot… not to have remembered about Festina. Jane got down. She tried to start her, because you never knew. Tried pushing her, tried cursing her and her descendants till the end of time or till all the oil on the planet had run out, whichever happened first. Because, at this rate, when she eventually reached the goose field not only would the old woman be tying baler band round her waist and positioning a piece of straw in her mouth just so, but it would be light enough to see Fergus's diesel level had dropped to zero.

IF he didn't get her up there soon, Roy reckoned, Sophie's housemates would be stirring.

JANE looked at Fergus, ticking over, his raised muck loader prongs, complete with scaffolding pipes, jutting into the still-night sky. Looked back at Festina. And couldn't help, for old times' sake, giving the corner between her windscreen and the driver's window a hug and whispering goodbye, before climbing into the cab and whamming the rev lever to full throttle and the loader lever to charge.

SHE looked bloody gorgeous, perched on the edge, lips damp with rosé, tongue tracing the rim. Roy took the glass out of her hand and put it on the bedside chest.

EVEN so, it took a bit of back and forth manoeuvring to get her to budge. For all the frustration, Jane couldn't help admire the way Festina refused to give in. But with a final push Fergus had her not just tipped over but on her back. Prongs pierced metal. One of the spikes was jammed into part of Festina's undercarriage. Fergus tried backing out but Festina clung on. Any further and he'd be in the ditch, dragging her on top. Jiggling this way and that, at last he managed to pull free.

Jane jumped down to inspect the damage. Fergus's wedge-end was intact but Festina was fatally wounded. She lay on her back, weeping what must be, by the smell, diesel. What to catch it in? Jane flashed her eyes around but no magic container materialised in the snow. She wrenched off a wellie and held it under the gash.

Every drop was poured into Fergus's tank. Nearly a legful. She screwed back the cap. No need to think of it as Festina's life's blood. She climbed aboard Fergus without a backward glance. After all, it wasn't even pink.

THERE was a rosy glow coming from behind her curtains. Simon knew they were her curtains because, when he'd passed in daylight, he'd spotted the pert-eared bunny on the windowsill. Sitting there, day after day, staring out at him. Grinning. Surrounded by a mountain of clutter that only Soph could have managed to accumulate in such a short time. Now it all merged into a silhouette stockade, with the fluffy bunny head sticking up two fingers. Fool that he was to keep going there.

SHE'D have to stop. No need to look behind. She'd seen there was movement even before the wheels spanned the lump. Jane climbed down. It was slumped in the middle of the road, one of its hind legs thrashing space. She leaned over. Dear God, make it stop. Still the leg kicked. How long had it been lying there like that? Please let it die. The rabbit caught sight of her, writhed its body in the frozen slush. Jane backed away.

She should find a stone. She scanned the snow-capped verge. Somewhere, under this veneer of loveliness, there must be something that would smash a skull. Or maybe there was something in the cab. She ran back. Nothing. Only the shovel, tied on the back with a hundred knots.

Numb fingers picked at one, felt in a pocket for the penknife. For a moment she wondered – but the blade was only sharp enough for cutting string. And if she cut the string now, she couldn't be sure the shovel would stay put till she reached the snow-blocked goose field gateway – unless there was enough room to wedge it. Groping under the seat to check, her fingers closed round the butt of the gun.

She crouched beside the twisted mangle. Raised her arms above her head. The rabbit stared with one staring eye, leg still. Was it dead? Please let it be dead. But she could see a faint trembling, an imperceptible rise and fall of the chest. Could see the whole mass of fur shaking, could hear the thump, thump of the chest, louder and louder, and the eye growing larger, ever larger, and the thud against her ribcage as the one unblinking eye sucked in the moon. And Jane's rabbit heart knew she could not do it.

She turned away. What now? Reverse over it? Could she hit it with the back tyre? It would die soon, anyway. Damn the thing, it wasn't her responsibility. She hadn't run over it. She hated that rabbit, hated it for being there, hated it for being alive. How much longer could it lie there unwrithing, uncrying, undead? Where was God when you needed him?

She slammed the gun against the tractor, over and over and – crack. There it was, broken. Not like the rabbit, broken beyond reason. She knew enough about the breaking of guns, the releasing of safety catches. Every last frigging detail, in fact, of Oliver's clay pigeon lessons. *Focus with both eyes for accurate depth perception.* She knew two cartridges in place when she saw them. *It all comes down to analysing the situation correctly.* She snapped the gun shut and walked towards the rabbit.

IT was over. What the hell was he doing here? Roy watched the lights tracking across the ceiling. He turned his face towards the window. The curtains were still open – they'd been in that much of a hurry, in the end – not hanging straight, but one dipping from the rail in a hookless grin, the other bulged up on the sill next to a bloody great stuffed rabbit, sat there, tail sticking up.

Shadows came and went across his face. His pupils must be whizzing from big to small and back again. Funny how you couldn't see what was right before your eyes. He closed them, and Jane stared back. He screwed them tighter, so her face broke into a thousand blobs of light that floated upwards and whirred into his skull, and kept on whirring even with his eyes wide open.

But it was only a motor ticking over, under the window, and the rabbit still sitting there on its fat backside and Sophie lying with her arse in the air. An arse he could sink his face into, even now, but just another arse, after all.

WHAT the hell was he doing here? It was over. Yet night after night he pulled up at the same spot, looked up at the same window. Simon fingered the gearstick. Tonight the curtains were open. So where was she? Not here, for sure. It was the only thing he could be sure of now. But had he ever been sure of anything, with Soph? It'd been a surprise when she'd posted on his spare key. He pushed it back in the ignition. Could you be sure of any woman? Even a girl like Jane... There was something about Jane he couldn't quite fathom. All that business with the tractor – quite sweet, really, her wanting him to have it. She knew nothing about engines, it was obvious, but it'd be fun teaching her what was what. Unusual for a woman to show such an interest. He smiled. She'd been so keen to see if he could get it started. Desperate, almost. His smile faded. What exactly was she up to?

JANE tied the gun behind the seat and shoved the short gear stick forwards. Better stay in the low range, even though that meant snail speed. At least she was moving. The road was too bad for ordinary traffic. Not a car in sight.

METAL crunched metal. Damn. A dented wing, at least. Charles shoved the Mondeo into reverse. He was damned if he was going to get out to see the damage. He'd probably get away with it. It wasn't as though there was anyone about. Not at this ungodly hour. He hadn't meant to stay this long. Must have dozed off, he was so damned tired. Tired of all this, if he was honest. He was pushing sixty, for God's sake. Time he was retired. God knows, he'd had enough of that, too. He was supposed to be a doctor not a damned businessman. Complete chaos, the way things were now. He'd had enough of chaos.

He swung the Mondeo clear of the line of cars along Jubilee terrace. Why should he lose his no-claims over that piece of trash? Of course he'd get away with it. Get away now. There might be a bit of white paint left on the yellow bodywork, but nothing that would tie him down. Not if he didn't come back. The Mondeo glided past number 28. Thirty two years of unblemished record wasn't to be thrown away. Not just for that. Charles glanced in his mirror for one last look.

SIMON was about to go when he saw a movement at the window. He got out of the car. Maybe he'd imagined it. No – something was different. What was it? He peered up at the dark pane. The rabbit's ears were tied in a knot.

ROY'S stomach lurched at the half landing. He was sure he'd heard something. He looked over the banister rail. Yes, there definitely was something at the bottom of the stairs. Something grunting – at least the guy was. The girl was lying close-lipped, head thrust back against the fourth step, eyes wide open, staring up at him. Roy stared back, unable to shift his gaze. He felt shabby. Felt that he, and the guy weighing down on her with his jeans round his knees, were lesser beings. She transcended them both with those forbearing eyes, grey in the grub of the hallway, grey like eyes he knew so well.

COULDN'T he go any quicker? She squinted at the throttle bar. It was as far up as it would go. Jane stopped. She wasn't going to get anywhere at this rate. She pulled the short gearstick towards her. She let out the clutch and couldn't help grinning as Fergus leapt forward.

A SMILE flickered over his lips as Oliver stirred in half-sleep. It had been bloody good. He reached across the bed. She must have gone to the bathroom. Maybe he should, too. No. It wasn't a pee he needed right now. He pressed his palm into the hollow where Jane had lain and waited.

THERE wasn't, Simon decided, any point in hanging around any longer. He had cut down a side road and gone right to the end of the narrow back street, wending his way between bins and boxes ready for tomorrow's collection. Cans, bottles, papers, the dregs of a fortnight's gratification. He kicked a straying coke can. It bumped across snow-capped cobblestones and was still, yet Simon could hear it reverberating down the street... a scuffling, scrabbling echo that seemed to be coming from something crouched on the top of the high wall that ran along the back yards. Too big for a cat, unless they bred them the size of leopards round here. He peered down the street.

IT was becoming difficult to focus, now the moon had turned on its dimmer switch. Even so, it was giving forty watts more than Fergus's one working headlight. Which was more than enough to see she still had miles to go.

GOD, it looked a hell of a long way. Probably no bigger drop than from the bathroom window onto the kitchen roof, but Roy had scarcely noticed that, so desperate was he to get away from a pair of grey eyes. Thank God she couldn't see him now. They'd been hurting enough, those eyes, these past few weeks, and he'd never found out why. His knuckles whitened as he tried to keep his grip between the broken glass jutting out from the mortar. He'd already skinned both knees as he shinned along the washhouse tiles and onto the tin sheets of the old lavatory. Now his legs, perched on top of the wall, were shaking enough to loosen the cobbles. Don't look down, for God's sake. He glanced away. Saw someone coming towards him. Jumped.

He didn't seem to have broken any bones. Not important ones anyway. Roy picked himself up and legged it, though what was at the end of this poky back street was anybody's guess.

WHERE – Oliver stomped out of the bathroom – the hell was she? Just when things seemed to be back to normal at last. He got back into bed. It was time she was made to see reason. He'd put up with a lot lately, with all her crazy goings-on. He pulled the duvet up to his chin. All that nonsense about the goose. Couldn't she see he was making the perfect Christmas? For her. God, he'd even arranged to spend it with her family. And what thanks did he get? Acted as though she couldn't care less. About anything. Except those geese. Well, she wouldn't be seeing them any more, after tomorrow. Not feathered, anyway. He tucked the duvet round his neck and closed his eyes. So – his lips gave the smile another flick – when she went past them yesterday morning, he hoped she'd waved bye-bye.

SO, this was it. Adieu. For one sole-lifting moment as he approached the lights, Charles felt a pang of regret. But, as amber joined red, he put his foot down and was over the cross roads before you could say go, swerving to avoid a light-jumper speeding towards him from the right. The Mondeo lost its grip, spinning sideways to face the oncomer. Charles braced himself, eyes closed.

When he opened them again he could see tail-lights disappearing into the depths of the mirror. Relief flushed over him, from the sunspots on his scalp to the calluses on his toes. He'd got away with it, apart from a telltale dampness in his Y-fronts. Although a bonnet-crunching encounter without witnesses, providing he didn't suffer whip-lash, would cover up a lot. Like the yellow paint there must now be on his left front wing and the scrape of green already on the right. Of all the rotten luck to have run into Jane like that. Or, rather, for her to run into him. Surely he wasn't going to be found out now, when it was all over? No, Jane wouldn't say anything – would she?

SHE couldn't tell exactly where she was. The only thing that was clear was that she wasn't there yet, or anywhere near. Jane slid to the edge of the seat and pressed down with both legs. Fergus pulled up sharp. She moved the long gear stick, right and back. Top, full throttle. She released the clutch with a jerk. Not a moment to lose. Fergus roared at the sky, tyres spinning.

She tried the other gears, the two in high range, three in low, with rubber grinding snow to polished glass. She tried reverse.

The tread gripped. Back went Jane, straining into the darkness, zigzagging between heaped verges, unable to see.

Not that that was going to stop her. Not till she was far enough from the ice sheet for Fergus to have a good run at it. Only this time she'd let the clutch out slowly.

ROY skidded round the corner and leant against the wall to catch his breath. He should have asked her, straight out. There was something on her mind, something so enormous it blocked out reason. It wasn't the Oilrag: he counted for nothing. He knew that now, he'd seen it in her eyes. And yesterday, those eyes had been screaming. Whatever it was, whatever mattered so much that it completely engulfed her, was about to explode. He must get to her. He'd hammer down the door of the flat, fell the Oilrag with a single blow. Nothing was going to stop him. Roy reached the end of the side street and wondered if there was a night bus.

THERE were headlights in the distance. That must be the bypass. She'd be there soon. Fergus must be doing about eighteen miles an hour now. Absolutely flat out.

HAD he slipped on the ice or tripped over one of the boxes? Simon pushed himself to semi-upright. Could he put any weight on this ankle? He winced. It must be sprained, at the very least. Every step was going to be absolute agony. But he had to make it to the end of this road. Because it was obvious there was a psycho on the loose, who, if he hadn't already done over Soph's place – and maybe Soph – would be going there next. Using the wall for support, Simon limped his way along the street. He stopped alongside the doorstep to Sophie's back yard, where the snow was trampled. Just as he'd feared. The psycho had landed right there. Simon peered at the upstairs windows.

NOTHING in sight. Nothing moving anyway. Only two lines of round-nosed polar bears, hump-backed and glistening under the street lights, fast asleep. All except one. Roy narrowed his eyes. He remembered that car, sticking out from the rest, snow scraped off its jutting bonnet and rear end. Simple Simon had probably stopped by for an oil change and she was letting him have one right now. Would have made room for a threesome if he hadn't got out in time.

He walked up to the car and scraped his hand across the ice until he could make out the letters behind the glass. What sort of nerd had his name in front of him on the windscreen? But the real question was – had he still got SOPH on the other side? Roy reached across. Then stopped. Because he was too cold to actually care. He stuffed his hand in his pocket, pressing his fingers against the warmth of his leg. Fingers that had just enough feeling left in them to make out, deep in the corner, the shape of a key. He pulled it from his pocket and looked at it. Looked at the Cortina, all pert-nosed with its bum sticking out. Just asking for it.

'OI! Hands off!' Oblivious to the possibly-seriously-ruptured ligament, Simon raced towards the car. He dashed in front, waving. Leapt sideways when he realised the Cortina – his Cortina – wasn't going to stop. He managed to grab the handle and wrench open the passenger door. It thudded into the snow mound in front, shaking off the bear-fleece and revealing a smashed headlight and a two metre gash of Screaming Scarlet along its skinned body. As well as slowing Colin down enough for Simon to jump in.

His 'What the hell do you think you're doing?' received no answer, which, now that he had a moment to think, might be just as well. He'd shut himself in with the psycho, a guy who, once he'd got onto the main road, would put his foot through the floor. And several other body parts. Simon opened the door but the car was travelling so close to the nearside line of parked cars it battered every one as it passed, leaving no room for escape. With a final crunch the psycho stopped and Simon swung round to face him.

JANE shunted Fergus round so he spanned the two lanes on the roundabout, his loader in front of the verge which fell away to the field. She'd made it. And somewhere under all that snow was the gateway. But she wouldn't have to shovel it out, now she'd found out what a loader could do. She pushed the lever forward. Fergus lowered his horns and headed for the biggest snowdrift.

NOW he'd got the damn thing shut, it wasn't going to open again. Ever. Even from the inside Simon could see it was well and truly buckled. Yet all this moron was going on about was that nothing had actually happened tonight with Sophie – looking at the little creep, Simon could well believe it – and that he was going to clear off ASAP. Simon curled his lip. Not in this car he wasn't.

With an eye on the jutting jaw line, Roy shot Simon a smile which he hoped, in this half light, looked nothing more dodgy than apologetic. Because he was sorry he'd caused a slight bit of damage. But the guy liked doing up old wrecks, didn't he?

YES! With a final shove, the gate was smashed from its post. Fergus was through, trundling his way over the felled five bars and into the field. Jane put her foot on the clutch and squinted across the snow till she had the ark directly in view.

THE two of them stared into space, waiting for the other to make the first move. Though maybe, thought

Simon, he was being sidetracked from what he really wanted. He reckoned he'd pick up a replacement without too much trouble. And make sure the little creep paid. Nothing more than a damn nuisance, Colin and – Simon realised this now – Sophie both. Meanwhile out there, crying out for a bit of attention, was something better. And – another realisation – he couldn't think Massey Ferguson 135 without thinking Jane.

SHE and Fergus were as one, a centaur galloping across the field towards the ark. Though presumably centaurs didn't make it to the original before Noah battened down the hatches. Jane hoped the old woman had fastened the ramp over the pop-hole properly. It would be fatal if it flew open when those metal fingers scooped up the jackpot.

THE Chrysalid was practically handing it to him on a plate. Roy glared past Simon through the side window. He'd been so caught up with Sophie he hadn't sussed out a suitable traffic island, never mind a roundabout, for the madcow sandwich board scheme. So – his eyes narrowed – where? Not in town, for sure, with insider-lane bikes and snap-happy dogs and people sticking their oar in like people always did. Roy's pupils twin-torpedoed through Simon's skull to some otherwhere place for two – like the little field they'd walked alongside that time. In fact, wasn't there a roundabout at the end of that field? He wasn't certain. But – his hand closed round the ignition key – he knew a way to find out.

JANE rattled the catch. It would hold, she was sure. The tricky part was going to be keeping the ark on the scaffolding pipes. She climbed back on board and double checked that the rope was there. It was a good one, as thick as cable. And as rough. It might well skin her fingers when she tightened it. But they were so cold she probably wouldn't notice.

HE'D soon know, one way or another. But Simon doubted Roy was as tough as he was making out. Either way, he wasn't going to sit back and do nothing. The little rat could keep Soph – though Simon doubted that as well – but he wasn't taking this car another metre. He grabbed the wheel.

Colin ricocheted between the lines of parked cars as the two men fought for control. Simon began thumping Roy in the chest, shoulder, ear. As he ducked away Simon belted him on the back of his head, so Roy's brain joined in the ricocheting, as he tried to fend Simon off with one hand and steer with the other.

'Okay, okay – leave off,' and Roy jammed his foot on the brake.

The car stalled. Simon reached over for the handle and bundled him out. But not before Roy had pulled the key from the ignition.

Simon was across the driver seat and out of the car before Roy's battered cerebellum could strike up any meaningful conversation with his hamstrings. Simon dragged him to his feet, would have shaken the little rat by the lapels if he'd had any.

'Where is it?' He hooked his thumbs into the button-down tabs on Roy's shoulders – did the rat think he was Napoleon or something? – and pulled him closer, though the effect was somewhat diminished by Roy being a good four inches taller. Definitely not Napoleon, standing there with both palms outstretched and the pocket linings of his jacket flapping empty. Simon unhitched himself from the epaulettes and thrust his hands into Roy's trouser pockets. He scooped his fingers round the contents and shoved Roy back with clenched fists.

Unclenching, he saw the car key, a screwed up poppy and an equally screwed up piece of paper. He looked up just in time to see Roy's right knee coming too close to his crotch for comfort.

JANE shoved the lever forward and the loader arm dropped down. She'd manoeuvred Fergus as near to dead centre as she could judge in the beam of his single headlight. Thank God the ark was set up on a couple of old railway sleepers. It would have been impossible to slide the prongs under with the ground so frozen. It just showed – second gear in the low box should do it – that this was all meant to be. She released the clutch.

SIMON slid down to the ground, back resting against Colin. The ice felt good.

'Look, mate, there's no way I'm in there.' Roy gave a backwards nod to the upstairs windows of the terrace. It was directed at Sophie's, but it would do no harm to include any others where the guy might have an interest. 'Take my advice and get along there now.' Leaving the old banger free for a quick roundabout recce. Simple Simon might have got back his spare key, but he didn't know that the original was safe in Roy's back trouser pocket. 'Trust me, mate, she'll welcome you with open arms.' To say nothing of – Roy shot a glance at Simon's face. Maybe give it twenty minutes.

God, he felt sick. Simon eased the seam under his zipper. Concentrate on something else. He looked at the piece of paper. Which took all the concentration he could muster, because the words going down the page didn't make much sense. He scowled.

A classic example, thought Roy, of a guy in need of distraction. He tapped the paper. 'It's Jane's.'

'Jane's?' Simon angled the paper, making best use of what light there was. 'Jane wrote this?'

'It seems,' said Roy, 'to be some sort of list,' and as a distraction device it scored ten out of ten. Or rather, six out of six, because, since finding the paper on the floor of the bog, he'd counted the items – *torch boxes sacks rope string pocket-knife* – several times.

'Could be her Christmas wish list.' Could even be a way of getting this guy off his back. Roy sighed. 'You know what, mate, Jane is the only girl in the world I want.' And he sighed again, this time inwardly. 'Except I don't really know –' why I'm telling you this, but now he'd started voicing his thoughts he didn't seem able to stop '– how Jane feels about me. It's obvious she doesn't give a toss for the Oilrag – you know, Oliver. You know Oliver, don't you?'

'Yes.'

'First class bastard, don't you think?'

And not only did Simon agree, but contributed several epithets of his own, two of which Roy hadn't come across before. He was really warming to the guy. 'She blanks out whenever he's mentioned. Yet her whole face lights up when she's going on about –' What exactly?

How about tractors, smiled Simon. Dream on, Roy Boy. You're not in with a chance. Jane would be fully occupied these coming months with the restoration of a certain MF135. With a man who knew a thing or two. Or would she? She was female, after all. Not so much interested in bodywork as performance. He couldn't help wondering how he compared – but Oliver would never have got her going as quick as that, even in daylight. And it was the getting going that had mattered. But it wasn't the Massey Ferguson, beaut that she was, that had roused such passion in Jane's eyes. Passion he'd seen once before, on that night in the car park when she'd been telling him something. He'd been too wrapped up in Sophie to really listen. Simon frowned. What was it –

– that Tony had said, when they'd been looking at those squiggles in Jane's diary? Roy's brow unfolded. Of course. *She's got a real thing about –*

'Geese,' said Simon. Or maybe it was Roy. The two men looked at each other. Whatever it was that Jane was up to, one thing was clear. She was up to it right now.

UNDER frozen knuckles, sweat seeped from Jane's palms onto the control knob. Fergus had his prongs jabbed under, poised for the thrust. Please God, let it work. She pulled the stick back.

Slowly, shakily, the ark rose. The ark rose and the dog slept on. She'd done it. He'd done it. She leaned forward and dropped a kiss onto the steering wheel before jumping down to find the dangling ends of the rope. A round turn and two, plus one more for luck, half hitches. Brown Owl had told her such a knot would come in handy one day. Unlike a three-point turn. Because there was enough room here to change direction without a backwards shunt. A wide arc – Jane gripped the wheel with grinning determination – for a wide ark. Then straight ahead to the gateway without raising so much as a whimper. Anyway, the collie was probably tucked up in the barn on such a night as this. Sweet dreams, Fido.

She put Fergus into forward gear. And realised she couldn't see a damn thing. She needed to lower the arm right down, so it just cleared the ground. Even then, she had to stand to see over the top.

When she'd approached the ark she'd been so intent on what lay ahead that she'd scarcely noticed the ground. After all, it looked as flat as a Christmas cake, albeit Grandma Bates's snow-effect one. Now, with the extra weight on the front, it was clear that the snow-effect was masking a depth variation last measured in rods, poles and penguins. Here she was, tractoring – Fergus might not represent the latest in technology, but he had the edge over your average team of oxo cubes – over one of the last tracts of Olde England. And every one of these overs was followed by a downwards lurch that threatened the ark's stability. It didn't need forty days of rain to expose these rigs and furrows for the bone-shakers that they were. And it was clear from the bumping sounds that other bones than hers were being shaken.

Even so, the sudden burst of cackling took her by surprise. Though cackling didn't really cover it. This was no under-cloak clucking of hags, killing time till a likely thane trotted by. This was a full-throttle twelve-pack cacophony fit to rouse the dead from their final resting place. Or a dog from its temporary overnight accommodation.

HE'D never looked on it as a permanent arrangement anyway. What he wanted, Charles decided, was the peace and calm of home. He'd reached that stage in his life when to be unneeded sounded downright comfortable. He'd jack it all in, the job – no-one could pretend it was a calling any more – as well. With Judith busy with her own life, he'd be left to his own devices. He couldn't remember the last time he'd gone sea fishing. Really gone, not let's pretend, stopping off to buy the occasional small cod or a couple of mackerel – not every time, he'd been careful to make it convincing, careful to cover his tracks. Nothing to connect him – apart from Jane. He must stay alert... Charles jabbed on the radio and scrolled for something loud.

SURELY such barking, enough to penetrate the sides of a bathyscope six miles deep, could be heard inside the farmhouse? Yes, lights were going on in the up – and down – stairs windows. Jane turned her head for another look.

Was that a torch beam tracing across the yard towards the barn door?

HE couldn't sleep. Oliver looked at the clock. No chance of getting off now. Anyway, she needed bringing back. Because he'd worked it out, while he'd been lying there. For God's sake, what if she was discovered mooning about outside that wooden goose hut? Those farmer types started early, didn't they? He reached for his vest. Could be up and about already, sharpening their knives.

SHE knew they were coming. But the way the ark was rocking about, she was going as fast as she dared. Not that they could catch her on foot, even at this speed. She turned her head. Saw the lights of a reversing Land Rover and someone dragging the farmyard gate wide open. Jane pushed the throttle stick as far as it would go.

Her hands welded to the steering wheel as she tried to keep a course in line with the rigs and furrows. But, Fergus's wheels not being two front pairs of oxen hooves apart, it was impossible to steer a level path. What the situation needed was every microgram of her concentration.

What it didn't need was the Hound from Hades to appear at fifty knots, intent on bringing Fergus to his knees by jaw-clamping one of his back tyres. How could she steer clear, when all she could see was a blur of heads and teeth trying to latch on before the treads sank into snow. The ark tipped this way and that as she fought one-handed to untether the shotgun from behind.

She had to turn and use both hands to loose the string. Thank God all this shaking had slackened it – she grabbed the wheel as the ark lurched over the next hump. Please God, let the rope hold. And let that damn collie clear off before it's squashed to guts and gore. She propped the gun against her chest, barrel pointing. But this dog wouldn't have flinched from task had it been facing the Armada, full broadside. As Jane tried to fend it off with the butt of the gun, she slid off the seat. She grabbed the steering wheel as one leg pitched through the gap where once a door had hung. Fergus took a dive to the right. He was seriously off course, and the Land Rover was gaining. In a few moments he'd be cornered.

Jane yanked the wheel at full lock and closed her eyes. She felt the full weight of twelve fat geese thud left but Fergus kept his grip. Which is more than the Land Rover managed. Glancing right, Jane saw its wheel spinning in deep snow near the fence, saw the passenger door open. Not a moment to lose.

Nor was there time to steady down and take the gateway straight. The loader arm was still rising when Fergus rammed the left side gatepost on his blind side. As one, the geese slid right. It was as much as Jane could do to stop him tipping over, never mind turn him onto the roundabout carriageway. She clung onto the wheel as Fergus charged ahead like a rabid Cyclops, across the two lanes, up the snow-compacted verge, over the wasteland. Nothing could stop him. Nothing except a crash barrier.

STEEL against steel. Bone against reinforced glass. Everything flash-bright and spinning blackness. Jane, salad tossed in somersaulting metal, was flung into a snowdrift as Fergus ricocheted from outcrop rock to buffer stop of saplings.

She pushed herself to sitting consciousness. Something jabbed her side. She felt and found the gun. *Focus with both eyes for accurate depth perception.* She stuck it in the ground to lever herself upright. She'd always known it would come in useful. Used it now, to side step down the slope to hell.

It all comes down to analysing the situation correctly. At the bottom of the embankment, the dual carriageway stretched out far each way, going places, north and south. And going nowhere was an arkful of geese smashed to kindling.

SHE picked her way among the bits of wreckage, trailing her shotgun crutch. She looked and saw three sets of headlights coming fast towards her, and looked away. Three cars were braking, blasting horns, pulling up with windows down to find out why. She listened to the silence of assassinated hope.

The closest got out first and straightened up, stirring aging bones to action. Further back, the next put weight onto a swollen ankle, cursing it to move. The one who'd been beside him struggled with a buckled door. Far behind, going as fast as road conditions would allow, came the final non-runner in the race to get Jane.

All around were bodies, battered and bleeding. She gathered one up in her arms, the one with the grey wingtips, and sat between shafts of wood and splintered feathers, rocking... *There's a ship sails away At the close of each day, Sails away to the land of dreams...* All dead. No, not all. Here and there she could see limbs twitch. *Mummy hugs him up tight...* Could feel his chest rise, clinging on. To what? After now, whichever way, lay nothing. *Daddy whispers goodnight, Sailor boy sail...* Burrowing into bloody feathers, she felt all semblance of control slipping through her fingers... *into sweet slumber land...* She stroked his head and he lay still.

The air was thick with shouts. In the distance the wail of a siren. And something else. Something she could hear above the headlines. She saw it rise on outstretched wings, higher and higher, far above the shadow figure cradling futility, one lone goose calling out to meet the day.

WHETHER it was one of her geese, or a wild one straying off course, she couldn't be sure. Whereas she knew the four men coming towards her only too well. Although they didn't, in actuality, know her at all. With accurate depth perception, she focussed both eyes on the one who was gaining. Back in actuality there would have to be some resolution. But would one cartridge be enough, even for a story? Because maybe life was just another line they'd spun her. It all came down to analysing the situation correctly. Either way, everything came to an end sooner or later. High above she followed beating wingtips disappearing through the cloud and out of sight. Now seemed as good a point as any to finish.